DANIEL M. BENSEN

INTERCHANGE

This is a **FLAME TREE PRESS** book

Text copyright © 2021 Daniel M. Bensen

FLAME TREE PRESS
6 Melbray Mews, London, SW6 3NS, UK
flametreepress.com

US sales, distribution and warehouse:
Simon & Schuster
simonandschuster.biz

UK distribution and warehouse:
Marston Book Services Ltd
marston.co.uk

Thanks to the Flame Tree Press team, including:
Taylor Bentley, Frances Bodiam, Federica Ciaravella, Don D'Auria,
Chris Herbert, Josie Karani, Molly Rosevear, Mike Spender,
Cat Taylor, Maria Tissot, Nick Wells, Gillian Whitaker.

The cover is created by Flame Tree Studio with
thanks to Nik Keevil and Shutterstock.com.
The font families used are Avenir and Bembo.

Flame Tree Press is an imprint of Flame Tree Publishing Ltd
flametreepublishing.com

A copy of the CIP data for this book is available from the British Library
and the Library of Congress.

HB ISBN: 978-1-78758-469-3
US PB ISBN: 978-1-78758-467-9
UK PB ISBN: 978-1-78758-468-6
ebook ISBN: 978-1-78758-471-6

Printed and bound in Great Britain by Clays Ltd, Elcograf S.p.A.

DANIEL M. BENSEN

INTERCHANGE

FLAME TREE PRESS
London & New York

For Kat, whose question inspired this world. Take the leap. Dive into unexplored waters. Who knows what awesome and fascinating forms you will discover?

CHAPTER ONE

The Bear, the Ring, and the Milky Way

Bamboo grass crunched and the mist curled away, revealing the bear.

Sunlight caught the gnats rising from its fur. Breath steamed from its black muzzle.

Its humped shoulders trembled. A plate-sized foot swung out, fringed with claws. Whuffling another plume of vapor, the animal approached.

Anne hardly dared to breathe.

"Raise your arms," Daisuke whispered behind her ear.

Anne twitched at the voice. So did the bear. Its forepaws struck the ground and agitated gnats billowed. Black fur bristled as muscles tensed, raising that great rugged spine. Claws spread at the ends of arms as long as Anne's legs. As long as the distance that separated the large angry carnivore from the incautious biologist.

The bear breached the surface of the mist, and the pale fur around its eyes, chin, and chest glowed as if spotlit. More display patterns. Threat displays, if Anne were any judge.

Its smell hit her, wet fur and urine, autumn leaves and rotting meat. Anger.

"*Oi! Deteike!*"

Anne and the bear twitched again. It was Daisuke, yelling.

"*Acchie ike!*"

Anne's boyfriend clapped his hands and the bear grunted.

Its eyes rolled. The bear was confused now, as well as angry, and deciding whether to become afraid.

You and me both, mate.

Panic reared up under Anne. Her toes tingled in her boots, telling her to run away. Her palms itched, as if for a stick. *Stupid monkey instincts. Totally inappropriate for this habitat and this species of predator. No bears in Africa.* Instead, she had to *think.*

"Raise your arms," Anne muttered through numb lips. "Raise your arms. Raise your arms!" Her hands shook, but she spread them out as wide as they would go.

The bear was looking at her again, breathing fast through its nose. Anne was too. Mammalian adrenal responses. Fight or flight or freeze?

She widened her stance, trying to look as large and intimidating as possible. Right, because the woman most often described as 'dumpy' might intimidate anyone.

Ah, there was the anger. Maybe she ought to try this threat posture on a few social media trolls.

"Get out of here!" Anne's ribs tightened around the shout. "Shoo! Go away, bear!"

Daisuke clapped again, and Anne tried it too. She jumped up and down, swinging her arms to bring her hands together. A star jump.

She felt absolutely ridiculous, but at least nobody was looking at her besides her boyfriend and a bear. At least there were no cameras or millions of followers here to critique every choice she'd ever made. She'd left her phone in Tokyo and that horrible body-cam on an alien planet.

"Don't you know who I am? I'm a global celebrity now!" Anne shouted. "I'm the queen of Junction! Now go away, or I'll star jump you to death!"

Another jump-clap. The bear flinched and whuffled. It shook its head. Fur and folds of skin flapped. It thumped back onto its forelegs and Anne felt an absurd rush of accomplishment.

"Yeah! Take that, bear!"

The bear did not strike her down for her hubris. It just hunched its shoulders and shuffled away like a grumpy uncle. It was anthropomorphism, but Anne couldn't help feeling it looked disgusted at her. As if she were much too off-putting, socially maladroit, and mediapathic to deserve a mauling.

Anne rubbed her face with trembling fingers. *Daisuke's right. I've been spending way too much time online.*

"*Ya!*" he shouted from behind her, and Anne jumped, fight-or-flighting all over again.

"For the love of god, Daisuke!" She turned, hand clutching at her heart. Her parka suddenly felt stifling. Her breath smoked in the autumn morning air.

Daisuke twitched his head and blinked at her. Hair mussed from sleep, red-faced and puffing from bear-scaring, he still looked absolutely fucking gorgeous. Oh, that sweat on his brow. Oh, the way the lower edges of his eyes scrunched up when he squinted into the mist. Those lips set in that firm line, as if to say *Once I've taken care of the forest creatures, I'll take care of my woman. And then, all the rest of the world's problems!* Slap that face on a jewel case, and you'd sell a million DVDs. Which was exactly what Daisuke Matsumori had done in his persona of 'the Iron Man of Survival'.

Daisuke had happened to be filming in New Guinea when Anne had found out about the wormhole just over the border in Indonesian Papua. She hadn't known it was a wormhole exactly, but she'd taken photos of it and sent them to everyone she knew. A couple of days later, Daisuke had been surviving a whole different kind of wilderness. And saving Anne's life.

"The bear." He gestured as if to direct the attention of a confused audience. "He might come back. He might still be curious."

Anne supposed Daisuke would know. She hadn't yet watched all of his old videos, but she recalled seeing a couple of bears in there.

"We should make more noise when we take walks in the morning." The Iron Man of Survival lifted his chin and squinted into the diffuse sunlight. "I'm sorry," he added.

"You're handsome is what you are. Look at you, with your hands on your hips and your jaw out like that." Anne put her arms around him, as if to stop him from running away. "You tell those bears, Dice."

Daisuke hugged her back. "Are you okay? Are you scared?"

She was, but not of anything in this nature park. It was just the outside world, all the outside worlds.

"Naw," she said, snuggling in under his chin. If the glory of nature and the fear of death wasn't enough to distract her from her stupid problems, maybe sex would work. Anne rubbed her hands up Daisuke's back. "Thank you for saving me from wild beasts."

"I'll catch breakfast for you too." Daisuke broke their embrace and leaned to pick up their fishing poles from where they had dropped them in the bamboo grass.

Anne considered, then grabbed him again and wrestled him back upright. "Breakfast can wait," she said. "Let's go where a bear can't find us."

A chuckle under her cheek. "I think you don't mean Sapporo?"

"Jesus Christ, no." She squeezed his ass. It resisted her fingers delightfully. "No civilization."

"Oh."

"No clothes either."

"Yes. I got it."

By the time Anne left their tent for the second time that morning, the sun had burned off the mist. The Ishikari Mountains loomed to the east like an autumnal wall.

She let Daisuke fuss with breakfast while she looked east. Light green deciduous trees shaded to red and orange as they climbed, giving flame-colored borders to the dusty-dark green of conifers. These broke up into huddled islands against the tan of alpine meadows, which shaded into gray rock, and, just at the top, snow. It hadn't been there the night before.

"Are you okay?" Daisuke asked.

Anne shook her head. "Of course I'm okay. I've got my wilderness, haven't I? My gorgeous mountains, my boyfriend who's grilling the fish he caught...." Words failed her, but Daisuke understood, the empathetic bastard.

"You're thinking that our camping trip is over. The dream is ending."

"I wouldn't put it like that, but I suppose so," she said. "We had a wonderfully uncivilized experience these last four days, but tomorrow we'll be back in Sapporo. And the day after that...."

The day after that they'd be back in Tokyo. The cars and buildings and people, the apartment, the internet, the whole massive, crushing rest of the real world.

And all the other worlds beyond it.

Daisuke smiled slyly over the fish. "I have a plan. I'll tell you later. Tonight."

"Yeah? What's special about tonight?"

"It will be very romantic," he promised.

★ ★ ★

Daisuke resolved to save Anne from bears more often. What a glorious day he'd spent, cooking for her, protecting her, making love to her. And what a romantic way he had to cap it all off. Daisuke had planned out everything.

He had seated her facing east, so she could look out at the forested skirts of the mountains. The stream was close enough for them to hear its burbling under the evening birdsong, and the breeze was picking up. Soon it would be the perfect temperature for cuddling.

Daisuke knelt on the picnic blanket and held up the little black velvet box. If Anne's face was the camera, he should tilt the box so the light from the setting sun would catch the diamond on the ring. Like so.

"Oh no," she said.

"Anne Houlihan," said Daisuke, "will you marry me?"

She burst into tears.

Daisuke's first thought was that he'd positioned the ring incorrectly. Then, that she thought sunset was an unlucky time of day to propose. Or had Anne been expecting the custom of the ring in the champagne glass? He had thought about that, but wouldn't packing champagne on a camping trip tip her off?

Daisuke had called Anne's friends and family and asked them what sort of proposal she would like. Responses had ranged from, "Not a clue, mate. Sorry," to "Oh, whatever you think is best, love," "Didn't you already propose?" and "What's the point of marriage anyway?"

Maybe Anne belonged to the last camp. Shouldn't Daisuke already know it if so? How could he so precisely predict the needs and desires of his audience, his director, his producers and fans, but not the woman he loved? Or was he being needy again? No, but he was performing. There were no cameras here. If only the sun wasn't in his eyes, he'd be able to see her expression.

"What's wrong?" he asked. A blind grope in the dark.

"Oh, nothing!" She rubbed her eyes and shook her head. Curls whipped. "It's just the whole world is crashing down on my head. Tomorrow it's Sapporo, then Tokyo the next day, and there will be all these emails waiting for me because you wouldn't let me bring my smartphone…and…just…!" Anne flailed her arms, hands like bats against the salmon and tangerine clouds.

Daisuke shifted his weight. This pose was becoming uncomfortable, and now he was wondering if it had been a good idea to keep the second phase of their trip a secret. Tears were not in the script he had prepared, and neither were emails. Maybe that was the problem. Anne had said she wanted him to be more spontaneous. He would speak from the heart, like she did.

"I don't like it that you're talking about email," he said. "I just proposed to you."

"I know! I'm sorry. I know you worked so hard to make this whole thing happen." She waved at the cooling landscape. "I wanted to play it right for you, but now all I can think of is that the scene is over and we have to pack up and go back to real life and I just can't!"

"Scene?" said Daisuke, but she wasn't wrong. "You knew I was planning this?"

"Well, yeah, Dice. It wasn't too hard to figure out."

Daisuke closed down his expression, trying to think. If she'd known all along, then what had her plan been? What was the purpose of this crying now? What could Anne be doing but telling him *no*?

"No, don't do the blank mask thing again. Don't…." Her shoulders sagged. "I'm sorry." She dropped onto the cloth in front of him as if she'd taken an arrow to the chest. "I'm just totally at a loss here, Daisuke. We were having such a good time. Catching fish. Having sex. You saved me from a bear! I've been looking forward to accepting your proposal for months! But then the time comes and I just fall apart! What the hell is wrong with me?"

Daisuke dropped his bitterness and grabbed at the question. "I think the answer is *fame*," he said. "Fame is wrong with you."

Daisuke had already been something of a celebrity in Japan before he became the face of the first expedition to Junction, and he had had a hard enough time adjusting to the increased public scrutiny. Anne's experience had been even more extreme.

She had been working on her first post-doctoral project when the Nun people, the local Papuan highlanders, had shown her the interplanetary wormhole in their back yard. Beyond the wormhole: Junction, the center of a web of yet more life-bearing planets.

A great deal of trouble had resulted, but Anne had survived for more than a week in Junction's patchwork wilderness, saved several lives (including Daisuke's), unmasked a murderer, foiled a military coup, and held up through the interrogations that had followed their rescue.

It was only when they'd come back to civilization that Anne had begun to flounder. Sleepless nights. Panic attacks. Delayed reaction? Useless boyfriend?

As he had learned to do on wilderness shoots, Daisuke suppressed his fear and uncertainty. He put his arms around Anne, and she turned and snuggled her back into his chest.

"This is nice," she said. "I wish we could do this all the time."

"We can do it all the time," Daisuke assured her.

"In Tokyo? Come on. Some days you wake up at 4am. Some nights you stay up *until* 4am. And you have to. There's always a party or a presentation or something else of Earth-shattering importance." She shook her head, sending curls flying. "And I just can't. Do you get it?"

More scared than he'd ever been sticking his hand into any hole the ground, Daisuke said, "No."

Anne thought for a moment. "I wake up and – wham!" She flailed her arm. "I reach for the cell phone, I turn off my alarm, and then I look at that screen."

"Yes?"

"And I think, 'What's it going to be today, the food pellet or the electric shock?'"

That took some thinking before the reference clicked. "Mm. Like a rat in a cage."

"Yeah. I'm like, 'Oh I was invited to give the keynote at a sustainability conference.' And someone called in a bomb threat because of something I said on Twitter. Or it's, 'Hurrah, you're invited to this fellowship.' But that one got defunded because the English department took offense at something else I said."

Daisuke tried to think of some useful advice. He really only had the one line, the same one he'd told her back when they'd met by the terraforming pools north of the village the Nun people had built on Junction. Tonight, he tried to put the message in different words. "It's not important what fools think. Don't pay attention to trolls on the internet."

Her sigh steamed, a pale flag in the dark air. "It's not the internet, Dice. It's everyone, every day. It's the human race, it's the planet Earth. It's running as fast as you can just to stay still, and I'm *failing*." She choked. Gasped. Forced more words out. "I'm the rat that gets a shock with every food pellet. So it just falls apart. Sits there shuddering in the corner of the cage."

Daisuke fought his own sense of panic. How had things gotten this bad? Should he contact a psychiatrist? Why hadn't he known? He was supposed to be the sensitive one. "No," he told her. "You can't look at it that way."

"Yeah, that doesn't help," she said. "I can't lie to myself, Dice. I'm not cut out for fame, like you. You can handle it, but I just can't." She pressed her back against him as if trying to push him over. "I should be a little worker bee humming away in the field, counting birds of paradise. Instead I'm the queen of Junction! And everyone wants a piece of me. Hurry up and fix the world's problems, Anne. Quick, before it's too late! Oops, it *is* too late! They burned down that forest and it's your fault for not stopping it."

Daisuke tried to get control of them both. He held her, and they rocked together on the picnic blanket.

"It's okay," he said, gathering up his courage again. This was hard to say. "It's okay. I love you."

She sniffed and turned her head so she could press her cheek against his shoulder. Daisuke's ears were starting to freeze, but the woman in his arms was warm. Infinitely precious. "I love you too. I'm sorry, Daisuke."

"Don't apologize."

"Okay. I won't."

The shadows of the trees reached out to swallow them and now it was night. Crickets sang their slow autumn song.

"I like this," Anne said. "I like it out here. We can just focus on day-to-day survival. Running away from bears and sleeping together in a tent under the stars...."

That *we* was a big relief. "It reminds me of what you love," Daisuke said.

"Yeah. And it isn't people." She jerked in his arms. "Oh, Dice! I'm sorry! I had this whole stupid nervous breakdown after you *proposed* to me! I shouldn't have let myself get sidetracked like…hang on. Didn't you already propose to me? Wasn't that the thing with the vacuum-spinner in the helicopter?"

The Nun had given him the enigmatic alien specimen, and he'd given it to Anne right after the American helicopter had rescued them. Anne had been so impatient to get the interrogations over with so she could get back to studying it. And the things she had discovered!

"The vacuum-spinner wasn't official," said Daisuke.

"You must have thought I was looking for excuses not to marry you," said Anne. "Oh, shit, Dice, I'm sorry."

She still hadn't said 'yes' yet, but Daisuke didn't tell her so. That would be tantamount to demanding that she say yes, and then what would the word even mean? Anne only said what she believed to be true, and Daisuke would no more dam up that authenticity than he would pour concrete into a mountain spring.

So he held her, enjoying her warmth and the starlight reflected in her hair, controlling his urge to rush into things.

The clouds were gone, and the Milky Way hung above them. With the sun behind the Earth and the lights of civilization far away, enough darkness had grown to make the galaxy visible. Between the brightest stars, more stars shone. Between them, yet more, and that was only the beginning.

"Just think," he said. "Those stars are all places."

Anne shifted in his arms. She was looking up too.

"Christ, that's lovely," she said. "I'm going to miss this."

All right, *this* was the time. "You don't have to miss it," Daisuke declared. "Let's go back to Junction!"

Anne went still. "But, they won't give us permission."

She was trying to convince herself that she didn't deserve to be happy. That meant Daisuke was on the right track. "You're the queen of Junction. Of course you'll have permission."

"I've seen the photos though. The army has destroyed so much. Are any of the biomes we explored still even there?"

Daisuke tried to remember the idiom. "There's only one way to find out."

She laughed. "God, Junction." Her hand found his, and clasped around it. "Can we stay there this time?"

"Yes," he said.

They kissed until the jewel box snapped closed on his thumb.

"Ow!"

"Well, give that over here." Anne took the box. "Now I can climb on top of you."

CHAPTER TWO

Vacuum-Spinner

The second phase of Daisuke's plan apparently began with lunch at an outdoor café .

Anne had to admit that this was no mean feat. Her previous experience with Sapporo had led her to believe the city had no such thing as an outdoor café. One could drink beer under the TV tower or have coffee in the glassed-in atrium of a crowded shopping center. One could even visit a restaurant called Auto Doa Kafue, which was neither 'outdoor' nor a 'café'. But Daisuke had found this place, under an overhang on the ground level of a hotel, sandwiched between a parking lot and another hotel.

If Anne turned her head and looked across the street, she could see a medium-sized cherry tree, a highly groomed little canal, and an even smaller and more highly groomed garden. A cedar tree and a clutch of red and maroon maples huddled under telephone wires and square, anonymous buildings. As Anne watched, a pair of young women gestured and exclaimed and took pictures of themselves in front of the trees.

"What are you thinking about?" asked Daisuke, and Anne realized she was being ungrateful. The café *was* outdoors, after all, and it *did* serve coffee, as well as small, expensive, extremely precious little pastries. Anne plucked at the unfamiliar weight of the ring on her finger, and fed her pastries to the pigeons.

"Pigeons," she decided to answer.

There were half a dozen of them jostling for space on the sidewalk, pecking up crumbs in the shadow of the overhang. Females scuttled away from males, which bobbed their heads and cooed desperately, throat feathers fluffed and shimmering with iridescence, fanned tails sweeping the concrete. Low-ranking birds loitered on the sidewalk, darting in to steal crumbs and hopping back out when their flock-mates nipped at them.

"Pigeons?" Daisuke asked. Was he really interested, or just faking it because he wanted to be a good boyfriend? Fiancé now. He'd be good at faking that too. How would Anne ever know?

"Specifically," she said, "color morphs." She tossed crumbs to the pigeons in need. The pavement-birds. "These pigeons are mostly wild-type. Dark gray heads and necks, light gray bodies. Four dark bars on the wings?" A few had wings checkered with dark feathers, but Anne didn't see any brown or pied morphs. "I'm guessing that means there are fewer domesticated birds in this gene pool than in Tokyo."

"You've studied the birds in Tokyo?"

Their life together in the city should have been a reward. *Good job, Anne! You survived, you stopped a war or something, you won the heart of a good man, so now you can just return to the rat race. Get running!*

She had tried gamely to fit into Daisuke's life, but there just didn't seem to be space for her. The obvious next step for him, career-wise, involved lots of parties, charity events, and international golf courses, none of which were Anne's preferred habitat. She could talk to two or three people at a time, or to a room full of fellow scientists at a conference, or to animals and plants, but any other situation left her floundering.

Recently Anne had been spending more and more time locked in their apartment, having increasingly vitriolic battles with people on the internet. The international NGO for the preservation of Junction had fallen apart and, privately, Anne was relieved.

But now everything was fine, right? She was engaged. Her fiancé would sweep her off to Junction. That had to be a good idea.

So she counted white rump patches. "Most of the pigeons have white feathers between the shoulders and hips. See? That's a defense mechanism to confuse hunting falcons."

She waited for him to translate her words back to her. *So, Anne, you're saying that there are probably more falcons here than in Tokyo?*

Instead, he said, "Ah. They're here."

Anne closed her eyes and took a deep breath. "You invited someone to meet me." From pigeon politics to people. She wished she could flash her feathers and dive to safety.

"Yes. You'll like them. This is my plan. Hello!" Daisuke stood and waved at someone across the street.

Hello? So he was addressing these mystery guests in English. That was both good and bad. The whole conversation wouldn't be over Anne's head, but on the other hand she couldn't just nod and smile and think of pigeon population genetics. Damn.

Anne twisted around in her rickety little chair and squinted at the man and woman walking along the canal toward her. Where these people his friends or business contacts or fans or what? Had Daisuke told her and she'd just been thinking about pigeons?

"What the hell is this, Daisuke?" she hissed.

He twitched his head to the side, confused. Then his TV-personality mask came down. "Relax. You'll like them."

It was impossible to tell whether that was a promise, threat, or order.

Anne licked her lips and rubbed her sweaty palms against her trousers, willing her heart to slow. *Bloody fight-or-flight reaction!* If they were still safely in the wilderness, she could at least scream and jump up and down and scare these people away.

Daisuke turned from the strangers and looked into her eyes. He gave her hand a squeeze. "It will be all right."

It was like he could smell her nervousness. And whatever crazy empathic powers Daisuke had, they worked on everybody. He would guide her through this interaction.

He stood, and Anne followed his lead.

The visitors probably weren't fans. The man was too old, and the woman was too well-groomed. She looked like a supermodel, and he looked like somebody's granddad.

No, make that somebody's wicked great uncle. The one who traveled the world and gave you a hookah for your thirteenth birthday. Skinny, energetic, face deeply tanned, hair and goatee brilliant white. He wore a shimmery gray suit that looked both comfortable and dapper as all hell. If he were a pigeon, he would be puffing his neck very far out indeed.

"Mr. Irevani!" Daisuke stepped forward to shake the man's hand, beaming as if he were addressing his dearest friend and most valued associate.

There was none of the awkward do-I-bow-or-shake-hands stumbling of a Westerner in Japan. Irevani seized Daisuke's hand in both of his and clasped it, his grin like a mirror reflecting the sun.

Uh-oh, thought Anne.

"Please, call me Farhad." He turned his smile to Anne, who squinted in the glare. Here was another member of Daisuke's tribe: the warrior-empaths.

"Professor Houlihan," the wicked uncle said. "It is an inexpressibly intense honor."

Oh *honor*! Anne had learned to be very careful about what honors she accepted. There were people who would call her a hero to her face, then turn around and sneer to their friends: 'She thinks she's a hero.'

"I'm not a professor yet," Anne told them. "I'm barely an associate professor."

"Oh, excuse me," Farhad said. "May I call you Anne, then? How gratifying it is to finally meet you. And in such a charming setting too. Sapporo is one of my favorite cities. And at this time of year, the foliage is just breathtaking, isn't it? Thank you, Daisuke, for making this happen."

Why was he still talking? Oh, he was holding out his hand for Anne to shake. Once she shook it, she'd be able to hold Daisuke's hand and find some stability in this cyclone of charm.

Farhad's palm was warm and dry because of course it was. He gave Anne's hand a squeeze just firm enough not to be icky and guided her efficiently up, down, up again. Release.

"Nice to meet you, uh...." What the hell was his name? Had Daisuke told her?

His gaze slid to Daisuke. "Kept me a surprise, I see? Don't worry, I'm a pleasant one."

So this conversation was going to be over Anne's head after all. Social cues were flying like badminton birdies.

"Farhad Irevani," he said. "Any way you want to pronounce it is fine with me."

Anne groped for Daisuke's hand and found it. She let out a breath, recited, "Pleased to meet you," and slumped, exhausted, while Daisuke elegantly explained both Anne and Farhad to each other.

"Farhad is interested in investing in your conservation work on Junction. He's a Silicon Valley entrepreneur."

"That would explain the American accent," said Anne.

"Do I have an American accent? Please inform my daughter!" Farhad's laugh sounded entirely honest and unrehearsed.

"And his administrative assistant is Aimi Garey," Daisuke continued.

Aimi gave him a perfect bow, then reached around her boss to give Anne a perfect handshake.

"Oh my god, Professor Houlihan, it's so good to finally meet you in person," she said, all slender calves, elegant cheekbones, and stylish brown hair. "You're such an inspiration to me and so many other women."

That couldn't possibly be honest. Anne shrugged. "Okay?" Nobody in the vicinity gave any indication of whether that had been the correct response or not.

Anne sat back down.

Farhad nodded approvingly at her. "I apologize for descending on you from out of the blue like this, but to make up for it, I have come bearing gifts. Or rather, Aimi has." He stepped aside, revealing the charcoal-colored box in Aimi's hands.

"And excuse me, Daisuke, but Aimi isn't exactly my administrative assistant. I prefer the term 'mentee', or possibly 'shadow'. Until she goes on to greater things, she keeps me honest."

"I also carry his stuff," Aimi said. She held out the box.

Anne tried not to think of engagement rings, attacking bears, and all the things her rumpled jumper and zip-kneed polyester pants weren't doing for her. This woman was the sort you got at film star parties. Daisuke's league.

She was looking at Anne. Everyone was looking at Anne. "Thanks?" she tried.

"Please, sit," said Daisuke. "Can I get you something?" Oh shit, he was going to go order and leave her with these people?

Farhad fluffed out his suit jacket and sat with his back to the pigeons. "Of course this is my treat, so what can *we* get you?"

Anne let Daisuke handle the social dance and stared at the box, panic rising. If it contained another engagement ring, the diamond would have to be the size of a lemon.

Aimi passed it to her mentor and went to order coffee, somehow talking Daisuke out of chivalrously doing it for her.

"Aimi is my best mentee yet," Farhad said. "She was the one who ran into Daisuke at the Independence Day party and laid the groundwork for this conversation."

"So Aimi manipulated Daisuke into manipulating me." Anne wondered if she should have said that.

Daisuke drew in a breath, but Farhad laughed. "Yes, this is exactly what I came for!" he said. "It's like you're allergic to bullshit. I love it! I'd hire you in a second to just sit next to me at pitch sessions and break out in hives."

She looked at him, resisting the urge to scratch.

Farhad's eyes crinkled. "I think you would appreciate it if we got down to business, hm?" The entrepreneur's hands caressed the box's black beveled corners. A manicured thumb pressed against a square on the front, and a green light came on.

"Aimi won't mind if she misses the big reveal. She's seen it before." Farhad leaned back as he opened the box, grinning like a carnival barker.

Inside the box was Anne's vacuum-spinner.

The alien specimen looked like a pomegranate covered in metallic scales, nestled on a bed of sheer gray silk. Except that the silk's shade changed depending on how you looked at it, and the scales were so tough it took diamond-tipped drills to penetrate them. Farhad had in his possession the remains of a space-dwelling organism, brought to Earth through at least two interstellar wormholes.

Anne felt dizzy. She remembered Daisuke holding this fascinating life-form out to her and asking to accompany her on her next adventure. Of course, what had actually happened was a couple of helicopter rides and a great deal of very dull politics. There had been a hundred opinions about what to do with Junction, none of them right, and when Anne said so, everyone got offended. Anne thought that at least she'd made sure she'd managed to get the vacuum-spinner into the safety of a proper research facility, but Farahad had managed to reverse even that tiny victory.

Daisuke squeezed Anne's hand, and she realized she'd been squeezing his.

"How", she asked, "did you get that?"

Farhad's eyes flashed up and down her face. "You must be angry. You wanted this thing safe in a museum."

"Well, yeah. The University of Sydney was supposed to keep that specimen safe from gallivanting billionaire dilettantes."

"Millionaire." Farhad smiled modestly. "Let's not get ahead of ourselves. Ah, and here's Aimi with the coffee. Aimi, I've screwed up. Observe my mistakes and learn."

"This isn't a joke." Anne pointed at the vacuum-spinner, her finger trembling. "What exactly are you going to do with this thing? Turn it into a hood ornament for your private jet? Grind it up and snort it off the back of a hooker?"

"Anne...." murmured Daisuke, which meant she was being rude. Was it the hooker comment? She glanced at Aimi, who did not so much as bat an eyelash.

"Defensive armor." Still holding her tray of coffees and food, Aimi spoke with the air of a doctor diagnosing a nasty case of shingles. "You had to build it up, with all the scrutiny the media is giving you."

Scrutiny such as the kind Aimi and her boss were focusing on Anne right now. She felt like a plasmodium trying to look back up the through the microscope lens.

Anne turned to Daisuke for protection, then remembered she was angry at him. "You knew I'd hate these people, which is why you didn't tell me about meeting them. And you told them to bring an alien organism because you know that's what gets my juices flowing."

"Let him give you the offer before you refuse it," he said, and didn't that just sound so reasonable!

"I told you we should have shown her a new species," Aimi said. "You can't swing a dead cat on Junction without finding a new species. The investors like the vacuum-spinner, but to a scientist, you just look—"

"Corrupt?" Farhad's fingers drummed impatiently on the box. "Professor Houlihan. Anne, I know you're not the sort of person to be won over by showmanship. I understand that."

"Clearly untrue," Anne observed.

"My intention was simply to get your expert opinion on the nature of this organism. The paper you published described it as a 'vacuum-dwelling autotroph'. In other words, a plant from space, right?"

"No. Well, plants do harness sunlight to make sugar, and indications are that spinners use light to spin them against a magnetic field, which must make sugar or something metabolically useful." Anne remembered she ought to be angry. "I mean, hey!" She poked her finger against the metal surface of the table, which wobbled. "You clearly *bribed* someone at the University of Sydney to let you cart this specimen all the way here so you could show it to me, so I could—" She flailed. "What do you even expect me to do? Hold it up and recite its vital statistics to the studio audience like I'm selling jewelry on television?"

Anne had to breathe at that point, and Farhad leaned forward like he was about to say something else stupid.

Aimi said, "Well," and he relaxed. "I understand you." But Aimi immediately disproved herself. "This is some sort of tiny spacefaring bio-ship."

"Oh my god!" Anne wanted to tear her hair. "No! Why do people keep saying it's a bloody spaceship? Why does everyone have to gravitate toward the dumbest possible interpretation? And then you stick *bio* on the front of it like that's supposed to— Look." She grabbed at the box, and Farhad's grip tightened.

"Relax, mate, I'm only going to turn it around so you can look at the organism." He relaxed, and she did.

"Look at it," Anne commanded. "Look at that shell. It isn't just hard, it's at least three centimeters of metals, ceramics, and polymers extruded in layers only two molecules thick, in a zigzag pattern reminiscent of tubulanes. It's harder, tougher, and more opaque to electromagnetic radiation than anything evolved on Earth. In a vacuum, that shell would inflate into a sphere, with a single point of entrance into the interior. And *that* is protected by a valve that's unlike anything we've seen, manufactured *or* evolved."

Farhad raised a finger. "Now imagine if we could reverse engineer that."

"Whatever," said Anne. "Don't look at me, Mr. Entrepreneur. Look at the spinner. Look at that fucking valve. It's blown open now, but when closed, its resistance to exiting fluid would have been ridiculously high. Going the other way, resistance is actually *negative*, which means that this thing is very slowly pumping air into itself, even though it's *dead*."

"And how—"

"You wanted the lecture, you listen to the lecture." Anne slapped the table, disturbing the pigeons. Her coffee spilled. "Right. So, the vacuum-spinner lives in a vacuum. But what's it doing up there? It's spinning. That's what we think the skirt is for. That's the silklike material that's extruded from glands around the valve. Quartz crystals doped with oxygen, nickel, iron – each crystal with nanoscale hooks—" she demonstrated with her fingers, "– linked together in a *very* specific order and folded and twisted and pleated like some sort of giant, inorganic *enzyme!*"

Anne unraveled her fingers, which she had folded and twisted together. Did she have their attention? Who cared? Either these people would learn something or they would go away and let her yell at Daisuke for getting her into this.

"I won't grab ahold of the stuff to demonstrate – and you better not have either – but if you pinch it between two fingers—" Anne pinched the air, "– it will either stretch like putty or resist like steel, all depending on the direction you pull. Now imagine if you spin it." She spread her fingers. "It forms a disk. A skirt. Microstructures on the surface of the fabric make it opaque or reflective to electromagnetic radiation depending on the angle the photons hit, and those microstructures alternate in these—" she groped for words, "– *gorgeous* bands that spiral out from the spinner. We're sure – well, *I'm* sure as hell sure – that the purpose of all of this is to spin the organism around inside its shell."

Anne's hands twitched. She longed to spin the organism on its stalk the way she had back on the American aircraft carrier, showing these dipshits how frictionless the motion was. Reverse engineer *that*, humans!

But no touching. With no mechanisms to repair them, the nanoscale structures that allowed these miracles broke. They broke a little more with each demonstration, and with each day. Magic, draining away.

Anne blinked away tears and forced her voice to stay level. "We mustn't cut this thing open. It's the only specimen of its kind on Earth. The Nun on Junction don't have any more, either. We have no idea how to get—" Her voice broke, and she swallowed and looked down at her hands. Damn it! Damn Daisuke for setting her up to fail like this.

He held her hand. His fingers were very warm. Somehow, he was stopping the others from interrupting her.

Anne took a breath. Let it out. "It's not a 'bio-ship'. It definitely didn't live in interstellar space. This thing evolved in microgravity and very low pressure, yes, but the valve wouldn't make sense unless there were some gasses for it to suck in. Not to mention magnetic fields to spin against. I think it skimmed the very upper layer of the atmosphere of an Earthlike planet."

"A planet like Junction," Farhad said.

Anne wished she could disagree, because now she understood where this conversation was headed.

"In your papers, you said this organism is adapted for life in an ecosystem unlike anything we've seen," said Farhad, "a low-orbit biome."

She nodded wearily. "And, since this specimen shows no sign of reentry burning or impact with the ground, there must be a wormhole on Junction that leads into space. Is that what you want me to say?"

"Yes," breathed Farhad. His eyes sparkled. "Yes, exactly."

Anne slumped back in her chair. She felt like she was back on Junction. 1.3 gees, and one of those stupid body cameras dangling off her chest, second-guessing every word she said and every thing she did. She felt like a circus performer. This meeting, her angry speech, it had all been on the script that these three had worked out between them.

"Please," she said, "return the vacuum-spinner to the University of Sydney. Whatever you paid them, it isn't enough to deny the world access to the things we can learn from the specimen."

Farhad gave another genuine-sounding chuckle. "You think that I'm greedy and controlling and I'll steamroll over any idiot stupid enough to get in my way as I suck all the world's value into myself."

She glared levelly at him, which he took as assent.

"But what I actually do is *create* value." He gestured at the spinner. "Those scales, the valve, the nano-manufactoring. And you didn't mention the radiation shielding. I would never deprive the world of this alien. I only borrowed it temporarily. Something to wow the investors with so that I can get the budget I need to explore these potentially world-changing discoveries. And so many more. You understand."

Anne didn't understand and didn't care. "Were your investors impressed by the show? I'm not. I know what the vacuum-spinner looks like. I've memorized its exterior features and everything that seismic tomography can tell us about its interior. I have *dreams* about dissecting this specimen, of—"

Anne stopped herself, but too late.

Farhad was leaning toward her, hands back on the spinner's velvet box. "You've had dreams—" he lowered his voice and Anne found herself leaning even closer to him, "– of seeing a live one. In space."

His face was much too close to hers, still grinning, wrinkles deep in the corners of his mouth.

"I am here because I need Anne Houlihan. And *you*", he said, before she could muster a response, "are here because you need a mission."

Again Anne found herself stammering, "I-I already have a mission."

Farhad leaned back, hands going from the spinner's box to his coffee cup. He took a sip. "You want to save Junction."

All Anne could say was, "Yes." She felt like a sheep with a collie at her ankles.

"Yes!" He beamed. "And where can that salvation happen? Here on Earth? Where's your leverage on this tired old planet?" Farhad swept a hand to take in the towering buildings, the tiny park across the canal. "Here, you're just another expert opinion for the media to ignore." His flat palm became a finger pointing upward. "But *there*, you can answer some of the questions we're all asking."

"You mean, are we going to fuck up Junction like we fucked up the Earth?"

"I...no." For the first time, they seemed to be off script. Farhad rubbed his goatee. "I was thinking of other questions, because what we do to Junction, you have the power to change that." He held his hands out at her. Coffee would have sloshed if there had been any left in his cup. "You can be the one who sets the policy on how we explore, not just on Junction, but on all the worlds it leads to."

"I'm no politician."

"Exactly. *You* know what you're doing." Farhad caught her eyes with his, and she couldn't look away. "Anne, on Earth you are wasting your time."

Anne clenched her fists and swallowed. The force of the temptation was almost palpable. A fishhook in her lip. On Junction, she could be queen.

"Are you planning anything big here on Earth?" Farhad asked. "Anything you can't delegate or do from Junction?"

"I tell her she needs to delegate more," Daisuke said, and Anne startled in her chair. For a second, she'd forgotten he was there. That he'd set this whole thing up!

And why not say it? "You set this up!"

"Yes I did. You need it." He looked into her eyes. "Why aren't we on Junction already?"

Anne should have said, 'Because of your career!' That would have been a good tactic, but she only thought of it a second after the words just fell out of her mouth: "They're destroying Junction. It's too heartbreaking to see it happen."

She hadn't meant to say that! But now it was out there, that truth, echoing between them. Why wasn't Farhad saying anything? He'd been quick enough to interrupt her before. Why was he letting the awful silence stretch now?

"Well?" Anne demanded.

"You're right," Daisuke said simply. "It is heartbreaking what they're doing beyond the wormhole."

And now Farhad put his oar in. Or maybe his demon's pitchfork. "No accountability, no planning, no vision beyond the next quick buck they can make. Idiots. That's why we need to be there, on site, supplying our more far-sighted, comprehensive vision."

Anne clutched the edge of the table, suddenly dizzy. She felt as if she were on a descending elevator. Like she was falling through the wormhole in Papua.

"My plan is a small expedition," Farhad was saying. "A compact but very powerful electric camper."

The plastic edge of his voice reached between Anne's ribs, pressed hard against her heart. She found herself massaging her chest, looking away from the tycoon and at the pigeons.

Those bizarre, beautiful creatures. As wondrous as any alien. Zippered keratin sheathing chalky skeletons rigged with protein puppet-strings. The whole organism bathed in iron-doped brine, four-hundred-million-year-old currents washing in and out of each cell, dragging oxygen from the atmosphere so that protons could be properly pumped.

A car swept by and the pigeons scattered. Wings slapped and syrinxes gurgled in alarm. Bones, muscles, and feathers slid across each other. Around them flowed the air, no less a product of biology. All that oxygen.

"Anne?" Daisuke said. She tried to ignore him, watching the pigeons swoop past the edge of the hotel and out of its shadow. They flared in the sunlight and vanished.

So that was why Daisuke had arranged this meeting. This was his engagement gift to her. His way to get her out of civilization, where she could be happy. To fix, if not her, then at least their relationship. *Oh, shit*, she thought. *It'll kill him if I say no.*

And Farhad was talking again. "What do you say, Anne? Can I take you back to Junction?"

★ ★ ★

"No," Anne said, and Daisuke swallowed the sudden lump in his throat.

She couldn't reject this gift. They couldn't go back to Tokyo. He had nothing to offer her there except some kind of nervous breakdown. Anne was like some sort of exotic creature. A cassowary. Beautiful and dangerous. Unappreciated and totally unsuited for life in a city. One way or another, Daisuke would have to reintroduce her to the wild.

If anyone noticed Daisuke's inner turmoil, they didn't show it. Farhad was leaning back, smiling, fingers laced over his belly.

"Finally, we come to the 'no'," he said. "It's good that you're unwilling to blindly sign on to my expedition in return for some vague promises of power to set environmental policy on Junction."

"Because you are in no position to grant me those powers," said Anne. "Unless you actually work for the American government."

Theoretically, the American army was only looking after the terraformed valley on Junction until such time as the UN could decide on a way to divide the territory up. A massively fortified emplacement had been built.

"God preserve me from the fate of working for the American government," Farhad said. "Don't worry, I have a much more humble project in mind to start with." He nodded at the vacuum-spinner. "Spaceflight."

"What?" Anne said, and Daisuke suppressed a sigh of relief. She had fed him the correct straight line. They were back on script.

"It's no easy feat," Farhad continued. "More eccentric millionaires have failed at getting into orbit than succeeded, and they had the whole industrial base of Earth to support them." He held up a finger as if to forestall any questions Anne might ask. "But! What if there was a way to get into orbit without all the fuss of rocketry?"

Anne folded her arms over her chest and just looked at him.

Daisuke's gut tightened with anxiety, which years of habit and training translated into a big smile. He spread his hands at his audience and said, "The Howling Mountain is home to a wormhole that can take us to space!"

Farhad deftly caught the cue and ran with it. "The native Nun people who gave you that spinner said it came from a 'Howling Mountain,' right? We've talked to the Nun and sent drones out in the direction they indicated and yes, there is indeed a mountain north-west of Deep Sky Base. Migrating toymakers have beaten trails to it. Toymakers are the alien life-forms that traded the spinner to the—" He caught Anne's expression. "But you know what they are, of course."

Anne's frown deepened. She had seen a man butchered by the little wood-shelled creatures. Daisuke restrained himself from filling the awkward silence.

Farhad did not apologize or otherwise acknowledge his gaffe. He simply talked on. Daisuke was reminded less of a steamroller than a huge American snowplow, clearing a highway.

"Even the *howling* part makes sense," he said. "Air escaping through the wormhole into a vacuum. You see?"

Anne waved a hand. "That's just speculation."

When she failed to elaborate, Farhad raised an eyebrow and tapped a fingernail against the vacuum-spinner's box. "What about this creature? Didn't it come from space? Is there any other way it could have gotten to you, other than through a wormhole?"

Anne looked like she wished she could say no, but she was too honest for that. "It's a hypothesis," she admitted.

"A very well-founded hypothesis," said Farhad. "There's no burn marks on this shell. No damage that might occur from a fall to the ground. If this specimen came from space at all, it came through a wormhole, and what more logical place for a wormhole to lead than from the surface of Junction to orbit around Junction?"

"Now that's *really* speculation."

"Would you like to join me in finding out the truth?"

"Right." Anne nodded, not out of agreement, but because she was assuring everyone she understood what was going on. "Right." Her eyes narrowed. "Now tell me the real reason you want to go to the Howling Mountain."

"Aside from the enormous potential value of a wormhole that leads to space, the human drive to explore, and my family's desire to get me out of the house for a while?" Farhad winked at Anne, who just looked suspicious. "In a word, my goal is bioprospecting. Junction has been accessible for barely a year, the politicians are squelching research as hard as they can, and still I already have dozens of patents filed based on the biochemistry of alien life. Your expertise in that field is unparalleled and would be essential."

"And profitable?"

Farhad answered as if the question hadn't been rhetorical. "Profits are a measure of efficiency, and my entire career has been about finding ways to make more efficient use of resources. Desalinization projects, bioremediation, genetic engineering, even seasteading. Junction has a better chance than any of these ventures of saving humanity."

Daisuke thought some translation might be in order. "The secrets of Junction might provide us with a means to save the Earth!"

"Exactly so," said Farhad.

Anne frowned. "*He's* already blowing enough smoke up my arse, Dice. He doesn't need help."

Daisuke blanked his face, not letting the sting show.

"We need to show people what an intact, unexploited Junction has to offer," Farhad said. "We need real exploration. Real, basic research. Sampling by someone who knows what they're doing."

Anne's eyes widened and Daisuke's esteem for Farhad rose yet further. An invitation to collect biological samples would sound like a dirty and boring chore to Farhad's investors, but Anne hadn't been in the field since they had returned to Earth.

"The area north-west of the glasslands is a wilderness," Daisuke said. "Everything we see will be a new species."

Farhad nodded. "There have been flyovers, but nobody has traversed those plains. No human feet have walked there, not even the Nun."

"There's probably a reason for that," Anne said, but Daisuke could tell she was looking for reassurance now. She wanted this mission to be real.

"The toymakers, now." Farhad held up his hands as if holding up a toymaker: a colony of alien worms puppeteering a wheeled wooden ship. "The toymakers have this periodic migration. And the Nun have agreed to loan us a contingent of toymaker wranglers to guide us."

"Okay," said Anne, and again it wasn't agreement. She planted her hands like cleavers on the table, rattling the coffee cups. "But why are *you* coming on this jaunt? No, let me rephrase that, you shouldn't be coming on this jaunt."

"Anne," murmured Daisuke, but Farhad held up his palms.

"I understand. You're worried I'll get in your way. Micromanage you. I promise you I won't."

"Uh-huh," said Anne. "Because you're the sort of workaholic executive who doesn't schedule every moment of his day and everyone else's."

Farhad grinned. "I prefer to think of myself as a work-connoisseur. This jaunt will be a palate cleanser for me. A vacation. I wasn't kidding about my family wanting a break from me. I'll be more than happy to sit back and watch you do…" he spread his hands and tipped them up, "…whatever it is you want to do."

"Bullshit," Anne said. "You don't hire someone and then not care what they do."

Daisuke kept his face blank, but he wanted to pump his fists and say 'Yes!' Anne's resistance was wearing down.

"What I do is I hire people who care what *they're* doing," said Farhad, "and then get out of their way. And I know you care very much, Anne.

You're the sort of person who will, when placed on an alien planet, take samples. All I ask in exchange for supporting your work on Junction is that I get to keep those samples."

Remembering his role, Daisuke cleared his throat. "Support?"

"Yes. Consider this a dry run. A first step. Once the mission is over and we've returned to base, I will have the resources to expand my presence on Junction." Farhad caught Anne's twitch and said, "I don't mean I'll open a hotel. I'm talking about a research and conservation station. A real one, not some military boondoggle that never actually gets built. And it will have you as its director."

Anne stared at him. Daisuke held his breath.

Farhad put his elbows on the table and leaned forward. "You're an explorer, Anne. Please, help me explore too."

Anne shook her head as if waking herself up from a pleasant dream. She thunked her index finger down on the table.

"I want a firm contract," she said. "And *in* that contract I want to be guaranteed independence. A lot of independence. You don't know what's interesting. I decide what's worth pursuing."

"Literally *pursuing*, I'm sure." Crow's feet deepened as Farhad smiled. "And I can't wait to see you chasing creatures across the landscape. You will have your independence, Anne. It's already in the draft contract. The only caveat is that you have to stay in or close to the mobile lab. Food and fuel constraints demand a strict schedule."

"And the NDA, of course," said Aimi.

Farhad did not so much as flicker an eyelash. "Of course."

Had the two of them rehearsed that reveal? If so, they hadn't included Daisuke in the loop. He leaned forward. "What are the terms of the NDA?"

"No announcement of new discoveries until we arrive back at Imsame. I have final say over the contents of the first press conference. After that, you can say whatever you want." Farhad turned up his hands, as if releasing birds.

"That sounds generous," Anne said.

Daisuke frowned. Was it too generous? But what a fool he would look if he set this meeting up, dragged Anne to it, then backed out now. He shook his head.

"All right," said Anne. "Who's my team going to be? You'll need a lot of specialists. Biochemists, biomechanics people, medical researchers if you want to do anything with drugs. I've been working with some people who I can recommend...."

She trailed off. Farhad had put his palms up and was shaking his head sadly. "Not on this trip, I'm afraid. I'm sorry, Anne, but you know the political situation. If the Farside Administration lets us field our big research team, they'll have to greenlight every other big research team, including those teams from, gasp, China. A big research station would give everyone an advantage, which means no advantage for one power relative to any other. Therefore every individual power will drag its feet, hoping to stumble across a strategic advantage that will allow it shove aside the competition and take the whole pie." He sighed at the foolishness of shortsighted politicians. "But the current deadlock can't last forever, can it? Some time soon the way will be open for civilian research stations. Like yours."

He cleared his throat.

"Then, of course you'll have your pick of the world's talent. For this expedition, however, we'll need to travel light. Aside from myself and Aimi, we'll have a crew of six, not counting the Nun. You and Daisuke are the last puzzle piece."

Emotions warred on Anne's face. She knew she couldn't do much real science without other scientists, but the last year had seen a chill set in between Anne and her colleagues. Envy, Daisuke said. Anne didn't know if he was right or not, but she had started inventing reasons to not appear at conferences.

That was why Farhad's offer was so important. This way Anne wouldn't have to bum around the army base. She could be out on the frontier. She could have Junction all to herself. She'd never have to leave.

"I'm not looking for a repeat of my last trip to Junction," Anne said, as if she'd heard Daisuke's thoughts. "I'm not in the mood for another life-or-death struggle with the aliens while someone tries to kill me, again with the aliens."

"Of course not," Farhad said. "I'm not even chartering a flight. My mission will be conducted in a nice, safe ground vehicle. A mobile lab and dormitory, supplied with everything we need and sealed against the elements."

"A caravan, in other words," said Anne, but Daisuke could tell she liked the idea.

"I believe the chassis was a Class A motor home, attached to what in the States is called a camping trailer," said Farad. "But I do like the word *caravan*. It has a Silk Road ring to it."

"The Wormhole Road?" suggested Aimi, scribbling on her tablet. "The Alien Way?"

"And it's fully stocked," Farhad said. "Microscope, dissecting table, liquid nitrogen, freezers, a mass spectrometer. Everything."

"What the hell would I do with a mass spectrometer?" Anne said. "Naw, ditch the mass spec, and add another freezer. Something that can go down to minus 190. And do you have a 4C fridge? And was that a dissecting microscope?"

Farhad grinned. "It certainly can be, Anne. Anything else you would like to add to your order?"

Daisuke couldn't help himself. "I'm so happy," he said. "This will be like a pre-honeymoon."

He didn't even worry when Anne looked shifty. Maybe she wasn't convinced that agreeing to marry him had been a good idea? Then Daisuke would convince her! Once they were back in the wilderness, he could do anything.

★ ★ ★

Farhad smiled and waved as the couple walked away. He projected calm, but his real expression grew under his mask of polite interest, what his wife called his 'manticore's smile'.

"All right," said Aimi. "All right. You did it."

Farhad looked up at the sky – no good if Houlihan turned and saw him grinning at her – and breathed out a great gust of air, as if to scatter the clouds. "Yes."

With his next in-breath, he gathered his energy, pulling it back into the safety of his body. As if aiming a cannon, he lowered his face and turned it toward his mentee. "Now tell me how I did it."

Farhad rubbed his hands together impatiently as she glanced down at her tablet. His fingers drummed on the vacuum-spinner's box and his knee bounced as if under a grandchild.

"One," she said. "What was the best outcome?"

Farhad checked his coffee cup. Empty. He really shouldn't order another, or he'd be unable to nap, and his ten p.m. with Fort Bragg would be suboptimal.

"Convincing Dr. Houlihan to come aboard," Aimi continued. "Check."

Farhad shook his head. "That wasn't the best outcome. What I wanted was to win her heart, but I failed. Why?"

Aimi frowned down at her tablet.

"The answer isn't in your notes," said Farhad, so Aimi looked up instead of down, cocking her head in a gesture that would look great on the cover of a women-in-business magazine.

Farhad had chosen Aimi to be his mentee partly because she was better than ninety-five percent of the other candidates, and partly because her looks put other people on the wrong foot. Women were envious of her, men of Farhad, and everyone assumed the two of them were sleeping together. They weren't, which made Farhad feel powerful.

"You didn't value-align," she said. "You only seemed to."

"Yes. Go on. Why?"

"Your black swans," Aimi said. "You told her hardly anything about the real mission."

"No more than her poor fiancé told her about this meeting. Why weren't we more forthright?"

"Well, because she would have said no."

"At the very least. She'd probably inform the authorities and have us arrested." Farhad's knee bounced. What he could use now was a walk. It was good to feel so much energy.

"Well, how do you value-align if you can't tell the other person what your real mission is?" she asked. "How do you build trust if you can't trust someone?"

"What you do is you change the terrain," said Farhad. "Here, on Earth, real synergy with Ms. Houlihan is impossible. On Junction, however, out of range of communications networks, things will be different." He stood. "Come on, let's take a walk. I'll need to work out some of this energy before my nap."

CHAPTER THREE

Holes

Under the ground of the highlands of Indonesia, a portal waited to open. Around that hole in the universe, pitiful human machinery clanked and gurgled.

Professor Dohyun Moon listened impatiently, his fists clenched, his teeth grinding, his eyes on a little red light. When would it ever turn green?

The light indicated the status of a hatch. The hatch blocked a portal that had sat here in the New Guinea highlands for as long as there had *been* any New Guinea highlands. A well of cosmic mystery, the greatest discovery since the stars themselves, and what had people done when they discovered it? Fought a territorial skirmish over it, then built this concrete nest on top of it.

The Indonesians had fortified the portal on their territory, dug the ground out from under it, lined the well they'd made with metal, and filled the well with water. Right now, that water was being pumped out according to principles understood since Archimedes. Never mind the question of how the portal knew when the water was gone. Never mind how it decided what should pass through it in the first place. The authorities were a bunch of narrow-minded primates who cared more about restricting the movements of other primates than about the destruction of *everything* Moon thought he understood about the cosmos and his place in it.

The speaker on the wall crackled. "Professor Moon? I'm sorry, I didn't understand that."

He'd been muttering. It would be a waste of time to explain why, and Moon had so little time left. He shouldn't have to waste his life on this hatch with its little red light. He shouldn't have had to tie himself in knots all through those interminable layovers between flights in primitive human aircraft. Moon should not have had to stand there, uselessly, in that hospital in Seoul, while his father took an unbearable eternity to die.

"Professor Moon?"

"It's not important," Moon said. "I was talking to myself." He tried to control his breathing. He gave up. "How much longer do I have to wait?"

"Any moment now, Professor."

In fact it was another two minutes before Moon felt the shift in his balance. His inner organs sank as the corridor seemed to tilt.

Moon stumbled, catching himself on the door, which had gained an apparent forward cant. A gravity gradient. The interaction between the Earth's vector of gravitational acceleration and that of a distant exoplanet.

And what the hell did *that* imply? That gravitons existed after all? That space-time didn't know it ought to warp until something came out of the portal and told it to? That this information could tunnel instantly under the horizon of the universe and turn the stomach of an impatient monkey on Earth? A monkey that would lose its mind before it died, as well.

It shouldn't be possible for a life to come so suddenly to a stop. Where did the energy *go*?

Moon made fists against the door, visor white with ragged breath.

"Professor Moon, please wait until the light turns green," said the voice from the wall.

He kept his mouth shut. Closed his eyes. Sight and speech were both pointless, and never mind the gravitons. Just calculate the vectors. Moon breathed. One vector points toward the center of the Earth, and the other points to the portal. Or rather, *through* the portal. To Junction.

Moon took a step back and his nausea abated. The pull of Junction faded. Another step back and he could hardly feel it at all. How did that work? How *could* it? Gravity should vary with the square of distance, forming an elegant asymptotic curve. Not this stupid little funnel. According to what Moon understood about how gravity worked, everyone on Earth ought to feel it when the portal opened and gravity from Junction leaked through.

Clearly, then, what Moon understood about gravity was wrong.

At least he had the grace to admit as much. *Wormholes*, the idiots in the media called the portals. If this thing in New Guinea really was two black holes joined by a throat, their gravity would rip Moon apart. He would fall forever into an inescapable gullet of stretched time. Outside observers would see Moon slow, but never stop; approach, but never reach the event horizon. Each breath taking longer to come than the last. The space between each heartbeat stretching.

And what would Moon, himself, experience? One might as well ask what Moon's father experienced as his disease converted his consciousness into noise. As useless a question as 'Don't you recognize me?' or 'Did you get yourself tested?' or 'Why did it have to be so soon?'

There was no cure for the disease Moon and his father shared. There were only the inescapable laws of heredity. You could scream your question into the sky, or a hole in the ground, but you'd never get an answer.

The speaker bleeped like a heart monitor. Moon started, opened his eyes to the fog on the inside of his visor. His biocontainment suit seemed to constrict around him, pinching him at elbows and knees. He itched to rip the pointless thing off.

"Professor Moon, you are cleared to enter the wormhole," said the speaker.

Yes. *Yes.* The light was green.

"Finally." Moon put out his hands and touched the door, which gave a heavy clank as interior bolts drew back.

He pushed, grunted, then realized the problem and pulled, feeling like an idiot.

"There is a ladder inside," the voice said. "Climb down the ladder to the wormhole."

"I know!" said Moon. Climb down the ladder, meet Farhad, get out of range of the American army's surveillance, and then, finally, begin his experiments. Crack portal physics.

The metal rungs slipped in Moon's gloved grasp, but he gripped harder and slowly leaned out over the edge of the door. The ladder descended a meter or so, then seemed to stretch, bulge, rip apart, and recombine itself. Moon might have thought he was looking at a reflection in a warped mirror, except for the fact that his own image was missing. At the far end of the shaft, light shone through an open doorway on another world.

Moon forced his hands to stop trembling. He had no time to waste on awe or dread. He just had to *go*. Leave the Earth like he had left that hospital room. What would have been the point of saying goodbye? His father had been entirely unresponsive to the voices around him. The outside world fell into the man's eyes, and nothing came out.

"Professor Moon? Please proceed through the wormhole."

Moon twitched. "Yes. Of course."

Furious with himself for wasting time, Moon swung himself through the door and onto the ladder. It wobbled slightly under his new, nearly doubled weight. Where did that energy come from? Where did it go?

Nothing about portals made sense. Things just went through one face and came out the other, no matter where. A portal could take him a million light-years away. A portal could take him to the past, or to the interior of a black hole.

His blood pounded in his ears and his weight continued to increase. He should be torn apart and crushed under a falling sky. He *would* be, if this were a real wormhole, if everything Moon understood about the universe were true.

How, then, was his understanding wrong?

Moon descended, imagining someone climbing down through a portal into a black hole. And then, impossibly – miraculously! – leaving.

★ ★ ★

The rows of cages extended for maybe thirty meters. That was smaller than the defensive perimeter around the Farside Base, smaller than the length of the plane that had flown them into the New Guinea highlands. To Anne, though, if you added up the flight from Sapporo to Jakarta, Jakarta to Jayapura, Jayapura to Nearside Base, and the wormhole drop down who knew how many light-years to the planet Junction, the walk between the animal cages was still the longest.

The cages had been stacked three or four high, and lined up to form a sort of gauntlet along the path that led from the Farside Base to what once had been the village of Imsame. Made of green saplings cut apart and tied back together with wire or wickerwork, the cages gave any jet- and wormhole-lagged newcomer an excellent view of the animals inside.

Here was a land-aster from the Lighthouse biome, like a giant plastic-shelled starfish. There, a scaly bug-like reaper from the Sweet Blood biome stood under the dried skin of a dire shmoo from the glasslands. Anne had watched one of these things kill somebody, but looking at this spiny silicone sack, she felt only exhausted sorrow. She registered a turtle and a shivering tree-kangaroo before she had to close her eyes. But still the animals cried out. They stank. They suffered, palpably.

"What's this?" asked Daisuke, and Anne put out her hand to push him forward.

"Don't stop," she said. "Don't look. Don't engage or someone will try to sell you one of these poor things." Then what would she do, caught between the moral imperative to relieve suffering and the market incentive she would create if she gave this bastard any money? She weighed an extra twenty-five kilos on Junction and she wanted to lie down.

"Hello!" said an Indonesian-accented voice. "You like that eagle?"

"Hmm," Daisuke said, which wasn't a no at all.

Anne opened her eyes so she could glare at Daisuke's back. "What, is this your first animal market? I said don't engage."

"You might be interested in this bird," Daisuke said, and you could practically hear the cash-register noises from the merchant.

"No, Daisuke. I'm trying not to look at it," Anne ground out. "If I do, I'll feel how bad *it* feels, and I'll want to fucking buy it."

"Bad?" The merchant's breath puffed on her face and Anne's eyes popped open. "They don't feel bad," he declared. "My animals are all safe."

Anne cursed. Behind her, Farhad chuckled.

"That's a bad marketing strategy, my friend," he informed the merchant. "You should tell her that your animals are in constant misery, so she'll feel compelled to save all of them."

Aimi cleared her throat and the tycoon chuckled. "Excuse my insensitivity. Anne, would you like me to buy all of these creatures and set them free? Then we can find the caravan."

"No!" said Anne and the merchant at the same time. "Someone would just capture them aga—— What?"

"I said no," the merchant repeated.

The dealers in illicit animals Anne had met previously had been walnut-faced old villains, infinite in age and cynicism. This guy, though, couldn't have been more than twenty-nine. He was small and twitchy, with a sharp-featured face and a haircut that made Anne think *military*.

"You don't set them free," he ordered. "You take care of them in your laboratory. Scientists, right? You're not army."

"Yes," Daisuke said.

"Does the caravan have room for an eagle?" asked Farhad.

"Uh," Aimi said. "Anne, would your research be improved by this specimen?"

Anne didn't answer. The creature had indeed caught her attention.

It was not an eagle. Not at all.

"Oh," said Anne. "Oh wow."

Rather than a beak, the animal had a fluffy, tapering snout. Brown fluff covered its body, which terminated in a nubby little tail, from which sprouted a pair of ribbonlike white plumes. It had no talons, which meant it didn't use its feet to hunt.

Anne looked up at the merchant. "Can I get a look at the forelimbs?"

He was still explaining to Farhad. "For soldiers, I say, 'You take good care of it. It's a pet of the barracks, right?' Of course we don't transport them to Earth. We're very moral here. We follow *Ibu* Anne's protocols. The natives.... Ah? What did you say, ma'am?"

"Can I get a look at its forelimbs?" Anne said impatiently.

The merchant fished around in his pocket. "Oh, yes, this is very interesting. Have you seen what happens when you give it food, ma'am?"

He produced a dusty twist of dried meat, which drew a grunt and a hard yellow stare from the non-eagle in the cage. "You've seen this species before, ma'am? You've been to Junction before?" His expression faltered. "Only I don't recognize you. Ma–*ow*!"

The non-eagle didn't poke its beak through the cage to peck at the food the way a bird would. It reached out with its wings, and the feathers folded back to reveal two pairs of long, knob-jointed fingers. Four wicked little claws poked out between the wires and hooked the merchant's distracted hand.

The non-eagle ignored the human flesh and stuffed the jerky into a mouth lined with tiny, backward-slanted teeth.

"Oh, yes. Very interesting," said Daisuke. "A dinosaur."

"A what?" Farhad said. "Since when does this planet have dinosaurs?"

"I think he means it's a dinosaur-like alien?" Aimi suggested.

Anne turned to her. "Oh, of course not. Would you find something this similar to an Earth animal evolving independently on a completely different planet? Daisuke was just being dramatic."

"So this planet does have dinosaurs?" Farhad asked.

Anne peered back into the cage. "Well, yeah. All birds are dinosaurs, and here it is on this planet. What's interesting, though, is just when this thing's ancestors split off from the rest."

"Wait, you're *Ibu* Anne!" cried the merchant, lunging for Anne's hand. "I mean, Professor Anne Houlihan!" He shook it. "I'm very, very happy to meet you! And to work with you!"

"I'm not a professor," Anne said. "Your hand is bleeding."

"Work?" Daisuke repeated.

"Just a…a thing. A little wound. You're Matsumori Daisuke! I'm so excited! We have to take selfies!"

"Ah," said Farhad. "You must be Turtle."

"What turtle?" Anne asked.

Without letting go of her hand, the merchant bowed deeply. He looked like his captive non-eagle, hunched over its meal. "My name is Evan Sudiarna, but everyone calls me Kura."

Anne blinked, then remembered the word in Indonesian. "*Kura* means turtle."

"Yes! I'm very, very happy to meet you! You're heroes!"

"I'm pleased to meet you." Daisuke bowed, then turned to Farhad. "Is he one of your employees?"

"Did Boss Rudi send you to meet us?" Aimi asked the man, who looked nothing like a turtle.

He shook his head, still clasping Anne's hand. "Rudi's with Professor Moon. Mr. Irevani, Ms. Garey! We didn't expect you until tonight. I wanted to find someone to take care of my animals before we go."

Farhad waved his hands. "Wait, wait, wait. There are dinosaurs on Junction? Aliens can be dinosaurs? Surely I would have read reports about this. Clarify this for me, Anne?"

"Didn't I already?" Anne struggled for patience. "The portal has been here for a hundred million years."

"Anne means that the animal in the cage is from Earth," Daisuke said, and held up his hands, forestalling whatever bone-headed misapprehension Farhad was going to come out with next. "That is, its ancestors came from Earth very long ago. Before the dinosaurs went extinct."

"Before the non-avian dinosaurs went extinct," corrected Anne. "And here, they didn't. Or at least, some species from outside Crown-Aves survived." How could she be sure? "Apparently," she corrected the correction. And would Farhad know what 'Crown-Aves' meant? Who cared?

Anne turned to Turtle. "Can it fly? And let go of my hand already."

"Can it fly? Yes? Not like an eagle though," he admitted. "More like a chicken."

"Why not call it a *phoenix*?" Farhad suggested. "Those tail feathers? Mythology always makes the best marketing."

Turtle beamed. "*Ibu* Anne, may I give you this phoenix?"

"No." Anne pulled her hand away from Turtle, who looked crushed.

Daisuke rushed to smooth things over. "She means we can't take care of it. We will stay in a small caravan, I think."

They all looked at each other.

"You are rescuing these animals?" Daisuke asked. "Alone?"

Turtle slumped. "Yes. They bring them to me every day. The natives catch them, or soldiers on terraform duty. Before, they just ate them, but I said they might be valuable scientific specimens." He swallowed. "For scientists. Scientists come every Tuesday, so I bring out the cages. I didn't think— Let's go to Boss Rudi."

"Wait," said Farhad, who had been murmuring with Aimi. "We'll buy them."

Turtle blinked. "All?"

"Yes," Farhad said. "There's, what, about a couple dozen specimens here? Twenty dollars a pop. Let's say five hundred for the lot?"

Anne looked at the tycoon suspiciously. "And what the hell are *you* going to do with them?"

"A zoo." Farhad put his hands on his hips and squinted off into the distance. "The Irevani Zoological Preservation Institute. IZPI. ZIPI?

Aimi, make sure that's not a slur in any popular language and see if you can register the domain name."

"This is wonderful," said Turtle. "Thank you very much, sir."

Anne sidled closer to Daisuke. "What the hell is happening?"

"I think you helped our new friend save the lives of many creatures." Daisuke rubbed his chin. "Do you think the phoenix would make a good mascot for our mission?"

"Yes. Perfect," Farhad said.

"What? No! I can't adopt that thing as a pet."

"I was thinking we could keep it on the grounds of the new research station," Farhad said.

Anne gaped at him, trying to untangle her feelings. Was she angry at this idiot who bought décor for a building that wasn't built yet? Or furious at a villain who thought of animals as décor? Or, just, hopeless? Because this animal didn't have the choice of life in a research station or life in the forest. There was no more forest.

The Mekimsam River, 'the water in the sky', had once flowed through terraforming paddies, yam gardens, and stands of southern beech, karakas, pear-fruits, and *Alyxia* shrubs. All very homey to an Australian biologist, and now, as far as that biologist could tell, gone.

They had crossed a wooden bridge to get to this side of the valley, but the rutted margins of the river testified to a time when soldiers had simply plowed their jeeps through the water. That would explain the failure of the terraforming pools, the flushing of toxic alien biomaterial downstream, the swath of dead ground along the river, and the smell.

Behind Anne, the Mekimsam River flowed in cloudy, scummy folds over sterile rocks. Pale gray tree roots stuck out of sharp-edged gouges in the riverbanks, their soil contaminated and washed away. Matted hummocks of reeds bleached in the sun, unable to rot.

Here, the ground was mostly just mud and dust, stretching to the airfield and a military compound that might have been copy-pasted from Iraq or Afghanistan. Away from disturbed ground, the few plants were fat-leaved succulents, adapted to live in alien-contaminated soil. Once, they had grown only around the terraforming pools, at the edges of the Earth biome.

Those edges were mostly gone too. The ground north of the airfield had been burned and poisoned. Only high up the mountains to the north did the blackened barrens give way to the acid-green alien plants that had spread out of their own wormhole. Above the green began the chocolate-brown of yet another biome. That was Junction. The patchwork world.

"There it is," said Farhad proudly, and for a second Anne thought he meant the wreckage civilization had made of this valley. Then she saw he was pointing at the parking lot.

To be fair, it wasn't just cars that were parked on the asphalt plain. There was construction and earth-moving equipment there too, as well as motor homes and caravans. The largest, she assumed, was Farhad's.

The fifty-foot caravan gleamed like nothing else in this wasteland: white with black honeycomb patterns on its sides that after a moment of squinting resolved themselves into photovoltaic panels. More panels hinged up from the roof like half-open books, angled to the south.

Farhad led the way, saying, "It's a hybrid design. Cutting edge! Solar and hydrogen fuel cells, although we do also carry a diesel generator for emergencies. Bunks on the upper level, laboratories and storage in the back segment, common spaces in the front. Two four-seater electric ATVs clipped to the back. Very suitable for a week of what you might call 'roughing it in luxury'."

"How the hell did you get it here?" Anne asked, trying to keep up.

Behind them, Turtle wrestled the phoenix into a wheelbarrow.

"It was cheaper than you might think." Farhad held out his hand as if weighing a pouch of gold coins. "I only paid a fraction of the shipping and reassembly costs because I sold the design to the army. This is just the sort of self-contained mobile platform they'll need to secure their territory on Junction."

Anne banished the image of an army of these things churning across the landscape. "What do you mean *their* territory? The Pizza Treaty doesn't give sovereign control to anybody other than the Nun."

"If by 'Pizza Treaty' you mean the Treaty of Junction, the United States isn't even a signatory. They never promised to stay off of other territorial wedges. All they've done is promise not to shoot first." Farhad shrugged.

"Water?" asked Daisuke.

"That is the limiting factor, yes. There's a brown water recycling system and a collector we can use to catch rainwater, but the tank can only be so big. The Nun assure me that we can find enough water along the way to top up, but you might want to take your shower now."

Anne wondered where the Nun were. Not anywhere around the Nearside Base in Indonesia, that was for sure. Apparently they'd been pushed out of their village here as well.

"How did you know it would have fingers?" Aimi asked.

Anne started and turned around. Farhad's secretary or mentee or whatever had snuck up on her. "What? Fingers?"

"I mean the phoenix." Aimi gestured toward Turtle, who was trundling his wheelbarrow toward them.

Daisuke cleared his throat and Anne tried to be more personable.

"Um. Because it had no talons on its feet?" Anne said. "No big teeth or hooked beak. It would need to rip flesh with something, you know?"

"How did you know it ate meat?"

Anne shook her head impatiently. "It's eagle-sized. Too big for an obligate insectivore and herbivores usually have a big fermentation gut. It could have been an omnivore or something that doesn't actively hunt, or have some sort of novel digestive system, or the insects here could be abnormally gigantic, but, you know. That was the hypothesis I was testing."

"Amazing." Aimi gushed. "You know they call you the Alien Sherlock Holmes here?"

"It's not an alien." Anne hated the way her cheeks were heating up. *Sherlock Holmes*? "And plenty of my guesses have been dead wrong. Like when I thought that the springy coil inside treeworms was metallic, but it turned out to be sugar crystals! The worms juggle ethanol and water concentrations to move sugars around and fix them in place." She looked back up at the thin band of green on the mountainside. "Or at least they used to."

The Nun people had been walking back and forth between Earth and Junction for the last forty thousand years, and they'd always known that human spit dissolved treeworm structural sugars. The army had found out that laundry detergent worked even better.

"There are still treeworms on their home planet," said Daisuke.

"Yeah," Anne said. "For now. There's no telling when someone will decide to claim the Treeworm wormhole, and then where will we be?"

"You'll be here," Farhad said, striding ahead of them. "That's where you'll be. In charge of a research station, instructing those bad guys to cease and desist."

Anne rolled her eyes.

"*Hei! Siapa di sana? Kura? Kenapa ada karavan? Siapa orang-orang—* Mr. Irevani!"

A short, portly man came bustling out of the caravan. He hastily zipped up his camouflage-patterned jacket and smoothed down his comb-over, shouting, "Mr. Irevani *datang awal*, but it's all okay! Everything okay!"

"Boss Rudi?" Farhad asked as the man lunged at Farhad's outstretched hand.

"I am happy to meet you, sir! Very happy! Even if you, uh, earlier, *semuanya*, uh, everything is ready and we can depart ASAP. Haha! Or have party, right? *Kura goblok, kenapa tidak panggil aku.*"

"*K-karavan....*" said Turtle, while Anne scrunched up her brows in concentration.

"'Stupid Turtle, you didn't radio ahead?'" she translated, and Farhad cocked an eyebrow at her. His smile widened.

"Everyone, this is Boss Rudi, our chief bodyguard and driver."

Anne thought the man looked more like he should be managing an accounting department than guarding an interplanetary expedition.

"I'm sorry we didn't warn you," Farhad was saying. "Don't worry at all, there's absolutely no need to change the schedule. No need for a party. We'll sleep and take showers."

"Ha!" Rudi said, "and then the party. *Bagaimana 'jangan sungkan' dalam bahasa Inggris?*"

"'Take it easy,'" answered Anne and Turtle at the same time.

"I insist!" Rudi roared, and turned to greet Anne. "*Anda pasti Ibu* Anne. *Senang bertemu dengan Anda. Selamat datang.*" He clasped hands with Anne while slapping his free palm against his chest. "Welcome back to Junction!" he continued in Indonesian. "Or maybe *you* should welcome *me*? Haha!"

Anne tried to figure out how to say 'Junction isn't mine' in

Indonesian. She got as far as "Junction *bukan...*" before her words were swept away in the deep, swift torrent of Rudi's effusion.

"Let's have a truly excellent expedition together," he said. "Have you heard of my private security firm, Aunty Anne? It's actually the most highly rated firm for this sort of small, unusual, but very important mission! Indeed, I *personally* guarantee safety, security, and no worries to all my clients. That's to all of my clients, but to Aunty Anne, I am delighted to promise even more! You are a celebrity! A most distinguished scientist, and of course a beautiful young lady."

Or something like that. After a year with very little Indonesian and quite a lot of Japanese practice, Anne was having trouble remembering which end of a sentence was up. "Um," she said. "*Terima. Saya akan... melihat...binatang-binatang?*"

Boss Rudi roared with laughter. Anne felt as if she were cooking in her jacket.

"I just want to say that I am here to make sure that you enjoy every minute of this grand adventure," Rudi said, and whirled away to give Daisuke, then Aimi, the same treatment.

Turtle gave a fractured bilingual explanation of his phoenix. Or perhaps it was Farhad's phoenix, or Anne's. What was to be done with it? No, not on the caravan, and no, the Americans won't take it, not unless you have the proper paperwork for little alien dinosaurs. Haha!

With no decision made, Rudi switched subjects to arguing with Farhad over whether or not they should have a party tonight. Despite the fact that Farhad said no, it turned out that they *would* have a party, which seemed to please Farhad a great deal. Nobody but Anne was surprised by this.

"Is there a bed for me?" she asked Rudi, once she had constructed the sentence in her head and triple-checked for errors. "Or a shower?"

"Of course it would be my honor to show you to your bunk, but—" Boss Rudi cleared his throat, "– the moon is in the shower."

"*Apa?*" said Anne, and repeated back what she thought she'd heard. "*Bulan sedang mandi?*"

He waved his hands. "*Bukan bulan. Kubilang* Moon *segang mandi.* Professor Moon. Ah!" A laugh. "Good joke!"

"Ah," said Farhad. "We're a day early and he still managed to get in ahead of us. No time wasted with Professor Moon."

"*Siapa?*" Anne shook her head. "I mean, who?"

For the first time, Farhad looked less than completely self-assured. "He's our physicist."

"Our *brengsek*," muttered Turtle.

Jerk, that meant.

CHAPTER FOUR

The Caravan

Anne's laboratory was surprisingly well-equipped. Small, but of course it would be, and Anne didn't think she'd be spending much time in it anyway. She planned to spend as much time as possible in whatever alien biome they were driving through. *Don't call it 'being antisocial', Anne*, she told herself. *Call it a 'pre-reward'*. This was a payment for the time she'd have to spend indoors once the research station was built. Enjoy the wilderness that's left before you buckle down to fix the places that have been ruined. A honeymoon.

"Hm," said Anne, plucking at her engagement ring. In the gleaming surface of her lab bench, her reflection looked troubled. Anne shook her head and went to explore the storeroom.

It was the largest space in the rear half of the caravan, and it smelled like new plastic. Here were the gloves and face masks and chemical sprays, as well as several worryingly large boxes of first aid equipment. Although, on reflection, wouldn't it be more worrying if there wasn't any first aid equipment? And it was good to see that the place had been stocked by someone who knew you could never have too many sampling vials. There was a tank of liquid nitrogen here too, and a 4C refrigerator, as well as—

Anne jumped back and bounced painfully off a stack of fuel tanks. She swallowed, hands to heart, blinking at the bubble-headed...no. That wasn't a person lurking in the closet, it was her own face reflected in the visor of....

"Hey?" she called. "Farhad? Why is there a space suit in here with me?"

Footsteps approached down the hall and Farhad answered, the smile plain in his voice, "Why do you think, Anne? Why did you think I needed your measurements? You're going into space!"

Another wave of gooseflesh. "I didn't know you needed my measurements."

"Oh." An uncomfortable pause. "Well, I'm sure the numbers Daisuke gave me were accurate. The suits were made specially by the company of a friend of mine, fitted for you, Daisuke, and Moon."

"Right," said Anne, still looking at the suits. "And what will we be doing in space? With a physicist?"

"We will be doing work of scientific value," someone else said. "For once on this farce."

"Oh dear," Farhad said. "Aha, Professor Houlihan, would you please come out and say hello to Professor Moon. I wanted to introduce you."

Anne poked her head out of the storage room to see Farhad standing in the corridor with a skinny, long-faced Asian man. He had the spiky hair of the recently showered.

"So you're Moon?" Anne asked. "Where do you work?"

The man regarded her from under his lashes, shoulders up as if bracing himself for a fight. "Until a few months ago, CERN." He had a thick American accent.

"So you really are a physicist? I thought Farhad was just confused and you were a physiologist or something."

Moon continued to look at her, his face less a mask than a statue carved in granite.

"You should shake hands," Farhad suggested.

Anne did so, annoyed at herself for obeying. "Just what the hell does our expedition need a physicist *for*?"

Moon's chin twitched. "What does it need a biologist for?"

Shit, she'd insulted him. Anne released his hand and waved hers, trying to recover her balance. "I mean, what are you going to study?"

"Portals, of course," he said.

Anne felt like an idiot for not figuring that out on her own. "Oh, right. Of course. Wormholes."

"Portals aren't 'wormholes'," Moon said, as if this were the fifth repetition of some tired old argument. "They have no detectable mass of their own. They can't be wormholes."

Farhad cleared his throat. "What he means is that *wormhole* is a technical term. It refers to some kind of warp in space that punches a hole in space-time."

"Ugh!" Moon made chopping motions with his hands. "Why do you have to dumb it down? An Einstein–Rosen bridge is exactly what it sounds like. It's a solution to Albert Einstein's field equations, but who cares about that now because *portals*—" he jerked his head to the right, presumably indicating the Earth wormhole, "– prove that Einstein was wrong!"

Farhad cleared his throat. "The way Professor Moon has explained it to me is that black holes are like horses. We've seen them and we know they exist. Wormholes are like unicorns; we can imagine them but we've never seen one. But a portal is a Lamborghini. It does broadly the same thing as a horse but much better and by completely different means."

"Hm," Anne said, because she had realized something. Not about Einstein–Rosen bridges. She didn't know enough about the physics to form an opinion yet. What she had realized was that Farhad was Moon's Daisuke. He was trying to translate the scientist's words into Normal Human speech.

Unlike Anne, however, Moon was not attracted to his translator, and was therefore less patient. "What I *said* was that portals are like cars because someone *made* them."

"Aha," said Anne, "the Zookeepers."

"If by that you mean that I think that the portals are artificial, of course I do," Moon said. "How could they have just happened to come into existence, otherwise? By natural selection?"

Anne actually had always assumed that the wormholes on Junction were artificial, but now she questioned that assumption. Moon was the sort of person who made her want to disagree with him.

"I don't know what to think yet." She was very proud of herself for closing her mouth on the rest of that sentence: *except that Turtle was absolutely right about you.*

Moon was a *brengsek* right enough, but instead of telling him so, Anne turned to Farhad. "Why not a chemist or a geneticist, is what I'm asking. What tests can you actually perform on a wormhole that don't require a supercollider or something?"

Moon opened his mouth to make some retort that would further lower Anne's opinion, but Farhad held up a hand. "It sounds like you have good staffing ideas for your research station, but to answer your question, and the one before that, come to think of it, Moon's primary experiment won't take place until we arrive at the Howling Mountain and use those space suits."

Moon grunted as if in frustration and Anne thought about using those space suits. The toymakers had collected the vacuum-spinner from Howling Mountain, and the vacuum-spinner seemed to have evolved to live in space. What must its ecosystem be like? What would Anne give to find out?

But she had to be sure. "Use the space suits to do what?" she asked.

"Well, to start with—" Farhad spread his hands, as if releasing white doves from his lapels, "– you'll launch the nanosat."

Anne scowled. "The what?"

"You can see how revolutionary it would be if we could put a satellite in orbit without actually launching it."

"It won't be in orbit," Moon said. "Not around Junction."

"What difference does that make?" asked Anne.

Farhad winked at her. "Moon says that if the wormhole opened up somewhere else in the universe, somehow that wouldn't make it a perpetual motion machine. I don't understand the logic there, but Moon is very upset about it."

Anne decided she was being side-tracked. "Fine. What I'm upset about is that nobody said anything about satellites before. It's all well and good if we're going to go explore the wonders of space-life, but if we're going to be chucking artificial junk at it. I mean we shouldn't bloody chuck artificial junk at it."

Farhad winced. "This is an uncomfortable place for this conversation. If you're ready for a debriefing on our full mission, why don't we go to the bridge?"

'The bridge' turned out to be the driver's cabin of the caravan, a roomy cube with wraparound windows and swiveling chairs set behind the driver's seat. It reminded Anne of the front end of a luxury bus.

Boss Rudi was already behind the wheel, going through a checklist with Aimi. They both looked up as Farhad led Anne and Moon into the cabin.

"*Ibu* Anne," said the driver in Indonesian, "you tell this miser that we won't save any money by setting out today. One less night hooked up to Imsame's electricity and water in exchange for one more night of food? It doesn't make sense."

"Uh," Anne said, "Boss Rudi doesn't think we should set out tonight." Then she thought about what she'd said and a thrill went through her. Leave tonight? That might get her into the wild faster.

"Don't worry." Farhad nodded at Rudi. "We're not 'setting out', we're just driving down the valley to pick up the Nun. It wouldn't be a party without them."

"'Bring your own meat', huh?" Boss Rudi asked Anne, still in Indonesian.

"The Nun aren't cannibals," Anne snapped. "The wormhole and this valley are theirs."

"Oh. Sorry, *Ibu* Anne."

He didn't look sorry, but Anne didn't have time to unpick his racism right now. One old man at a time. She turned to Farhad. "I don't like that I wasn't told about the nanosat. How can I be part of a mission whose basic objectives I don't know?"

Boss Rudi said something about Anne's heart being hot, and "Last-minute changes and secrets make for terrible security. You tell him I said that."

"And Boss Rudi isn't happy either," Anne said.

"Then allow me to rectify my mistake," Farhad held a hand out to Aimi. "It's time for the drone photos."

"Now?" Aimi's fashionably bushy eyebrows rose. Apparently this was another last-minute change. She passed her tablet to Farhad, without another word.

"Thank you," he said. "Now call Daisuke and Turtle, please."

"I haven't issued walkie-talkies yet, but I'll find them." She slipped past Farhad, who sat in one of the chairs.

"Please take a seat. You can swivel them around so you're facing me." Farhad flipped up a lecture-hall-style board from the armrest of his seat and placed the tablet on it.

"I considered turning these little tables into touch screens, but Aimi says those things are a gimmick." Farhad poked at the tablet until it spat up a grainy green-and-brown image. "All right, cards on the table. This, subject to any last-minute changes I might have reason to make, is the first day of our itinerary."

Anne sat and leaned forward to look at the photo. "Looks like an aerial view of a valley. This valley, from the chlorophyll-green color. I suppose this photo was taken several months ago, before the ecological destruction was quite so total?"

Farhad hummed as if impressed. "Yes. Very good. And here's photo two." He slid the image aside to make way for a new one: a valley with one yellow side, one green side, and gray mud in the middle. "The Death Wind valley, where we'll meet and make merry with our native guides. Well, I should say the managers and handlers of the toymakers, which are our real guides. They periodically migrate to the Howling Mountain, it seems, and although the Nun have never made the trip themselves, some of them were willing to accompany us. For a generous payment, of course."

Anne wasn't listening. She thought about the lack of deadly mist and the gouges clawed into the vegetation on the eastern end of the valley.

"What took this photo?" Daisuke asked. "A helicopter?"

"Military drone," Farhad said. "We had it fly all the way down our planned route."

After the crash of Anne and Daisuke's survey flight, drones had become all the rage on Junction. The problem was that, on a planet orbited by no human-made satellites, that radio-controlled devices lost contact when they went over the horizon.

As far as Anne had heard, the best that anyone had been able to do was send up relay balloons, which expanded a drone's operational radius to about three hundred kilometers. The circle of Junction geography thus revealed consisted of several parallel north-south mountain ranges, with dry flatlands to the east. They had yet to discover an ocean on Junction.

Daisuke, Turtle, and Aimi arrived and took their seats as Farhad said "...then over the Outer Toymaker range and into the glasslands. That's still as far west as anyone has explored. Welcome, Daisuke and Turtle. Take a seat. Have a look."

He dragged his finger across the tablet, bringing up a photo of shiny purple plains. Anne bent closer. Lavender, maroon, burgundy, and blue, with subtle red striations and the occasional shocking pinpricks of yellow sporulation tiles.

"The glasslands," she sighed.

"We'll be traveling a bit north of the path that you took on your previous expedition," said Farhad. "Right through here." He slid his finger again, showing another purple landscape. Not a plain though.

The overhead view made it hard to judge depth, but the ground seemed to rise into jagged red ridges. Anne was reminded of pictures she'd seen of the Tsingy karst plateau in Madagascar, except here it wasn't green forest between gray rock, but cloudy water between blue-red glass.

"Not something we'd want to drive over," Farhad said. "But we can visit on foot." He tapped the screen and it zoomed in on one particular column of rock. Something glowed there, spherical and blue.

"Oh," said Anne, who had been thinking about biogenic acid erosion. "The climax *would* be around the wormhole, wouldn't it?"

"I'm afraid I don't understand," Farhad said.

"A climax ecosystem is where the plants have lived for a long time," Daisuke translated. "Anne means that someday, the flat glasslands might grow into that crater?"

"I see," Farhad said. "The wormhole at the heart of the biome."

Moon grunted.

"I mean, the *portal*, of course," Farhad said.

Anne had no interest in further pedantry. Another question had occurred to her, so she leaned forward and tapped the edge of the tablet. "Right, so why are we driving through all this stuff? Why aren't we flying?"

Farhad's face went blank before he chuckled. "If you think space is tight in this caravan, let me tell you something about helicopters."

"If you could fly a drone over our whole route, it's well within range of a military helicopter, and if we did have a helicopter, we wouldn't need a mobile lab," Anne pointed out. "We could fly in and then back to base."

Farhad was shaking his head. "Doing that every day for a week would be prohibitively expensive."

More than the caravan? But Farhad was still talking.

"…and one of our mission objectives is to survey the route from the ground." He raised his eyebrow. "Anyway, I thought you'd appreciate not flying after what happened to you last time."

Daisuke nodded emphatically, but Anne said, "Not so much. The crash was a freak event, and anyway we survived it. I'm not scared of flying."

Farhad winked at her. "Well, you'll pardon me if I make things a little easier for us mortals. And this way, you can take samples from all of the biomes between here and the mountain. I thought that was the major draw for you."

It was. Anne couldn't wait to see whatever lay beyond the glasslands.

"We'll be in unexplored territory within three days," said Farhad, tempting as the devil, and flipped to the next picture.

Hilly green fields, their color slightly deeper than one would expect on Earth.

"That isn't grass," Daisuke said.

"No," Anne agreed. "Look at the stripes in it. Some fractal stuff going on there. And those odd rectangular shadows. Are they some kind of trenches?" She spread two fingers on Farhad's screen, trying to zoom. The image only got grainier.

"I think they're the shadows of something," Daisuke said.

Anne imagined something broad and narrow, covered in the same green stuff as the ground. "Some sort of green slab?" she wondered out loud.

"Some kind of tree?" Turtle suggested.

"Trees that grow around wormholes, if so," said Farhad, sliding to another photo. A similar ring of slabs, visible only by their rectangular shadows, encircled a dark sphere.

"No, go back." Anne slid her finger across the screen. "It looks like those rings are only at the crowns of hills. See here? Those are animals there." Again, they were mostly visible by their shadows: many-legged and serpentine. Some were forked at one end. "Maybe what we're seeing is nests, rather than trees," Anne guessed.

"How large are those animals?" asked Daisuke.

Farhad chuckled. "It's good to see you're so excited."

"Do they have two heads?" Turtle asked.

Anne wasn't listening. Her finger had pulled over the next photo, which showed a sharp demarcation between green and orange. "Lovely stuff," she said. "Interesting there isn't much dead land between it and the grassy-hilly-slab biome. That's the smallest border zone I've seen."

"Yes." Farhad sounded aggrieved. "We believe that orange stuff is a forest."

"Well, of course it's a forest. See the exclusion zone around each tree's crown?" She peered at the photo. "Weird. This looks more like a subtropical forest than cold-temperate."

"Are the trees far enough apart to drive the caravan through?" Farhad asked.

Anne blinked up at him. "I have no idea. I shouldn't think so."

"Then do you have any ideas that will help us bushwhack through it?"

Anne looked around. "Off-road this thing through a forest? Not too likely. I say don't bother trying. Turn north and go around the edge of the biome. We can take sampling trips on foot."

Anne looked up to see Farhad rubbing his beard and looking at Moon.

The physicist shook his head. "It will take too long."

"I'm serious," Anne pressed. "We can't drive through that forest. We'd have to cut a whole road into it."

"And how long will that take?" Moon demanded.

"Don't worry," said Farhad. "We'll have time. We'll make it to the mountain one way or another. You never know what opportunities will come up."

"Maybe," Anne said, "but the prudent thing to do is to assume the worst." She met Farhad's eyes. "If it comes down to keeping your timetable and protecting the integrity of the ecosystem in front of us, will you let the timetable go?"

Farhad held her gaze. "Yes," he said.

Anne had no idea how to tell if he was lying. She glanced at Daisuke. He was smiling now, but that didn't mean anything either. Aimi had a similarly uninformative expression, and Turtle was whispering something to Boss Rudi, probably a running translation. Moon looked like he was doing vector equations in his head.

Ugh. Humans. Give Anne a bird of paradise and she could tell you whether it was angry or horny or what. She could even make a decent stab at predicting an alien organism's reactions and get it right more often than mere chance. Humans, though. Humans lied. *Does he know that I know that he knows?* It was tedious as hell.

"Let's fast-forward to the main event." Farhad flicked ahead on his tablet and Daisuke gasped.

Anne squinted. The image showed a silvery object, roughly square in outline, blotched here and there with brown, green, orange, and purple. It looked like a lichen-covered rock. Except those dark patches were the shadows of clouds. A very large rock, then, photographed from very high up. Further shadows darkened two triangular faces of the rock. The image reminded Anne of something, but she couldn't put her finger on it.

"That's a pyramid," Daisuke said.

Farhad's voice was very smug. "That, my friends, is the Howling Mountain."

★ ★ ★

"The Howling Mountain!" Daisuke said, trying to cheer Anne up.

They were stretched out in their bunk, which was only about a meter high, but as wide as the caravan. Windows on both sides gave generous views of the moving scenery.

"We've set off on our adventure," he tried again.

Anne growled like a bear and rolled over. "Sleeping."

"We'll be at the Nun encampment soon." Daisuke rubbed her shoulder. "We'll see Sing. And Misha and the baby."

"Yeah. That'll be nice." Although she didn't sound happy.

Daisuke thought. He couldn't ask 'What's wrong?' That would be tantamount to a demand for Anne to be happy. It was his job to figure out why she was unhappy. Find the problem and fix it.

"I'll massage you," he decided.

"Okay."

He smiled, even though there was nobody to see his expression, and climbed up on top of her.

"Oh, this extra gravity." She moaned. "No, stay there. I like it."

So did Daisuke. He put his thumbs between her shoulder blades.

"Yeah, I'm feeling a little b— *Ohh!* That's good."

She was worried about Junction's environmental degradation. There wasn't anything Daisuke could do about that, but he could change the focus of her attention, couldn't he?

"Turn your head," he said. "Look out the window."

The Deep Sky valley rolled past them. Silver-tan grass rippled up the slopes of the western mountains, dotted with dark islands of wind-tossed tree-ferns. From her perspective, Anne would be able to see all the way up to the peaks, fuzzy and brown against a powdery lavender sky.

Daisuke scooped out the hollows on each side of her spine, and Anne groaned. She would be saddened by the development in the valley. The destruction of the terraforming pools and the felling of the trees by the river. She didn't know how to appreciate what she had. How to stop reaching for more.

"Do you see the trees on the mountain?" he asked.

"Hmm. Rhododendrons," she murmured. "The bushes are probably *Coprosoma*." She raised herself on her elbows and her voice took on some animation. Daisuke loved how her back felt when she moved.

"The big trees with crowns shaped like toilet plungers have got to be podocarps of some sort. Lots of stumps."

Daisuke understood her anguish. That ache between the way things should be and the way they are. His own ambition had carried him far before it burned up his first marriage. No, he shouldn't say that to Anne. She wouldn't understand how good that destruction had been. Daisuke's life had fallen apart, and then he'd found Anne. If only he could do the same for her. Shoot her out into the wilderness where she could find out who she really was.

"Don't wait for things to be perfect," he said. "Focus. Focus on what's good."

Like Anne. If Daisuke searched for imperfections with her, he'd find them. She could do the same with him. A hairy mole here, a flabby pouch there. All that proved was that they were real and alive.

Could he tell her that? It would be best to leave out mention of moles and flab.

The caravan passed jogging soldiers in uniform, Nun tribesmen leaning against their three-meter spears, a pair of civilians playing with a dog.

"Ha," Daisuke said. "A dog on an alien planet! It's good, right?"

"It's bad, Dice!" Anne said. "I can't lie to myself! Invasive species, clear-cutting, the looming total collapse of this ecosystem, not to mention what will happen on Earth if someone chances upon the wrong alien microbe." Her back tightened up right under Daisuke's hands. "I can't just bury my head in the sand and pretend this world isn't falling apart around me. I've got to do something!"

Daisuke's hands hovered over Anne's re-tightening back. He considered the job in front of him. No, don't be clever. Just go back to the top of her spine and start again.

"We will do something," he said.

"What, Dice? What will we do?"

"I don't know yet." This was hard to say even in Japanese. How would he make it work in English? "'What should we do?' We ask that question until we understand the answer. If we don't have the answer, we keep asking. After we have the answer, we stop asking."

"Well, obviously," said Anne. "That's like saying things are always in the last place you look."

A flock of birds flew up past the window. Little dark wings flashed. Daisuke kept massaging.

"We're explorers, right?" he said. "Our job is discovering new things. Maybe one of the new things we will discover...." Daisuke lost track of his sentence. Anne's hips were so wide and her waist was so narrow. "I mean that we can discover the answer."

Daisuke's hands rose and fell with Anne's deep inhalation.

"I hope so," she said.

"I hope so too."

"I'm sorry," Anne said after a while. "I'm not properly enjoying this romantic trip you planned for me. I'll try to be happier."

His chest tightened, but Daisuke focused on the feel of her skin on his. "Don't worry. I am a patient man."

She snickered into her pillow. "Is that a hint? Maybe you should slide up me a little more so I can feel how patient you're being."

Daisuke did so with great relish. This would be a very romantic trip.

CHAPTER FIVE

Ladder to Orbit

The Sweet Blood portal shone blue and green above a mound of raised ground, almost the only color on this denuded hillside. Standing at the base of the plinth, Moon felt the pull of the Sweet Blood planet's gravity like a hook through his chest.

"Oh, that's better." Misha grunted. "I often come here. Helps with my back." The enormous man stretched like a sleepy bear, all muscle and facial hair in army surplus fatigues. Moon wondered whether those enormous round shoulders and bowlegs were the result of extended living in Junction's 1.3 gees or if the man was simply a mutant.

Perhaps the latter, since none of the natives looked so mountainous. The Nun people tended more toward short and wiry, with curly black hair and heavy features. They walked between the army tents that dotted this muddy hillside, tending to their pet aliens.

Toymakers, they were called, and Moon could see why. The little wooden constructs trundled about the camp or bobbed in the air like balloons. The wheeled versions ranged in size from hundred-centimeter tubes to one-fifty-centimeter cubes, usually with smaller ones pulling the larger like clockwork draft animals. Humans also did this chore, especially where the mud got thick enough for legs to work better than wheels.

Daisuke must have been watching Moon's face, because he said, "Toymaker users," as if he were providing voiceover to Moon's thoughts. "Witches. It seems like there are more of them than before."

"The proper word is *wrangler*," said Misha. "And yes, there are more than before. We've adopted most of the toymakers from the forest on the ridge."

According to the materials Farhad had given Moon, this Misha person had once been a pilot, smuggler, and spy for either the Americans or the Russians, Moon wasn't sure which. Now he was a sort of fixer and unofficial liaison between the Nun and everyone else. Supposedly, he was Anne's friend, although she didn't seem very happy with him now. Maybe the biologist just treated everyone like that.

The biologist had worn a scowl since she'd disembarked from the caravan, but now her expression deepened further. "What is it exactly that you need those toymakers for? What the hell has happened to the Nun, Misha? And what the *bloody* hell has happened to the Sweet Blood biome?"

Moon hadn't studied the ecology of this place in any great detail, but he had the vague impression that it had once been rather lush. Something Earthlike, hadn't it been? Giant bugs and lettuces or something like that. Mostly mud, now.

"It's been hard." Misha looked out over the encampment and Moon followed his gaze.

Rainwater had carved runnels into the hill's thick black mud, which stretched from the riverbank up to the bulbous brown trees that crowned the mountain. Here and there, pale blobs that might have been dead alien plants lolled flabbily down the slope like bleached air mattresses. Only on the top of the portal's mound was there any sign of life.

Yes. Right. The portal. What, if anything, could Moon do with it?

"I can't believe they've pushed you off your land," Anne said.

"It's more like the Nun can't stand living next to the soldiers," Misha rumbled. "Most of the land in Imsame is legally tribal property, but we're still working on convincing anybody to pay us rent."

"Haven't you been able to get the Nun to somewhere safe on Earth?" Daisuke said.

"Like Sing and the other mothers, you mean?"

Sing was Misha's wife. A woman of unusual taste, but gone now, along with most of the Nun women, to enjoy the comforts and medicine of civilization on Earth.

"Our job is to make this place fit for our wives when they come back."

Moon was dubious about that. So was Anne.

"Some job!" said Anne. "You can't live in the Sweet Blood biome, Misha."

"We *do* live in the Sweet Blood biome."

"Killing every non-Earth organism on this hillside in the process!"

"Better them than us."

"Yeah, and what'll you do now that you've eaten all the tortoise-hogs and all that's left is mud?"

Misha cleared his throat. "There's talk now of moving through the wormhole. At least the Nun can still hunt there."

"You *hunt* there?" Anne sounded horrified.

"Come on, Anne."

Moon rolled his eyes. He had better things to do than listen to this spat. He walked up the mound toward the portal.

He was afraid someone would try to stop him. Some native with a taboo. But everyone on the hill ignored him as he climbed. The pull of the Sweet Blood planet grew stronger.

Behind him rose Anne's voice. "Why does this keep happening? I'm here." Mud splashed. "I'm standing in the middle of a blasted fucking hellscape! But I say, 'This is bad,' and everyone acts like I've used the tablecloth as toilet paper!"

"Anne is very afraid," said Daisuke.

"Way to leap to my defense, Daisuke. I'm not afraid. What I am is angry!"

And look how little good that emotion did her. Moon tried to ignore his ears and use his eyes.

There was no ladder running through this portal, no government facility planted on top of it. The result was an object that looked utterly impossible. An optical illusion hanging over Moon's head. The browns and blacks of the hillside warped, twisted around into a rim that then untwisted into a view of pulpy green plants under a blue sky.

"It's all right," came Misha's rumble. "I'm sorry I lost my temper. I'm just an angry ex-spy who hasn't smoked weed in over a year and I'm trying to be a good brother-in-law, but nobody listens to me."

"Yes, Anne has the same problem," Daisuke said, oily facilitator that he was. "We will work together. We'll do it."

Moon paced out a circle around the portal. As he did so, the clouds, the pale blue sky, the yellow hills across the valley, seemed to twist. Colors smeared as if viewed through rippling glass, or maybe a more apt comparison would be images seen through the edges of a whirlpool.

Objects seemed to shrink, compressed into an infinitesimally thin ring. The ring expanded out again toward the center of the portal, decompressing into an image of the Sweet Blood planet. This view too, shifted as Moon circumnavigated the portal. It was like rotating a periscope. Or walking around a sphere that contained an entire world.

Within that world, something moved.

Moon stopped. His feet slipped on the mud, his weight a fraction of what it should be. He suddenly felt as if he was being drawn into a trap. What had they said about predatory aliens living in the Sweet Blood biome?

The thing in the portal stretched spindly legs toward Moon, its hide camouflaged, the pads of its feet oddly regular.

Moon exhaled. Boots. He was looking at a distorted, fish-eye view of someone lowering himself through the other face of the portal. A native, it appeared, short and dark-skinned, wearing military boots and pants but no shirt. A long yellow wand protruded from his unzipped fly. The decorative penis-sheath was of the same material, though thankfully not as long, as the yellow spear that the native clutched in one hand.

He slid to a stop in front of Moon, eyes narrowed suspiciously. "*Gu danya?*" he barked, then switched from the Nun language to Indonesian and English. "*Siapa!* Who!"

"Yunubey-*o*! *Ibu* Anne *yak-lem-bak.*"

Moon looked over his shoulder to see Misha waving.

"*Er ara* Moon *bikanya,*" the Russian said.

"Moon," the native repeated, and bared his teeth. "Good. Hello." He put his hand to his chest. "Chief Yunubey."

Ah, the Russian's brother-in-law. Maybe he could be useful. "Hello," said Moon. "I have questions about the portal."

"*Dan?*"

Moon turned and shouted back down at Misha. "Tell him I have questions about the portal."

The big man was apparently as happy to abandon Anne and climb the mound as Moon had been. He exchanged a few words with Yunubey, who poked his spear at the portal.

"He asks if you want to go through it. He says it's allowed."

"*Yak-lum*," Yunubey said, and turned to lead the way back up the mound.

Moon quashed his frustration. If people would just listen to him, everything would be easier. "No. I actually have questions. I want to know about the edges of the portal."

"Edges?"

"Ask him if I can borrow his spear."

Yunubey stopped at the translation and looked around, smirking like he couldn't believe how stupid Moon was. He said something that made Misha snicker as well, but tossed the spear down to Moon.

It was very smooth, more like ivory or plastic than wood. Moon walked up the mound past Yunubey and stuck the spear into the portal.

It went in the same way Yunubey had come out. On the Sweet Blood planet, a hole in the ground would now have a sharpened yellow pole sticking out of it.

Moon moved the spear laterally. It approached the edge of the wormhole, seeming to bend as if seen through a lens. The farther toward the edge of the portal he swung it, the more the spear warped, until....

Thump. The spear hit the soil of Planet Sweet Blood and rebounded. The same thing happened when Moon swung the spear in the other way.

He imagined the perspective from the other side: a pit in the ground on Planet Sweet Blood with a portal at the bottom. A spear sticks up out of the portal and waves around, hitting the sides of the pit, just like any normal object would.

"Oh," Misha said. "Edges."

"The edges of a pit in the dirt! That's not what I meant." Moon hissed through his teeth. Why was there always something in the way? If he could just grab a portal and move it out into empty air....

Yunubey said something, and Misha translated: "He says the wormholes have no edges. They are not holes like the ones you find in the ground or in skin. They are not holes at all. They are... uh... just a second."

Misha asked Yunubey something in his language. The Nun chief made a cage of his fingers, as if holding a ball, and spoke.

"They are like the hydrogen envelope of the toymaker blimp," translated Misha.

"They're a volume," Moon said, nodding. So the native knew what he was talking about, even if Misha didn't. Good. Now for a question the answer of which he hadn't already predicted. "Can anything bigger than a person go through a portal?"

"Yes," came the answer, "but only something shaped like a bird or a fish."

A what? "I don't understand," Moon said.

Misha and Yunubey discussed the matter. Yunubey steepled his fingers and poked the air with the wedge they made.

"He says that the only big things that can go through a wormhole are fish or birds...? That's not true. There's a word he's using that I don't understand."

"That's all right," said Moon. "I think I understand."

Moon stuck his spear into the portal and walked around in a circle, watching the perspective change. Size. Volume. Edges.

Moon recalled a joke paper he'd read in college, claiming that Earth's topology was actually concave. According to the author, rather than living on the outer surface of a sphere or rock surrounded by infinite space, humans lived on the inner surface of a bubble of space surrounded by infinite rock. The geometry that described the real world worked just as well that way. The only problem was that you had to make the speed of light become exponentially slower as it approached the center of the bubble. Space only seemed big because it took so long to penetrate.

"And what am I going to see when I go through there?" It was Anne. She was still in the mood for useless argument, apparently. "More ecological disaster?"

"More people trying to survive," Misha said.

Moon knew better than to engage. Talking hadn't worked in the hospital, and it wouldn't work here. He climbed higher up the mound, feeling his body grow lighter, until he could stretch his whole arm through the portal. He put in his other arm, so he was up to his elbows in another planet.

Aside from the gravity differential, Moon felt nothing. No resistance. Not even a tingle as his blood and nerve signals flowed across the cosmic distances.

Or perhaps the Sweet Blood planet, and all the space between it and Junction, was right here, compressed infinitely small. Perhaps the same was true of Earth, and every other planet on the other side of every other portal. Perhaps the only real, uncompressed space in the universe was here, and only Junction was real.

He separated his arms, and the portal's diameter grew. The edges knew where they should be. Moon had read every paper and report on 'wormholes', and not one of them had mentioned that they could change size.

"There's still the whole planet beyond the wormhole," Misha protested.

"Put a wall around it," said Anne. "Put a wall around all the wormholes unfortunate enough to be our neighbors."

★ ★ ★

Anne lowered herself onto her grass mat, careful not to spill her food and drink as she pressed her back up against Daisuke's. He felt hard and very warm.

She allowed herself a small sigh of contentment. A good, cold bottle of Little Creatures beer in one hand, a tray full of canned ham and instant porridge in the other – frankly, the food was pretty terrible. But! A good man at her back. Good things.

"This is the life, eh?" said the figure hulking on the other side of the stove. "Maybe it makes you want to emigrate? Join the Nun tribe. Initiation rituals are a steal at ten thousand US dollars and only a very little bit of physical torture."

The much thinner man next to him said something in Nun.

"Well, if you can understand English well enough to know I'm insulting the tribe, you can say, 'Shut up, Misha.'"

"Shut up, Misha," repeated the man. His name was Yunubey, the chieftain of the Nun, and Misha's brother-in-law.

The smuggler and the witch, Mikhail Sergeyevich Alekseyev and his wife, Sing, were the only two other survivors of last year's expedition. Misha had stayed on Junction with Sing's people, helping them negotiate with the soldiers, moving their camp, and, apparently, reproducing as well. His wife was with Misha's parents in the United States, raising the baby.

Anne had asked why Sing hadn't given birth at the American army base. Didn't the Nun need Sing's skills? But apparently the military doctor there had taken one look at the size difference between the parents and recommended a C-section. And even if they could convince the army to fly in a team of obstetricians, there were, as Misha said, "No alien trees that grow diapers."

Was this how all the Nun's births would go? Would the mothers ever bring their children back to Junction? Or would they exchange the end of infant mortality for the end of the tribe?

Misha hadn't wanted to answer those questions, so for now, they sat in peace on the northern slopes of the Outer Toymaker Mountains. The air smelled of cooking ham, human and pig body odor, a sewerish pong that could either be those same humans and pigs or else the exotic chemistry of the Toymaker biome up the hill, and, just faintly, bananas. That would be the ghost-scent of the Sweet Blood biome, which the Nun had almost entirely destroyed in the less than twelve months they'd been living here.

There were no more extrusion-pines or packing-peanut-bushes. Last time they'd been here, Daisuke had flirted with Anne and eaten a banana-flavored bug he'd caught in a stream. That stream was gone now, and its miraculous filter-wall. People sang and stumbled between cooking stoves, pigs, tents, and the military surplus kit they'd scattered over the hillside. The caravan was parked at the edge of what had once been the Death Wind biome, and was now an expanse of polluted silt.

It was better to look across the valley at the golden glow of the Lighthouse biome.

"Do you remember when we came here?" Daisuke asked.

Anne remembered stumbling out of the toymaker forest that capped this mountain. Colonel Pearson, the American soldier who'd stranded them in Junction's wilderness, had died. Tyaney, the Nun chieftain who'd shown Anne the Junction wormhole in the first place, had been chopped to pieces by the same toymakers who'd shot a miniature balista bolt into Daisuke's chest. They'd had no supplies left and no clue what to do. But they'd looked across the valley to see those illuminated trees.

Crystal boughs reflected and redirected light from the Lighthouse wormhole, spreading it across the mountain's middle elevations.

Walking through that forest had been like walking across a giant stage, lit with spotlights.

Misha held up his bottle. "A toast to fellow travelers."

The three of them clinked and drank, and Yunubey held up his tin of meat.

The trees of the Lighthouse biome seemed to grow brighter as the mountain under it darkened. The heart of their web glowed brightest, a wormhole shining with the blood-orange light of a star much older than the sun. The Lighthouse planet. Up the hill behind Anne floated the Sweet Blood wormhole. Those were just two of the worlds linked to Junction.

If Junction had as much land area as Earth, and the regular grid of wormholes they had observed in this region extended over the rest, that would mean about five hundred thousand worlds. Not counting whatever was waiting for them in space.

"It's funny," Misha said, "the first time we were here, I was terrified. Panicking. Remember the monsters in the fog that tried to eat me? But now I just remember falling in love." He glanced at his brother-in-law.

Yunubey grunted in an 'Oh, *do* you?' sort of way. He was squatting on his mat, feet covered in thick woolly socks and grass cape bristling on his back. His bare chest and face were caked with translucent aerogelly, collected from animals in the Lighthouse biome. His penis-sheath was another of that biome's products: a tapering rod of yellow plastic as thick as Anne's thumb and as long as her arm. His toymaker floated on the fishing line through his belt loops like a tiny wooden blimp.

"*Tekenak nunja, goma* 'love' *ara talenalum, hong yu ara senalum dara.*" He showed his large, square teeth and jerked his chin toward Anne and Daisuke. "*Pelum.*"

"He says, if I want to find love with him, I should shave my beard.'" Misha said. "The Nun word for my beard, by the way, is *nose hair*. Not *their* beards, just mine."

Anne savored the sensation of Daisuke laughing against her back.

"I am glad your brother-in-law has a sense of humor," he said.

"*I'm* not," said Misha.

"But no," Daisuke continued, "I was thinking about our first party, where Anne and I met. In Imsame. Old Imsame, I mean."

"You mean the village that's now the parking lot of the American military base?" Anne said bitterly. "Couldn't you do anything to protect them, Misha?"

"Obviously," Misha said, "I couldn't." He took another swig of beer.

Yunubey said something, his expression bleak.

Anne's little spark of anger guttered out, and the smell of the tinned pork on her lap turned her stomach. "Would you tell him I'm sorry? For bringing this down on his people?"

Yunubey didn't wait for a translation. "*Tekena nunja malye uwado. Soko Im Taramak ang* Anne *unggula. Pelum.*"

Misha nodded. "He says, 'Things have always been hard. Anne doesn't own the Deep Sky Country.'"

"That's not what I meant."

Daisuke pushed against her, a sign that he would translate for her. Not English to Nun, but Anne to Human.

"Thank you for helping us now," he said.

"You are welcome," Yunubey said in English, hand to his chest. "Thank *you* for money."

"Yeah. Is it true that this Mr. Irevani is paying for your own private research station, Anne?" Misha leaned forward, eyes shiny with speculation.

"Not *my* own private," she said. "*His* own—"

"What about a hospital?" Misha interrupted.

"Yes," said Yunubey.

Anne swallowed, thinking of those babies. "Er, look, Farhad isn't Santa Claus. He's more like one of those evil genies who turns every wish bad."

"That isn't fair, Anne," Daisuke said.

"All right, maybe." Anne took another drink. "I'd just like to see one of his promises come through before we start trusting him to make more."

"We *are* on his mission."

"Yeah, Dice, but what's it a mission for?" Anne thumped her bottle against her knee. "Not pure science, that's for sure. First it's 'Oh, we're prospecting for new species.' Then it's 'Oh, we're testing out this new satellite launch system. Oh, is that what I said? I meant that we're trying to see how wormholes work.' Then it seems we're also surveying the land for a new international treaty?"

Misha scratched under his beard. "Yes. I did wonder why we weren't flying to the Howling Mountain. The Americans have an AgustaWestland AW609 that could make four trips there and back before it needed refueling."

"Right?" said Anne. "I don't like the way things keep changing." She realized as she said it that that was truer than she'd thought. Anne liked none of the changes that had befallen Junction since her last visit.

Daisuke's back tensed. Somehow, Anne could tell he was making a fist. "We will make good changes!" he declared.

"Yeah. *Ganbatte*," Anne put aside her dinner and took another drink instead, trying not to think about Junction's problems and her lack of any plan to deal with them.

Daisuke was right. These weren't the same firepits or the same food or place, but there were the plastic codpieces on the men and shaved heads for the women. The ginger-tinted sunlight, the gravity, the tensions and uncertainties. The feeling of something waiting for them to discover it.

Could they discover a way to move forward? A good future? Anne pictured green spreading back down the slope of this mountain, holes healing in the web of lights on the opposite slope. Maybe down there in the valley, where the Death Wind biome had retreated back to its home planet, they could build a research center. They could plant it with nothofagus trees and dig terraforming pools into the riverbed. Anne could stand on the roof, surrounded by three healthy biomes and the Nun village, and direct the further study and protection of this world.

Anne raised her head and looked east through the Death Wind pass to the mountains that cupped the Deep Sky valley. Shadows climbed their slopes like dark water, but apricot light still warmed the peaks. A trio of kelp-tree balloons flashed like copper against an indigo sky. A line of bright sparks was visible.

They were not stars.

Junction was ringed in wormholes. They orbited the planet like beads on a necklace or cars in a train, presumably placed in orbit by whatever forces had created Junction. The Zookeepers, some called them. Aliens? Gods? Something stranger? Something a hundred million years old.

And Farhad wanted to send Anne up there. She clenched her fists, a feeling in her chest like a blunt knife prodding her heart.

"I want this so terribly," she said. "It scares me."

A silence fell around their stove. Daisuke broke it with a quiet request.

"Yunubey, would you show your toymaker to Anne?"

Anne looked around to see Yunubey's chin up and his narrowed eyes on her. His gaze slid to Daisuke, and the chief smiled and nodded as if a grand master had challenged him to a chess match. He held out his hands, palms up. "*Eng udirobak.*"

"Of course," translated Misha. "It would be an honor."

Yunubey reached up and grabbed the creature in two hands as if it were a rugby ball. Solemnly, he passed it to Anne.

Her suspicion that the boys were playing some kind of social trick on her evaporated as her fingers brushed its surface. Wood, or something almost like wood. A rhinoceros horn made of fused filaments of lignin, rather than keratin. Or maybe a better comparison would be the shell of an ancient cephalopod.

Yunubey released his hold and sat back. Anne gripped the shell harder. It had the mass of a liter bottle of beer, but thanks to its hydrogen gas envelope, its weight was negative. The shell of the toymaker gleamed darkly in the light of the stove, like polished walnut, smooth and fibrous. It narrowed gently toward the front, where a bubble of glass had been cemented. The cockpit.

Careful not to lose her grip, Anne rotated the toymaker until she was looking into its eyes.

Everyone called the Nun's floating and wheeled pets *toymakers*, which was like calling cars and planes *people*. Technically, the blimps and land-galleys and so forth were the toys. The makers lived inside.

They peered from their dark, syrupy growth medium like calamari rings smothered in chocolate sauce. Eyespots glittered on rings of pale flesh. Hoops of muscle turned themselves inside-out and outside-in, flashing tiny teeth, knotting and unknotting, coupling with each other to spin gears of chewed wood.

Tlink-tlunk!

The whole blimp vibrated with the force of the signal, like a clock filled with mud, powered by self-twisting rubber bands. The underslung spring-ballista shuddered.

Glong! Glong! Glong!

Yunubey chuckled and said something that Misha translated as. "The little...rascal? Is begging for food. Would you like to feed him?"

Anne sniffed and nodded, not trusting herself to speak. Finally, here was an alien. Not dead. Not in danger of dying. Just hanging in there.

Yunubey untied a flask from one of his belt loops and held it out. The liquid inside smelled absolutely revolting, but Anne smiled at the memory. The carved cap on the flask fitted perfectly with the valve on the upper rear end of the blimp. It clocked and clunked as Anne fed it. She assumed those noises indicated contentment.

"It's possible he remembers you," Misha said. "That was Sing's toymaker before she went to Earth. The one she tamed," he pointed, "right up there."

He pointed and Anne twisted to look up the hill. Sunset light had turned the toymaker forest a rich whiskey-and-oak color. Gold highlights gleamed like hair after a very expensive shampoo. Trees like tethered balloons swayed and rubbed against each other, flag-leaves snapping in the wind.

Anne found herself grinning. The toymaker forest was still there. Still swimming with strangeness and bristling with danger. And tomorrow they would set out for even wilder lands.

★ ★ ★

Daisuke felt triumphant rather than relieved. Anne was only really happy away from civilization, and they were on the edge of civilization now. If he could keep her attention focused westward, they'd be all right. Their joyous adventure was just over the mountains.

And when they came back? Maybe something unexpected would happen before then.

Perhaps the thought made Daisuke more observant. On the lookout for opportunities. In any case, he was the first of their group to spot the beer.

"Oi!" Daisuke waved. "We're here!"

Moon and Aimi climbed up the hill to them, bottles in hand.

"There you are!" Aimi yelled. "You drink alcohol, right?"

Daisuke waved his bottle in answer and moved to make space on the mat. "Where are Mr. Irevani and the others?"

"Not drinking. Smoking a lot." Aimi maneuvered Moon into his place between her and Daisuke. The physicist was carrying a cooler.

"Wise men," said Misha. "I always tell Yunubey that alcohol has killed more recently contacted people than any army." He held out his hand. "So you can give me his share of the booze."

"You must be Misha. I'm Aimi, Farhad's protégé." She gave him two bottles of Bintang.

"The pleasure is all mine."

"Chief Yunubey," she said. "I look forward to working with you."

Yunubey asked Misha something, and Misha shrugged, then shook his head. Daisuke suspected the exchange went something like 'Is she married?' and 'I don't know, but don't try yet.'

"So," Aimi said, "what conversation are we interrupting?"

"Anne was raking me over the coals for failing to preserve her alien wilderness," said Misha.

Daisuke could feel Anne's back muscles tense up. Last year, she might have made some kind of outburst, but recently her tendency had been to grit her teeth and curl in on herself, simmering in rage. Daisuke didn't think this new development was at all healthy.

"Anne has experienced a frustrating year," he told Misha. "She has fought to preserve the Nun *and* the alien wilderness—"

"To no apparent effect at all," growled Anne.

"But that isn't true!" Aimi said. "I've followed your work in more detail than anyone, Anne, and I know how much you've accomplished since you came back from Junction the first time."

"What, you mean all of the new social anxieties I cultivated?"

"I mean your international non-profit! You're getting scientists and specialists into Junction, doing important research—" she raised her voice to stop Anne from interrupting, "– and most importantly, you're highlighting the value that Junction's intact ecosystems have. With every photograph of a treeworm or a toymaker, you're creating interest back on Earth, changing the public dialogue!" Daisuke felt Anne shiver. She hated praise like this because she never knew how to respond.

He did his best to help. "And please extend our deepest thanks to Farhad, who has made it possible to do so much more."

Aimi's teeth were bright in the gathering darkness. "I made some personal donations as well." She turned to Misha and Yunubey. "And I plan to raise the subject of Nun cultural preservation with Farhad. How about a cultural center in addition to a research station and zoo?"

Misha grunted. "Well, consider *me* bribed. But give me a moment to pass the buck. Yunubey-o, *dan ern adya yuang ara wik kwanamsnanan?*"

"Mm!" Yunubey rubbed his hands together and rattled off what sounded like a list.

"A lot of Indonesian and English words mixed in there," said Anne. "I got 'infirmary', 'school', 'electric generator', and 'ceiling'."

"We'll write up a list for you," Misha said.

Aimi winked at him, and Daisuke entertained a fantasy that this fabulous wealth might actually materialize.

"What if the Nun had a hospital and a school?" he asked.

"And, for whatever purpose, a ceiling?" Anne said.

"He means a building with ceilings. A dormitory or barracks."

Aimi leaned into Anne's field of vision. "What's your perfect future for the terraformed valley, Anne? What does it look like?"

That was a very good tactic. Daisuke would have to remember it.

"I don't know," Anne said. "I suppose what would be best for the Nun and the valley would be a sort of little town. It would be surrounded by terraforming pools and nothofagus forests? If the Nun have somewhere comfortable to live, we could get them off this hillside, anyway."

Daisuke winced.

"Damn it, Anne," Misha said. "The Nun have bigger problems right now than getting off your hillside."

She wiggled against Daisuke's back, waving her hands. "You know what I mean! It doesn't have to be life for *either* the Nun *or* the Sweet Blood biome. The Nun's ancestors lived here for forty thousand years without harming their neighbor biomes."

"No, they just had to use very slow processes to harm their neighbor biomes. And they kept dying here and being replaced by more poor exiles from Earth. Now that they have flamethrowers, they stand a real chance!"

Anne overrode him. "When the Nun can move back into their own valley, we can repair this one! You transplant vegetation from the Sweet Blood planet and coax the native fauna back. Do the same for the Lighthouse and Treeworm biomes. Instead of having one big mess where everyone is dead and miserable, we could have lots of little functioning biomes that all work!"

"A win-win situation, you mean," Aimi said.

"I mean something sustainable," Anne said.

Moon snorted. Aimi elbowed him. "That's exactly the sort of solution that Farhad is trying for," she said. "That's the direction we're all pushing in."

"Usually, I'd say a castle made of chocolate would be more realistic," said Misha. "But I'm just drunk enough for optimism. Hand me another beer or two and I might work my way up to idealism." He laughed and took the bottles that Aimi handed him. "Just take me home before I reach mysticism. Cheers!"

The sky to the north had become the sullen slate color of the North Pacific, but the warmth of the setting sun had turned the western sky tropical. When Daisuke looked up the valley, in the direction they would travel tomorrow, he saw the sort of clear turquoise you get over a coral reef.

Aimi held out her bottle, gleaming against the turquoise. "To the mission!"

What followed was the corporate drinking familiar to Daisuke from a hundred projects. Everyone tried to get so plastered that when they woke up the next morning with both kidneys, they concluded that they must be surrounded by trustworthy comrades. Aimi seemed to already have Moon well in hand. He was blushing furiously and gave more than one-word responses to Daisuke's questions.

"So," Daisuke said, "you studied in America?"

"I went to Tufts."

"I was at the University of Montana. I hear the weather in Boston is very snowy."

"Ask him what he thinks he'll learn from the portals," said Anne.

Daisuke hesitated. Why didn't she ask her own question? Clearly, she didn't feel comfortable talking to the other scientist, and Daisuke didn't want to highlight that fact. The best thing to do would be to stay silent and wait. Moon would pretend Anne's question hadn't been weird, and smooth over her faux pas.

Moon said nothing. He just looked sourly at Anne until Aimi said, "I'm curious too."

Moon took another swig of beer and shrugged. "Everything."

Aimi gave him a gentle shove with her shoulder. "I knew that. The theory of everything, right?"

"Hm," said Anne.

"Ah?" Daisuke wished he had studied for this interview. "I don't know what that is."

Moon looked down into the mouth of his bottle.

"They'll understand," Aimi said. "I understood when you explained it to me, didn't I?"

Moon looked at her and straightened his shoulders. Daisuke hid his grin. Misha didn't.

"Well." Moon's voice was suddenly softer and deeper. "On the one hand we have gravity." He thumped his bottle on the mat. "Einstein and so on. Relativity. The interactions of huge things over vast distances. On the other hand we have quantum physics." He chopped the air with the edge of his left hand. "Uncertainty. Fuzziness. Tiny things over tiny distances. One predicts the movements of planets and stars." *Thunk* went the beer bottle. "The other predicts the behavior of electrons." *Swish* went his hand. "But neither system can explain the other. Plug quantum-scale objects into Einstein's field equations and you get a divide-by-zero error. At least one of these systems is wrong." Moon took a drink. "Probably both."

Anne hummed again, and Yunubey asked Misha to translate. Misha gave a belch and a one-word response that couldn't possibly be a translation.

Daisuke decided to dig deeper. "I think I follow that, but what does it have to do with portals?" He was careful to use the expert's preferred terminology.

"Obviously, portals are the key to transcending the quantum and relativity models because they violate the rules of *both*." Moon waved his bottle. "They fly in the face of pretty much everything we've discovered for the past hundred and fifty years."

"And yet here they are," said Anne. "Here *we* are on another planet." She moved against Daisuke's back and the others looked up. She must be pointing at the sky. "And there's a ring system made of wormholes."

Daisuke looked up.

It was as if someone had organized the stars. White, red, yellow, blue, the wormholes followed each other in lines that curved gently across the southern sky, fading into the last light of the sun. If Daisuke waited long enough, he would see those points of light move up the sky, or wink in or out of existence as something – what? – passed through them?

"*Ch!*" Moon said. "Do you expect me to deny their existence? I'm not an idiot. I know when I'm looking at proof that I'm wrong."

"But back in the caravan you said that the wormhole in the Howling Mountain won't lead to orbit around Junction."

"It won't."

"Well, where's it going to go other than up there?" Daisuke felt a jerk against his back as Anne gestured at the Nightbow. "We have a wormhole on the ground that spits out space-dwelling creatures and a ring of wormholes in orbit, swallowing space creatures."

"If you say the creature you found comes from space, I suppose I have to believe you."

"Goddamn right you do," Anne said.

"But it can't have come from the Nightbow. Not from anywhere we can see in the night sky."

"Wait," said Misha. "You mean our expedition *isn't* going to the wormhole that leads to space?"

Yunubey must have understood that, because he spat a question at Misha, who stammered an answer in the tone of 'hell if I know'.

Aimi cleared her throat. "What you mean, Moon, is that while you do believe the Howling Mountain wormhole – portal – leads to space, you think that space must be somewhere very far away?"

"Somewhere with the same momentum as the Howling Mountain," Moon agreed. "Because otherwise you'd be squashed."

Daisuke startled. "Squashed?"

"It's the only way momentum can be conserved," Moon said.

Misha wiped his hand down his face. "How am I supposed to translate that?"

"But you always come out of a wormhole with the same momentum you had when you went in, relative to the wormhole," Anne said.

"Bullshit."

"What's bullshit?"

Aimi gave Moon another shoulder-bump. "Would you explain it to them like you explained it to me? The ladder to orbit?"

Daisuke smiled to see the physicist's spine straightening.

"Oh. All right. Look." Moon held up two fists side by side, as if holding an invisible ladder. "Let's say you climb to orbit." He moved his hands as if pulling himself up rungs. "That would take a lot of energy, right?"

"Yes?" said Daisuke as Misha stumbled through a translation. "But what does that have to do with momentum?"

Moon turned his head and scowled off at the eastern mountains, hissing between his teeth. "Because momentum is mass times velocity," Moon said eventually. "And when you change momentum, that's mass times acceleration. Force."

"Think of a rocket taking off," Aimi said. "That's a lot of force you need to get from the ground to orbit, right?"

"And where does it come from?" Moon demanded.

"Well, it comes from the wormhole, of course," Anne said. "It must add or subtract the force to you as you travel through it."

Moon raised his hands as if beseeching the heavens for a blessing. "In what time? The time it takes to transit a portal is so small we haven't been able to measure it. That means that the force *applied* to you in order to *change* your momentum would have to be *enormous*."

"It would squash you," Aimi summarized.

"Slow down," Misha said. "I'm still working out how to translate *rocket*."

Anne threw up her hands. "Then congratu-fucking-lations, Moon, you've disproved that wormholes exist."

"Wormholes *don't* exist! Why do you think I call them *portals*?" Moon took a deep breath. "The only way a *portal* might work is if the momentum on both of its faces is equal."

"Wait," Anne said. "You're telling me you think that the wormhole in Papua, which is spinning around with the Earth, which is spinning around the sun, which is going wherever the sun is going… that wormhole is moving in exactly the same speed and direction as the Earth wormhole over there?" She moved, probably pointing back into the Deep Sky valley.

"Yes," said Moon. "It has to be. Otherwise we'd be squashed."

"How does that make sense?" Anne asked. "You said that there are no special reference points. The Earth wormhole is spinning around the center of Junction as the planet turns, and Junction is spinning around its sun—"

"So how can it have the same velocity relative to those reference points as anything else?" interrupted Moon. "Exactly! It can't."

Anne swore and Moon looked startled. Misha had given up and was sucking on his bottle while Yunubey pestered him for more translation.

"He means you're right," Aimi said. "The place on the other…did you say the 'face' of the portal? It must not share any reference frame at all with the near face."

"Exactly. Junction must be outside the Earth's light cone."

"Light cone?" Daisuke asked.

"He means Junction is outside of the universe that's observable from Earth," Anne said. "Yeah, I read *A Brief History of Time*. But if Junction and Earth are in different universes, then Junction and, say, the Lighthouse planet must *also* be in different universes, and while the Howling Mountain wormhole might take us into space, it'll be space in yet *another* universe. So that's one new universe per wormhole?"

"Maybe."

Anne rocked behind him. "That's ridiculous. You're saying it's impossible that an infinite force acts on you inside a wormhole, so to solve that problem you postulate an infinite number of universes."

Aimi cut off Moon's sputtering. "Isn't that what we're going to test? We go through the Howling Mountain wormhole—"

"Portal!" said Moon.

"– and we see whether Junction is on the other side or not. Farhad's nanosat will transmit a signal, and if we can pick it up on the ground, it will prove Moon wrong."

Moon hissed air through his teeth. "It would prove that things make even less sense than they seem to now. We'd have to throw out *all* physics, not just the last hundred years."

"And when you figure out how to explain it, you'll become the father of the *new* physics, won't you?" Aimi said.

The warmth in her voice should have melted Moon like butter, but instead he shuddered, shoulders drawing in, air hissing through his teeth.

Daisuke's bottle stopped on its way to his mouth. Why had the compliment frightened Moon so badly?

Aimi seemed to know. "Oh, Moon, I'm sorry! I didn't mean to mention your father."

"You didn't. I should go." Moon pushed off the mat, but stopped halfway up, wobbling.

Aimi caught him. "Don't you dare. You owe me at least one more drink. Daisuke, Anne, more beers?" She lowered Moon back to the mat. "Something stronger?"

Daisuke smiled in recognition of Aimi's tactics. Revealing terrible secrets was an excellent way to bond. He'd steer Anne in that direction too, bring her out of her spiny shell, and this whole trip would go much more smoothly. Did Moon have a famous father? There was time enough to find out.

"Let's drink!" he said.

Aimi was a pleasure to work with. Between them, they kept the alcohol flowing, guiding the conversation to hiking, life in America, and the exploration of Junction. It turned out Misha and Moon had the same taste in music, and Aimi's maternal grandfather came from the same village as Daisuke's best friend from high school. Everyone but Aimi and Yunubey agreed that root beer was disgusting, then Anne attempted to defend the concept of Vegemite. Even Misha's anecdotes seemed funnier.

"Okay, okay," Aimi said much later. "Okay. New game. Tell me something you're afraid of."

After consultation with Yunubey, Misha declared that the Nun chieftain was afraid of nothing. He, Misha, was afraid of Yunubey. "He is the *worst* boss!"

"Ha!" said Aimi. "You know what I'm afraid of? Not having a boss anymore. Now you, Anne."

"The destruction of Junction, of course."

Daisuke decided he was sick of hearing about that topic. "I am afraid," he said before Anne could elaborate. "I am afraid alien monsters will eat me."

Anne cackled. Her head was in his lap now. "Dice, that's what you're *not* afraid of! That's what you jump on."

"So, what do you jump *away* from?" Aimi asked.

Daisuke considered lying. But he understood what Aimi was doing. They should build trust.

"Yes. I'm afraid that I'm bad for Anne," he said. "I'm afraid I can't protect her." He looked down, caught her eyes, and jerked his gaze back up. He took another drink. "I came to Junction to prove that I can protect her."

"At least you two are together," Misha said.

"Well, shit," said Anne, and Daisuke's face heated. He'd put her in a terrible position.

"It's okay," he told her in Japanese. "I'll work hard, I said. It's okay!"

"Daisuke, I don't know. Shit." Anne fell silent.

Aimi leaped into the silence. "Whoa! That's way better than mine. Let me try again: I'm afraid I don't have it in me, too. I'm afraid all of my accomplishments are because, you know." She framed her face with her hands. "I'm pretty. People are programmed to be nice to me. I'm not sure if anything that happens on Junction can convince me otherwise."

Moon swayed closer to her, clearly having a very hard time focusing. "You're not sleeping with Farhad?"

"No. And you see my problem. You assumed I was." She shushed his slurred apologies. "Now you've got to tell me the truth about you, Moon."

"The – well. I don't know."

"Moon. Tell me. You insulted my honor. This is how you make up for it."

Although she must have already known, to have maneuvered Moon back into this position. This drinking game was intense!

"I suppose I am afraid that I won't make my name," said Moon.

Daisuke looked back at Moon, his brain seeming to slosh around in his skull. "Is physics a young man's game then, like math?"

"For me it is." Moon looked at Aimi and shook himself. "It's fine. It isn't a secret," he declared. "My father is dying of Alzheimer's disease. Early onset. Hereditary. If I want to discover the new physics, I don't have much time." He made a bitter sound in the back of his throat. "Soon, I won't be able to discover my own shoelaces."

Oh. Not a famous father. Daisuke had faced death right on this hillside, and it seemed Moon was doing the same. Except the physicist seemed to have no hope that he would emerge from the contest. So why would he choose to spend his limited time here?

Silence around the stove. Aimi raised her glass. "Then here's to the time we have left."

"That's *beautiful!*" Daisuke looked down at Anne. "This is how you bond with people! You get destroyed with your new coworkers. Then, when you wake up in the morning with both your kidneys...."

"Daisuke, I am too drunk to translate that in my head."

"Was I speaking Japanese?"

"Yeah, you still are." She lifted herself out of his lap. "That's probably a sign that it's time to get you home, big guy. Come on."

She stood in front of him. Daisuke hugged her around the hips and buried his face in her crotch.

"Goddamn it, Dice!" She shoved him into Moon.

"Hey, Moon," Daisuke said. "You're good. Thank you for letting me..." What was 'lean on you' in English? Oh, right.

"Lean on me," Daisuke sang, "when you're not strong..."

Moon smiled back at him. "...If the mountains, they should crumble to the sea."

Aimi hit the mat with her bottle. "That's 'Stand by Me', you pencil-necked atom-smasher, not 'Lean on Me'!"

Daisuke reached around Moon and prodded the air with the neck of his bottle. "Be nice," he warned her. "Be nice to Moon."

"Misha, Daisuke is absolutely legless. Help me get him back to the caravan."

"Why should I? Why should he get to sleep with a woman when I can't?"

"Misha, I swear to God...."

Daisuke felt arms under his elbows. He needed to tell Anne he loved her. She would never regret marrying him.

"I thought you proposed to her a year ago," said Misha.

Had Daisuke spoken that aloud? He hoped it had been in Japanese.

"Shut up, Misha. No, you pull and *I'll* push."

"Do you know how much I envy you?" Misha asked.

"No envy," Daisuke said. "You have a baby."

"Dice, he was talking to me. Misha, you're drunk."

"So are you, Anne. Drunk with your lover. Going to bed with

your *lover*! Sing is on another planet and her brother hates me. You know what he calls me?"

Daisuke felt himself pushed and pulled. Misha's hair was in his nose. "Good night, Aimi," he called. "Good night, Yunubey. Good night, Moon!" For some reason, that made Aimi and Misha laugh.

"So why don't you abandon Junction like Sing did?"

"Be nice, Anne." Daisuke waved his hand and nearly fell off of Misha's back.

"What do you know about Junction? I was keeping the Nun alive while you were getting into fights on the internet."

"How do you know about that? Does *everyone* know about that?"

"It's the internet, Anne. Its whole point is to tell everyone everything."

"Everything bloody stupid!"

Daisuke squinted against sudden lights.

"Who's shouting out there? *Ibu* Anne?" That was Turtle's voice.

"I like Turtle," said Daisuke.

"You screwed up, Misha," Anne said. "I left Junction with you for a year and you fucking let it run to ruin."

Misha swayed under Daisuke. "Fuck you! Yunubey was right, you do think you own Junction."

"*Ibu* Anne?"

"No, I don't! I'm *responsible*."

Misha spun toward Anne. "You think—"

Daisuke retched and Misha dropped him.

It hurt so, so much.

CHAPTER SIX

Dangerous Unknowns

The rising sun cast the shadow of the caravan across the glasslands.

At first glance, the surface under them might have been a sea. Sunlight sparkled off a million tiny knobs and divots. Hummocks rolled by like the backs of dolphins. Swarms of glittering creatures rose around the caravan like spray before a Viking longship cresting the waves.

So was Anne on a Viking raid, then? She shook her head and closed her eyes. She concentrated on the warmth of the mug in her hands, the gentle rise and fall of her seat as the caravan drove up and down the ripples in the ground. In the driver's seat, Boss Rudi whistled approximately along to a sappy love song playing on his phone.

When the motion sickness got too much, Anne opened her eyes, focusing through the wraparound windows to the northern horizon. The ripples there rose higher and steeper than any wave, and the shapes that crested them were not foam. No sea on Earth had ever bloomed with algae of quite this grape-candy color, either, and even a frozen sea wouldn't reflect the sunlight so harshly.

"Driving on this surface feels very strange," said Boss Rudi. "You say it's made of glass?"

Anne clutched her coffee, grinding through the Indonesian sentence. "This land...planting glass plants."

"This land *grows* glass plants," the driver corrected. "I don't see plants. Unless you mean those things on the tops of the hills? Or that giant donut?"

"What donut? Oh, that's a *wheeler*." She used the English word. "It's an animal like a sheep."

"Donut sheep? Amazing! What does it eat?"

"Um. *Tiles*." Another English word. "They are the plants of glass.

They have six...." Shit, what was the word for *side*? "They are like beehives." That was a word she remembered, but possibly not very helpful. She didn't know the word for "cells of a beehive" either.

"Do you mean that they're hexagonal?" Boss Rudi asked. The word in Indonesian was apparently the same as in English.

"Yes," Anne said. "They are hexagonal. Inside they have purple jelly, which makes food from sunlight, like the leaf of a plant. Under, they have hard roots like pipes." At least she *thought* she'd used the right word for *pipes*. Anne remembered the way those chalky tubes had crunched when she twisted a tile loose. "And the shell is made of glass."

Or more likely some more complex shell of silicates embedded in silicone. *Remember how they had tented up during the rain, so that water rolled to their edges? The way they gave just a little under your foot?* Had anyone actually taken a dissected glasslands tile under a microscope? And here Anne was with a dissecting microscope. Hmm.

She sipped her coffee, thinking about the forces that created that landscape and last year's trek through it.

The hexagonal plates of glasslands plant life rose and fell in gentle undulations, forming low east–west ridges crowned with purple growths shaped like cockscombs. How inconvenient those things had been, when the lost expedition had been trying to drag old Pearson east toward home. A couple of times every day they'd had to drag the sledge up one of those glassy slopes, shatter the combs on top, and descend into the next valley. And all of it in heavier-than-normal gravity and thinner-than-normal air. How the hell had Anne done it? How had she managed to fall in love while doing it?

And was it the combs that made the ridges, or the other way around? Were the combs the same organism as the plate-shaped ground cover? Were the plates genetically distinct, like clumps of grass, or were they clones like coral polyps? Did any of those comparisons make sense with aliens? What tests could Anne do to determine that?

Anne plucked at her ring. That was improvement, right? She'd hardly been able to do any science at all the last time she was here, what with all the geopolitics and murder by wildlife. Their party had been shocked, cold, half-starved, dragging a dying man over those siliceous hills. Half of them had been waving guns around and threatening the other half. A wrong step would have killed them, literally. Why would anyone miss that?

"Good morning, everyone!" Farhad strode onto the bridge and spun a seat toward him. "What a lovely country we've found ourselves in. The sky and the land under it, like a frozen ocean of red wine. It'll play well in California, for sure." He settled himself into his seat and inhaled the cardamom fumes from his tea. "What's our status? Boss Rudi, are we moving fast and breaking things?"

"We drive straight north, sir," said Rudi. "Ahead of schedule."

"Excellent! And Anne! I hope you slept well after what I hear was an intense party. Planning out your experiments for the day?"

Anne took another gulp of coffee. If Daisuke were here, he'd come up with a way to make friends with Farhad, turn him to a more virtuous life, and plan their day all at once.

"Yes?" she essayed.

Farhad laughed. "I'm sorry, Anne. Don't let me push you. I'm told I have trouble with downtime. Feel free to relax a little."

"Actually I *was* thinking about an experiment," Anne said. "I was thinking of figuring out what those tiles are made of."

He blew on his tea. "Not simply glass, I assume?"

"*Ibu* Anne knows a lot," Boss Rudi contributed.

"That is why I hired her." Farhad sipped and hummed with satisfaction. "I'm sure you're appreciating this landscape on a different level than anything I can manage. You did hike across it on foot, after all. What's the word I'm looking for?"

"*Death march*?" suggested Anne. "That's what it was, what with the shmoos and the sporulation plates."

"Ah, yes, the dreaded dire shmoo." Farhad rapped his armrest. "You don't need to worry about predators hurting this thing."

"Rather the opposite." Anne wiggled her ring. "What is the weight of the caravan doing to the tiles under us? Not to mention whatever contaminants are caught in our tires."

He was looking at her. Why was he looking at her?

"What?" Anne said. "I'm worried."

He nodded. "Yes, you took the changes in Imsame very personally."

"Destruction," said Anne. "Not changes. Destruction." She

gestured at the window with her coffee cup. "What can we do to prevent this place from being destroyed too?"

Farhad tilted his head up and waggled his chair from side to side. "I'm considering how to address that. Maybe if I had an egg on me, I could show it to you. Look how beautiful it is, I could say. Look how smooth the shell is. How perfect the shape. Why would anyone want to break it and make an omelet?"

Anne's heart sank.

He chuckled. "You probably think I'm a wicked old capitalist who cares about nothing but money."

"Well," said Anne. "It does look that way."

His nod was more like a little bow. "Thank you for speaking your mind. I really do appreciate it. If you just kept quiet about your beliefs about me, I wouldn't be able to tell you that you're wrong."

Farhad took another sip of tea. "Money is just a way for people to communicate their needs. How much would someone pay for a chance to come to Junction and see a lovely view like this? A research station? A new cancer drug or antibiotic distilled from the blood of native animals? How much would they pay for—"

"A parking lot?" Anne said.

"I was going to say, 'How much would people pay for a safe place to live?'"

The hairs on the back of Anne's neck rose. What the hell was Farhad talking about? How would Daisuke phrase that?

"What", said Anne, "do you mean?"

Farhad tilted his head up and frowned at the ceiling, as if there were instructions written up there. After a moment, he nodded to himself and said, "When I was a teenager, I smuggled myself into Turkey in the back of a pickup truck. That was only the start of the struggle that led me here."

"...yeah?" Anne said, for lack of any better response. Farhad sounded like he was answering the questions of an interviewer who wasn't here.

He held up a finger. "My parents supported the Shah, which means nobody trusts me in modern Iran." A second finger. "My grandfather fled to Iran in the first place because he was a wealthy land-holder in Armenia when the Red Army came." A third finger and a smile. "My great grandfather was not a favorite of the Ottomans, either."

Farhad turned up his palms. "Before that, history doesn't say, but you can be sure that whatever my ancestors were doing, the regional power at the time thought they were wrong."

Anne wasn't sure what she was expected to say about that. She noticed that Rudi had stopped singing along to his phone.

Farhad nodded as if Anne had said something. "My family has survived because we played outside of the rules, and we made sure to get out before the revolutionaries took control of the transportation network. So when I tell you that Junction might save humankind…"

"You're telling me you don't care if we smash a big hole in Junction's ecology," Anne said.

"I'm saying that this planet is important." The twinkle in Farhad's eye was less jolly grandfather now, and more targeting laser. "Yes, we will do a non-zero amount of damage to Junction as we move through it, but there's more to life than avoiding damage."

Anne didn't, but Farhad didn't pause to explain.

"What if Junction is our only life raft when things on Earth go to hell? Isn't our continued survival worth a couple of squashed glasslands tiles?"

Anne's chest grew tight and cold, as if someone were buckling her into refrigerated armor. She could pull out now. Leave the caravan and walk back to Imsame and Farside Base. Then back to Earth. Except that wouldn't stop Farhad, only deny Anne the possibility of balancing out his destruction. The armor had a collar and lead attached.

The silence was broken by Daisuke's voice. "*Natsukashii naa.*"

Anne looked around to see him standing behind her, his own cup in one hand while he stabilized himself against the doorframe with the other.

"Ah, Daisuke. Thank you for joining us," said Farhad. "You're already looking better. Those pills I gave you working?"

Daisuke nodded, then appeared to regret the motion of his head.

"What does that word mean?" Farhad asked. "I always wanted to learn Japanese, but alas…."

Anne forced herself to un-bristle. Farhad wasn't trying to butt in on her and Daisuke's tender moment. Well, he *was*, but he wasn't doing it maliciously. And he was Anne's employer. "*Natsukashii* means *nostalgic*."

"Nostalgia for your last death march here?" Farhad chuckled. "I suppose I understand that."

"The trip was very hard," agreed Daisuke, lowering himself into the seat next to Anne. "But, hard times…" he curled his hands around his own cup, "…bring people together. Bonding. Me too, and Anne." That dazzling smile flashed through his hangover. For a moment, Daisuke looked like a little boy who'd just gotten the best present for Christmas, and knows exactly how he'll play with it.

Anne felt herself blushing. "Stop doing that. You flirted with me shamelessly on that trek too."

"And in comparison, our relationship has gotten boring?" He sipped his coffee, and met her eyes over the brim of the cup.

"That's not what I meant at all." Anne glanced at Farhad and blushed harder. "Don't misinterpret me."

"It's all right, Anne. Romance. You need romance." He nodded to himself and clunked his cup on his seat's armrest. "And I can give it to you. *Romantiku na otoko dakara ne.*"

Anne had been about to tell Daisuke what an idiot he was being. She'd been talking herself into taking him back to bed, and here he was, casting doubt on their relationship. *Oh no, the spark is dying, Anne. You keep demanding all these romantic gestures from me, and I'm such a great guy, I'll keep giving them to you.* But whenever he said something in Japanese, Anne had to drop whatever she was thinking about and translate it.

He'd said it with a sort of macho swagger, but now that Anne translated it, it sounded a little unsure. Maybe Daisuke wasn't annoyed that Anne was demanding too much of him, he was worried he wasn't giving enough to her. Or maybe Anne had the wrong end of the stick entirely and she just had no idea what he was trying to tell her.

Anne needed more data. She finished her coffee, and leaned toward Daisuke. "What are you talking about?"

"A date," he said, and put his hands around hers. "Remember the day we went looking for water and you showed me all the tiny creatures? Let's do that again."

That did sound suspiciously perfect. "That's a great idea. I bet there are a dozen new species we can discover five minutes walk from the caravan. Oh! And I've been thinking about the combs."

"Combs?" Daisuke ran his hand through his hair, and made it look great.

"I mean the bush things growing on the tops of the ridges. I have a theory to test. Come on, Daisuke, let's go look at them." Anne stood.

"Perfect," said Farhad. "Go earn your keep! I can't wait to see what you discover."

★　★　★

The wheels of the ATV hummed over the nubbled surface of the glasslands, throwing up clouds of glassy fliers. Larger animals rolled away like animated wheels, balls, beanbag chairs. Clouds raced across a lilac sky, reflected in the grape-candy ground.

"Oh my God," said Daisuke. "This is much better than last time!"

Anne laughed. He was right. And she was doing the right thing, coming here. This landscape, this wilderness, was where she belonged. Where she could do some good for once! Anne didn't have to force herself into her computer chair and pound herself against global society in order to make a difference. She could come out here, between the ground and the sky, and finally *learn* something.

The muscles in Anne's chest and belly loosened. As Anne drove their ATV north, the land sloped gradually down, but the hills grew taller. This forced them into an up-and-down path which, combined with vibration in the seat and steering wheel, gave Anne the impression she was riding some sort of Swedish luxury roller coaster.

She turned west, running them along the length of the ridge they were on. She left behind the caravan and its file of Nun and toymakers, and imagined for a moment that she and Daisuke were alone on Junction, speeding toward the mountain.

"That one?" Daisuke asked.

She let out a breath. "What?"

"What comb will we see? That one?" Daisuke pointed forward and left, to a particularly large, Merlot-colored crown. "It's beautiful."

"Yeah. It's a beauty all right," laughed Anne. Daisuke the nature show host. She steered in for a closer look.

From a distance, the comb looked like a glass sculpture a meter and a half tall and maybe five long. On closer inspection, however, the surface wasn't smooth, but ribbed with soft undulations that marched up from the root to the tips of its flanges. Anne was reminded of the walls of Kings Canyon, but those formations had been eroded from layers of sandstone. These layers were more like tree rings or the ridges in a seashell. Not ground down, but built up, layer by microscopic layer, over what must be hundreds of years.

Anne ran the tip of her fingernail up the comb, feeling the vibration of keratin on glass, watching the color of the gel inside brighten from dusty violet at the roots to ruby red at its comb-tips, outlined with gold as the sun shone through them.

Daisuke crouched down next to her, hip touching hers. "*Mite*," he said. "Things are moving."

Anne refocused her eyes, and saw that he was right.

Every five or so growth-ridges, there was a partition like a floor in a skyscraper. There were even glass elevators running through the comb's structure, branching tubes visible only because of the organisms using them. Tiny pale capsules rose through this circulatory system like bubbles in champagne. Higher up, rows of darker capsules descended. Larger organisms – organs? – glided slowly across the inner surface of the glassy shell.

"What am I looking at?" Anne wondered aloud. "A tree infested with termites? A colony *built* by termites? A little building, complete with window washers?"

"A fish tank," said Daisuke.

She bumped him with her hip. "Be serious."

"I don't want to be serious. This is discovery!"

Anne grinned, remembering what they had discovered the last time they were on a ridge in the glasslands. The gentle snow and the explosive sporulation that had followed it. The life that boiled up from the ground to struggle and mate and die. Daisuke taking her aside and telling her about…what was it? Anne couldn't remember, only that they'd kissed for the first time.

"What do you think we'll discover this time?"

Instead of answering, Daisuke pressed a finger to the surface of the comb.

It noticed him. A blob the size of a postage stamp stretched itself flat against the glass opposite Daisuke's fingertip, bubbling with black eyespots. Screw-shaped organisms homed in on him like tiny missiles. Motes sparkled in the gel, and the comb around Daisuke's finger flashed yellow.

He snatched his hand back. "Oh!"

Anne held her breath, but the warning colors on the comb had dissolved back into the normal purple color of glasslands photosynthesis. The plant had got itself back down to the business of turning sunlight into life. Anne should get on with her work too.

"All right!" Anne clapped her hands to her thighs and stood. "We've got science to do. Tell me if you feel like your throat is closing up."

"Anne, what's wrong?" Daisuke followed her to the ATV.

"Nothing physical," she assured him. "It's just...." She thumped the vehicle's door. "What changed, Daisuke? The last time we were here, I was afraid sometimes and angry sometimes, but it was...." She looked over the purple plains. "I don't know. Thrilling. I was worried because there were so many unknowns. *Dangerous* unknowns, yeah, but I could discover them, right? And discovery is what I'm all about." She watched the caravan, grinding slowly west, the Nun and their toymakers trailing behind. "I should be happy now."

"I don't understand," said Daisuke. He gave her a blank look. Another mask.

Anne hadn't used to notice those. Now, she wasn't sure what to do about them. Another chore she had to see to before she could dissect anything. "*Yes*, Daisuke, I know I'm throwing your romantic gesture in your face. I'm sorry."

It didn't work. Daisuke frowned. "I want to understand."

Was he actually trying to find the problem or just managing her? Anne had no way of knowing.

But maybe she'd been spending too much time online, where 'I don't understand X', was code for 'I hate X'. Maybe she should give her boyfriend the benefit of the doubt. Fiancé. Whatever.

"I don't understand either," she said. "I should be happy out here with you on Junction but I can't manage it. I don't know why."

"'I don't know'," Daisuke repeated slowly. "That's not so bad. You don't know how aliens work and you don't know how your brain works." He poked the side of his head in illustration, then grinned like a sunlamp. "But we can learn, right? Discovery is what you're all about."

Anne thought about that. "Huh."

"So!" Daisuke nodded briskly. "Where does the sadness come from? When you look at the comb, how do you feel?"

Anne snorted. "Don't I need to be lying on a psychiatrist's couch for this?"

"Huh? Oh, I get it. No, just tell me." Daisuke's eyes widened in an expression that he somehow kept from being utterly ridiculous. "Explore yourself."

Anne considered that instruction.

The comb stood like a frozen splash of sunrise on the crest of the hill. A process of exuberant growth. A tiny, climbing current in the otherwise downward-rushing river of entropy. A flame in the darkness. Hopelessly fragile. Anne's chest tightened.

"Tell me what you're thinking," said Daisuke.

"I'm...." Anne rubbed her sternum. "I'm worried. No, honestly, I'm scared. I'm scared that the next time we come here, this beautiful thing will be gone." She blinked, found there were tears in her eyes. "Daisuke, what if someone destroys it?"

He closed the distance between them and enfolded her in his arms. He didn't say 'They won't destroy it', because who could know? It was an unknown. Something worth discovering, like the source of Anne's fear, and therefore her mission.

She shuddered in Daisuke's arms and hiccuped, feeling stupid. But when Anne took a breath, that band of tension loosened. She took another, deeper breath.

"I have to protect this thing," Anne declared into Daisuke's chest. "I have to protect Junction. I'll figure out how."

Daisuke was silent for a while, rubbing her back. "Maybe it would be good to ask Farhad?

Anne pushed away from him. "*Farhad?*"

"He knows how to do things."

Anne grunted. "What he knows how to do is look at you

patronizingly and make pronouncements he thinks are deep. Not very appealing to me, but maybe he reminds you of your granddad."

"No, you remind me of my granddad." Daisuke laughed. "Farhad reminds me of myself."

"Huh?"

"We're both good at knowing what people want to hear. We have both...." he searched for words. "*Kore made iro iro na mondai ni okorarechatta.* We have been hurt by bad things. We have learned that we need to do something big with our skills. Bigger than ourselves."

Anne shuffled back from him. "But maybe you need to do something bigger than yourself that's also *good*?"

Daisuke looked at her blankly, then his face cleared. "That will be my goal. I will convince both of you that the other one is also good. We have a long trip in front of us, right? We have time to teach him."

Anne blew out a breath. "Steady on, Dice. One grand project at a time. Fix Farhad, fix *me*...."

"Learn what's going on inside that comb?"

Anne smiled thinly at him. "It's transparent, for one thing. Like you."

Daisuke grinned and held his hands up as if holding a video camera. "And... action!"

Anne rolled her eyes, but she couldn't help smiling back. "Well, the comb has a glass shell, right? Just like the hexagonal plates on the ground. The tiles. The difference is that this organism is vertically oriented. You'll notice it's presenting its wide face toward the path of the sun." She swept her hand to the south. "What strikes me as odd, though, is that the best orientation for this southern exposure just happens to line up perfectly with this little ridge. If it was just this hill, that would be one thing, but there are so many of them." She pointed at the shorter ridge they'd ridden over to get here. Beyond it, there was another, even shorter, and then another. The land rippled off toward the caravan, and each ripple was crested with its comb.

"It looks like waves breaking on a shore," said Daisuke. "Only...I should get my binoculars." He reached into the ATV and extracted the very compact, very sensitive instruments. These he trained on the landscape sweeping out to the south.

The ripples weren't the only feature of the glasslands. Their orderly march was disturbed by stands of screw-trees and steaming pits where spore tiles had recently exploded. Animals skated across the plum-colored surface as well: spiky land urchins, donut-shaped wheelers, an unfamiliar creature like a giant snail shell on stilts. A middling-sized shmoo rolled lazily up to a steam-hole, scattering a flock of glittering fliers. The animals buzzed up, hung between the sky and the ground, settled.

"Ha," said Daisuke. He had turned around. "I was right. The land is like a bowl."

"What's that?"

"The combs are all the same height," he said, handing Anne the binoculars. "Look."

She pressed the eyepieces together and fitted them to her face. "What are you talking about? The combs are smaller to the...huh."

He was right. The combs to the south were 'shorter' in the sense that their tips were closer to the ground, but that was because the ground itself rose in that direction. The tips of all the combs that Anne could see looked to be at the same height, as if they had grown up against an invisible ceiling.

No, as if they'd stayed in the same place as the floor had dropped out from under them.

Hadn't Anne been thinking about erosion? Maybe those ridges on the comb weren't growth lines after all; maybe they were marks of the shape's *excavation*.

Anne shoved the binoculars back into Daisuke's hand and turned to inspect the roots of the nearest comb. Careful not to touch the organism, she knelt to see where it emerged from the tiles that covered the ground. The tiles grew smaller close to the base of the comb, more rounded, and spinier. Some were misshapen, some dead and gray. Their chalky roots had clearly been broken, regrown, and broken again. Under the roots, the shell of the comb continued.

"Yes!" Anne said. "I was wrong! Look, Dice! Look at the comb! It didn't grow out of the ground, it held on to the ground, which was eaten away everywhere else!"

"Eaten?" asked Daisuke.

"Eroded, I mean. We knew that the ground cover tiles secrete acid that dissolves the rock under them. But this other organism, the comb, forms a protective coat over the rock, kills the tiles, stops them from eating away the ground. Over time, the surrounding terrain sort of drops out from around it. Lovely!"

Anne held her hands out, letting them fall, imagining what the land would look like after—

"Of course!" she shouted. "The drone footage! We saw what the climax stage of this ecosystem looks like!"

She looked up at Daisuke. "Don't just stand there grinning at me, train your binoculars north and tell me if the ground keeps falling away. If I'm right, we should see a sort of bowl with the combs turning into columns."

"They look more like pyramids," Daisuke said after a moment.

Anne whooped. "Ha! Up till now it's been either tourism or feelings and crap, but *this* is starting to look like science!"

Daisuke was standing on tiptoe, peeking through the gaps between two of the combs' tips. "It's like a forest of pyramids," he said. "Narrow pyramids. Spikes? *Kenzan mitai ne.*" He looked down at Anne. "What's the word in English? The thing with spikes that holds flowers. You put flowers on top and it holds them."

"I have no idea, Dice," said Anne. "Let me see with the binoculars."

"*Kenzan.*" Daisuke put his binoculars back to his eyes. "Kenzan bowl. A kenzan crater? I see the wormhole...." Daisuke twitched. "*Masaka!*"

Anne frowned. As far as she knew, that word meant something like *What the hell?*

"What?" she said. "What do you see? What about the wormhole?"

"No," said Daisuke. His brows scrunched down over the binoculars and he fiddled with the focus. "*Ano*, yes. The wormhole is there. But also, I see people. Three...four people."

Anne screwed up her mouth. "There are other people out here? Soldiers or something?"

Daisuke removed the binoculars and shook his head. "I saw the other ATV. They're from our caravan."

CHAPTER SEVEN

The Pyramids of Doom

"Farhad," said Anne. He'd changed into khaki slacks and a black turtleneck. If she could just figure out a way to shoot death rays out of her eyes and through these binoculars....

"What the fuck is he up to? Drive faster!" she shouted.

Daisuke had taken the wheel because he had more experience with off-road vehicles. The problem was that his experience was all with driving off-road vehicles *safely*, and not in the pursuit of nefarious millionaires.

"Faster!" Anne shouted again.

"Sit down!" They crashed over a ridge, spraying shards and gel.

Anne thumped into her seat as Daisuke twisted the wheel and accelerated. Electromagnetic torque and heavier-than-normal gravity combined to blast their vehicle down the gully between two ridges.

Anne imagined the kenzen crater. A funnel filled with water, pierced with stone spikes. Pyramids. The mature form of the comb organisms that formed these ridges. That meant the pyramids would be in east-west lines, just like the ridges, presenting their broadest sides toward the sun.

"Right," Anne said. "Keep driving east until we're past the crater, then we'll loop around and come at Farhad with the grain of the land."

"The what?"

"Just drive straight!"

They barreled down the gully between ridges, scattering flying animals like winged batons. The ground dipped, then rose again. "We've passed south of the kenzen crater," said Anne. "Just a little farther."

The land rose until the tops of the ridges were level with Anne's head. She stood up, balancing against the upper edge of the windshield, and twisted to aim her binoculars north-west. "The other ATV is parked at the edge of the crater, and there's a rope bridge leading to the stone spike in the center. Do you have a clear path north? Take it!"

The ATV twisted under her and Anne's stomach lurched.

"What will we do?" Daisuke asked. Stubby ridges juddered the vehicle. "We can't attack them."

"What else are we going to do? Yell at them through the walkie-talkie? Actually...." Anne plopped down in the passenger's seat. "Drive faster while I yell at them. When we're level with the crater, turn left and blast down that gully, got it?"

Anne didn't wait for a response. She tugged her walkie-talkie off her belt, fighting motion sickness, trying to figure out which buttons did what.

Daisuke swerved west and Anne's vision swam. She closed her eyes, fighting the urge to vomit, and of course that was the moment Farhad chose to answer her squawk.

"Yes? What is it, Anne?"

"Hey Farhad!" Anne yelled into the walkie-talky. "Just what the fuck are you up to?"

A pause. "What do you mean?"

"What do you mean what do I mean? Mate, I can see you."

She didn't need binoculars now. The other ATV and its occupants waited for them at the end of the gully, like a target in front of a cannon ball.

"How can you see me?"

"Stop stalling. You're right in front of us. You're between the two ridges that pass through the center of the kenzen crater."

"'Kenzan crater,'" said Farhad. "I appreciate the alliteration. Professor Moon, you have about sixty seconds."

"Who the hell cares about alliteration?" shouted Anne. "What's Moon doing?"

Farhad didn't answer her. He didn't need to. Anne and Daisuke sped west down the gully that deepened into the kenzen crater. Steam rose beyond Farhad's ATV. Above the steam towered a tapered stone column – a pyramid. At the pyramid's tip floated the glasslands wormhole.

Anne dropped the useless walkie-talkie and used both hands to hold the binoculars to her eyes. She recognized Farhad, Moon, Aimi, and Turtle. They were gesticulating at each other. Arguing?

Their ATV bucked over the honeycombed ground. The acid-etched rock to either side of them rippled in strange fractal shapes, like rivers or blood vessels. The combs on either side had grown into spindly pyramids, solid stone at the base shading to glassy red at their sunlit tips. Shadows grew as they drove deeper into the throat of the biome.

"What are they doing? What is that?" They were close enough now for Anne to make out the rope stretched from the nose of the ATV to the tip of the nearest pyramid, which was connected to the next pyramid down the line, which led to the central pyramid and its crowning wormhole. The upper slopes of the glassy tower glowed with the light of the glasslands world. Rose-lit steam drifted around a clutch of heavy, round objects slung around the pyramid's neck like charms on a very ugly bracelet. Barrels?

Why would Farhad have his men tie barrels around a pyramid, then call them back to his ATV, where one of them was now…Anne squinted…handing his boss a device? Were those wires running from it to the rope? Two wires running down a rope to a black barrel of what Farhad had told her was emergency fuel.

"He's rigged it to explode!" Anne cried and Daisuke slammed on the brakes.

Anne jumped out. Daisuke was yelling something but she pumped forward. Strange, frilly organisms curled into tubes at her passage. Sack-like blobs climbed ladders of spun glass, escaping the invasion from Earth.

She couldn't run fast enough. She wouldn't get there in time. She slid on the glassy ground, slow as a nightmare, screaming, "Don't do it! Farhad! Moon! Don't you fucking *dare* blow up that wormhole!"

Farhad flapped his hand at Turtle, who twisted around in his seat and waved his arms at her. "Stay back! Danger! Explosion!"

Anne didn't waste breath on answering. She dug deep into the bottom of her soul and ran harder.

"Cover your ears!" shouted Turtle.

And Daisuke caught her.

An enormous weight yanked Anne off her feet, swung her around so her face was pointed up to the glowing tips of the pyramids, and her back hit Daisuke, who hit the ground.

He said something like "Pah!" And they were down. He struggled to breathe and she struggled to get back up.

"Wait!" Anne screamed. "Daisuke let—"

The barrels went off like the beginning of a rock concert. *BAM. BAM. BAM.* The air punched her in the face. Knocked her back into Daisuke's arms. Her vision went gray and her ears squealed with the terrible assault. Gravel pinged off her head. Daisuke gasped under her.

So he wasn't dead. Neither was Anne. The ATV ahead was still upright. The ground was not collapsing.

But the central pyramid sure as hell was. The spike of rock was visibly tilted out, a big charred hole in its side. Anne could hear the stone cracking from here. Nice to know she still had her hearing.

"Look," shouted Moon. There was more emotion in that one word than anything Anne had heard from him before. "It's *stationary!*"

He couldn't mean the pyramid he'd blown up. That thing was not stationary. It was toppling.

But as it toppled, it carried its wormhole with it.

That's what Moon meant. The wormhole stayed in exactly the same place relative to the tip of the pyramid, tilting and falling along with it. That was Moon's purpose here. His experiment was designed to answer the question 'can a wormhole be moved?' The answer was 'yes'.

The central pyramid was falling now, sweeping its wormhole toward the slightly shorter pyramid on its far side.

Like a pendulum in a high school physics demonstration, the wormhole traced a perfect arc, ending at the tip of the second pyramid.

The tip pierced the wormhole. Passed through. Kept going.

"Yes!" crowed Moon as the central pyramid continued to fall, dragging the wormhole at its tip down the height of the second pyramid. The pyramid widened toward its base, and so did the wormhole. The circle of warped colors expanded as it fell, swallowing ever-increasing tons of rock. It flashed once, twice.

There was no explosion this time. Anne simply blinked, and both pyramids were gone. Two stony stumps protruded from the steaming water that filled the Kenzan Crater. They had been truncated along a perfect circular arc.

The wormhole was gone too.

★ ★ ★

Anne closed her eyes hard, pinching the skin between her eyebrows, clenching every muscle in the upper half of her face until a shimmering black-and-red checkerboard took shape before her straining retinas. Visual noise foamed and spun around the glowing black circle in the center of her visual field, burned there by the explosions.

"Anne?" Daisuke asked.

"Give her a moment," came Farhad's voice. It was the last straw.

Anne ripped herself out of Daisuke's embrace and rose to face her enemies. "What—?" Dizziness pressed against the sides of her skull. She shut her eyes again. "The *fuck* did you do?"

"That—" Moon's answer was cut off and his boss spoke instead.

"We performed an experiment. An important one. We've discovered—"

"Bullshit! You destroyed a wormhole! You *destroyed* a *fucking* wormhole! We can never, *ever*, visit the glasslands planet again."

"It wasn't great," said Moon. "It's just lava and rocks."

Anne choked on her rage. Literally, her throat closed as if against an allergen. Her eyes squeezed shut again and when she opened them, everything was tinted with red. She'd burst a blood vessel.

Pain sliced across Anne's forehead, as if Moon had physically attacked her.

"Moon, you're not helping," Farhad said.

"No, this is ridiculous." Moon's voice grew louder as he walked toward Anne. "One day you say we should put walls around the portals so we don't get our unclean human hands all over those pristine alien planets, and the next you're screaming at me because I did just that."

The unfairness of it was like a slap to the face. Anne wasn't screaming. She was strangling herself to keep the screams in.

"This is not what Anne wanted," Daisuke declared.

"She should decide what she wants, then. I saved that planet, didn't I? Isn't that what Anne wants?"

Anne imagined her fist going through Moon's face with such hallucinatory force she almost felt like apologizing. Instead she said, "Don't you talk over my head."

Moon and Farhad were standing in front of her, Turtle and Aimi in the ATV behind them. "Anne, just take a moment and calm down," said Farhad. Now Daisuke was rubbing her back, tacitly agreeing that Anne was the real problem here.

And meanwhile Moon kept talking. "I'm sick of tiptoeing around Anne and her crazy demands. Is she in charge of this expedition? Is she in charge of this planet? You promised she wouldn't interfere today."

"Moon, shut up," Farhad hissed.

Anne pressed her hand to her forehead. She didn't feel any blood. The headache was probably more from fury than...wait. "What?" She looked up at Farhad. "You promised—" She whirled to face Daisuke. "Our romantic date was *Farhad's* idea?"

Daisuke's features went blank, but not before Anne caught the flash of shame.

"He used you as a distraction, didn't he! A babysitter while he went off and— Goddamn it!" She stomped and pain lanced through her forehead. "I trusted Farhad. I trusted *you*, Daisuke!"

Anne pressed her palm into her skull. She couldn't cry now. She couldn't let Moon beat her. He'd been waiting for this. He'd prepared his arguments at the same time as he'd been wiring the wormhole up to explode, and he'd completely blindsided her. Blasted her supports right under her so he could watch smugly as she self-destructed.

Fuck him. Fuck what he thought of her. Fuck what any of them thought of her!

Nearly blind, vision swimming with red, Anne slapped away Daisuke's hands, and came at Moon, hands curled into claws.

Farhad stepped between them. Her eyes met his, and his expression hit her like a ton of pulverized mountain. *Compassion.*

"I'm sorry, Anne," Farhad said, and it sounded true. The old man really did sound as if Anne was breaking his heart. But what did that mean? Anything?

Anne reeled. She didn't want insight into her enemy's psyche.

She didn't want to feel what Farhad was feeling, or look at herself through his eyes. Because what she saw was a red-faced, squalling dwarf. *How dare you lay a finger on Junction? Junction is mine!*

Anne pressed her forehead between her palms again, as if to literally get a hold of herself. She felt the way she had when she'd stomped on a sporulation tile in the glasslands last year. She'd bulled forward into a territory she didn't understand, lost her temper, and drenched herself in hot acidic water full of alien allergens.

Anne had to do what she had done last year: slow down and explore these dangerous unknowns.

"...further discussion for an hour," Farhad was saying. "We can all rest and get something to eat, then attack this problem with clear heads. How does that sound?"

Anne took a long, shuddering breath. "Oh no you don't." She tried to make eye contact, couldn't, and spoke anyway. "This was why you hired Moon and—" The idea burst upon her like a geyser. "And why you put us in the caravan instead of flying. You wanted to play with the wormholes along the way."

Moon sneered at her. "Hardly play."

"Well, it was hardly science, was it?" Anne said. "You're a little boy sticking firecrackers in an anthill."

Moon blinked, reddened. She'd pissed him off, as easy as pressing a button.

Good.

Anne pretended she was participating in a particularly aggressive Q&A at a conference. "How do you know you haven't destroyed the entire glasslands planet? Or turned off all the other wormholes? Did you do small-scale tests? Simulations?"

"Of-of course not." Moon took a step back. "How can we simulate something like a portal? Based on what math?"

Anne folded her arms. "Right, because you don't know how they work, do you? You have no idea what you're doing, Moon. You could have killed us all. What if the wormhole had blasted us all with X-rays as it died?"

"What if it had sprayed candy out of it like a piñata? There's no reason to assume any danger. There comes a time when you simply have to make a decision," said Farhad. "Either we consider every possible outcome, or we accomplish our goals." Anne was about to ask what the hell those goals were, when Moon turned to his boss and murmured. "Although it might be illuminating to place sensors around the area next time."

Anne lost it. "Fucking *next time*?" spluttered Anne. "Right, because Junction is huge, isn't it? There's a wormhole every ten kilometers or so. Always more where that came from!"

Moon opened his mouth. Closed it. Straightened, and looked at Farhad.

Who said, "Well."

Anne instinctively stepped back. Shit, she'd lost the initiative. Found one button on Moon and pressed it, but now Farhad was looking at her like her soul was a keyboard and he was about to launch into a concerto in B-flat.

He clasped his hands in front of his chest and angled his face downward. The tech mogul could not have appeared more reasonable and conciliatory. "I was not aware of the size of the risks Moon took. However, those risks were a price worth paying."

"Because you know now how to destroy wormholes? What good is that possibly going to do anybody?"

Only then did she realize that she'd asked *why?*, which was exactly the question that Farhad wanted to answer. She sounded as if she were pleading.

"This is the first step to saving the human race, of course," Farhad said.

"Uh," said Anne. "What?" This wasn't a concerto after all, but some weird modern art performance where nobody knew who the audience was.

"What happens when people need a new place to flee to, and Earth is all used up?" Farhad asked. "The future of humanity depends on Junction. Don't you see?" Farhad lifted his face to the dusty sky, eyes glittering. God help her, Anne almost believed him.

"No!" she said. "That's insane. The Earth biome can't support the number of people on it now, let alone refugees from this dystopian world of the future you're envisioning."

"That's the beauty of it!" Farhad grinned. "We don't need to colonize Junction. We'll have other planets. Destroying a portal is the first step in *creating* one!" He spread his hands like a stage magician. "Think of it! We could colonize space!"

Anne refused to be dazzled. She was in control of herself. She knew exactly what to say. "No. Absolutely not. This is it. We're turning the caravan around and going home. And to jail, some of us."

Moon snorted, and Anne realized what an empty threat that had been.

Farhad, however, was in a much better position to threaten. "Well, I'm afraid I cannot accept that." He clapped his hands together. "You're in no danger, Anne, but you can't go back to Imsame before I do. That just isn't going to happen."

Anne stared at him. What could she do? He had all the money, guns, and politics. How could she convince Farhad that he was wrong? Manipulate him? Lie to him? Turn herself into a slimy shmoozer?

Anne lowered her face so Farhad wouldn't see her expression. "I'm sorry," she said. "I'll stay. We'll stay. We'll help you with this saving humanity thing."

"I'm so glad to hear that, Anne," said Farhad.

He sounded perfectly honest.

Anne hoped that she sounded honest too. What she really wanted to do was run away screaming.

She was trapped in the alien wilderness with a madman. *Again*!

CHAPTER EIGHT

Change of Plans

The western border of the glasslands lay like a battlefield before Misha and the Nun. The flat-topped hexagonal tiles had given way to spiked, fishbowl-shaped growths surrounded by sand and shattered glass. Past that, purple spheres clustered on jagged rocks, growing smaller and smaller until no sign of life remained. Fuzz on the hills in the distance might indicate the plant life of the next biome, but with the setting sun in his eyes, all Misha could see was blood-red.

"So," he said. "Your boss destroyed a wormhole."

"Not my boss!" Anne replied.

"Our boss," said Daisuke quietly.

Misha turned, bringing into view his friends, his tribe, their toymakers, and the caravan that carried all of their food. He swore at length in four languages.

"Yeah," Anne said. "It's a fucking disaster." She stared down at the sand as if she wanted to bury herself in it.

Misha scratched under his beard. "We could kill them. Farhad and Moon. I suppose we'd have to kill the Indonesians too. Maybe only lock up the woman?"

"No." Daisuke looked horrified. "No, Misha!"

Misha looked at Anne, who took longer to respond. "No," she finally said. "I was thinking you would just tell the Nun—"

"And let *them* kill your boss?" Misha snorted at the pair's shocked expressions. "Of course Yunubey will want to kill them. Of course we *should* kill them. This is war!" He slapped his chest. "Farhad blew up one of our wormholes!"

"It's not a war," Daisuke protested.

"Obviously we're not going to make a formal declaration. We'll tell everyone another story or something. Farhad was eaten by a shmoo." Misha gestured behind him. "Or whatever lives over there in the castles, okay? Then we'll go after Moon...."

"I'm not a murderer. Anne, you too."

"She's not the one you have to convince." Misha put a hand on Daisuke's shoulder. It was an old habit from his time in Jayapura. "You gonna stop me?"

"Boys! Enough!" Anne snapped, which only made Misha squeeze tighter.

"Misha," Daisuke said. "You're scared, but you're using anger to hide from fear."

Misha blinked at him, hand relaxing. "Huh. You're good at that."

"We are all scared."

Daisuke flicked his eyes toward Anne, who said, "Well, good! Anger is the most appropriate emotion for this fucking situation."

He blanked his face at her.

"What? You look like your brain's been flushed down the toilet, Dice." She stomped her foot and looked away. "But you're right. We can't murder anyone."

Misha puffed out a breath. The air was getting colder. The Nightbow hung in a darkening sky. "When I tell the Nun what happened, they'll massacre the caravan no matter what I do."

"*Dan ara pedirolum?*"

Misha's head jerked around. Yunubey had materialized behind him in that awful way he had.

"Nothing." Misha answered his question. "We're not talking about anything important."

Yunubey grinned. "I think you were talking about the bomb that the Them exploded earlier today."

Misha jerked back.

"What is it?" Anne asked.

Misha closed his eyes. "They know that Farhad blew up the wormhole."

"Well, what do you have to look glum about, hey? Didn't you want to massacre everyone?"

Misha glared at her. "Shut up. I *am* scared, all right? Let a man have his machismo for five seconds." He glanced at the rest of the camp. "But Yunubey might seriously kill someone."

"Only if he finds out what really happened," said Daisuke.

"Stop talking to the Them and tell me what they're saying," Yunubey said. He wasn't grinning anymore.

"I can't lie to him, guys."

"You're a spy," Anne pointed out. "You lie professionally."

Misha rolled his eyes. "Okay, let me try again. I *won't* lie to Yunubey, okay? I'm his only good link with the non-Nun, and every time I do a less than perfect job, the extinction of my wife's people takes a step closer and—"

Yunubey did not grab Misha's arm. He did nothing more than shift his weight onto the balls of his feet, jangling the tools carabinered to his belt. Misha found his eyes drawn to the tip of the man's spear.

"You will tell me," Yunubey said slowly, "what the Them are saying."

"Uh, yes, my brother!" Misha swallowed, flashing back to his time in the army. "Farhad and his people have destroyed a wormhole. Anne and Daisuke tried to stop him, but he was too clever for them."

Yunubey grunted, apparently unsurprised. "Ask them if they know whether the wormhole really is dead, or if it's just hiding."

It was a good question. Wormholes turned off whenever they were surrounded by anything other than breathable air. The Americans and Indonesians used that fact to control traffic to Junction.

"I think it's gone for good," said Anne after Misha had relayed the question.

Misha translated that while Yunubey looked at him as if the Russian was a misaligned gear in a toymaker's drive mechanism.

"She only thinks she knows. Tell her to only tell me the facts of what happened."

Anne and Daisuke did, starting with how they'd spotted the other ATV, backtracking to what they were doing out on the glasslands, pausing to more precisely translate the concept of 'a date', then forward to the shape of the glasslands and the kenzen crater.

They ended up reenacting the destruction of the wormhole with Daisuke's steepled fingers representing the tip of the pyramid and Anne's fist, the wormhole.

As he listened, Yunubey's fingers tightened around his spear.

"It expanded to swallow a whole column of rock and I guess it... choked?" Anne finished.

"Forbidden!" Yunubey spat.

"Yes," said Misha, "but please don't—"

Yunubey flashed his spear up, pointed at Anne's chest. "Swear that you had nothing to do with this *malyelya*."

It was a new word for Misha. "Do you mean 'making something bad'?" he asked.

Yunubey responded through gritted teeth.

"He wants you to swear that you had nothing to do with the, uh, *desecration* of the wormhole," Misha translated.

"Desecration is right!" said Anne. "Of course we didn't. We tried to stop them, but we were too late."

In the light of the Nightbow, Yunubey's eyes had become pits.

"Please don't kill anyone," Daisuke told him. "Don't be angry."

But Misha knew that Yunubey wasn't angry. Yunubey looked like any of Misha's handlers and commanders did when they'd made a hard choice.

"Can we kill Farhad in battle?" he asked. "Does he have guns?"

"I think so. I think he's stronger than us," Misha answered.

"Find out for certain." The chieftain banged his spear on the ground and turned as if to walk away, the Nun equivalent of 'That's an order, soldier'.

"What did he say?" Daisuke asked.

Misha tugged at his beard. "He wants us to figure out a way to kill Farhad."

"Ha!" Daisuke laughed, which surprised Yunubey enough to turn back around.

Daisuke pounded his fist into his hand. "We can't give up. I have a way we can achieve our goal. We stop Farhad and Moon from destroying anything. Misha stops the Nun from killing anyone. We go to the Howling Mountain and discover all the wonders there. We go home and use the things we learned to protect Junction. And nobody dies!"

Misha stumbled through a translation.

Yunubey sneered. "We will kill Farhad. Or else we will force him to go back to the Them's country."

"I tried that already," Anne said, and Misha translated.

"Or else we will abandon him and go back home."

Misha turned to look back the way they had come. "Do we have food for the trip back?"

"Yes."

That was news to Misha, but he translated dutifully. "We can still turn back. The Nun will take us home."

"No way are we running," Anne said. "This has got nothing to do with our safety. We're trying to stop Moon from laying waste to Junction. Any more than he already has. And, yes, Daisuke, quit looking at me like that. Without killing him, obviously."

"Then how?" Misha asked. "You can't reason with him. You won't kill him. Are you suggesting we maim him?"

"Watch," Daisuke said. "We should watch him. Tell Yunubey that you and I and Anne will follow Moon around. We won't leave him alone. He can't do anything."

"A rotating guard?" asked Anne as Misha translated. "Moon won't like that."

Daisuke rubbed his hands together. "Only if he finds out about it."

★ ★ ★

Moon knew something was wrong the moment he saw Anne. The biologist was sitting in what Farhad called the 'breakfast nook', a little table between the caravan's middle door and the accordion joint that connected the two halves of the vehicle. Her head swiveled to track him as he passed her.

He didn't bother wishing her a good morning. Moon just turned to the espresso machine opposite the table, feeling Anne's eyes on the back of his neck as he measured out coffee grounds and tamped them into the portafilter. His hair stood on end, as if electrified by her hatred.

Anne clearly wasn't just pissed that Moon had conducted his experiment without an ecological impact study first. That temper tantrum she'd thrown yesterday didn't have its roots in any rational policy of environmentalism. Anne was an animal, snarling at the intruder in her territory.

And what happens when an animal attacks an intelligent human? The thought brought no comfort. Where would Moon's intelligence be in twenty years? He twisted the knobs on the machine and filled the kitchen with noise. Let Anne hate him. Moon had work to do.

The walk down the length of the caravan to the bridge reminded Moon uncomfortably of the previous night's dream. Corridors and confusing streets. Moon had been a ghost, sliding as if on tracks around some hybrid of Meyrin, Switzerland, and Cambridge, Massachusetts. He'd been looking for his body, but couldn't think where it could be. Had he died in bed or in a hospital or in the lab? What would the most efficient search pattern be? And the street layout kept changing.

Anne's fiancé was waiting for him on the bridge.

"Good morning," said the entertainer, sweet and false as diet soda. "What are we going to do today, Moon?"

"The same thing we do every day, Daisuke." That was Aimi. She giggled as if she'd made a joke, and although Moon didn't get it, he found the corners of his mouth tugging up. More animal complications.

"Heh, but actually we've all got marching orders this morning. Farhad thinks a more structured schedule will prevent any more unpleasant misunderstandings." Aimi patted the chair next to her. "Sit," she said. "And drink your coffee while I tell you the plan."

Moon did so, looking out past the empty driver's seat over the new biome.

The barren, broken rock under the caravan's front bumper acquired a layer of red clay. Ahead, green stains on the clay developed into elaborate spirals, which merged into a thick, grasslike carpet that extended into the hilly distance. Water glimmered out there, then dark woods, and finally, on the horizon, a blunt blue cone. The Howling Mountain.

"I want to help," Daisuke announced. "Professor Moon, if you plan to go out into that grass, I'd like to accompany you."

That offer would have rung false even if Moon hadn't seen the expression on Anne's face this morning. So the idiots thought they could keep him from his next experiment, did they?

Moon considered saying, 'I don't need company,' or something, but why bother? What good would communication do here?

"It might be dangerous out there," said Daisuke. "You should never go into unknown bush alone."

Moon sipped his coffee.

Aimi cleared her throat. "Yes. That's why Farhad wants Turtle to accompany Anne on her field expedition today. We want to begin surveying this biome as soon as possible. And Turtle is a tremendous fan of Anne's and he wants to see her work."

Aimi winked at Daisuke before turning to Moon. "This morning you're assigned to Misha and the Nun. The toymakers apparently need some kind of refurbishment before they can cross into this biome, and your technical skills will be useful there."

Toymakers? Moon knew three programming languages and wasn't entirely at a loss when it came to repairing electronic equipment, but the toymakers were just wooden tubes filled with worms. What was he supposed to do with them? He opened his mouth to say so, but Aimi met his eyes and he lost his train of thought.

"All right," Daisuke said. "Should I go with Moon or with Anne?"

"Actually, Farhad and I have something to discuss with you here." Aimi smoothed back her hair. Was she nervous? "Actually it's Anne."

Daisuke's brows came down. "Anne is right."

"Well, you know I agree with you, but this is a difficult situation. I don't want to—" Aimi glanced at Moon and frowned. "Why don't you go see Misha now?"

Moon jerked in his seat. What was she playing at? Aimi wasn't on the side of the idiots, was she?

Human relationships! Are you on my side? Can I trust you? No! Obviously, always, no. Physics you could count on. Your understanding might be imperfect, but at least there was something that you *could* understand. There was solid ground out there, somewhere, if only Moon could find it.

He sucked down the last of his coffee. To hell with Aimi. And to hell with Farhad if he thought Moon would spend the morning playing with toymakers. Moon had his own plans. The bucket and shovel he needed were already in the ATV.

The air outside was colder and drier than yesterday, with a new scent like fish and smelling salts. The sun shone from the south-east, just slightly the wrong color.

Moon walked along the caravan to the rear, where the ATVs were mounted. He ducked under the window of the breakfast nook. No sign of Anne or Daisuke. All he needed. He might just be able to—

"*Annyeonghaseyo.*" An enormous shadow fell across him, as if one of the ATVs had detached itself from the back of the caravan and risen up on two legs. Misha.

No sense asking him what he wanted. Moon just stared at the Russian, who cracked his knuckles.

Well, what the hell was he supposed to do now? Dodge around to the back of the caravan and try to start his ATV before this goon grabbed him? Go back into the caravan and find a heavy wrench or something?

"Ah, Moon, there you are!"

Misha's head jerked up and Moon spun to see Farhad hopping down from the caravan's middle door. "What are you doing back here?"

"Trying to get to the ATVs," said Misha.

"ATV, surely," Farhad said. "Singular. I sent Boss Rudi out this morning to scout for sources of water."

"What?" Moon said. "Did you send him in my ATV?"

"I sent him in *my* ATV," Farhad said mildly.

Moon ground his teeth. "I mean," he said, "the one I want to use." He'd explained this all to Farhad. Had the old man forgotten? Some senile memory lapse? No, that Moon's father, not Farhad. And Moon, himself.

"You are supposed to accompany Anne and Turtle on their biological survey," said Farhad. "Remember?"

Senile indeed! Or insane! Another component of Moon's life failing when he needed it!

But Moon couldn't exactly say 'Today I plan to desecrate another wormhole,' with Misha watching. Damn these complications! "Which ATV did Rudi take?" he tried.

And failed. Farhad waved a hand. "Never mind about that. What you need to do this morning is build bridges with Ms. Houlihan. She is your colleague in the caravan and, outside it, she's your superior. You'll do nothing without consulting her first, is that clear?"

Moon's lip curled.

"This attitude is going to be a problem. Come talk to me, son."

Talk, talk, talk. It never made a difference. As a teenager, Moon had thought the problem was the Korean language. Maybe it wasn't expressive enough. Then, in college, he'd decided his English must be imperfect. But his German too? His French? Finally, Moon had realized that no level of language proficiency would make another person agree with him. Other people were just too stupid.

No matter how well or thoroughly Moon expressed himself, the hairy stinking animal crouching behind the other person's eyes would make some snap decision and that was it. Fire bad! Banana good! Further discussion was pointless.

Farhad took Moon by the shoulder and turned him away from the hulking Misha. Moon had no choice but to let the old man pass him to Anne, who was just emerging from the caravan's central door.

"Thinking about prospecting those hills to the north-west?" Farhad asked. "Good, good. Moon and Turtle can help you carry sampling containers."

"No," both Anne and Moon said at the same time.

She recovered from the surprise first. "You think Turtle will distract me while Moon makes a run for it?"

Farhad gave her a look of put-upon patience. "He's not going to make a run for it, Anne. Where would he run to?"

"This biome's wormhole, obviously."

Moon's skin crawled. She knew.

"Why, are you trying to stop him? Keep an eye on Moon, perhaps, without him knowing?"

Now Anne looked like Moon felt. Secrets writhed like worms under an overturned rock.

The old man raised his hands. "All right. Come with me, Professor Moon."

He made as if to climb back through the door, but Anne dodged in first and yelled down the length of the vehicle. "Hey Dice! Keep an eye on these dipshits, would you?"

"There's no need for personal insults," Farhad said. "I was planning to talk to Daisuke anyway. Have fun, Turtle."

The Indonesian boy looked extremely guilty as he followed Anne out into the shaggy hills. That expression finally convinced Moon that Farhad was up to something.

"Did Rudi take the ATV with my shovel and bucket?" Moon asked, voice low.

Farhad frowned at him and shook his head. He watched Anne and Turtle recede out of earshot, then whispered, "Wait at the south-west corner of the caravan. Stay low so we can't see you on the bridge. And trust me, all right?"

Moon scowled, but Farhad winked at him. "I haven't had this much fun since I smuggled myself across the Turkish border. Go. Make this time count." He climbed back into the caravan, saying loudly, "All right, Daisuke, you have me and Aimi at your disposal. Let's talk about how we can—"

Moon glanced at the hills and the rear corner of the caravan. Anne and Misha were both out of sight.

"Idiots," he muttered. Wasting his time with their cloak-and-dagger nonsense. He should be halfway to the wormhole by now.

Keeping himself low to the ground, Moon scuttled around the front of the caravan and waited there, out of sight, thinking.

The Junction face of the Sweet Blood–Junction portal had been at the top of a mound. Its Sweet Blood face had been at the bottom of a pit. The same had been true of the Earth–Junction portal before humans had excavated around it. Why?

If matters were as simple as the sum of the gravitational vectors from both faces of the portal, you would expect every portal to be at the top of a mound. The particles of soil under the portal would be pulled upward increasingly as they got closer. But that wasn't what was observed.

Instead, there seemed to be some relationship between the difference between the gravity of each face of the portal and its height above or below ground level. Relatively low-gravity Sweet Blood planet and Earth versus high-gravity Junction had generated pits on Sweet Blood planet and Earth, and mounds on Junction. The glasslands–Junction portal had rested in a shallow divot on the top of a column of rock, like a golf ball on its tee.

Except *rest* wasn't the right word. It wasn't as if the portals themselves had mass and were sinking into the land. Whether they were at the tops of mounds or the bottoms of pits, portals never actually rested against anything. They just sat there, fixed in empty space. Fixed how? Fixed relative to what? Moon's hands itched for the shovel.

And here came Rudi now, driving Moon's ATV, bucket and shovel all ready for the next experiment.

CHAPTER NINE

The Mongol Feint

Moon wasn't back by lunchtime. When Farhad signaled his walkie-talkie for the fourth time and nobody answered, Anne slapped her knees, stood, and walked off the bridge. Whatever the bad guys said to her, she ignored it.

"Come on, Dice!" she called over her shoulder. "Misha!" Thank God they still had the other ATV.

The stiff, grasslike stems that grew from ammonite-coiled rhizomes had lost some of their stiffness in the heat of noon. They flopped over like half-cooked spaghetti, paler than their morning pine-color, and squelched sadly when Anne stepped on them, releasing fishy-smelling grease. That would be the tertiary amines, which indicated all sorts of things about these plants' relationship with nitrogen, but Anne wouldn't be able to figure out that puzzle, because she had an idiot to catch.

Good thing the ammonite-grass was there. Sickly-green noodles lay squished in two parallel bars that curved off to the hilly north-west. Anne tried not to mourn the plants Misha killed as he drove them in the same direction.

The land rose and fell under them, not like the ripples in the glasslands, but in a random, water-sculpted way Anne couldn't help but feel was more 'natural'. Limp grass hung down the slopes of miniature canyons like sweaty hair, and crenellations crowned many of the rises. Anne watched the rectangular silhouettes slide past each other as the ATV drove, black against the lavender sky.

"Anne," Daisuke asked after a while. "Are those castles on the hills?"

Each slab was three meters tall, flattened and roughly rectangular, and the rings they formed were more like henges than fortresses. Some tighter-coiling, shorter-noodled species of plant covered their faces and tops.

"No, they're like trees," Anne said. "Turtle and I examined one of them. The funny thing is that the ground around them is lower than the rest, like it was dug out...." She realized what Daisuke had done and whacked the dashboard. "Don't distract me! I came here to rescue Moon, not look at aliens."

"I think you came here to look at aliens," Daisuke said.

"Well now I can't, can I?" She hadn't been able to concentrate during her brief walk with Turtle, she'd been worrying so hard about Moon. Worries that had been more than justified, it turned out. "Some prison wardens we turned out to be. We couldn't keep track of Moon for thirty minutes!"

"Look at it this way," said Misha. "Maybe he blew himself up."

"Or got eaten," Anne said, then considered. Based on the critters she'd scared up on her morning hike, this biome's animals had evolved from a segmented ancestor like a centipede or polychaete worm. Nothing large enough to harm a human, unless venom was involved.

"Hm," she said, watching the grass rustle. "More likely poisoned."

Misha made his own thoughtful noise. "If he is dead, it might be tricky convincing Farhad we didn't kill him."

"But *we* all have alibis." Anne laughed bitterly. "Farhad made sure we each had something to do when he sent that dipshit physicist sneaking off into the bush, didn't he? Committing unspeakable acts with wormholes. I almost do want to kill him."

"If we rescue him, maybe he'll listen to us," Daisuke suggested.

"Ha," said Misha. "I know how to make him listen. I hold him and you two punch and kick."

Anne was in the mood for neither optimism nor humor. She watched the squat, menhir-like trees pass, close enough that she could see the green whorls on the red clay. How had that clay gotten into that shape? She wished she could get out of the ATV and touch a tree. Run her hands through the ammonite-grass again. Figure out what it was.

"I think I can talk to Moon," Daisuke said.

"Contrary to all evidence thus far collected," said Anne.

"You know," Misha said, "if we make it look like an accident—"

They rounded a flat-topped tree-wedge and Anne said, "Shit."

The other ATV sat in the grass ahead of them, facing them. It was unoccupied.

Misha braked and turned the wheel, bringing them up alongside the abandoned vehicle. An animal the size of a python uncoiled from its resting place on the driver's seat and reared, legs along its sides rattling against each other like clapsticks.

"Maybe it bit him?" Daisuke hypothesized.

"Let's see," Misha said, and the joking tone he used when merely talking about assault and battery was gone. "Come with me. Anne, stay here."

Anne popped open her door. "Don't go all macho on me. It may be that that...clapstick-python just found a nice place to bask after Moon left the ATV so we couldn't track him."

"Track him where? The ATV is facing toward us. Back toward the caravan," said Misha. "That means he was on his way back from wherever he went when he was attacked."

"How do you know he was attacked?" Daisuke asked. "I don't see blood."

"Look for footprints. Careful of the python."

Anne ignored the men. The hairs on the back of her neck were standing up, and it wasn't because of the articulated python. The air smelled oily and sharp. Tertiary amines and regular old ammonia. Something whistled just on the upper edge of hearing. The animals rustling in the grass had gone silent.

She looked down the trail behind them where the flat, wall-like trees concealed so much. "You think whatever attacked Moon is still...oh."

Something moved behind a wall-tree on the hill to the north. Something else cast a shadow from behind a tree to the east. Anne cursed.

Misha whirled on her. "Quiet!" he whispered. "You'll— Oh what the fuck is that?"

The animal undulated lazily up the trail behind them, cutting off their means of escape. Its forward end split in two, the upper half curving up like the tail of a scorpion while the lower one wagged from side to side. Meter-long hooks spread. The ammonia smell was like a spike to the nose.

"Shit," said Anne, "I was right."

A piercing, teakettle shriek shattered the air, and the ambushers fell on them from all sides.

Anne tried to jump out of the ATV, but only got as far as unbuckling her belt when something that felt like a serrated tusk smacked into her back. The force of the blow knocked her into the other tusk, which dug into her front. Anne looked down at sharp little saw-teeth, snagging in the tough material of her jacket.

Pincers, she had time to think before a terrible force yanked her up and sideways.

A gun went off. Another whistling scream. Was Misha *armed*? Or Daisuke?

The air was full of a complex, acrid smell, like burning lime juice. Anne grabbed the pincers around her torso and held on as her feet were pulled over the passenger-side door of the ATV. There was no way she could force the jaws to open. And there was a horrible pressure on her right arm, as if someone were pinching her biceps between gardening shears.

The world shook around her. When she twisted her neck, all she managed to see was another set of shorter, sharper mandibles and the narrow, axe-shaped skull of the animal's…upper head? Her arm screamed in pain as she was hefted higher, turned sideways, and wrapped in spiked segments like a mouse in an iron gauntlet.

Anne leaned, trying to get a look at these things. What she got a look at instead was the nose of the ATV and Misha's back as he grappled with the mandibles of another ambusher. Its head was a meter tall, but only ten centimeters wide, protected on each side by scratched, mottled brown carapaces. An eye like a bunch of black grapes stuck out and up from the top edge of the head, with another bunch sticking out and down from the other. Below that….

The other head?

Misha kicked it, and the second head, broad and platelike on its own segmented neck, curved away. Three pairs of sickle-shaped mouthparts gaped and it gave a low hoot of pain.

Anne's captor swayed under her. It moved as if on stilts, making little forward-and-backward motions as it turned. Its broad, sickle-jawed second head swung back and forth under Anne, as if panicked. The lime smell was eye-watering. The narrow, hook-jawed first head remained steady, however. It had coiled Anne up within its neck, squeezing her no harder than necessary to keep her motionless. A gentleman. Chivalrous.

Chivalrous? What was Anne's subconscious telling her? She watched reflections of sky and hills sweep across its black grape eyes, thinking of what wasps did with the insects they captured.

Anne twisted her head the other way, looking down the length of the animal. Its body was made of vertically flattened segments. Pale wrinkled flesh pulsed between vertical plates of shell, as if a chain of giant clams had been set on their edges. From the top of each segment grew a short spike, while from the bottom protruded a long, smooth limb, jointless as a tent pole. Alternating limbs curved out to the right and left, creating a cage that could support the animal against the ground. Anne remembered her first look at her ambusher. How it must undulate its body, galloping across the ammonite-grass like a serpentine, segmented...horse?

Light dawned. The worm under her was like a horse. The sort of animal ridden by a chivalrous, castle-dwelling, ambush-setting knight.

Anne bunched herself up within the cavalier's mandibles. She tucked in her legs and twisted her spine. The grip stayed tight around her, but Anne's weight was now entirely off the edge of the mount, along with most of the rider's coils. The mandibles squeezed at her and the animal – *both* animals! – puffed and scrabbled as they tilted farther sideways.

The mount swayed under them, unsure what to do. Anne waited until it swayed away from her, then kicked her legs out and torqued herself and the rider right off the side.

They hit the ground with nearly identical *oof*s, the air knocked out of what must be two fairly similar respiratory systems. Now, it was possible that the rider would scissor her in half with its mandibles, but Anne bet that it would be more interested in remounting.

She was right. The pressure around her torso vanished. She rolled out of the way as the cavalier raised its axe-shaped head, waving stubby, useless peg-legs. This creature couldn't walk without aid. It let loose a piercing whistle.

The mount wheeled around, graceful as a swimming otter. Its peg-legs hit the ground, flexed, and bounced back as it undulated up to its rider. The platelike head lowered, and the rider reached out with its own little legs. Anne had bought herself about a second and a half.

She spun around to see the ATV and the men. Misha was trapped between the jaws of another cavalier, but the animal was having trouble lifting him. The mount strained under it, stilt-legs bowed so far it seemed they might snap. Daisuke, probably remembering his crocodile-wrestling experience, had grabbed the mandibles of his assailant and forced them together. The worm shook its head, but its muscles were designed to powerfully close its jaws, not force them apart or pull them from the grip of an angry human. Its mount could have sliced open Daisuke's legs with its mandibles, but didn't seem to want to.

"Daisuke!" said Anne. "It's like a man riding a horse! Twist it off the big worm underneath!"

Another whistle from behind her.

Daisuke turned around, saw Anne, and gave a whoop. It was much too happy a sound for a man seeing a bloodthirsty predator bearing down on his fiancée.

Anne spun and put up her hands just in time to catch the scissoring mandibles of the knightly worm whom she had so dishonored. The mandibles clacked together between her hands.

And stayed there. Immobilizing the cavalier took much less effort than Anne had expected. Like arm wrestling a ten-year-old. The creature squealed, wriggled in her grip, but could do nothing more.

Anne let out a whoop of her own.

It was answered by more teakettle shrieks from the castle up the hill.

★ ★ ★

Daisuke let out another whoop. It wasn't just because he'd had no idea what to do with the horrible screaming centipede creature once he'd forced its mandibles together. It felt so good to work together with Anne again. To help her figure out what made this or that crazy biome work.

He had wondered what to do if the lower head attacked him, and had been ready to stand on one leg and kick it. Thank goodness for Anne, who had realized the heads belonged to two separate animals. Thank goodness she had stayed calm while being almost bitten in half.

Daisuke's heart thudded. It felt like he'd been shot there with a crossbow. He could actually *see* those enormous mandibles as they scissored through her body, cracking ribs and spinal column, forcing out an explosion of blood that would be the last thing to come out of her mouth—

Roaring, he wrestled his worm to the ground, then abandoned it as it cried for its mount. Even now, more of those things were slithering down the hill toward them.

"Anne! Misha!" he shouted. "Into the car. Let's go!"

"Shut up," said Misha, although he was probably talking to the centipede he had unseated. It waved its head back and forth and whistled when he kicked it. "I'm fine, by the way," Misha grumbled as he slid into the driver's seat.

"I bet we can outpace them," Anne said, sliding in next to him.

Daisuke stopped himself short from ordering Anne to come sit with him in the back seat. He wanted to put his arms around her and never let go. He compromised by grabbing her hand as Misha put his foot down on the accelerator and slewed around Moon's abandoned vehicle.

"Anne, are you all right?" he asked.

She breathed out and nodded. "I seem to be. Bruises on my front and back." She rubbed her right shoulder. "Probably a blood blister over here. I don't think it punctured the jacket though."

Daisuke envisioned punctures in her skin. Poison. Injection. Allergic reaction! All Anne needed was for the centipede to breathe on her, to shed its skin-flakes on her. He shuddered. "Anne, do you feel allergic? Itchy?"

Misha scratched himself. "Of course I do, now that you say it. Shit!" He hauled on the steering wheel and jerked them out of the path of a gaping rider-centipede. "Thank God these things don't have spears to throw at us."

"Anne," Daisuke insisted. "Are you allergic?"

"Steady on, Dice. We have more important things to worry about," she shouted over the enraged whistling. Mandibled heads writhed in the grass behind them.

He let go of her hand. He would hurt her if he squeezed too hard. Daisuke wanted to bundle Anne back into the caravan. This adventure wasn't supposed to get dangerous!

They were still traveling north-west, following a double trail of tire tracks that wove between the slab-topped hills.

"We should turn around," Daisuke said.

"Wait, Dice's right," said Anne. "Moon was captured by those cavaliers on his way *back* from whatever jiggery-pokery he was up to with the wormhole. Which means we've got to turn around and find out where they took him. And I bet I know where."

She pointed back the way they'd come, at the hill where they'd been ambushed and its crown of slab-like trees.

"You mean that stone henge thing?" Misha turned them in a wide loop, sweeping Daisuke's anxious vision across the landscape to the north. More slab-trees dotted the slopes. On the tops of hills, the sides of gullies, and other defensible positions, they grew in rings. Daisuke remembered the medieval fortresses he had seen in Spain. Squat, blunt, ugly buildings designed by people who lived in continuous war for a thousand years.

He rubbed Anne's shoulder and she said, "Ow! Damn it, Dice, I said I had a hurt shoulder."

"Sorry." Daisuke cursed himself. He wanted to grab Anne somewhere, but he contented himself with squeezing the back of her seat. "Do you think the cavaliers are intelligent? They have horses, and castles."

"Lords and ladies?" Anne snorted. "Naw. I mean, who knows what's intelligent, but no spears, like Misha said. No tools at all. No language. I mean, maybe they were reciting intricate ballads with smell or something, but I don't think so." She spoke animatedly, happier than he'd seen her since their disastrous date on the glasslands. "You don't have to be a genius to evolve into mutualism with something. Ants have 'domesticated' aphids, after all. So, yeah, I don't think they took Moon for an audience with their liege lord. I think they took him to the same place they were trying to take me, like adult paper wasps carry prey back to the nest for their grubs to— Ow!"

Daisuke snatched his hands back from her shoulders. "Sorry. Sorry." He forced his hands into his lap and his expression blank.

"Hell, you're doing it again, aren't you?" She was turned around in her seat, frowning at him. "You've got your mask on. Stop it."

Daisuke took a shuddering breath. "Yes. Sorry. I am...." He tried to pin down the frantic, scrabbling thing in his chest and dissect it into words. "Scared. I'm scared, Anne. It almost killed you."

"Me?" she said. "You big men are the ones who almost got killed."

"I had everything under control," said Misha.

"Yes," Daisuke said. "You understood that the cavaliers ride the other worms. But only after you were bitten. What if that first bite killed you with an allergy?"

She looked at him. "I don't know what to tell you, Daisuke. Yeah. We're on another planet. It's dangerous."

Daisuke thought of how Anne had torn her heart apart back in the glasslands because she was afraid she might hurt the *aliens*. That couldn't be a healthy attitude, but before he could figure out a way to say so, Anne said, "Give me cavaliers over Farhad any day of the week. Frightful alien beasts at least I have a chance to understand."

"Misha and I can go to the castle and rescue Moon," Daisuke pleaded.

"How about we don't and say we did?" Misha said. "With luck, the cavaliers will take care of our Moon problem for us."

Daisuke opened his mouth to argue and closed it, wondering if maybe Anne would agree to go back to the caravan if Moon was dead. He shook his head, disgusted at himself. He had to rescue the physicist. He had to keep Anne safe. How could he do both?

"It's a lovely thought," said Anne, "but it just wouldn't be right, inflicting Moon on those innocent alien worms. We've got to rescue him, gentlemen."

They rushed toward the castle, and Anne's grumble became a shout. "Full speed ahead, Mr. Alekseyev! Let's move fast and break things!"

★ ★ ★

Anne held on as Misha weaved the ATV around the henge-trees.

A creature like a fat butterfly the size of a basketball launched itself backward off one of the plants as they passed, and flashed by too fast for Anne to tell if it was gliding or flying or jet-propelling or what. Damn it!

"You want to drive right into the castle?" asked Daisuke. "That's dangerous!"

"Well what do you want to do, abandon Moon?"

"Shut up, both of you," Misha said. "You're not military historians."

"What the hell does that— Argh!"

A cavalier worm lurched out from behind a henge-tree and snapped its hooks together on the space where Anne's arm had just been. It withdrew, neck coiling into a heron-like S-shape, aiming for her torso. Before it could make another strike, Daisuke reached out and grabbed its mandibles.

"Turn left!" he shouted, and Misha turned, yanking the cavalier off its mount.

Unfortunately, this maneuver put their ATV broadside to another cavalier, which snapped its hooks around Anne's shoulders.

Terrible pain sawed at her deltoids as the cavalier heaved her from her seat.

"Oh no, you don't," said Misha, and accelerated them forward. The cavalier squealed as its mount fell out from under it. Legs like curved ribs grasped in vain at the side of the ATV, trying to find something it could ride.

"*Hanashite!*" Daisuke shouted.

"Shit," said Misha. "Shit! Daisuke, get that thing off her."

Daisuke pummeled the cavalier's head and sides, which did as much good as the animal's scratching on the door with its legs. Humans weren't built to punch through cavalier armor with their fists, the same way cavaliers weren't built to ride ATVs.

Hm.

"Daisuke," Anne said, "stop hitting it. I have an idea."

She leaned to the left, pulling the cavalier farther into the vehicle with her. A cloud of rotten citrus smell engulfed her as jointless legs scrabbled over the side of the door. She could see how they were curved to fit around the body of a mount. There would be a strong instinct there to grasp whatever fit.

"What the fuck are you doing?" Misha said. Her head was nearly in his armpit. Daisuke grunted with the strain of keeping hold of the captive cavalier's mandibles.

"Just keep driving."

Ignoring the cursing from the men and the pain in her shoulders, Anne twisted farther. She was hunching over in her seat now, with her head pressed up against Misha's ribs and the head of the worm upside down in Daisuke's grip behind her. The segmented body fell against her, and its limbs closed like the rings of a binder around her waist.

The cavalier gave a low whistle and stopped struggling. It breathed slowly, in great deep drafts like a human fighting panic. It humped its way up Anne's back, settling in. The lime smell grew weaker.

"Anne!" Daisuke called, still gripping the worm's head. Anne was bent double with her elbows on her knees. "Are you all right?"

"Fine," she said. "Just…being ridden."

"You jealous?" asked Misha. "Ha ha— Ow!" He swore in Russian and the car swerved under them. "I thought your pet cavalier would tell the others we're friends now. *Ubezhat' ublyudki takiye!*"

Another swerve.

"Forward," Anne ordered. "This vehicle is faster than their mounts, and their jaws aren't designed to grab people out of ATVs anyway."

"*Eto khorosho.*"

"They're still following us," said Daisuke. "I count fourteen."

"Yes. The whole cavalry is chasing us." Misha sounded back in control. "Now, my friends, you see what's so great about my incomplete bachelor's degree in history."

Daisuke patted Anne's shoulder. "Anne, are you sure you're all right? Is the worm hurting you?"

"It's calmer than you," Anne pointed out. "I'm fine. The riding legs don't squeeze very tight. I am getting a pain in my back, though, and I wish I could see what's going on. Will you take pictures of this thing up close for me?" She was trying to picture the cavalier's body in her mind. "I'm thinking about something like a row of clams all strung together. Or a pelagic polychaete turned on its side, one set of setae functioning as legs and the other as dorsal spines?"

"Shut up!" Misha said. "You get to lecture all the time. Now it's my turn. You bond with your new pet and listen, because this is a Mongol tactic, what I'm doing now. You ride up to the castle. You pretend to attack, and all the knights inside come rushing out. You turn and gallop away. Angry knights chase you."

"Should I keep holding this worm's jaws?" Daisuke asked.

"Quiet. Now, Mongol riders are faster than armored knights. Mongols ride knights to exhaustion, turn around, run past knights and plunder the castle, which has no defenses." Misha whistled to himself. "It's good to finally put my liberal arts education to use."

The cavalier jerked on Anne's back and she heard its jaws snap shut. "What was that?" she asked.

"It's okay," Daisuke said. "I held my jacket up and the cavalier grabbed it. Now I will tie its mandibles closed."

"You weren't listening," Misha complained. "Anne, the next time you tell us about alien creatures, I'll make rude jokes the whole time."

"So, no change then?"

The ATV raced across the ammonite-grass, trailing monsters behind it. Despite the thudding hoof-pegs and snapping mandibles, Anne felt her mouth stretching in a smile.

The wind buffeted in her face, and the worm held her tight, smelling of chalk dust and low tide. The tires bumped and his curved limbs clutched tighter around her ribs and shoulders.

Misha whooped. "Eat dust, aliens!"

"Turn now," shouted Daisuke. "We have to get Moon!"

Cackling madly, Misha spun the wheel and they all slewed sideways.

Anne laughed as the worm whistled in distress. "Just hold on, mate," she told him. "Hold on!"

The hills and their castles slid past each other as her perspective changed.

"I think I'll call you Lancelot," she told the worm.

The ring of henge-trees, when they reached it, turned out to be less *castle* than *corral*. Mount-worms undulated gently across nautilus-grass cropped so short it was little more than green spirals scribbled on red clay.

The same ocher material seemed to cover the trunks, but when Anne looked closely at the henge-trees, she could see that they were constructed from the same clay as the ground. Rain had carved runnels between the swirls of the growth that covered and sealed it. There were smooth places where a tool like a builder's putty knife had spread more clay to repair old damage.

Anne thought of mandibles, but the cavaliers' mouth parts were all about hooking and slicing. Their mounts had sickle-shaped instruments for cutting grass. What sort of creature had built-in spatulas? A tree-top browser? A beaver- or termite-like creature that made its own raised gardens?

"So what are you?" Anne wondered out loud, twisting her head to look up at Lancelot. "A knight? A squatter? A landlord? Curiouser and curiouser."

A tug on her arm. Anne looked around, annoyed. "Hold on, Daisuke. I'd best find a new mount for Lancelot." She looked around. "Or are the other cavaliers coming back?" Guiltily, as she remembered what they were supposed to be doing here, she asked, "Did we find Moon?"

To his credit, Daisuke didn't sigh or say 'Focus on the real world,' or anything. He just jerked his head to where Misha was arguing with, yes, Moon. Anne realized they'd been doing so for some time, and she'd just tuned out the noise.

Her working hypothesis had been a wasp-type situation and she'd been ready to find Moon head-down in a giant larva. Instead, their physicist-in-distress had been locked away in a tower.

CHAPTER TEN

Strange Mutualisms

The tower was a short one, slightly tapering toward the three-meter top. Henge-trees had been planted – built? – in a small circle, then pushed inward so they rested against each other. Their upper edges had all been fused together, but triangular gaps opened toward the ground. It was through one of these gaps that Moon was shouting.

"I don't care! Just get me out of here!"

Lancelot hissed as Anne ignored his commands. Rather than grazing contentedly, she stomped over to Moon. "You bloody stupid, arrogant dipshit. You hurt?"

"Not enough to teach him a lesson, clearly," said Misha.

Moon's face was a pale, blank oval in the shadows of the tower. "Help me."

Anne knelt down next to his triangular window. Lancelot rocked and hissed on her back, like an anxious pressure cooker. "What were you doing out here?" Anne demanded.

"Experiments, he says," Misha said.

"We don't have time for each of you to individually interrogate me," Moon said. "You can hear my discoveries when I tell Farhad."

Misha growled something about snotty little twerps, but Anne knew there was only one way forward. "Are you hurt?"

"Nothing serious," said Moon. "Now stop wasting time. Please."

"Please? Your pride must really be wounded," Misha said.

"How are we going to get him out?" Anne wondered.

"Quickly," Daisuke added.

Something whistled. Not Lancelot.

Anne felt her cavalier's weight shift as he twisted his neck around, looking beyond the henge.

Daisuke gave the tower a shove. The grassy clay failed to topple.

"We need rope," he said. "Wait. No, we don't." He backed up, flexing his arms and legs, preparing to jump. Of course that was exactly what he was going to do.

"Wait a second," said Anne. They needed more information. She raised her voice. "Moon, what's in that tower with you?"

"Monsters!" Moon shouted. He had wedged his shoulders through the triangular window, but it was much too small for him.

"That's not very illuminating. Let me see." Anne pushed Moon backward and stuck her head in with him.

There were mount-animals in here with Moon, which would suggest the tower was a corral or barn and not a larder. Except...Anne blinked and squinted, letting her eyes adjust. Moon was shouting at her, which was distracting, but yes, there were things riding the mounts. Not cavaliers though. These riders were only the length of Anne's arm, and had the same platelike flattened heads as their mounts. Except these...jockeys had tiny, useless-looking mandibles and enormous eye-clusters. She was reminded of the drones of honeybees.

Moon stood and hissed in frustration, and something whistled in the darkness. Another mount, this one riderless. It hooted again and inserted itself into the space between Moon and the jockey. Its neck bent backward until it was resting its head on its spine. Its throat lay bared at Moon, breathing holes gasping.

Anne grinned. "Now, that is never a threat response." For all Anne knew, those breathing holes were getting ready to spray her with acid snot or something. But, looking at Moon, she didn't think so. The mount was quivering just like the man. They were scared, but brave. Protecting what they loved?

"He's right, Anne." That was Misha's voice. "You can't fit through."

"I'm not trying to fit through," said Anne. "I'm trying to figure out what we're looking at."

"Everybody?" Daisuke' said. "We should hurry!"

"We could just leave him," said Misha.

Anne slid her head back out of the window and rose carefully to her feet. Lancelot released a smell like old fish, which she assumed was a sign of happiness.

"Okay, I think I know what we're jumping into, and that we can jump back out."

The breeze shifted, and a scorched citrus smell washed past Anne's nose. Lancelot whistled and more cavaliers answered from every direction.

Daisuke's expression turned fearful. "Misha, protect Anne."

He took three steps back, then leaped forward.

His boots hit the sloping sides of the tower and propelled him upward with a grunt and a shower of fish-smelling plant material. Another body-length upward, and Daisuke's feet slipped, but he flung his hands up and hooked his fingers over the edge of the hole at the top of the tower.

Clay sagged under him.

"What are you doing?" Moon demanded as Daisuke hauled himself up on bulging arm muscles.

"Hup!" he said, and vanished headfirst into the tower.

Only then did Anne remember her theories about wasp larvae. "Dice! Are you okay?"

"Okay," Daisuke answered. "Moon, please let me lift you up."

"What?" said Moon. "Oh, a boost." In a moment, his hands appeared over the wall of the tower. With an unathletic grunt, the physicist pulled and was pushed out.

"Okay," Daisuke said again. "Now turn around and give me your hand."

Moon frowned. "Oh, so you can climb out." He looked around, squinting.

The shithead was considering letting Daisuke rot in there.

"Hey!" Anne shouted. "Don't be a shithead."

Moon shot her a look of contempt. "You have no idea—"

The cavaliers attacked.

They came from all directions, whistling and thrashing atop their mounts. Four of them attacked the ATV and the rest went after Misha.

"Anne!" Daisuke screamed. Anne turned to him, and so didn't see Misha thump up behind her like a rugby forward and scoop both her and Lancelot into his arms.

Three huge steps and Misha threw Anne up the slope of the tower, then pounded up after her. Lancelot squealed as Anne flung out her arms and legs, grabbing at the shaggy ammonite-grass. She slid, nearly overbalanced, but Lancelot swung his head in the other direction, and halted their motion. Of course he would be good at that sort of thing.

Anne looked up. She, Misha, and Moon clung to the upper slope of the tower, just above the snapping jaws of the pack of cavaliers that surrounded them.

"What's going on?" Daisuke called from inside the tower. "Are you safe now?"

"No, you idiot," said Moon, and the tower collapsed under their weight.

★ ★ ★

Daisuke felt a little silly for how loud he screamed.

In fairness, it was Anne's name on his lips when the ceiling fell.

He realized that actually he was the person in most danger here and jumped back from the wedge of clay that came smashing down in front of him. Sunlight flooded the tower, and an animal squealed in pain.

The squeals were echoed outside. Over the edge of the now much shorter tower, the necks of three enraged cavaliers whipped. The humans had destroyed their animal pen and crushed one of their sheep.

Or perhaps, thought Daisuke, as creatures slithered and undulated past him and into freedom, *we've started a prison break.*

He shook his head, loosing a cloud of brick-colored dust and dry grass. *Focus. Protect Anne. Get out of here.* He stepped onto the broken wall, which sagged perceptibly under his weight. This was far too much like the aftermath of an earthquake, but at least Daisuke had some training for this.

"Anne!" he called. "Can you move? Can you come to me?"

Misha and Moon obeyed, but the real object of Daisuke's worry stayed where she was, curled into a ball with that horrible centipede creature warbling on her back.

Lancelot waggled from side to side, trying to gape his muzzled mandibles, the breathing holes on his fat lower body wheezing like a phlegmy accordion.

"Anne! Are you hurt?"

"Mmph!" came the reply, smothered in grass and clay rubble. "Trumphing sumphing."

"What?"

"She's trying something," Misha said, clambering down to join Daisuke and the jail's remaining creatures. "Some animal behavior magic, I hope? Work fast, Dr. Dolittle!"

Even as Misha spoke, the other cavaliers approached. Their mounts didn't appear to like stepping up onto the broken roof, but one creature managed to bully its way up. The mount squeaked as its rider squeezed it with riblike legs, but it found its footing on the crumbled clay. The rider swung its mandibles toward Anne.

Who stood.

★ ★ ★

Anne stood astride the fallen tower and looked down at the cavaliers.

They watched her back. Heads cocked and swayed, running her image across one eye-cluster then the other. Inner mandibles clattered together as outer mandibles gaped. Spikes twitched down spine and throat. Breathing holes contracted with indrawn breaths. Bowed limbs squeezed around lithe, segmented bodies.

Whistling, they came.

Clods of clay flew from stilt-tipped feet as the mounts rippled up the ramp of the collapsed tower wall. Plate-heads and axe-heads bobbed in unison, segments expanded and contracted in identical sequence, as if rider and mount shared the same blood and brain.

They really are like one animal.

For a moment, Anne's heart soared. Not only because the cavaliers were beautiful, but because she understood them.

She pictured a field of clay, looped about with noodly ammonite-grass. Sickle-jawed grazers picked their way over the ground cover, slicing it and packing it into their mouths. Too many grazers and the grass would get eaten up, but things would never get to that point because axe-headed predators waited in ambush behind trees, ready to decrease the grazer population.

Except. Where did the trees come from? The trees didn't grow; they were built by something with mandibles shaped like a bricklayer's trowel. The builders stacked clay into slabs so tall that the grazers couldn't eat the plants on top of them. A standing stone, facing south, presenting its broad face to the sun. A garden for the builders, out of anyone else's reach. Anne imagined a giraffe with eye-clusters and peg-legs.

Now, if predators ate too many grazers, there would be no need for builders to build the henge-trees that the predators needed to hide behind. If the cavaliers ate builders, on the other hand, they would free up space for grazers. The result that emerged from the needs of these three species would be a sort of savannah, with henges scattered across grass.

So far, so Earthlike, but population dynamics didn't explain the fences, hunting blinds, and prison towers. Why would builders shift their behavior to benefit the cavaliers? Why would mounts allow cavaliers to ride them? There were some weird mutualisms going on around here. There had to be a balance, and a way to negotiate it.

Anne remembered the way the mount in the tower had stood between her and the jockey, baring its throat, offering itself up. For sacrifice?

Big grazers carry little grazers on their backs. Big grazers sacrifice themselves for little grazers. Now, put the predators literally on top of that. The predators – cavaliers – ride the grazers, their mounts. Not on the hunt, because mounts willingly let themselves be slaughtered, but to defend their territory from *other* cavaliers!

The wind picked up, smelling of limes and snow. It blew Anne's hair out as she stood taller.

This! This was what Anne was meant for. This was her *job*! You watch the aliens. You figure them out. You use what you know to save people. She wanted to spread her arms out and shriek. HA!

But no! That would be a human threat display, and Anne wasn't playing the human now. Nor was she playing the cavalier. Lancelot was on her back and Anne was his *mount*.

So she reared, thrusting out her belly, inflating her lungs, hoisting Lancelot up on her shoulders. He waggled in protest, but Anne put her fingers in her mouth and whistled as hard as she could.

The attackers stopped.

Mounts pulled up, rearing, grasping at the sky with their cages of legs.

They rocked back to the ground, shivering, snorting foam from the spiracles running down throat and spine.

Cooling secretions, Anne's brain supplied. *Like sweat.*

The cavalier's head reared back, tracking not Anne's face, but the face of her rider, Lancelot. Lancelot gave a sharp, up-down head bob and vocalized a single low toot.

One by one, the mounts arched their heads back, exposing their throats. Anne bent herself backward as well, as if doing the limbo.

She grinned, panting with adrenaline. Why couldn't she make these sorts of deductions where people were concerned? Maybe she could.

The air was thick with the smell of butter and fish.

"So, Daisuke?" Anne called, still limbo-ing. "Are there other cavaliers in there in the pen with you?"

"Cavaliers?" said Daisuke.

"Pen?" said Misha.

"What's going on?" Moon demanded.

"Yes. Walking alone, a human looks like prey. In the ATV, we looked like rivals. But if we have a rider...."

"I get it," Daisuke answered, and switched to the aren't-you-a-beauty tone he always used when talking to animals. "*Ii ko. Ii ko da ne. J ba shiy ka? J ba?*"

Anne waited. The muscles in her back started to tremble.

Daisuke made the *yo-issho* noise, as if hoisting something heavy. A pant. A low whistle. "Okay. Okay. I have a rider."

"The only rider." That was Moon's voice.

"What about us?" Moon asked.

"Misha, you should, uh, *onbu! Kataguruma!*" Daisuke flailed for English and Anne's back burned. "Piggyback! You should piggyback!"

Inspiration hit Anne like lightning. "Misha and Moon!" she shouted. "Imitate a builder!"

Both men cursed. Oh, right, they didn't know what a builder was.

"Stand as tall as you can!" Anne shouted. Pain sparked up and down her spine. "Reach up with your hands like you're imitating a giraffe!"

She had to straighten. Groaning, Anne pulled her torso forward. Would she be sore tomorrow. But the cavaliers weren't attacking. They bobbed their heads at her rider, and Daisuke's.

It wasn't exactly a cavalier or a jockey. Its neck was stubby and its body was bloated, more like a maggot than a centipede. Instead of the tortoiseshell plating of the other cavaliers, Daisuke's rider was covered with thick, puffy pads, like the amusement park mascot version of a cavalier.

But when the mascot bobbed its head, the other cavaliers bobbed back. No abject submission, but not an attack either. Those mandibles were right at the level of Daisuke's face.

"Bow, you asshole," came Misha's voice.

"I *am* bowing!" said Moon.

"Not with your *head*, bow with your arms. We're imitating a giraffe, remember?"

Anne looked over her shoulder. Now her neck muscles hurt in addition to those in her back and belly, but she caught a glimpse of Moon riding Misha's back. With one arm, the physicist hung on. The other was stretched up, imitating a giraffe, or maybe that was meant to be an ostrich?

"This is ridiculous and we're all going to die," Moon said.

"Walk forward, Misha," Anne told him.

He did, and the cavaliers backed away.

"Lead the way, Misha," she said.

"What are we going to do when we get to the ATV?" asked Moon.

"Uh, I haven't thought that far," Anne said. "We'll just get in and see what happens."

Not much happened, at least when Misha and Moon climbed into the vehicle. The cavaliers swept their heads back and forth, as if wondering where the builder had got to.

Misha closed his door. The click of its latch seemed very loud.

Mounts balked, but cavaliers reached their heads out and stroked the backs of the skittish beasts. Or was Anne just anthropomorphizing?

"There are cavaliers behind us too," Daisuke whispered.

The heads swung back to Anne and Daisuke and the bobbing began again. The scent on the air shifted from fish to smoke and citrus.

"Don't worry. Just one step at a time," said Anne.

The nearest cavalier urged its mount forward. The big animal bowed its plate-shaped head in Anne's − or more likely Lancelot's − direction. The cavalier on its back bent in the opposite direction, baring its throat. Anne felt her own rider do the same.

"What's happening?" Daisuke said.

"It's okay," Anne said. "Just more submission behav—"

The cavalier in front of her snapped its body forward like a catapult, chopping its head down onto the neck of its mount. With a polytonic squeal, the creature tumbled to the ground, spraying blue-green blood from the stump of its neck.

"Shit," said Anne. "I didn't expect that."

And Lancelot's head smashed into the back of her neck.

★ ★ ★

Daisuke's heart nearly stopped.

He took a step forward, and the cavaliers around him stiffened and gaped. He didn't care. He would tear them apart and let them tear him apart if—

Anne started swearing.

Her cavalier, Lancelot, let go of her back and humped awkwardly away. The creature whistled and wagged its head, which – thank goodness – still had Daisuke's jacket wrapped around it.

Anne swore again. She had toppled forward, and her face was in the grass. This rendered most of her words inaudible, except for, "– your neck, Dice!"

Daisuke looked up to see the nearest cavalier bring its jaws down on the neck of its own mount. Aquamarine blood splattered him, and he felt his puffy rider shifting its own weight.

He brought his hands up and laced them behind his neck just in time to feel those mandibles tear across his skin.

"Now fall over like you've been decapitated!"

Daisuke did. With a sigh, the puffy rider on his back let go.

"Okay," Anne said. "Now we slowly crawl to the ATV...hm."

Daisuke leaned toward her, whispering. "What's wrong? Is it safe?"

"Huh? Oh. I don't know. I'm just wondering whether I can snag one of these dead mounts," Anne said. "I'd love to get my hands on something I can dissect."

CHAPTER ELEVEN

Moon's Mission

"If only I could have got both species," Anne said as the ATV sped out of the henge.

The mount's head was in her lap, wrapped in Daisuke's much-abused jacket. The body was in the back, draped over Daisuke and Moon, who was looking very sorry for himself.

"If we were going to share our ride with an alien, why not bring a live one?" Misha asked.

"Keep Lancelot as a pet, you mean? What would we feed it?"

"No, please," Daisuke said.

Anne tapped her teeth, looking over her shoulder at the cavaliers that had gathered to watch them go. "And are the riders and mounts even different species? I've been assuming predator–prey population dynamics, but how would things look if they were different castes? Sexes? Something epigenetic? Hm."

"I'm glad you're not hurt, Moon," said Daisuke.

"I'm...." Moon trailed off. Anne twisted around, trying to figure out what was going on with the physicist's expression. Was that gratitude? Or just relief and exhaustion?

Moon hunched and looked away from her. "Thank you," he said.

The alien centipede-knights had been much easier to domesticate, but maybe there was hope for Moon as well.

"You're welcome," said Anne. "Any time. Now, I want to know what you were doing out here, Moon."

Daisuke said, "Anne...." as if she'd made a faux pas, but Misha grunted in agreement.

"Anne is right. We risked our lives for Moon. *He* risked *our* lives for what?" He glanced over his shoulder. "You tell me, Moon, or maybe you walk home, huh?"

Moon made one of his annoying *tssh!* sounds. "First, I didn't risk your lives. You followed me. You were trying to interfere again."

"Us meddling kids," agreed Misha.

"Misha and Anne are only worried," Daisuke said. "You might have died, Moon."

Another *tssh!* followed by, "Yes. I know. But second, I don't need to walk home. I need to recover my ATV and my materials."

"What materials?" Anne asked. They'd reached the bottom of the hill and the other ATV was right there.

"Let me off here," Moon said. "You can stop the—"

Misha braked hard and they all rocked forward. The big man didn't give Moon time to settle in his seat before he turned around and grabbed him by the front of his jacket.

"What", Misha growled, "materials?"

"Misha, please," said Daisuke. "We're friends here." Did Daisuke really believe that?

Moon sure as hell didn't. He looked down at the fist bunched in his shirt. Back up. "My bucket," he said, expression set, "and my shovel."

Misha didn't let go. "What were you doing with a bucket and a shovel? I thought you'd be looking for the wormhole to the Cavalier planet. What did you need the tools for, Moon?"

"I didn't do anything to the wormhole to the Cavalier planet."

Anne didn't know what to make of that, but Daisuke said, "I see. It wasn't the Cavalier planet on the other end of the wormhole."

Moon's eyes widened. Daisuke was right! How did he do that?

Admiration kept Anne's mouth closed, while Daisuke said, "Professor Moon, we deserve an explanation, don't we?"

The physicist slumped. "I don't suppose you'll let me out of this vehicle unless I tell you."

"We will let you out," said Daisuke. "We will follow you to find your bucket. And I think you will feel better after you talk to us. You can't talk to anyone, can you?"

"That's not important." But Moon went on. "The planet on the other side of the wormhole I went through wasn't anything like the biome where I was ambushed and captured."

"And rescued," Misha grumbled. "You're welcome."

"Misha," said Daisuke. And more gently, to Moon: "What was the planet like?"

"The planet on the other side was not the Cavalier planet," Moon answered. "No grass, no worms riding worms. The ground was covered by dark purple spongy stuff, like a mattress."

Anne's fingertips tingled. "What does this mean? Either you're just a dipshit who can't tell one biome from another, or..." she twiddled her fingers, "...or there was some sort of terrible extinction event on the cavaliers' home planet and their entire biosphere has been replaced. Or it really is a different planet that Moon saw and the cavaliers are invasive in this area of Junction."

"So the cavaliers did to this biome what we're doing to the Sweet Blood biome?" asked Misha. "Are you sure the cavaliers aren't intelligent, Anne?"

"Yes! No, I have no idea!" Anne scratched at her hair. "Shit. We've got to do a better survey of the Cavalier biome, collect samples on both sides of the wormhole and compare them. And, maybe, we drive around the edges of the Cavalier biome and see how big it is."

"Unless Moon is lying," Misha said.

Would Moon make up a story like that? Could he? Anne turned to Moon. "Did you make any other observations our biologist might want to know about this sponge?"

Moon shrugged. "I think the spongy stuff was transparent, and the things living in it were purple. They wriggled away from me and the ground lost its color."

"Yeah?" Anne reached her hands out to him. "Then what happened?"

His Adam's apple bobbed as he swallowed. "I turned around and came back."

Anne's fingers curved into claws. "For Christ's sake, Moon."

"I didn't have time to take samples. As if you would thank me for taking any."

"Wait," said Daisuke. "Why did you have a bucket and shovel?"

"The shovel. I used it to demolish the wall around the portal."

Anne started. "There was a *wall* around the portal?"

"Yes. Like the tower I was in, but a cylinder rather than a cone. Those clay slabs, but all fused together. A wall."

"They built a wall around it!" Anne turned around in her seat. "We've got to see this thing!"

"No," Moon began, but Anne spoke over him.

"You can get in the ATV and drive yourself wherever you want, Moon. Or come with us, or stay here with Lancelot and his friends."

Moon looked at Anne, up the hill, and back. With sudden decisiveness, he kicked the door open, slithered out from under the dead mount, and ran flat out for his ATV. The engine hummed to life and the tires spun against the clay and ammonite-grass. Moon tore off for the west in a plume of fish-smelling dust.

Anne groaned and again grabbed a safety bar as her ATV lurched into motion as well. "Don't worry!" Misha shouted. "We're hot on his trail!"

"We won't let him do anything," said Daisuke.

Anne rubbed her face. "Anything *more*, you mean. We can't post a watch on Moon. And we can't save his life, make him our friend, and convince him to stop poking wormholes."

"I thought we should try to be kind to him," Daisuke said. "At least he didn't blow up this wormhole."

"Not because of anything *we* did," Misha said. "I guess the cavaliers ambushed him before he could finish his experiment?"

"He was lying," Anne said. "Right, Daisuke?"

"I think he wasn't telling us everything," said Daisuke. "Maybe we can discover more if we look at the scene of the crime?"

They rounded a crenelated hill to see all of the Nun squatting in front of a broad cylinder of clay.

"Too late," Misha said.

Moon's ATV slid to a stop. They could hear his cursing from there.

The cylinder was the same height as the henge-trees and Moon's tower, which suggested a maximum height for builders. A rim of blue and purple showed just above that wall, the air around it bent. Purple, Moon had said. It certainly wasn't the color of the plants of the Cavalier biome. So what was Anne looking at?

"What are the Nun doing?" asked Daisuke, spoiling Anne's concentration. "What's the word? A sit-in? A strike?"

Misha slowed their approach, yelling something in Nun. The

nearest men yelled back, making go-away gestures and shaking their spears. Nobody stood up.

"They're saying we should go away. We're interfering with an important discussion," Misha translated.

"They're pissed off because we let Moon desecrate another wormhole, aren't they?" Anne asked. "Tell them it wasn't our fault."

"It *was* our fault," said Misha, but he said something to the Nun, who reacted by variously rubbing their faces with their hands, shaking their spears, or turning their faces away. Yunubey, still crouching, shouted something in very slow, clear words.

"He doesn't care?" Misha asked. "He knows what Moon did? It wasn't desecration, he just drove an ATV in and then out again. No problem."

"Tell him we'll stop him next time," Daisuke said. "Tell him—"
Anne gaped. "He drove into *where?*"

"*Bilulum!*" Yunubey bellowed, half rising from his squat with the effort, "*Pergilah!* Fuck away!"

"I think he means 'Fuck off,'" said Misha. "Let me smooth this over." He popped his door open, and all the Nun yelled in unison.

Anne looked out at the grass. It was standing erect again in the late afternoon cool, shading the tops of toymaker land-cruisers. It stirred in places.

"Misha," Anne said quietly, "there are cavaliers all around us."

They rose from the grass like lions. Mounts with their scything jaws, riders with their axe-shaped heads suspended on segmented necks like the stingers of scorpions. Clusters of pinot noir eyes turned toward them.

Anne realized how silent their gathering was. The Nun weren't speaking and the cavaliers didn't whistle. The only sounds were the panting of the mounts and the ticktocking of the toymakers.

"What's that signal mean?" Anne whispered.

"Double-tocks," Misha said. "That means 'ready' or 'stand by' or 'safe'."

Were the aliens speaking? How much information was actually being given and received? Was this language? Were these people? The Nun always said no to both questions. Could Anne believe them?

She shuddered. *Can I trust him to trust me to trust him? Does he know that I know that he knows?* The endless, exhausting mirror maze of consciousness. Much better to leave that tangle to the xeno-psychologists, or whatever it was people called themselves who studied alien minds. Their first task would be to determine whether the psychologists themselves had minds. What would the objective test for that be, exactly? The wise would run away screaming.

"Anne, what's going on?" Misha asked.

"I was hoping you'd tell me," she said. Their escort had surrounded them, but the cavaliers' mandibles were closed, and she couldn't smell any ammonia or lime. "No aggression or fear displays that I can recognize. Not that that means anyth—"

Daisuke grabbed her shoulder.

Anne looked up in time to see the pair of animals bob out from behind the fenced-in wormhole. Stilt-legs moved in placid ripples, supporting long, curved necks, graceful as any swan's. Two heads rose and dipped, displaying Swiss Army-knife mouthparts. Anne's eyes registered branched antlers, broad shovels, miniature combs, flat-tipped spatulas....

"Anne, what are they?"

There was a distracting tremble of fear in Daisuke's voice, which Anne chose to ignore. She imagined muscles running through those mouthparts. The shovel going rigid to dig into the clay-like soil. Those trowels flexing back and forth, scraping clay off the shovel and onto a henge-tree.

"Builders," she said, suddenly happy Moon had dragged them here. The builders looked just like she'd predicted they would.

"What are they doing here though?" Misha asked.

"Repairing the fence, obviously," Anne said. Her gaze went back to the toymakers.

"'Ready', they're signaling," said Misha, "and 'stand by'."

Cavaliers bobbed their heads at the toymakers, the Nun, and the ATV. One of the mounts curved its neck back, showing its throat.

"Uh...huh," Anne said.

The toymakers ticked faster, like a drumroll, and the cavalier beheaded its mount.

The Nun jerked backward, spears bristling. The other mounts had more or less the same reaction, but Anne had seen it all before.

So, apparently, had the toymakers. The toymakers began a three-tock signal.

"It means 'seek'," said Misha. "Or 'food'."

A chop sounded from the grass, like a flint axe striking flesh. This was followed by another.

Daisuke moaned, and Misha said, "This is Tyaney all over again."

"What're you talking about?" Anne asked. "The toymakers are just butchering their gift."

The cavaliers swung their mounts toward the ATVs and Daisuke said, "Drive, Misha. Drive!"

Misha shifted into reverse.

"No no!" said Anne. "Daisuke, hold up your corpse. See?" she shouted at the cavaliers as Daisuke grappled with the long, limp body. "We've already got one!"

The air smelled like butter and fish, which was probably a good thing. And to make matters even better, the display spooked Moon, who backed past them and sped away.

"Should I follow him?" Misha asked.

Anne had been thinking about selfish genes. She shook her head. "Huh? Naw. Whatever's in his bucket, he can't get it now. There's nothing he can do that he hasn't already—"

Something exploded in the sky above them.

Anne looked up in time to see a second toymaker blimp detonate. Acrid soot rained onto the grass.

"Oh," said Anne. "Right. They expect the sacrifice to be mutual." She sniffed. Whatever had been in that blimp smelled like burned sugar. Bananas? "Where have I smelled that before?"

"Sweet Blood biome plants," Daisuke said. "When they burn, they blow up."

"A big, flashy, purely symbolic thing? Or valuable nutrients? What exactly just happened?"

"Something good," Daisuke declared. "Wondrous."

★ ★ ★

Daisuke was glad to leave Misha with the Nun. It meant that he could get out from under the dead mount and sit next to Anne.

She looked better, more like herself, with the wind in her hair and a smile on her face as she drove and turned theories over in her mind.

"That ritual we saw," he said. "Do you think it was like going through customs?"

She hummed to herself, steering between hills. "Bribing the border guards, paying tolls, or sacrificing to the god-king. But then why did they give *us* gifts? A gesture of submission? Weakening yourself, like rolling over and showing your vulnerable tummy? But then why expect the same of us?"

She swerved to avoid the cavalier that jumped up on the left, but that brought them closer to another on the right. It didn't attack, though, just glanced sideways and pulled away to keep its distance. Had it been looking at the body of the mount in the back?

"Do you think our dead animal is scaring them?"

"Hm," said Anne. "Maybe that's the purpose. They know we've already paid the toll. Or got our passport?" She sniffed. "Or maybe I'm anthropomorphizing again. I guess we'll see whether they attack us or just escort us back to the caravan."

As they drove on and no attack came, Daisuke allowed himself to relax. He was trying to figure out something romantic to say when Anne started humming again.

"What are you thinking about?" he asked.

"What was Moon doing back there? What was he trying to discover?"

"I wish we could explore the crime scene." Daisuke reviewed the sentence. "Could have explored, I mean."

"We didn't need to. We know he drove his ATV into the wormhole. That's what he was trying to discover."

Daisuke wondered if he should change the subject. They had so little time out of Moon's shadow. But soon they would be back at the caravan and the man himself would be waiting for them. Solving the problem was better than ignoring it.

"He already knew that the wormhole would expand to swallow something larger," said Daisuke. "Why did he test it again?"

"I guess Farhad told him to?"

Daisuke cocked his head, thinking. "Farhad wants to save his family. Or maybe the human race. He wants to colonize Junction."

Anne shivered. Daisuke worried he'd done nothing but allow her to ruin her mood, but she shook herself and muttered, "Keep exploring, Houlihan! Lift up that rock and see what squirms out from underneath." In a louder voice: "Okay, what purpose would blowing up a wormhole serve Farhad's cause? Driving through one, okay, that would get more colonists through faster...."

"Stress tests!" she and Daisuke said at the same time.

"He's also understanding what doesn't work," Anne said. "Can you pile people into a pyramid and drop a wormhole on them? No. It will explode. But what if you drive an ATV through?" Her voice dropped. "Experimenting on wormholes. But I experiment on animals, don't I? Yeah, and how different is that from Farhard's thing about eggs and omelets?"

Daisuke saw a place where he could help. "The difference is sustainability. You don't crack an egg until you know that there are more eggs in the world."

That seemed to relax her. "Right. So they've set an upper limit on what a wormhole can swallow. What'll they do next? They'll try to get closer to that limit."

"This is good," said Daisuke. "We can tell Misha that we know what to expect in the next biome. Moon will drive through the next wormhole in something bigger?"

They looked up. Ahead of them, the caravan sat at the edge of the Cavalier biome like a huge and very hungry caterpillar.

CHAPTER TWELVE

A New Course

Anne clapped her gloved hands together over the dismembered corpse of the mount. "*Itadakimasu!*"

From behind her, Daisuke snickered. "You're not planning to eat it, are you?"

"What I feel like is a starving woman who's finally been given a goddamn sandwich." Anne repositioned a light and bent over the carcass on the worktable in her barely used laboratory. "Hand me a magnifying glass. I want to get a look at this stump."

The middle mandibles of the cavalier had severed the animal's neck like a pair of gardening shears, compressing before cutting. That meant Anne had to do some decompressing before she could get a look inside. She held out a hand. "Forceps."

"Ah?"

She made pinching motions with her hand. "Like big tweezers."

"*Kanshi?* Pliers."

Anne didn't look up. "Yes. Sciency pliers. Forceps."

Cool metal was pressed into her palm. Anne hooked a thumb through the tube that ran down the middle of the animal, pinched with the pliers, and gently pulled. The inside of the mount's neck turned out to be very interesting.

"Okay," said Anne. "We've got your basic tubes-in-tubes body structure, like any honest Earth coelomate. Outermost layer is some sort of tough, wrinkly tissue. I'm reminded of elephant hide. It even has hairs."

"What about the exoskeleton?" Daisuke asked.

"Not exoskeleton. It's embedded in the skin. Some kind of armor." Anne rapped a plate with the pliers. It clunked. "We'll have to wait until we can get these samples to a real lab, but I'm guessing we'll find out that it's a scleroprotein like keratin. You can see the growth rings, like a turtle's shell."

She tapped the shell again, adding percussion to the run of her thoughts. "Lots of proteins in this biome. Did I tell you the sample of ammonite-grass turned out to be full of nitrogen too? More keratin, maybe? Actin? Freakin' gluten? That'd be a laugh."

She straightened, looking at the lights that hung from the ceiling on their jointed, adjustable arms. "All of which might indicate some sort of super-duper nitrogen fixation, if the plants have all these nitrates to waste. It would explain the smell, too."

"Nitrogen is what's in fertilizer, right?" said Daisuke. "If the plants here can get it from the air—"

"Nitrogen-fixing bacteria on Earth already do that for beans," Anne said. "And rice and sugarcane and a whole bunch of other things. The enzyme they use is— Hmm...nitrase?" She cocked her head, searching her memory of university lectures. "Is that true or did I make the word up? Anyway, whatever they've got on Earth, this biome's got something light-years more efficient. Maybe. I'm speculating."

Daisuke's voice was eager. "Maybe we can figure out how they do it. That could be valuable knowledge."

Anne's gut tightened. "Ick. You sound like Farhad. You can tell him how to make money off of ammonite-grass, but I'd rather not talk to him." Ever again, if she was honest. But failing that, she could at least bury herself in biology for a while. Try not to worry about things.

Anne shook her head and put her hands on the alien. "Okay," she said. "Under the...what I'll call for now the 'epidermis'... we get a living layer of 'let's-pretend-it's-dermis', some stuff that looks very much like fat, then..." she counted, "...six, seven, eight longitudinal muscles."

"Is that strange?" Daisuke asked.

"It's what I expected. It took an enormous amount of leverage for the cavalier to lift me." Anne rubbed her shoulder, which was bruising up nice and purple. "These muscles must run down the whole length of the body. And yet these animals are also as flexible as earthworms. No bones, okay, but then how can the animal support its own weight? Maybe they have tissues that expand as well as contract?" She poked and prodded. "Proteins resistant to pressure, but not tension…. Oh! Well, here's something you don't get in an earthworm."

Daisuke leaned closer. "What is it?"

Anne enjoyed his breath on her cheek. "*Kanshi*, love. Little mineralized clamps. Look here." She pinched the edge of a shell with one hand and squeezed her forceps around the severed end of a muscle cord. When she pulled, the corpse on the table curled, stilt-legs splaying, tail scraping around the opposite edge of the table.

Anne let go, but the body stayed curled. Even when she put both hands on it and tried to bend it back in the other direction, it refused to budge.

"It's a winch!" Anne crowed. "I can't straighten it. It takes energy for the tissues to relax, so this thing picks something up, locks its muscles, and just stays like that."

Anne waited for Daisuke to say something along the lines of 'We could sell this and make a fortune,' but he didn't. Instead he said, "It looks like a centipede. Or an ocean worm."

"A polychaete. Correct." Anne put her hand out, palm down. "Take a swimming worm and turn it on its side, so half of the bristles become legs and the other half dorsal spikes." She turned her hand into a blade. "The side-to-side undulations that moved the worm through water are now an up-down galloping motion."

She pointed her fingertips up, as if making a karate-chop. "That also explains Lancelot's head, which was laterally flattened, remember? There was one eye-cluster on the top of the head, the other on the bottom, stuck out on short stalks that angle either up or down to bring the eyes closer to the body's midline." She pointed to the appropriate places on her hand.

"But that's not what the mount's head looks like," Daisuke said.

Anne glanced at it. It was about the size of a serving platter, round on the edges but flattened at the front, with three pairs of mandibles shaped to cut grass and shovel it into the mouth.

"Right," she said. "This animal's head is dorsoventrally flattened. A secondary adaptation. To grazing, it's clear."

"Why didn't the mounts just turn the right way around, like centipedes, with the legs on both sides?"

Anne shrugged. "Evolution does funny things like that all the time. Nobody's in the driver's seat; you just end up somewhere. Now, these limbs."

The limbs began as little yellow hooks along the animal's throat, one for each pair of armor plates, each hook with its own puckered, mucosal breathing hole. Moving down the neck, the hooks grew larger and straighter, until they were each the length and thickness of a walking stick.

Anne grabbed one of these stilt-legs and gave it a wiggle. It bowed slightly out from the body, like a rib the color of carrots and the texture of ivory. "Now, this isn't just protein. It's mineralized in some way, but we won't know how until I carve off a sample. Which, glory be, I can do right now." Anne held a hand out to Daisuke. "Scalpel me."

Anne got her scalpel and used it to dig into the limb, which turned out to be softer than ivory. Maybe horn was a better comparison. Proteins, after all. And.... "Oh! It's hollow. There's a sort of pith inside and...wait just a second here."

She moved her fingers up the limb to where it joined the body. "Hm. The breathing hole here might indicate a biramous ancestor, or am I just flashing back to trilobites? Never mind about that now...." She cut into the tough hide and found what she was looking for. "Another muscle cord!" When she pulled it, the limb bent, just a little.

It was hard work. Anne strained for a moment before she released the tension with a gasp. The limb returned to its normal shape.

"Whew!" she said. "That was like stringing a bow. So the stilt-legs aren't entirely stiff after all. They've got some spring in their step. A lot of spring, actually. Fascinating!"

The walkie-talkie on her belt squawked.

"Anne?" Farhad called. "Would you come to the bridge?"

Anne could feel the muscles around her neck clench. Like her spine had been caught in a winch. "I'm working. For the first bloody time on this jaunt, Farhad."

"Then I'm very sorry to interrupt you."

What did the mad mogul want now? Had he discovered a tree that grew money? Maybe the emperor of the cavaliers had invited him to tea? The rest of the party had formed a union? Ha. If only.

"Tell me what you want," said Anne. "Daisuke, give me a sampling container for the spectrometer."

"I don't believe in multitasking," Farhad said. "When you're dissecting, you should focus on dissection. When you're advising me, I want your full attention."

"Then bugger off until I'm done."

"I'm afraid that the decision I need to make is time-sensitive," Farhad said. "And I think you would like to have some input."

"Anne," Daisuke said, "I think we should go to the bridge."

"Yeah, yeah." Anne threw down her forceps and snapped off her gloves. "Why can't they just make a decision without me babysitting them?"

Then she remembered what Moon had done the last two times she wasn't babysitting him. "Shit. We'd better go."

★   ★   ★

They found the bridge crowded with Farhad, Aimi, and Boss Rudi, who was in the driver's seat.

"We no break wall," he was saying. "Break caravan."

"All right, what is it?" asked Anne.

Rudi turned in his seat. "*Ibu Anne, bilang* Mister Farhad *kalau kita tidak bisa menabrak dinding pohon. Suspension tidak bakal tahan.*"

Anne blinked, trying to force her brain to switch languages. The main points were, 'tell Farhad', and 'the suspension won't hold'. She'd had a lot of conversations in Indonesian about vehicle repair. But *dinding pohon*? "Uh, what's a tree-wall?" Anne looked past Rudi's head. "Oh, I see what you mean."

It was the same basic structure as the fence around the wormhole and the wall of the tower where Moon had been imprisoned. It's just that this one was much longer. The tree-wall was a continuous, three-meter-high slab of clay with ammonite-grass growing on top of it. The clay had been excavated right there. Anne could see where the ground dipped as it approached the wall. The depression had filled with water. Plants grew in it like tubes topped with dark green hair.

"You see why I had to interrupt your work." Hands clasped behind his back, Farhad inclined his head at her. " Anne, would you please tell us what we're looking at?"

She folded her arms and drawled, "Yeah, I'd say it's a tree-wall, all right."

Farhad sighed.

"It's even got a moat," Anne said. "Hm. And a wall. If this country wasn't the cavaliers' original territory, they must have come here and conquered it, for lack of a better word. Okay, fine, but then why didn't they conquer whatever was west of this wall?"

"The orange forest," Aimi informed her.

Yes, it would be, if they were heading north-west from the Cavalier biome. This was the ecosystem that she had wanted to drive around.

She squinted up at the top of the wall. Beyond the noodly plant-tubes, there curled something orange and spiny. Barbed wire laid over the top of a prison wall. "We ought to ask ourselves why the cavaliers had the forest walled off."

"What are they protecting?" Daisuke clarified. "What are they protecting themselves from?"

"Yes, very ominous," said Farhad. He put a hand against the windshield. "But what I want to know is whether we can just ram through it."

"What?" Anne said.

"No," said Rudi. "*Ibu* Anne, *beri tahu dia.*"

"I sure as hell will!"

"Anne?" said Farhad.

"No," she said. "You can't ram through it."

"Indeed!" Boss Rudi said.

"All right," Farhad said. "So, we'll have to knock a hole in the wall."

"Yes," said Rudi, and turned to Anne. "Tell him that that's okay," he said in Indonesian. "Moon only needed an hour with a shovel to break down a wall like this."

Anne's teeth snapped together. She opened them slowly. "No. You cannot make a hole in the wall, Boss Rudi." In English she said, "I told you before we should drive around this biome."

"Not possible. We have a schedule we need to keep," said Farhad.

A muscle started jumping along the side of her nose, but Anne would not lose her temper. She would...she would...why the hell wasn't Daisuke helping? Saying something manipulative?

Anne visualized the caravan turning and driving north. What would get them moving that way?

"Maybe there will be a way through the wall?" Anne looked at Daisuke and pumped her fist. "We shouldn't give up!"

He blinked at her. So did Farhad. "You think we'll find a gate? A border crossing?"

Anne abandoned her impersonation. "I think your schedule can stretch to a little reconnaissance, in any case. Exploration is what we're here for, isn't it? Drive north along the wall. Slowly. No, better yet, wait until the Nun overtake us." She was starting to sweat. Moving Farhad's mind was like pushing a car uphill. "The toymakers have been coming this way for a long time, right? Even if the Nun don't know how to cross the border, the toymakers must do."

Farhad stared out the window. "The toymakers. You saw them do something yesterday, didn't you?"

"Well, yes," said Anne, surprised at the deduction.

"Some sort of negotiation with the cavaliers? The report I got from Moon was confused on that point."

Oh, so not a deduction at all. Anne hated to agree with Moon, even in absentia. His analysis was a gross oversimplification at best, and more likely to mislead them than not. But it would push Farhad in the right direction. Bleh. Shmoozing.

"That is the hypothesis I'm testing, yes," Anne said.

"So the cavaliers you saw really were escorting you?" Aimi asked.

"Mostly likely," Anne said, but where had the sudden tension in the air come from? Both Daisuke and Farhad were looking at Aimi with narrowed eyes. Her own eyes widened. Was the supermodel scared? Why?

"All right. I was watching you." Aimi looked at Daisuke under her lashes and brushed a lock of fine dark hair behind her ear. "I was worried about you. The two of you."

Anne looked from Aimi's face to Daisuke's, suddenly lost. Stupid humans and their stupid mind puzzles.

"Sir," Daisuke said. "I think we should let the Nun go in front of us. Their toymakers are very useful."

Farhad nodded slowly, still gazing out the window. "All right, Anne. I defer to your expert opinion. Boss Rudi, please wait until the Nun and the toymakers catch up with us, then follow them." He turned to Anne. "Do you have any more advice for me?"

"Don't go through that wall and leave the orange forest alone?"

Farhad examined her face. "Anne, would you and Daisuke extend your break from your work and sit with me for a minute?"

He sat, flipping a hand at Aimi. "Would you make some tea for us? And bring in Moon."

Anne's neck stiffened so fast her vertebrae popped.

As if he had heard the noise, Farhad turned his smile back to her. "I know things have become strained. I'd like to fix the problems between you two."

Anne looked at Daisuke, who was nodding unhelpfully. "Uh," she said, "yeah. Thanks, but I have this alien corpse I'd like to get back to dissecting."

"This won't take long, I promise." Farhad steepled his fingers. "Think of this as just another part of the postmortem."

★ ★ ★

Moon sat on the bridge with Anne, Farhad, and Daisuke, pretending to listen.

"Professor Moon told me how grateful he was to you for saving his life," Farhad said.

Moon's eyes tracked across the toymakers as they streamed around the caravan, rowing on oars, floating under gas-filled envelopes, or pulling on reins attached to other toymakers or humans with strained expressions.

"Yeah, he looks grateful as hell," Anne said, "but what was he doing, Farhad?"

"Why, research, of course," Farhad said and coughed. "Boss Rudi, would you tell Turtle to stow the solar panels and prepare for departure?"

"What research?" Daisuke asked. "What did you send him out there for with a bucket and a shovel?"

"That was to move dirt. To break through the wall that the – did you call them *cavaliers*? – that they placed around the wormhole."

Moon's fingers twitched. Farhad was much more sanguine now than he had been yesterday, when Moon had told him the cavaliers had stolen back the bucket. Even now, something hard and sharp gleamed behind Farhad's grandfatherly mask, like the shell of a scorpion.

Whatever. There were more buckets in the caravan's storage room, and another portal ahead.

Moon watched the cavaliers, pacing alongside the larger toymakers outside. The aliens clacked their mandibles, paused, clacked again. The nearest humans waved their arms, lips moving as if speaking.

"Is he even listening?"

Moon glanced around to see Anne had stood. "I don't believe this! I don't believe *you*." She blocked Moon's view, hands on hips. "Moon, what the *hell* were you doing with that wormhole?"

Moon met her eyes. So Anne was angry. When wasn't she? It was a disgusting display of self-indulgence, like taking your dieting friend to a sweet shop and stuffing a whole cake in your mouth.

"I'm not going to tell you," he said.

Daisuke sighed and Farhad let out a groan. "All right, boys and girls—"

"No!" Anne slashed her hands through the air. "I can't do this, Farhad. I can't stand by and let you send your minions out on evil missions!"

Farhad rubbed his beard. "So you think I'm some kind of super-villain?"

"This is my working hypothesis, yes."

"Anne," said Daisuke.

"No, no," Farhad said. "It's all right. I understand. Anne, I know you're frustrated—"

She stomped her foot. "I am going on strike! If you try to drive *this* machine through *that* forest, I am locking myself in my room and not coming out."

Moon snorted. "You can't lock yourself in. He has keys to all the rooms."

"Moon!" Farhad glared at him.

"Creepy," said Anne. "But irrelevant."

Farhad sighed. "Anne. Please don't make ultimatums. It's bad strategy."

"Oh is it? What do you think you can do to me? Drag me outside and force me to hypothesize at gunpoint? Even if you torture me—"

Farhad held up his hands. "Please, Anne. For god's sake, I'm not going to torture you. You're not my enemy, or my slave or my prisoner. If anything, you're holding *us* hostage. If you don't help us spot potential danger, we might be killed."

"Yup," Anne said, "sounds like a good reason to keep your caravan on this side of the wall."

In the silence that followed, Moon stood. "I should go," he said.

"No hold on," said Anne, but Farhad said, "Let him go."

The biologist turned on the tycoon, and Moon slipped off of the bridge.

Farhad gave him an exasperated look, but what part did Moon have to play here? He didn't care whether Anne or Farhad won this pissing contest. Moon had work to do. His experiments would continue until the portals either yielded up the secrets of space and time, or, as was looking more likely, Moon went mad.

He'd driven off alone into the alien wilderness, gotten blisters all over his hands, been imprisoned by monsters and nearly killed, and what had Moon accomplished? Nothing but the discovery of another superficial layer of the Zookeepers' user-interface system.

That was the real humiliation here. Not being rescued by Anne or defended by Farhad. They were monkeys playing monkey games of territory and dominance. What did that make Moon though? He was nothing but a monkey too.

Let a monkey play in a sports car and it might eventually find the starter button. It could press the button and all the other monkeys might hoot with glee at the bright lights and loud noises. That brought nobody any closer to understanding internal combustion.

None of which changed Moon's plan. Portals were still the most promising path to the new physics. Nothing else so completely failed to obey the old physics, after all. As ever, there was a wall between Moon and the truth, and he would continue to scratch away at the surface until something gave and he broke through.

From the outside, there was no way to tell how thick it might be. All he could do was dig faster, while he still had his shovel.

★ ★ ★

"Why don't you tell me what you are afraid will happen if I drive the caravan through the forest?" said Farhad. "Aside from you going on strike, I mean. What will the natural consequences be?"

"What do you mean 'What's going to happen'? You're going to cut down a whole bunch of trees."

"Why would I do that?"

"To make room, obviously!"

Farhad frowned at the tree-wall. "Do you think the forest over there is that dense?"

"Of course it is!" Was he teasing her? Anne was tempted to just storm off the bridge, but what if Farhad really didn't know? "You're the one who showed me the drone photos. Didn't you see the exclusion zones around the crowns?"

"I hate to admit it," Farhad said, "but I only pretended to understand you. What are exclusion zones?"

Anne couldn't help but sigh. She knew she probably sounded like she couldn't believe how stupid Farhad was, but actually she was just relieved. "You didn't know how dense the forest is? You thought you could just drive through it?"

The tycoon shrugged. "I usually go camping at Redwood National Park. You can drive a camper between those trees."

Anne took a deep breath. "Yes, but the trees over that wall aren't redwoods. They're much shorter and more densely packed. More like an artificial tree plantation than an old-growth forest, now that I think of it. Although if people planted them you'd expect the trees to be in rows...." She shook her head. "You can't drive the caravan through without cutting trees down, and no way am I going to allow that. Especially when it would be so easy to just drive around."

"More to the point, it would take more time to cut the trees down than to drive around." Farhad stroked his goatee, watching her. "All right, Anne. You win. I agree to your terms."

Anne sagged. "Oh. Okay. Thank you."

"You're welcome," Farhad said. "And I'm very sorry things had to come to this pass. You shouldn't feel like you have to engage in combat with me in order for me to change my plans." He clapped his hands together. "Now, what was that you said about artificial plantations? Do you think somebody *made* that forest?"

Anne shrugged. "Not enough information."

"How could we get that information? On foot? With what supplies? Will ATVs pass between the trees, do you think?"

"Of course they will," said Anne before she realized what Farhad was doing. "I mean, wait, what about driving around?"

"I'll double-check, but I think going straight through, even on foot, will still get us to Howling Mountain faster."

He just wanted to get at the wormhole, the bastard. Anne looked to Daisuke for help, and he suggested, "What about a compromise? Anne, I, and the Nun will walk through the forest, and everyone else will drive around it in the caravan?"

"Ah," Farhad said, "a compromise." For a second, his face pinched together in a way that almost looked sad. Disappointed. Then he smiled and turned up his hands. "If that's what it will take to keep you happy, Anne, I'll do it."

"We will tell you everything we learn in the forest," Daisuke said.

Farhad nodded. "Of course you will. I'm very much looking forward to finding out what you discover."

Boss Rudi pressed the starter button and the caravan hummed to life.

CHAPTER THIRTEEN
City of Gold

The gate, when they came to it the next morning, was refreshingly inhuman. No arches, no arrow slits or murder hole. Not even a door. There was just a gap in the clay wall and a mound where a pile of clay had been dumped into the moat.

The toymakers had waited for sunrise before they began to trundle across this crude bridge. At their lead was a mobile fortress the size of a mini-fridge, towed by a team of land-galleys. A quintuplet of tethered zeppelins hung over the fortress like arm-length wooden wasps, orange with caked-on clay and glittering with mica.

Anne stood outside with Misha and Daisuke, and watched the delegation approach the gate. Beyond the toymakers lay a thicket of those barb-wire tendrils. They sprawled and coiled like a saffron-colored blackberry bramble, except....

What was so wrong with them? What gave Anne that fluttery feeling in her belly when she looked at them? A real bramble – assuming it was growing in its native habitat and wasn't taking over some defenseless South Pacific island – should make her feel calm and eager. What sort of birds would be nesting in it, etc.

These serrated orange curlicues, though, filled her with dread. Anne examined her reactions and found that the reason she hated these plants was because they looked artificial.

The gates were symmetrical. Each spiral and loop of vine mirrored around a midline. Anne hugged herself, thinking of the wrought-iron vines on the gate of a Victorian-era train station. *All aboard. Hurry up and wait. Better run or you'll miss your connection. Welcome to civilization.*

"Something is moving," said Daisuke.

Anne raised her binoculars and zeroed in on the disturbance in the hooked and looping vines. Behind them was what looked like more vines. The tangle was so thick that Anne couldn't see anything past it. But the toymakers and cavaliers were all clacking, and yes, there were small, mouselike animals fluttering away from....

"Oh!"

Anne had thought that mass of fronds was a plant. Maybe some kind of fruiting body. Now, though, it came twisting out of the bramble, as if umber staghorn ferns had rolled themselves into a cigar.

Fronds brushed against vines, curled, contracted, and a head emerged. It was blunt, with the cross section of a five-pointed star. The star twisted as it was drawn out, creating five equally spaced ridges that spiraled down its body. Two of these ridges sprouted contractile limb-fronds. Another bore eyes like black beads. The fourth was just raised bristles – maybe other sense organs. The fifth bore a row of interlocking, triangular teeth.

Which *unzipped*. The tube-shaped body became a spiraling ribbon, fronds splayed like the bows of a monstrous birthday present around the slick, blue interior surface. A thrumming noise reached Anne, such as might be produced by an oboe the size of a Bengal tiger. Maybe something more like a bassoon.

The toymakers clacked, and a hatch on their land-fortress opened. From this angle, Anne couldn't see what was inside, but the zipper-animal stopped its display. It smoothed out its fronds and bent over the toymaker delegation, the unzipped front of its body dangling like an elephant's trunk lined with eyes.

"Tock-tock!" signaled the toymakers, and the forest animal struck. The tooth-fringed ribbon buried itself in the toymaker fortress.

Anne could feel the other humans tense, but the toymakers made no alarm clacks.

The creature convulsed. A wave of motion traveled up its body, the zipper-teeth opening and closing in rhythmic ripples.

"Is it vomiting?" Daisuke asked.

"The opposite, I think," Anne said. The animal was sucking something from the toymaker cruiser. Food? Drink? She debated with herself about running forward to take a closer look.

The animal reared up. Its nose zipped itself back together and Anne's diaphragm fluttered in sympathy to another deep vocalization. A pair of smaller animals stuck their heads from the brambles and slithered up to the first.

158 • DANIEL M. BENSEN

"Are they kissing it?" Misha asked.

To Anne, it looked more like they were plucking something from its body. She quashed her impatience. There would be time to make more observations.

All three animals withdrew into the brambles, leaving the toymakers to wait.

Anne's walkie-talkie gave a squawk and Farhad's voice asked, "What happened? Did we make it?"

The creepy, symmetrical brambles did not swing back like doors on hinges. They didn't even uncoil. They lurched up and rotated away, as if they were potted plants whose pots had been turned and shoved out of the way.

Beyond the gates shone a city of gold.

★ ★ ★

"But I don't want to call it 'El Dorado'," Anne said later.

"Yeah, I think you've named your fair share of things already." Farhad dropped another pack of water bottles next to the ATV and straightened, massaging his back. "Everything's a blob-worm or a slime-snake to you. At least call the animals here 'serpents', for pity's sake. And would a 'dragon' here or there kill you?"

"And what's that, then?" Anne pointed past him, across the belt of umber lawn to the forest of towering trees beyond. The nearest specimen looked like a mad Gothic baron had built a cathedral out of cheddar-flavored Legos. "A Rapunzel tree? A Tree of the Knowledge of Good and Evil?"

"Yes!" The mogul was practically drooling. "Good lord, Anne, can you imagine the sort of press we'd get?"

"Can you imagine the backlash on Twitter?"

Farhad was holding up his hands, and Daisuke, walking up with a box of supplies, was shaking his head at her. *Well, screw 'em!* Anne pushed on regardless.

"Right," she said. "We can't plaster our mythology all over this planet. We'll get every creationist and his sister-wives in here, chewing on the scenery."

Farhad flapped his hands. "Fine, fine. I take your point, Anne, yes.

No religious allusions. But 'Rapunzel trees'? That's brilliant! Although—"
he tapped his chin, "– if this place is El Dorado, we really ought to have a
conquistador theme. Feathered snakes and doubloons and so forth."

Aimi looked up from the box she was digging through. "I think that'll
get us social media backlash as well. Colonialism."

Anne winced with the pain of someone who'd been called a colonial
apologist on the internet.

Farhad nodded, but said, "At a certain point, backlash is publicity.
Better to lean into it. But feathered snakes! What were they called?"

"Kukulkan? Quetzalcoatl?" Aimi smiled at Anne's look of confusion.
"I majored in anthropology."

"That's great. The second one. Let's shorten it to *coatls*." Farhad pointed
down to the ground just in front of them, where the lichen-encrusted clay
gave way to an orange – for lack of a better word – lawn. "How about
that little plant on the ground? What's *grass* in whatever language?"

"I don't actually speak Nahuatl, Farhad," said Aimi.

It was clear that the plants of the lawn weren't grass. They grew at least
a meter tall, forming a tight, springy orange net that visibly bent under the
weight of the humans and larger toymakers on top of it.

"Doubloon-grass?" offered Daisuke.

Land-galleys scuttled across the stuff easily enough though. The little
wooden cylinders hooked their oars into the ground cover and rolled
on little gear-toothed wheels, shuttling between the big cruisers and the
coatls that clustered at the edge of the forest.

"That's the spirit, Dice! Now, Aimi, talk to me about how we can get
these names trademarked."

Anne wanted to scoop out her eyeballs, this conversation was so
excruciating. Like a drowning woman clutching a piece of floating wood,
she knelt to examine the plant.

The organism that she would absolutely never call *doubloon-grass*
reminded her of a twig from a juniper or a frond of *Corallina* algae. It
was composed of flattened oval yellow-tan segments, each around half
a centimeter long. At the base of the plant, these segments followed one
after another like beads on a necklace, forming a stalk. Farther up, one
row branched into two, each of which branched into yet more, forming
a fan shape.

"What are you looking at?" It was Daisuke, squatting next to her.

"Tired of copyrighting the bounty of nature already?" Anne asked.

Daisuke sighed, which made Anne feel bad. By way of apology, she said, "What I'm looking at is a nice Fibonacci growth pattern."

"Fibonacci? Ah. *Fuibonatchi-su*. One, one, two, three, five, eight? That one?"

"Yeah, that's the one." Each new number was the sum of the previous two. "The same numbers that gave the nautilus-grass its curve. Not to mention Earth nautiluses. Math is universal, but the problem is...." She put out a finger and waggled the little yellow fan. "Look. It can put out more shoots from the tips of its branches, but it can't thicken its base." Already, this plant was bending under its own weight. She found what she was looking for.

"Here, look at this," she said, and crouch-walked away from the corporate types and their naming game.

Anne pointed to a hand-sized fan of doubloon-grass bent into a bridge shape, with its segmented branches burrowing into the dirt. The broad upper surface of the bridge was spiky with new, upward-growing shoots. More fans stretched up from the leading edge of the parent plant....

"And that."

Anne pointed farther west still, where the lawn began. Triangles begat triangles, yellow branches cascading out across the ground.

"Another mathematical shape," said Daisuke. "What was it called? *Kōkō sūgaku nante mukashi no hanashi dana ... Shierupensukii no Gyasuketto dattakke?*"

"The Sierpinski Gasket," Anne said, too ashamed to admit she'd only ever heard the phrase in a Jonathan Coulton song. "Sierpinski-grass. There. Much better than *doubloon-grass*." She remembered that that name had been Daisuke's idea and hid her chagrin by peering more closely at the plant.

"Oh!" There was an animal clinging to a branch of the sierpinski, camouflaged in umber and tangerine blotches, a bit longer than Anne's pinky fingernail. Its shape reminded her of a computer chip: a long flat rectangle with its long side fringed with tiny teeth.

Or perhaps legs. When Anne disturbed the plant it had wrapped itself around, the animal dropped off and rippled away, its body bowed to allow the triangular pegs to dig into the soil. When Anne bent to touch the creature, it curled into a spiral, tooth-legs meshing, and inverted itself into a sphere. The orange upper surface of its body was now on the inside, and its dark blue ventral surface formed the skin of a little ball. It oozed milky fluid that was probably some kind of defensive toxin.

Anne wondered if the creature could invert that sphere, and put the toxins on the inside. Subdue prey inside that cavity? Digest food? And hadn't she found it spiraled around a branch? A quick inspection showed that, yes, the branch of sierpinski-grass where the pinkie-nail had perched was scored in a spiral pattern, like the red line around a barber's pole.

"Aha! That's one way to evolve a coelom," said Anne.

"What?" Daisuke asked.

"Never mind about that. Look how they *stack*." Anne waddled deeper into the biome. "The sprouts on the top of one sierpinski fan out, then bend, then root themselves on the top of another bridge and so on."

The lawn thus formed stretched to the forest and continued, filling the space between ornate tree trunks. Deeper into the forest, the wedge of sierpinski-grass rose three or four layers high before it put up blue stalks – fruiting bodies? Gaps in the layered ground cover indicated where herbivores had torn chunks out and…ha!

Anne got up and jogged to the place where two wedges met. "Look at this." She pointed at a bare line in the ground. "It's the border between the two competing sierpinskies." The line jagged off into the forest like a bolt of lightning, branching and converging, marking the history of a million tiny battles.

"And that's only one solution to the problem of supporting growth." Anne turned in a slow circle, pointing. "Those domes, look how every other branch dips back toward the ground. Those… telescope…bamboo…things. Look how the rings of stem-segments sprout from the ground around an upward-growing core. Or you just don't branch much at all, and you get these long, coiling whips. Barbed bramble."

"I like that name," Daisuke said.

"Thank you." Anne turned and looked back east across the lawn that separated the tree-wall and the forest.

The edge of the forest wasn't clean, of course. Shrubs grew up from the sierpinski, scattered around the lawn like very ugly hedge sculptures. Rather than the globular or conical shape of most understory plants, these things looked like they'd been hacked apart and glued back together by surrealists. One was a wiggly, spiny U shape with a horned blob on one end. Another was an overturned barrel with legs.

Anne watched a forest animal slither out of this shrub to threaten a passing toymaker land-galley. The little craft stopped and raised its forward oars.

"Anne! Daisuke! We're almost ready to go." That was Misha, striding across the springy mat of sierpinski.

"There's something odd about the oars on that toymaker," Anne said.

Most toymaker oars looked like flattened chopsticks, but this land-galley was equipped with segmented orange sticks. They looked very much like they came from this very biome.

"Eh?" said Misha as the toymaker flapped its orange sticks in semaphore. Its wooden shell shuddered as some internal mechanism clunked into a new position. A sound cue? Some visual thing that Anne couldn't see from this angle?

The forest animal nosed closer.

"Is it talking to that coatl?" Daisuke asked.

"Toymakers don't talk," Misha said. "But I don't know what that one is doing."

The toymaker rushed forward, then stopped. It rushed forward again until it was almost kissing the...yes, might as well call it a coatl. The toymaker held out its front oars like a toddler asking to be picked up.

The coatl unzipped its snout and plucked the oars off the toymaker. The serpentine alien slithered off into the forest and the stranded toymaker clacked.

"What?" said Anne, and the Nun started calling to each other.

Misha cocked his head. "That's the signal to move out."

"Great!" Daisuke clapped his hands together. "We'll load the ATV and meet you at the wormhole."

"Farhad's still going along with your plan, is he?" Misha narrowed his eyes toward the gate and the caravan beyond. "Are you sure you can trust him?"

"I think so," Daisuke said, while Anne thought, *Not on your life.*

CHAPTER FOURTEEN
Get Rich Quick

Farhad did not kneel to pray, not when at work.

He'd been fired for it, once, back in his first job in Los Angeles. His manager had walked in on Farhad during his lunch break, and they'd put him on probation a week later. Farhad had held on for two months before he came to his senses, gave them an excuse to fire him, and started his own business with a fellow Iranian. But Farhad hadn't prayed in front of that guy, either. Farhad's relationship with God was nobody's business but his own.

Now, if anyone saw Farhad sitting with his eyes closed, tea mug steaming in his hands, face turned toward the eastern window of the caravan's bridge, they'd think nothing of it. The old man was just enjoying his tea, or perhaps he was meditating.

That would be an interesting inversion of the truth. Several of Farhad's friends did practice transcendental meditation, and they were forever talking about 'reaching out to the cosmos'. That was the exact opposite of what Farhad was doing, which was opening himself up to let the universe flow into him.

The caravan bumped. Aimi and Turtle whispered together while Boss Rudi, perhaps coincidentally, crooned a romantic ballad from forty years ago. Ginger sunlight shone through the window and onto Farhad's face, which was turned east toward the wormhole that led back to Earth.

Farhad saw his world in all its beauty and vulnerability. He saw his grandfather's tomato garden, and the irrigation channels the old man had dug out between the plants. When the water came, the cracks in the soil darkened first, then brimmed.

Farhad listened to the blood pulse in his temples. *Should I give up?* He asked. *Should I stop pushing and turn us around? Go back to Earth and, I suppose, do something about its problems?*

The answer came as the sensation of a shadow falling over him. The skin on Farhad's neck prickled as he felt the Howling Mountain looming up at his back. A massive cone, too regular in shape to be natural. It radiated cold from the wormhole at its peak. What lay there? What waited at the top of the tower?

Fear. Suffering. Sacrifice. The transformations Farhad would have to create in order to climb that last mile. A reward to make the climb worth it.

The wormhole. The escape valve. And so little time was left.

Farhad opened his eyes. He had his answer: stay the course. Climb the mountain. Reach the finish line by whatever means necessary, and rest when you're dead.

He took a long, slow sip of his Earl Grey. Its heat spread down his body and pooled in his stomach. A center, a tunnel back to simpler, more dependable times.

Farhad clinked his cup down on the arm of his chair. Aimi understood that this sound was a signal for her to stop what she was doing and pay attention. Before Farhad could say anything, though, Moon arrived.

"We have to turn around right now," the physicist demanded.

Farhad quashed his annoyance. Why couldn't Moon be his enemy and Anne his ally? That would be easier, emotionally. "All right," he said.

"The math is simple. The closest portal is the one in the middle of the Dorado biome. I need it. We don't have time to detour to get another."

"All right, I said." Farhad looked up at Moon, who was pacing back and forth on the bridge like a caged leopard. "I'm agreeing with you."

Moon stabbed a finger at him. "For now, maybe, but what about after Anne's next tantrum?" Farhad clinked his mug again, wishing it were a gavel. Beyond the windshield, the Dorado forest still slid slowly by on the left. They were still driving north along the border of the Dorado forest, as Anne had demanded.

"I can't believe you gave in to her threats," muttered Moon, but Aimi cut him off before he could work himself up any further.

"If we have the Howling Mountain," she said, "and the co-operation of Ms. Houlihan, we still have the secondary and tertiary missions."

"No!" Moon smacked the back of a chair and pushed off for another lap. This pacing must be making the man terribly carsick. "It isn't enough. All we've done so far is prove we can destroy a portal!"

"Phase two was successful," Aimi pointed out. "Isn't that something?"

Moon stopped pacing. "It is *nothing*!" he hissed. "Pure research doesn't matter anymore. I'm not a scientist anymore. I am a monkey in a Ferrari and I need the key in my paw!"

Farhad noted Aimi's flinch from Moon's raised fist. The poor boy. A pity he didn't consider himself a scientist anymore, because he wasn't a man, either. Maybe this outburst was Moon's way of telling Farhad that. A cry for help.

"Professor," Farhad said, "I understand. And I agree with you. We've already destroyed a wormhole. That information alone will turn international politics upside down, but if we want any leverage from which to bargain, we must complete the primary mission. And for that, you need your wormhole."

"Portal!"

Farhad waved his hand, more annoyed with himself for forgetting Moon's foibles than at Moon for having them. When a man's dog bites someone, you don't blame the dog, you blame the man.

"We must reach our goal at any cost," Farhad told them.

"Yes, and we have to tread lightly while doing it," said Aimi. "We can't just steal the w— I mean…the portal from the Dorado forest. Not if we want Houlihan's co-operation."

"What co-operation?" sneered Moon. "What's she going to do to us? I need that portal, Farhad."

Farhad hid his annoyance by putting his cup to his lips. It was empty. He looked down at it, suddenly tired despite the caffeine and the lingering smell of bergamot.

He laced his fingers around the teacup and looked from Moon to Aimi. "All right," he said. "Unless one of you has a better idea, I think the time has come to engage in some light treachery."

Both of his people slumped, but Aimi's faint scowl indicated sorrow and anger. Moon just looked relieved.

"Aimi," ordered Farhad, "go to Boss Rudi and tell him to turn around. We go south and east, back to the Cavalier portal. Moon, figure out where the next closest portal will be."

"Obviously, the two closest portals are the Cavalier and Dorado portals. The most direct path is to just push past Anne and take it."

"No," Farhad said. "I told you, the costs are too great. If we can visit two portals and come back here before Anne and the others realize what's happened, maybe we can salvage something."

Moon smirked. "Once I'm done, it won't matter what we salvage."

Farhad leveled a finger at him. "This is the attitude that made you think you could drive off alone into the Cavalier biome. This lack of caution lost us one portal already, so learn from your mistakes, son."

Moon flinched. Farhad hated to use such crude tactics on the man. Poor Moon was crushed between his dead father in the past and his own ruined mind in the future. Reminding him of that would only hasten his breakdown.

But maybe Farhad didn't have to care. All he really needed was to postpone the breakdown for two days.

"Let's go, people." Farhad stood, and sent up a silent prayer that he would not be incentivized to commit any worse acts than this one.

★ ★ ★

The Dorado wormhole did not sit above a mound or at the bottom of a hole. This wormhole was trapped, pierced by the branches of the trees, and crawling with activity.

Spiky orange limbs as thick as Anne stuck out from a ring of mighty Dorado trees and went right through the wormhole, presumably interconnecting to a matching ring on the Dorado home world. Coatls formed rushing conga lines across these bridges, a pulsing stream of activity that reminded Anne of ants in columns. Or maybe one of those time-lapse pictures of stop-and-go traffic.

Except ants and cars didn't suddenly peel off in a different direction or slam into each other and...fight? Mate? Start dancing? It looked like all three at once. Tangles of wrestling animals formed, grew, then scattered without apparent signal. Phalanxes would coalesce, clear paths through the melee, then dissolve and join it. Swarms harassed loners, loners gathered guards around themselves, individuals in both groups switched sides, all apparently at random.

Creepy. Strange. Interesting. Anne found her fingers clenching as if to rip open this forest's secrets.

"What am I looking at here?"

"We'll protect it," Daisuke declared, his hand on her shoulder. "Even if Farhad was lying—"

"He was lying," said Misha.

"Even if he comes through the forest," Daisuke said, "we will be here. We'll be waiting for him."

"Don't say that, Dice." Anne gestured at the Nun and their toymakers, which were still filtering in from the eastern forest and arraying themselves in protective circles around the wormhole. "If Farhad comes through the forest, that'll mean he's leveled the forest."

"I thought he would use the ATV," Daisuke said.

Misha crossed his arms. "Yes, that's my most likely scenario. Farhad sends his goons in the other ATV, along with guns and chainsaws."

The Nun would kill or die to protect this wormhole, Anne knew. Or more likely, kill and then die, because the vast majority of their food and water was inside the caravan.

"What about food?" Anne asked. "Farhad can starve us out."

"Probably not," Misha said. "He has a schedule to keep. We have enough supplies that starving us out will take him longer than driving around the forest to the Howling Mountain and blowing up its wormhole."

"Shit," said Anne, who hadn't thought about that possibility. "And if he's willing to just leave us here, he can traipse across the landscape, experimenting on whatever wormholes he wants."

"If he leaves us here, we'll just walk back to our village," Misha said.

"Do we have enough food for that?"

Misha's big, florid face went suddenly stony. "You let us worry about that." And in a more normal tone of voice: "Of course, Farhad will try to stop us from getting back to civilization before him. He won't want anyone to know what he's been doing out here."

In the past few days, Anne had almost forgotten about Junction's extra third G of gravity. Now she felt all of her extra weight and more. "Agh! I hate thinking like this," she said. "I hate people and their politics and scheming!"

"Then you have come to the wrong place, *dorogoy*," Misha said.

Anne blinked, looking back up at the rush-hour traffic on the Dorado trees. She knew that Misha meant that the humans had brought politics with them, but now that she thought of it, wasn't there something city-like about this forest?

"Yeah," she said. "That's what keeps creeping me out."

"What do you mean?" asked Daisuke.

Anne found herself smiling. Daisuke was banishing whatever nerves he might have twinging and letting her bounce speculative biology ideas off him. She could feel guilty about that, or she could lean up against him and enjoy his warmth and solidity.

"The more I look at these trees, the less sense they make." With a sweep of her hand, Anne indicated branches that formed ramps, bypasses, flying buttresses, braces – more architecture than physiology. "Look at those two trees. There's a *bridge* between them!"

"Maybe that growth is accidental," Daisuke said. "Sometimes trees grow together." He rubbed two of his fingers together. "The wind makes them touch and the bark comes off...."

"This isn't accidental," Anne said.

"So it's planned, then?"

"Well obviously it's not *planned*," Anne said, although there was nothing obvious about anything here. "But it is sure as hell co-ordinated. Like the tunnels of an anthill. Except ants just *dig* tunnels. I don't understand how these structures could have grown this way. All right, so a mangrove can grow stilt roots and a banyan can grow prop roots, but – but look here." She pushed herself off Daisuke and walked up to the nearest flying buttress. "Imagine a branch that grew up from the ground and curved to meet this trunk, or maybe a branch that grew from the trunk and curved down to hit the ground. Why am I sure that's *not* what happened here?"

Misha only rolled his eyes, but Daisuke was smiling. "These little shapes in the bark."

"Correct. The bark is segmented, just like the vines and the grass. Made of lots of little elements. But the elements in this buttress didn't grow up from the ground or down from the trunk, they're not even coiled or in bands! That would be very un-Earthlike, but at least I could understand how it grew."

"What's so strange?" Misha said. "Haven't you ever seen bricks in an arch?"

"Misha, if these elements are actually little bricks, then who stacked them? Or here." She pointed to the base of one of the forest giants that pierced the wormhole. "Look at these chains of segments that ring the trunk. They're like the hoops around a barrel. How did they grow like that? Those segments aren't connected to anything but each other. Are we looking at a distinct plant? Some kind of symbiote? A parasite? Or is it exchanging structural support for something?"

"I still don't know why you're worrying about this," said Misha. "Do you think that if you can figure out what makes this ecosystem tick, you can use it to do something to Farhad?"

"That would be great!" Daisuke said.

"I've had about five minutes to examine this biome," Anne grumbled, squinting into the forest. "What the hell do you expect? A tree that I can plug my brain into?"

"Maybe we can just relax and learn about aliens," Daisuke said.

"Maybe we can." Misha looked back toward the Nun's defensive ring. Yunubey was walking around it, talking to his men and giving each what looked like a handful of dust. "Ugh. They say they're throwing the go-home dust. Another ritual I don't need to see. All right. Let's go exploring."

They walked past the first ring of trees. The trunks were as densely packed as Anne had predicted from the drone photos of the canopy. She hadn't thought the trunks would be this thick, though, or so gothic. Limbs twisted and spread toward a canopy so dense it was almost black. The only light came from the exclusion zones between one tree's crown and other, like irregular rings of fire.

Even the shadowed patches under giant trees had their own extravagant growths. The closest of these was roughly the dimensions of Anne, a monstrous lump of tangled tendrils with two huge curved branches protruding from the top.

"Odd. It doesn't seem like there'd be enough light for this bush to grow here," she said. "Maybe it's some kind of parasite? A fruiting structure? A flower?"

There were certainly lots of animals climbing on the bush's curlicue branches. Anne counted four distinct shapes of coatl. Species or growth stages or sexes or some even stranger determiner of morphology. Columns of the animals marched to and from the plant, paying it no less attention than the trees around it. She thought about the ecological web. Lines connecting nodes. Coming together into...what?

"It doesn't look like a flower to me," said Misha. "It looks like those hedge sculptures we saw back at the gates. The yellow devils with horns."

Daisuke tilted his head to the side. "I think it looks like a giant ant."

"It's not *art*, guys," Anne said. But now that Daisuke had said it, she couldn't unsee it. A hedge sculpture, just like the ones they'd seen back at the gate. And hadn't one of those hedges also looked like this? Those two huge serrated mandibles. Those eyestalks.

"Oh shit," she said. "It's the head of a cavalier."

A little searching found other hedge sculptures. In addition to cavaliers, there were legged barrels that looked an awful lot like toymakers, as well as stars, fern fronds, mouths with teeth, and a dozen other abstract objects. At least, Anne hoped they were abstract.

"What do you think they're for?" Misha asked.

Anne looked up. She'd been studying a baroque tangle, as if an octopus had been planted head down in the ground, then persuaded to grow hands instead of tentacles. "Hell if I know. I guess I can't claim to think these shapes are coincidental."

"Cargo cult?" asked Daisuke. "They worship alien visitors?"

"War training?" Misha asked. "Maybe they ritually destroy these sculptures."

What Anne wanted to do was stake out an observation blind and spend the day watching. She'd need cameras and a team of people to help analyze the videos. Samples. Dissections. Radioisotope tagging would be lovely.

Wasn't that the point of this whole expedition? But Anne didn't have time for any of it, and she was beginning to despair that she ever would. Even if Farhad came through with his promise of a research station, who could guarantee that this ecosystem would survive his attention long enough for Anne to study it?

Her worries about Farhad and Moon and Junction in general loomed up, and she pushed them aside. Best to focus on one thing at a time.

"All right," she said. "Do you see that spike growing up out of the ground over there? It looks as if it's growing up to meet that other branch that's coming down and form a new buttress."

"So now you know how they grow?" asked Misha.

"No! How does the tree know where these two branches are supposed to meet? Pheromones?" The air of the forest was redolent with *something*. The closest Anne could come to describing the smell was *resinous*.

She approached the tree, watching a pair of coatls twist their way toward each other, one from each end of the half-made buttress. Each of the spikes was made of orange elements stacked like bricks, but the elements at the tip of each spike were blue, shining brilliantly in the curtain of light that slanted down from a crack in the canopy.

"The elements that make the rings and the flying buttresses and the trunks of the trees are all the same," Daisuke said, and Anne saw that he was right.

Some of the thumb-sized, knobbly segments grew in regular rows, each born from the tip of the last. Others, though, were sideways or poking out as if someone had placed them there. There was also something odd about the colors. Yellow, orange, umber, brown, with clusters of iridescent blue. Contrasting colors?

A coatl screwed its way out of the sierpinski-grass, its zipper-mouth stuffed with more red objects. They were cylindrical, about the size of Anne's thumb. Rough cylinders, ridged on the outside as if they had been extruded by a machine. Anne thought of churros. Or maybe a child's building blocks.

Or bricks. Those red objects were the wrong color, but otherwise they looked a great deal like the segments that made up the trees. And the objects the toymakers had given the coatls guarding the gates.

Anne watched as the coatl slithered up the lower spike of the unfinished buttress. It reached the tip and pressed its conical face to the blue elements there. It withdrew long enough for Anne to see it had clipped a red segment into place on top of a blue one. The possum-sized creature inserted the tip of its snout into the center of the segment, which began to flush purple.

"Ha! It *is* a fruit," Anne said. "Or some sort of flower. Or that mouth isn't a mouth at all, but an ovipositor, and the purple segment is filling up with eggs."

"Are those things fruits?" asked Daisuke.

"Hold on just a second." Anne reached out to touch a blue segment at the tip of the lower spike of the future buttress.

An oboe keen and the coatl flared its fronds at her.

"Oh, sorry." Anne stepped back. The coatl stayed where it was, staring at her through its spiral line of eyes. Now another coatl climbed up to stand beside it.

The first twisted its head around. It unzipped its mouth, flashing the blue interior, then it shifted its grip on the tree and flared its fronds at Anne. The second coatl mimicked the first. The first went through the same routine, and again the second mimicked it.

"Weird," said Anne. "Am I watching a threat display or a mating dance or what?"

The first coatl seemed to kiss its own body, then the mouth of the other. Anne saw a dull red object pass from the tip of one snout to the other, and the first coatl was slithering away up the tree. The second animal, though, stayed, flaring its fronds at Anne.

"A guard?" Daisuke asked.

"Who knows? I don't." But Anne's cheeks burned. It was ridiculous, but she felt embarrassed. As if she'd just brushed up against security at a fancy office building.

Anne took a step back. Another. The guard-coatl quested around with its nose, as if confused or bored. When Anne stepped behind another tree, the little animal smoothed itself out and wandered away.

"That's right," Anne said. "Go about your business." Business. Now, why did she think that word?

"Okay, here's a theory," she said. "What if, instead of growing a fruit to tempt animals to pass seeds through their digestive systems, a plant grows a structural element. The element refuses to give up its nutrition until it has been used to build something?"

"It makes the animals wait? How?" Daisuke asked.

Anne hummed to herself. "I'm thinking about the toymakers, which seem to have been carrying those segments around since their last visit to the Dorado biome. They must have waited for a long time indeed. But how long did that coatl wait? And why go through the trouble?"

Anne thought of the way coatls passed segments to each other. Of the trove of segments the toymakers had given over at the border crossing. The covetous way the coatls had hoarded this treasure....

"Holy shit," she said. "I think we've discovered money."

"It's about time," said Misha, who had been watching the Nun and the toymakers. "What are we talking about?"

"The coatls pay each other with tree segments," Anne said. "They even accept payment from toymakers."

Daisuke cocked his head, eyes pointed up, thinking out loud. "What if we paid them to spy on Farhad for us?"

"That's stupid," Misha said, but Anne's eyes widened.

Could she get some of the forest's currency and figure out how to use it in one night? She turned toward the nearest Dorado tree. "So let's get rich quick."

★ ★ ★

The forest hummed with commerce. It throbbed.

Flying creatures like bees or hummingbirds zipped between flowers like gaudy wrought-iron cages. Others twirled down from the canopy, spinning on stiff little wings. Coatls, ranging in size from leg- to hand-length, streamed around boar-sized creatures that growled over the sierpinski like armored troop carriers.

Now that Anne knew what to look for, she saw that even the trees moved. A cluster of animals would condense around a blue-tipped limb and scatter, leaving it longer. Others would snatch elements from existing structures, or gather into larger groups to besiege and disassemble entire plants. Entire leaf-bearing branches would be unplugged from trunks and snapped into new positions. Over the course of the day, spots of light opened, closed, and shifted as the forest canopy was re-engineered. Everywhere flashed the blue and orange of negotiation.

The coatls didn't flock, exactly, or swarm, but their behavior was clearly emergent from something. It reminded Anne of ocean waves, except these waves were from and going to every direction.

Anne remembered sitting at her apartment's window – Daisuke's apartment's window – watching the pedestrians on the busy streets below. Every little speck had its own place to go and thing to do. Rushing, rushing, and never arriving. *Those pitiful little idiots*, she had thought.

Now, why would Anne's cheeks flush at that memory? Was she ashamed of comparing humans to animals, or the reverse?

She cleared her throat and the men looked at her. "This place *is* a city. It's Shibuya at rush hour."

"I think Tokyo is better organized," Daisuke said.

Anne stepped around a long, skinny coatl, which opened fronds like skirts to reveal shimmering sapphire bristles. "Times Square, then."

"What's the word?" Daisuke asked himself, looking up at bustling branches. "Trade? Commerce."

"I don't get it," said Misha. "How would a squirrel tell a dog that it wants to buy something? How would the dog understand it? Do the coatls *talk* to each other? Can they, like, negotiate contracts?"

Anne had seen a dozen alien species held up as potential sapients. They'd all proven to be disappointments. Even toymakers had performed worse than rats in creative problem-solving, and their supposed 'language' consisted of five non-combinatorial signals. Coatls, though....

"How do you negotiate an exchange of money for services unless you have language? That would be an interesting question to answer." Anne peered around, eyes narrowed. "Maybe if I could get my hands on one of those detachable...segment...element...brick things...."

"Doubloons?" suggested Daisuke.

Anne looked up sharply. Had she really hurt Daisuke's feelings when she rejected his name for this plant? His face said he was teasing her, but his face lied all the time.

"Fine. If I had some doubloons, I'd be able to experiment."

Misha growled. "You and your experiments. We are not scientists here; we are defending the forest from Farhad."

Anne looked at him, trying to think of something to say more helpful than 'Shut up, Misha'.

Daisuke cleared his throat. "I think that Anne has a plan. She will probably find out something about this forest that will help us."

"You mean like we could pay the forest creatures to attack Farhad? This isn't a cartoon, man."

Anne decided to let them argue. She didn't want to think about Farhad or what he might be planning. She just wanted to see what was up with that bush shaped like a fish standing on its head.

Like the rest of the forest, the fish-bush was constructed of orange segments. She grabbed one between thumb and forefinger. The doubloon did give a little when she wiggled it, but before she could pop it free, a coatl rose from the bush, humming at her and shaking its fronds.

"Just knock them away," urged Misha, who, Anne noticed, was not offering to tackle any aliens himself.

"I'd like to get past them without hurting them," she said.

"Ooh." Misha rubbed his hands together. "A heist. I'll be the getaway driver. Daisuke, you're the muscle."

Daisuke looked at the bush uncertainly. "I think I don't want to rob a bank."

"Even just a little *branch* office? Eh?" Misha looked from Anne to Daisuke. "Nothing? Fine." He sighed. "I wasn't thinking about anything violent. Just bribe the guards."

"Bribe them with what, genius?" Anne said. "We haven't got any money. That's the whole point of this experiment."

Misha shrugged. "I always use drugs or alcohol."

"Always?" repeated Daisuke.

"I mean I used to. I'm a happily married Nun now, and now I'm sure I couldn't even tell the difference between a twelve-year-old Hakushu and industrial alcohol mixed with black tea in a Hakushu bottle." He coughed. "For example. Anyway, there must be something that those guards want more than money. Food? Sexual favors?"

"No!" said Daisuke, but Anne wondered if she might combine two investigations into one. She had no idea how coatl reproduction worked, and wouldn't it be nice to find out? But wait. What had Misha said about alcohol? Tea? Happily married?

"Oh, I'm an idiot." She slapped her forehead. "Misha, ask Yunubey. The toymakers got all of their doubloons from somewhere. How did they do it?"

Misha frowned, but Anne's priorities now were to study the

forest and save it, not untangle the ex-smuggler's feelings about his brother-in-law. Grumbling to himself, Misha walked back toward the wormhole grove.

"How do they do it?" she asked herself. "How do animals invent money?"

"Well, we did," Daisuke said.

Anne shook her head, but shelved the argument. Misha was on his way back, leading Yunubey. The chieftain held the tether of a toymaker blimp like a wooden party balloon.

"Hard work," Misha said. "That's how they got the doubloons. The toymakers put themselves out there and got jobs. That's what Yunubey thinks, anyway."

Misha said something in Nun to his brother-in-law, who gestured at the wormhole grove and at Anne and Daisuke.

"What's he saying?" asked Anne.

Misha looked sheepish. "I've been playing too much with you."

"Ignoring your duties as a Nun?" Anne asked.

Misha's face clenched up, as if she'd angered him. "I thought what *we* were doing was important, but now that you mention it, yes, maybe I should spend more time with my tribe and leave the safety of this biome up to you."

"She didn't mean it that way," Daisuke said, which made Anne want to ask him how she *had* meant it. But she was getting that hot feeling behind her eyes that meant it was time to let Daisuke drive, so she just folded her arms and tapped her foot. The whole purpose of keeping Daisuke around was so he could handle people and their squishy emotions, right?

The thought squirmed queasily in Anne's mind. She dropped it. "Does your tribe need you?" Daisuke asked. "I'm sorry if we've kept you away from your duties."

"Eh. Duties," said Misha. "Yunubey is angry at me because I spend more time with you than with him, so my status is falling. I need to bring home some bacon. Instead, I'm asking for more."

He turned to Yunubey, who launched into a long lecture. Misha's expression grew glummer as this continued.

Yunubey pursed his lips and clicked his tongue twice. His blimp double-clicked back. Yunubey tongue-clicked three times, put his hands around the little wooden vehicle, and thrust it toward the sapling. The coatl guards fluffed their fronds and hooted again, but with a clunk of gears, the toymaker's forward windshield turned blue.

"How the hell did that happen?" Anne leaned in toward it. "Is that a shell or something they're pressing up against the inside of the glass?"

A coatl twisted toward her and hooted. The toymaker clacked four times, Yunubey snapped something, and Misha said, "Uh, Anne, move back a little."

Anne took a step back, and the nearest coatl turned its corkscrew head away from her. It bent around and plucked something from the fronds that covered its body: an orange doubloon. The creature stretched its serpentine body out toward the toymaker, and tapped the doubloon against the blue windshield. It tapped again. And again, robotically.

"I think it looks confused," Daisuke said.

"Supernormal stimulation," said Anne. "Like a bee landing on a picture of a flower. That's just what coatls do whenever they see something blue. They try to clip a doubloon to it. Maybe this trading behavior was exapted from a mating ritual? Or feeding young? If – oh."

The coatl had broken out of its tapping loop. Still holding the doubloon, it darted away from the toymaker and down the branch. It stopped, reared up, and attacked the empty air. Four jabs of its mouth before it slithered up to its partner and made as if to pass its doubloon to the other animal. The other animal followed the doubloon with its snout, but the first slid back to the toymaker, which it tapped with its doubloon again. Finally, the coatl curled itself up and sat, as if waiting for the toymaker to do something.

The toymaker clunked and clocked and the blue flag vanished from its windshield. The little wooden alien made three decisive tocks and waited. It made another three tocks.

Yunubey spoke and Misha translated, "It's hungry."

"What's hungry?" Anne said. "The coatls or the toymaker?"

Misha shrugged. "It's impossible to say. Three clicks just means 'seek' or 'get'. It's the noise the toymakers make when they're hungry, but it could just as well mean that the coatls are hungry, or that one of them is hungry, or that there is some resource around here that the toymaker wants."

Anne reconsidered the little dance of the coatl and said, "Huh."

"What?" said Misha and Daisuke.

"Hey guys," she said. "Look around for something to feed the coatl."

"What does it eat?" Daisuke asked.

"Meat, I'd guess from the way it mimed hunting." Anne pulled gloves out of her jacket pockets and slipped them on.

The first thing that she noticed wriggling, she snatched.

When the wriggler failed to explode, spit venom, or otherwise try to kill her, Anne brought the creature up to her eyes. It flexed between her fingers, the front part of its body peeling back like an automatic banana. More of those zipper-teeth, except these were in a straight line down the length of its body. Less a banana than an empty sleeve, with button-eyes and a fur of little tentacles.

With the front third of its body unzipped, the animal now looked like a sleeve with its cuff undone. Or probably a better analogy would be a cobra with its hood extended. The inner surface of the sleeve was dark blue, shiny with some mucus that Anne didn't want to get on her skin.

She rose. What would happen when she fed this thing to one of the coatls? But before she could put her experiment into action, the sleeve-snake in her glove clenched and spat something out of its body cavity. Surprised, Anne relaxed her grip, and the sleeve-snake hit the ground along with the object it had expelled. A pellet of waste? A distraction, like the tail of a gecko or the guts of a sea cucumber?

The pellet hit the sierpinski and bounced. It was roughly cylindrical, thumb-sized, burnt umber in color, with flattened sides and warts protruding from its pocked shell.

"Holy shit," said Anne. "It's a doubloon. The little bugger tried to bribe me."

"Grab it!" Misha said.

She was too late. The doubloon bounced to a stop and the sierpinski erupted in animals. Forms like twisted ribbons, chains of starfish, and flying correa flowers swarmed over the doubloon.

"Hey!" Daisuke kicked at the swarm. "*Itta!*"

He yanked his boot back, dragging with it a trout-sized animal covered in plump tentacles. The creature writhed up Daisuke's boot, exposing the serrated wedges of its zipper-teeth.

Daisuke winced as the trout-a-pus gnawed on his boot. Yunubey rose and stepped away, saying something sharp to Misha, who ran forward and gave the animal a kick. It let go with a shriek and plopped back onto the sierpinski. With flailing tentacles, the fish-shaped creature squirmed back under the protection of ground cover. The doubloon was gone.

"Damn it, Daisuke," Anne said. "What if that thing had bitten your foot off?" She put her hand to her thundering heart, and found something crawling there on her shirt. She grabbed it, and held up to her eye an animal as long as a lima bean. An armored head with a collar of legs, followed by a leathery, fluted structure that unfolded into wings as the animal tried to fly away. A burrowing flier, maybe in the beetle or cockroach niche? Maybe something the coatls found tasty?

Before anything else could happen, Anne reached toward the hungry guard, offering up the flower-shaped creature. The guard pulled out its doubloon and waved it at her.

"Visual signals and mimicry," she said. "Is that really enough to negotiate an exchange?"

Yunubey's toymaker tocked twice, Yunubey said something, and Misha translated. "Now it's saying 'ready'. That means it thinks its job is done, I guess."

Something slapped Anne's hand. She jerked her attention back to the coatl, which had snatched the roach and deposited the doubloon onto her palm.

The coatl unzipped its mouth, brought together the tooth-fringed edges of its body, and squeezed down on the roach. It crunched.

Anne held up the doubloon and looked at it. Less a cylinder, now that she looked closely, than a rough hexagonal prism. Its hard shell was marked with raised lumps and lowered divots.

"A doubloon," she said. "Wave your doubloon around to indicate you want to pay for something. Show off your blue internal surface if you want to work for pay. The buyer goes through the motions of what it wants done, and the seller mimics that behavior until the payments stop coming. There's no need for symbols. Aside from the doubloons themselves, maybe? Hm...."

The toymaker tocked twice, and Misha said, "I think we have another customer."

A second animal approached, waving its own doubloon. The coatl danced, miming hunting, and waved its doubloon again. Another dance. Another wave. It stopped, body pulsing, then launched into the display again. Dance wave, dance wave, dance wave.

"That's three," Misha said. "The coatl wants three more bug-things."

"So they can count?" Anne wondered. What she wouldn't give for a lab where she could study these things for a few years. Oh, right. She'd given a lot, and Farhad had demanded more.

For once, Daisuke didn't notice Anne's mood.

"Oh, I know this game," he said, and pressed the toe of his boot into a gap in the siepinski. He jerked back when the trout-a-pus flared its tentacles at him.

The burrower hooted and pulled back a flap of skin over its mouth, revealing brilliant blue flesh. It gaped its mouth in what Anne was beginning to realize was not a threat display, but a merchant's call.

"Is it offering itself up to us?" she asked. "Why would it want to be eaten?"

The animal closed its mouth and vanished into the ground cover, only to return a moment later with another roach struggling in its tentacles. It flashed blue again.

"It doesn't want to be eaten. The little bastard is sticking itself into the middle of our transaction," Misha said. "'Oh, Misha, don't turn me in. You know I'm your man if you have a job.' There was this guy in Jayapura *just* like that."

"What?" said Daisuke.

"The trout-a-pus is telling us that it will only let us hunt for roaches in its sierpinski if we give it a doubloon," Anne said. The sentence felt a bit like reciting Lewis Carroll's poetry, but Daisuke seemed to get it. He bent and took the roach from the trout-a-pus, gave the roach to the coatl in the bush, got his payment, and passed the payment on to the trout-a-pus, which went hunting again.

"Net profit: zero," observed Misha.

Daisuke held up his hands. "This is very slow. If we want enough money to do what we want, we must work harder."

Misha sniggered. "Step back, and let an old criminal show you how to really make money. Anne, bribe that guard to leave his post."

Anne held her hands up to the coatl she'd fed. It threat-displayed.

"Bribe. Right." She held up her orange doubloon and mimed lowering something to the ground. "I'll pay you to leave your guard post. How about that?"

The guard followed Anne's motions with its multi-eyed snout, then went into its own mime. It pulled a doubloon from its fronds, put it back, pulled it out again, and so on until Anne lost count.

"That is one expensive bribe," Misha said. "I'm glad you don't work at Indonesian customs, little dude."

Anne ignored him, waving her offer as she mimed carrying the coatl to different spots on the ground, different branches on its tree, a spot on a different tree....

The coatl hummed and pushed its nose toward the next tree over, like an eager ferret. Its partner perked up, and pointed to the same place. Two passengers.

"Tell them to pay up front," Misha suggested.

"How the hell do I do that?" But the coatls were ahead of Anne. They released their grip on the bush and fell into Anne's hands, dense, frond-covered cylinders like feathery hot dogs. One of them snapped up the doubloon she was still holding.

"Hey," she said.

"Maybe he thought you would stiff him," said Misha.

The little animals just looked at Anne until, ashamed of herself, she carried them to the next tree over.

"Misha," she whispered, "pull doubloons off of that branch this bush was guarding."

"I already am, of course. Although next time, you let me do the negotia— Oh no!"

Anne turned to see Misha stagger back from the bush and the dachshund-sized coatl that had just slithered up its trunk. Fluting in rage, the animal unzipped its head to display a spiral of sharp teeth and gleaming digestive surfaces.

Misha cursed. "Middle management!"

Anne was about to ask Misha if he'd managed to steal any doubloons when a horrible, atonal blatt sounded from the branches overhead. She looked up to see three weasely bodies race out of the foliage. Two coatls were chasing a third, and while all of the animals looked identical to Anne, she could guess the identities of the pursuers.

The murderers! The two coatls Anne had bribed caught the third, grabbed it by each end, and twisted. With a sickening crack, the victim-animal broke, dropping a handful of segments onto the sierpinski.

One of the murderers rushed down the tree trunk to snap up the fallen plunder, and fought off the animals that emerged from under the ground cover to steal its ill-gotten gains. The bleats and hoots of the scuffle drew other coatls from the tree, which saw the first murderer chewing on the flesh of its victim. It gave out an alarm-call and its partner twisted up from the ground, holding most of the plundered segments inside its helical body.

The two criminals met on the tree trunk, looked toward Anne, and waved a doubloon at her.

"Ha!" Misha laughed. "Who's the getaway driver now?"

"What?" Anne was frozen to the spot. Had these little aliens *manipulated* her? They'd tricked her into becoming their accomplice.

With a grunt, Misha strode to the trapped criminals and held out his hands. Each coatl spat out three segments, then three more once Misha had delivered them safely to their home sapling.

"Triple prices for emergency job," he said, palms full of doubloons. "Half payment on delivery. How civilized."

"Did we just get away with murder?" Daisuke asked.

"Oh, good idea." Misha hopped back to the scene of the crime, where the murder victim's body had fallen onto the sierpinski. Misha snatched up the little corpse just as a trout-a-pus rose from the depths, tentacles spread to snatch the meat. Misha shook his finger at it. "*Niet, moi drug.* Hey, who has something blue I can show this guy?"

Anne could almost convince herself that the trout-a-pus's tentacles clenched with frustration. But as soon as Misha flashed Daisuke's Chapstick at it, it dragged itself farther into the open and unzipped its mouth to offer up payment. Misha received his doubloons and deposited the dead coatl. The trout-a-pus seized the meat and vanished back into the grass.

Anne looked at the bush, where the manager coatl was dispensing doubloons to the two guards. Paying them for their successful hit on the guardian of a rival tree? Or maybe the two criminals were flush with cash now and demanding higher wages.

"So," said Anne, "the first interactions we try to have with the eco-economy and we get suckered by evil possums."

"We're strange-looking aliens nobody has ever seen before. What legitimate employer would hire us?" Misha stuffed doubloons into his pockets, grinning. "Now, come on, let's find some more crimes to commit."

CHAPTER FIFTEEN

Tempting the Serpent

Farhad leaned forward in his chair, steepled fingers tapping his nose, watching the gate to the Dorado biome as it grew larger in the windshield.

"I'm not sure what's more disturbing," he said, eyes still on their destination. "The fact that you thought I might strand Anne and the others and leave them to starve to death in the forest, or the fact that you hesitated to bring me the recordings from our bugs."

"I'm very sorry, sir," said Turtle. "When the caravan started going east, I didn't know what to think."

"We had plenty of time to accomplish our mission and still pick them up before their supplies ran out," Farhad said, but who knew if the young man would believe him? This was the problem with a reputation for villainy. It eroded trust, necessitating further villainy.

If not for all this distrust floating around, Farhad wouldn't have had to depend on the bugs he'd planted on Anne's and Daisuke's clothing and equipment.

"'If we had doubloons, we could pay the forest to attack Farhad,'" he repeated to himself. "Oh my, oh my." Rage was an indulgence worse than alcohol. Farhad would not scream or stomp. He was not that kind of man. When Farhad Irevani killed, it was with kindness.

He made sure his expression was warm, then turned his head. "You did well, son. We turned the caravan around. Anne and the others are in no danger of starving and the mission can move forward anyway. Everyone gets what they want."

Turtle nodded, but his brows were still pressed together when Boss Rudi brought the caravan to a stop. Ahead lay the gates to the Dorado forest, and Farhad knew just what to do with them.

Farhad rose to his feet. His knees popped. His neck hurt too, but in many ways he felt younger than he had in years. He'd built his reputation on slow and steady progress. No corners cut, no dashes slapped. And yet sometimes the time came to make an executive decision. You burst into a sprint or they caught you and killed you.

"Turtle, Rudi, you're with Moon. Do as he says." Farhad walked to the door. "Aimi. Follow me."

"Yes, sir."

He turned as the door opened and gave his mentee a smile. "No need to 'sir' me now. The fact that two thirds of my expedition is in open rebellion is no reason to fall back on hierarchy."

"Isn't it?"

Farhad gave a short laugh and stepped out onto the ground. The wind was blowing cold from the north-west, and the resinous scent of the forest filled his nose. The yellow and orange forest might have been the larches and aspens around a Northern Rockies camping resort, but the smell made Farhad think of spice markets. Although maybe that was just his plans affecting his perceptions.

"We should have done a better job of value alignment," Aimi said. "I should have worked harder to get Anne on our side."

"Don't say, 'I should have,' say 'Next time I will'," Farhad said. "And in fact what we should do next time is not hire someone whose interests diverge so sharply from our mission plan."

They reached the gate. Segmented orange coils blocked further progress, elaborate and lovely as Reyhan calligraphy.

"The problem is that this expedition is a one-off event," Farhad said. "There won't be a next time. I'm sure you're familiar with the game theory of this situation. The Prisoner's Dilemma. Non-iterated."

"Not a good game to play," Aimi said.

"And yet, here we are." Farhad examined the gates as well as his memory. "What was it Anne said? Wave your doubloon around to indicate you want to pay for something. An economy-ecology. Fascinating."

"But money isn't real," Aimi said. "It's a tool we humans invented to keep track of debt. How can animals have it? How could this evolve naturally?"

"Maybe it didn't." Farhad said. "Maybe this forest was intelligently designed." He looked around at Aimi's silence. "I mean some alien civilization built this place. You know. With genetic engineering, like in that one movie."

Aimi squinted at him. "You think the coatls were made by the Zookeepers? Like as pets?"

"Maybe the Zookeepers. Maybe someone else. But don't think pets. Think delivery drones." Farhad waved at the bustling forest. "You build robots to deliver goods to consumers. You build robot factories to make those robots. And robots to make those goods. Robots to place the orders. Robots to choose what consumers buy. Eventually, it's all just robots, going around and around."

"Living robots? Shaped like orange squirrels?"

"Well, I admit the color was a surprise. And the hooting." Farhad turned up his hands. "Maybe I'm wrong, and this really is all natural. Maybe money really does exist, like flight or vision, and many animals will evolve it independently. In any case...." He noticed his mentee's lack of expression. "What's wrong?"

She looked away, jaws working. Looked back at him. "Farhad, when I started working for you, you told me you hated cutting corners. Well what is this?" She spread her arms to indicate the forest between them and the mountain. "This is literally cutting a corner."

Farhad spend a moment meditating on the fact that what he hated more than cutting corners was being second-guessed. He said, "I'm afraid there's no other choice. We don't have time. But once we get Moon's wormhole, we'll have enough leverage to apply the brakes a bit."

"You mean we'll be able to threaten everyone else to back off while we entrench ourselves. But will we be entrenched in the right place?"

Farhad examined his feelings. *I am annoyed with Aimi. More than that. I feel betrayed. And I notice that Aimi is in my way.*

"We can't have this conversation now," he decided. "But you have until we reach the top of Howling Mountain to convince me there's a better way. Deal?"

"Deal," she said, but not happily.

Farhad breathed through the familiar annoyance of everyone piling their problems on top of him. He'd asked for this. He'd put himself in a position of power, and the price for that was that people looked to him to fix their lives.

And, to be absolutely honest, Aimi was right. This whole

enterprise *was* slap-dash, and it was only a matter of time until it fell apart. Farhad didn't like this feeling of riding the edge of collapse either, but what other choice did he have? If the American army wasn't storming toward the Howling Mountain right this moment, they soon would be. He'd destroyed a wormhole.

Maybe he'd get lucky. Maybe Aimi would give him a real alternative to this smash-and-grab. Until then, though, it was time to get grabbing.

As they approached the gate, a coatl slithered out of the vines and hooted at them. Yes, this would be why Farhad's plan hadn't been enacted before. The trees were involved in this economy. They controlled the money supply. Of course they would have guards.

Farhad didn't have any doubloons yet, but a search of the kitchen had produced a baby carrot. This had needed only a few minutes under Turtle's pen-knife to become counterfeit currency.

Farhad waved his vegetable coin, and the coatl's snout unzipped. Blue interior surfaces glistened. He had its attention.

"You brought the machete, Aimi?" he said. "Good. Chop at that thing if it tries to attack me."

Aimi chuckled. "The worker chops, the manager decides which tree, the leader decides which forest."

"Exactly." Farhad grabbed a structural element of the gate-vines, what Anne had called a doubloon. Immediately, the coatl rushed him. The alien was the size of a boa constrictor, but Aimi sliced it neatly in two.

Farhad had expected that. One of Aimi's hobbies was Filipino knife-fighting. What Farhad did not expect was for the creature she killed to be full of money. He didn't notice the orange lumps contained inside its tubular body until other animals boiled out of the gate and began stealing them. "Aimi!" he cried. "Kick those things away and collect that money."

"Next time, let's get the others involved," Aimi said as she chopped and kicked. "Ha. We should call these things 'piñata snakes'."

Farhad laughed. They were gathering money much faster than he'd expected. He tossed away his carved carrot. No need for counterfeits now. "Would you like to switch sides? Give the machete to the old man while you haggle with the client?"

"No, no, haggle away, old man."

Aimi gave him a handful of doubloons, which he waved at the next guard-coatl. The guard stopped, following his motions with its spiral-eyed snout. A flash of blue.

"Now the buyer goes through the motions of what it wants done." Farhad reached out, past the guard, and the tip of one of the curling vines that made up the gate. He gave a sharp tug, and off popped two doubloons and a half-grown sprout.

The supposed guard did nothing to stop him. It only watched, blue throat flashing in and out of view behind its flexing teeth.

"It's working," breathed Farhad. "We're tempting the serpent." He waved a doubloon past the coatl's nose and plucked another from the gate.

The coatl pressed its snout against the gate and copied him.

Farhad paid the coatl, then signaled he wanted it to do the job again.

Now both Farhad and the coatl were collecting doubloons. This part of the gate was starting to look thin. Aimi didn't need to use the machete anymore. The next guard that came to defend the plants was simply bribed into switching sides.

"It's working," said Aimi.

The more of the plants they disassembled, the more doubloons they had with which to pay for further disassembly. Farhad watched as his workforce grew and the gate melted away, unable to suppress his manticore's grin.

Beyond the gate, trees were beginning to sway. Farhad took a step back, watching, waiting for his chance to shout, 'Timber!'

★ ★ ★

The first sign of collapse was a massive increase in wages.

Anne heard it before she saw it. The toymakers tocked when dealing with the coatls, and the humans grumbled. As they stood there guarding the wormhole grove, the sun sliding across the southern horizon, the tocking and grumbling had begun to come more often.

"You greedy little bastard," said Misha. "Didn't I just pay you?"

Anne had been leaning against a tree, eating the last of the food. Now she straightened, ears pricking. "Something's wrong."

"Yes," Daisuke said. "We don't have enough doubloons to pay our guards. We're running out."

Anne rubbed her face. She had fallen into a trance, playing with phylogenetic trees for the coatls, spinning idle theories on their evolution and development, watching the forest darken as she contemplated adaptive radiations after extinction events.

"We will have to go out into the forest to find more jobs and get more money," Daisuke said.

The rat race. You couldn't avoid it in academia; what had made Anne think she could avoid working for a living on another planet? "Do we have time?" she asked. "Once it gets dark…." She looked up, her voice trailing off. Gooseflesh prickled up and down her limbs, as if she were one of the trees of the wormhole grove, and coatls were scurrying across her skin.

What was she feeling? What was wrong?

Anne twisted around and looked at the grove. No, the nexus of branches was normal, the orange-and-blue orb hanging above it like a clock over a village square.

The frenetic activity of the grove had not become any less intense either. There was still just as much rushing, clumping, and attacking as ever. What had changed?

Anne let her gaze go fuzzy. Focused on nothing, unblinking, her eyes accepted information as a red-orange blur. A blurry fountain of scurrying creatures. A fountain flowing down from the wormhole.

And that was wrong. The flow shouldn't be so asymmetrical. Anne blinked and focused, but the conviction remained. More coatls were climbing down the trees than going up. More were coming through to Junction than returning to their home world.

Anne turned slowly. Yes, most of that traffic was flowing away to the east. Anne caught her breath. The direction of the caravan.

"Farhad," she said. "Farhad's doing something." A coatl streamed past her foot. In the distance, something crashed like a mountain of pebbles. Light grew to the east, like a sunrise. The light had been growing, Anne realized, for some time.

Another shattering crash. The Nun were yelling, looking around.

"What the hell is going on?" Misha asked, either of God or of Anne.

She started forward. Stopped. Daisuke had latched on to her arm, the whites around his eyes showing.

"Don't go!" he shouted. He had to shout now, above a rumble like a waterfall made of wooden blocks.

The light grew steadily, and now Anne could see why. The canopy to the east was falling apart. Anne tried to pull out of Daisuke's grip as she watched a great, spreading trunk *melt*. Its limbs dwindled away even as they tilted and fell.

"Let go of me!" Anne twisted free and ran to the eastern edge of the grove. Her eyes darted, found a pair of coatls, focused on them as one animal waved extravagant bunches of doubloons at the other. When the second coatl flashed blue consent, the first lowered its mouth to the surface of the tree under it. It ripped loose a doubloon.

A tree shivered, then clattered the pieces. Another. The noise increased, like waves crashing against a beach of woodchips. Animals streamed past Anne, who stood staring as the forest ripped itself apart. Animals wailed, horrifically like the sirens of ambulances. Pheromones like burning pitch coated her tongue. The light was very bright now, almost like on a treeless plain. Anne wobbled in it, drowning in understanding.

We did this, she thought. *I did this*. She had thought she was winning this war, but wars destroyed. She had thought the righteous flame of her anger would only burn her enemies. Instead, the whole forest was burning down around her.

Farhad's caravan burst into view like the end of the world.

It glowed orange with the sunset light that shone through the rip in the canopy. Mighty trees trembled at its passage, bent away, withered, broke apart into lucrative rain. And through the destruction, damned, cavorted the coatls.

Animals weren't fleeing the destruction. They were flocking to it. Adding themselves to it. Ripping apart their biome in a frenzy of misaligned instinct.

"What is this?" shouted Daisuke.

"Farhad!" Anne said. "They think he's paying them."

Misha laughed. "And he thinks they're working."

The caravan slowed as it approached the wormhole grove and allowed the market crash to sweep past it.

★ ★ ★

Farhad flinched as another tree burst apart on the roof of the caravan. This couldn't be good for the solar panels.

"We're almost at the wormhole," he called, turning. "Are you ready, Professor Moon?"

Moon stood with Turtle and Aimi at the door. The physicist's skin looked pale, waxy, as if he were trying to replace sleep with caffeine. "You need to get Anne out of my way," he grated.

Farhad silently prayed, *God, save me from expert consultants.* Out loud he said, "I'm not going to kill anyone."

Moon made clawing gestures, as if fighting his way through cobwebs. "No, I mean I can't do my experiments while she's out there interfering. I don't care how you distract her. Just keep her away from me."

It was annoying to be told to do something one was already doing. On the other hand, this was an excellent chance to appear to be serving Moon. "Of course," he said, and brought his walkie-talkie up to his mouth.

"Anne," he said, "would you and Daisuke please board the caravan?"

He held the device away from his ear while his biologist spat a stream of invective.

"I need that portal," said Moon. Aimi shushed him, and he flinched. The young man had screwed up badly with her, and there wasn't time to fix things.

"Anne," Farhad said into his walkie-talkie. "Anne, please. Yes. Yes, I know. This is entirely my responsibility – fine! But it isn't safe out there." An idea occurred to him. Farhad kept the smile out of his voice as he said. "Daisuke, are you there?"

Silence from both of them while Moon made more demands. Farhad suppressed a sigh, took his thumb off the talk button and said, "Are you ready, Moon? Do you have your bucket? Your net?" This was so exactly like getting the children ready for school. Farhad resisted the urge to tell Moon to pee now before he left.

Maybe it was the memories of his children that caused the anxiety to spike up Farhad's belly. Anne and her followers were his responsibility, just as much as his loyal people. Would someone physically attack Moon? Would Aimi and Turtle protect him? In doing so, would they harm the rebels? Would the local wildlife eat them or bring a tree down on them? There had to be a better way to do this.

Farhad pressed the talk button and said, "Anne? Daisuke?"

"Will you allow us to come aboard?" came Daisuke's voice.

Yes, there was the weak link. "Of course, son, of course. Bring Anne and whoever else needs safety." Farhad would happily fill the caravan with angry tribesmen if Anne was with them.

"We're not doing anything with you," Anne growled. "Never! We're staying. We're fixing this."

Fix? How do you fix a market crash? You cash out, hunker down, and hold on to what you can until the storm passes. But that argument wouldn't work on Anne. Instead, Farhad spoke loudly and clearly, so that someone standing next to Anne would understand him. "It isn't safe, Anne! Would you rather live or die?"

★ ★ ★

Anne cursed and shoved the walkie-talkie back onto her belt. What was the point in talking to the slimy bastard? A waste of time, as useless as standing there, tears running down your face, just watching a forest rip itself apart.

A giant tree swayed as its flying buttresses melted away. The place where the branches came together had been heavily reinforced, wound around with linked doubloons like the hoops of a barrel. Now, those hoops burst, and the trunk split in great vertical cracks. Doubloons popped with sprays of sap. Even as animals leaped from the branches, they clutched at the tumbling red-orange segments.

Nearby, a large coatl sprayed money at its smaller employees, trying to find a price high enough to convince them to stay and protect their tree. Soon, the chief guard ran out of its own stash of doubloons, and started pulling them from the very tree it was supposed to be guarding.

Doubloons rained from the sky. Animals dove for them, attacked each other, attacked the attackers. The phalanx of coatls guarding the wormhole grove broke and reformed, inverted. They ripped into the bases of the trees.

The Nun and the toymakers were fleeing. Misha too. Daisuke made a grab for Anne, who stepped back. The humming and hooting of coatls had grown to a deafening siren of greed and alarm, rising and falling with the crash of trees.

"Shit!" Anne flinched away from the corkscrew proboscis of an enormous coatl. It was probably only about her mass, but with its fronds flared out, it looked the size of a polar bear. She hadn't heard its threat call over all the other noise.

Daisuke pulled her back from its zipper-teeth. "This isn't safe!" he shouted. "We have to go to the caravan!"

"Never." Anne threw all the doubloons she was carrying at the coatl, which dove like a porpoise after them. "No. We stay. We fix this."

There had to be a way. Pay the coatls to stand still and do nothing? Pay them to flee? Pay them to rebuild? But if you pay a coatl to build a tree, you lose doubloons both as currency and as building material. If you pay a coatl to destroy a tree, you free up cash to pay more coatls to destroy more trees.

Anne was fighting a runaway feedback loop. The disaster catalyzed further disaster, like a forest fire. So then what was the Dorado biome equivalent of dropping water from helicopters? A gas that knocked out coatls? Some sort of glue that stopped them from popping doubloons off of trees? You'd think the trees themselves would evolve a response like that.

Daisuke grabbed her arm.

"Stop fucking pulling on me," Anne said, twisting free again. She almost had it. Something to do with the trees. Like eucalyptus exfoliating their bark, filling their leaves with volatile oils, building up a layer of tinder for the fire that would open their seeds and fertilize the new shoots.

Spreading seeds. Shuffling doubloons. And from the ashes would sprout the new, red flowers.

Except here, in the Dorado biome, red wasn't an attention-getting color. Here, the trees used blue.

Anne darted forward.

"Anne!" called Daisuke.

"A stump!" she called. "I need to find a stump!"

There. Behind the caravan. The remains of a mature Dorado tree as wide around as Anne. It did almost look burned. As with charcoal, the disassembled stump had separated into chunks. In this case, it was a sheaf of closely packed hexagons, crumbling around the edges. Below the soil, the doubloon elements had fused together, and the coatls hadn't been able to pull them apart.

A coatl the size of a German shepherd bounded out of the forest and past Anne, almost knocking her over. Daisuke was still calling after her. He'd run to the caravan and opened its rear door. Now he slammed it closed and rushed toward her, eyes aflame with the mad need to rescue.

There was no time. Anne turned away from him and bent to inspect the stump.

"Yes!" she hissed through gritted teeth. There. Exactly what she expected to see.

The top of the stump was turning blue.

What were doubloons, after all, but the promise of nectar? That's how this whole crazy eco-economy had evolved in the first place. A doubloon, when plugged into the proper part of a growing tree, would produce nectar for the enjoyment of the animal that had put it there. 'Proper' in this case meaning 'blue'. By changing color, a tree could control where doubloons were placed.

All Anne needed to do was speed the process.

She turned and straightened just as Daisuke dashed up to her. "Daisuke!"

He grabbed her arm. "*Miro!*" he said. *Look!* Anne looked.

The coatl was the size of a rhinoceros. Its lower fronds were twisted together into temporary limbs that formed, stepped, and dissolved in waves down its body. It shook with each step, quivering with the weight, Anne realized, of what must be thousands of stored doubloons. It was a walking bank. A living moneybag. A forest kingpin.

The kingpin lashed a tail of braided tentacles and reared. Zipper-teeth strained to hold in the weight of cash inside its body as it stretched its twisted snout toward Anne and Daisuke. A spiral of eyes unwound, and orange fronds spread like a mane, antlers, grasping hands. Its church-organ call shook the diaphragm in Anne's chest.

"I can fix this," Anne promised, either to Daisuke or to the animal.

Daisuke only held on tighter, breathing hard. His face was like nothing Anne had seen on him. Not since the last time a Junction animal had threatened her life.

The forest kingpin understood her better. The giant coatl convulsed and vomited a stream of doubloons onto Anne's feet.

It was a big enough pile to tempt a crowd, even in the midst of a market crash. Little coatls flocked to the kingpin, flashing blue mouths as the animal, now as sleek as an elephant seal, twisted around and started plugging doubloons into the blue-blushing stump.

Anne felt like crying with relief. There was a way to rebuild.

Daisuke nearly pulled her off her feet. Anne shouted at him, but he kept pulling toward the caravan. The caravan?

"Oh! Yes!" Anne turned and ran with him. "Daisuke," she panted. "We need paint. Blue paint. Draw in more kingpins."

"What?" screamed Daisuke over the roar of the crashing forest.

"Kingpins! Investors! Bosses! Blue paint in the caravan. We need blue paint!"

Daisuke hit the caravan with his open palms, stopped himself, pushed, and spun around. His face communicated no understanding at all. "Go inside!"

"Come help me find that paint," Anne said.

He looked at her, face blank again. He took a deep breath. Smoothed his hair. "Yes. Yes, Anne. I will help you find blue paint."

He picked her up and threw her through the door and flung himself in after. He shut the door soon enough to stop all but a few of the kingpin's little helpers, which he stomped on.

Unnecessary. And watching the frustrated giant prowl back and forth on the other side of the door was also pointless. Anne could reverse the damage! She could save the forest!

It took her about fifteen minutes to figure out that Daisuke had tricked her. By then it was too late.

★ ★ ★

Animals swarmed across the devastation, flying, climbing, burrowing, side-winding across the rutted ground cover. Some fled, some struck out at each other or ripped new holes in the weakened landscape. Others simply lay where they had dragged themselves and wailed. Begging calls ululated like air-raid sirens.

Moon plugged his ears and slitted his eyes against the distractions. Relying on Turtle and Aimi to protect him, he looked up at the growth that Anne called 'the wormhole grove'.

A glance confirmed his expectations. There was the portal, a blue-and-orange sphere hovering over the nexus of five horizontal branches. *Branch* might not be the right word. They looked more like bridges, complete with support columns growing down into the ground under them. And traffic. Animals dashed back and forth through the portal, commuting between Junction and their home world like cars on the Zakim Bridge.

Interesting. What was *important*, however, was that like the Boston landmark, this bridge was multilevel. There were more branches *under* the portal. Between the portal and the ground, another five limbs came together. Nothing rested on top of them, but Moon bet there was something inside. His first task would be to get it out.

"Come on!" he shouted, and ran toward the grove.

Moon had to hand it to Farhad. His way was much easier than Moon's plan. Bringing down the forest had saved an entire day, and the wave of destruction neatly cleared the area of Anne's followers.

Now, though, the destruction was spreading to the grove itself. The five limbs slewed to the side, all set to drop Moon's prize into his waiting hands.

"Ready the net!" Moon kept his eyes on that nexus under the portal. The animals were disassembling those branches where they joined the main trunk, which should allow the whole thing to just fall into his net. Perfect.

A portal in a tree. Moon still couldn't believe his luck. A portal sitting normally atop a pedestal or at the bottom of a pit would have been no disaster, of course, but this way he could complete his next experiment in a moment. Which was good, because moments were all they had.

Turtle and Aimi kicked aside some tentacular bushes and spread a tarp to catch falling branches. Above, feathered serpents gnawed at modular wood. The portal was still in position overhead.

Moon watched it. He still had no grasp on the physics of the portals, but he had come to understand something of what might be called their 'design philosophy'. Whoever had made them – and he was sure it was a *who* – played things safe. Portals didn't explode, cut through things, or even allow bad air to pass through them. Moon was willing to bet that they didn't allow dangerous microorganisms, either, which bespoke a level of intelligence that was more frightening than any alien plague.

And when something unusual happened to a portal, it simply vanished.

He almost missed it. Blink and the portal was gone. Animals hooted in a chaotic ball, piling up on the suddenly empty branch nexus. Moon didn't care. A chunk of hollow branch hit the tarp, bounced.

"Close the net!" he screamed.

More animals bounded out of the way as Moon helped Turtle and Aimi close the net and tie it off. They had a bag now, weighing maybe eighty kilograms.

Turtle turned to him, "Do we—"

"Shh!" hissed Moon, watching the air above the bag. Waiting.

Pop. Like a bubble in reverse. The portal reappeared.

A giggle escaped Moon's mouth before he slapped his hand over his face. No time to celebrate. No time. The whole forest was coming down, and one of Anne's cronies might see that Moon knew how to do more than destroy a portal.

He knew how to move them.

"Take it back to the caravan," he ordered. "My laboratory. Now."

★   ★   ★

"Let me through, Daisuke." Even as she said the words, Anne realized they were pointless.

Daisuke had no interest in finding blue paint onboard the caravan, or letting Anne go back outside.

He shook his head, his face a pale mask. They were in the breakfast nook, standing before the door. Outside, the stumps slid past as the caravan picked up speed.

Anne should have predicted this. She would never have let herself be fooled, but she'd been in a panic. She'd grasped at anything that might save the Dorado biome, including the belief that Daisuke would help her.

Oh, he had pretended dutifully enough. Daisuke had followed her through the storeroom, her lab, the kitchen. It was just that he had no expectation of saving the biome. All he cared about was keeping Anne safe in the caravan.

"I said let me the fuck through!" A crumbling concussion shook the walls and floor. "They're dying out there!"

"You'll die," said Daisuke.

"I don't care!"

"I care!"

Talking was a waste of time. Anne took in his stance, arms and legs spread across the door. He had ushered her through this same door on their disastrous attempt at a date on the glasslands. Now she considered kicking him in the nuts. That would get her past him.

Moon elbowed her in the back.

Anne's foot kicked out, carrying her brain's last instruction, hitting empty air. She must have looked like a cancan dancer. *Idiot!*

"Watch it!" she shouted, as her brain caught up with her adrenaline-drunk body. "Where the hell did you come from?"

Moon didn't bother to answer, or even glance back at her. He was halfway to the bridge by now, but it was obvious where he'd come from. The rear of the caravan, with its door.

That door was blocked too. Turtle and Aimi were discussing something, casting glances toward the closed door to Moon's laboratory. They looked guiltily at Anne as she stormed toward them.

She hadn't heard the three come in, she'd been so focused on Daisuke. *Stupid!* She should have just dodged sideways and left the caravan through the rear door.

"Out of my way," she ordered Farhad's flunkies.

"Don't let her go!" shouted Daisuke. "It isn't safe."

Turtle opened his mouth, saw Anne's expression, closed it, and stepped aside.

"Please don't, Anne," Daisuke begged as Anne put her hand on the door handle. She gritted her teeth, kept her eyes forward.

She looked through the window set into the door.

The caravan had been moving all this time, heading west. Anne noticed the ugly ruts that the weight of the vehicle had smashed in the sierpinski. Then she raised her eyes and saw the wormhole grove. What had been the wormhole grove.

The trees had been reduced to blue-tipped stumps in a heaving sea of coatls. Doubloons lay in drifts ten centimeters deep on the ground, but frenzied animals tore each other apart for yet more. The scene was like something out of Hieronymus Bosch, but that wasn't what stopped Anne from opening the door.

The wormhole was gone. The stumps of the trees might grow again, but now the air between them was empty. Moon had destroyed this one too. The heart had been stolen from the Dorado biome.

The floor swayed under Anne. Her stomach heaved and the edges of her vision darkened. She clamped down on herself. She would not faint. She would not vomit. She would stand there, hand uselessly on the door handle, forehead pressed to the glass. She would watch.

She did watch, ignoring Turtle and Aimi, ignoring Daisuke. Later, she would have to talk to him. She would have to lie to him, manipulate him, to get the help she needed. She had been about to risk her life to save this part of Junction, why not risk Daisuke's as well?

But not now. For now, Anne would stand here by the door, and look out the window at the horror of her failure.

CHAPTER SIXTEEN
Join the Feast

The ruined wall ran across the northern border of the Dorado biome. The week before, it had probably been splendid: a row of inward-leaning Dorado trees. These had been braced by flying buttresses, supporting a sheet of interwoven strands of doubloons. Perhaps the wall had once been intended to grow into a dome, if one could think of an ecosystem as possessing intention.

Not that it mattered now. Panicking forest life had torn the walls down, removed the buttresses, let the trees topple. In the piles of now-worthless doubloons, little half-dome huts had sprung up in the shadows of the blue-crowned stumps. Coatls huddled in the shadows, noses quivering as if they couldn't understand why all the smells had changed.

Anne squinted against the diamond-sharp light and pulled up the collar of her jacket. Without the Dorado trees, this place was a tundra. A snowy graveyard.

"Well, I guess this is it," she said wretchedly. "We give up. We go back to civilization." She felt like she'd swallowed a quart of wet wool. "Remove ourselves from the equation and I guess starve to death on the way back, but I just *can't do this* anymore."

Daisuke rubbed his hand over her back. "All right," he said. "It's all right. I think we won't starve."

He looked so certain, but how could Anne trust him? Daisuke the actor, the liar, the manipulator. Tell people whatever they want to hear, pour oil over those troubled waters until we're all coated with black sludge, dying on the beach. Anne shuddered.

Daisuke said, "Look."

She braced herself for the follow-up. *Look, Anne, you know you're being a bitch, right? Look, this relationship isn't working. Look.*

Anne coughed. "Look what?"

Daisuke turned. "Look. It's the mountain."

He was right. High feathery clouds frosted the lilac sky, matching the color of the snow on the boulders at the foot of the Howling Mountain.

It was maybe an hour's walk away, a blobby, rounded cone capped in mist. Its lower skirts, tiger-striped with different colors of vegetation, rose and fell like a quilt, folded into deep horizontal and vertical crevasses. From this close up, the landform looked like no act of geology that Anne had seen before. Not architecture either. The mountain was alive, and horribly vulnerable.

If she left, Farhad would devour it. If she stayed, it would make no difference.

"No, we can't protect it," she said. "I can't, Daisuke."

He nodded sadly.

What? Wasn't he supposed to tell her it would be all right? But what good would that do? If he told her that, he'd be lying. If Anne said she believed him, she'd be lying too.

She pulled Daisuke's arm off her and turned away from the mountain.

The Nun squatted around a cluster of kerosene stoves, on which steamed pots. Other men were cleaning empty toymaker shells. Others were stacking them like hollow logs, well out of sight of the living toymakers.

"Good morning!" Daisuke called out. The Nun mostly ignored him, but one parkaed figure raised a hand and growled back.

"Daisuke! Anne!" called Misha. "Come to join the journey? Heh. Or just join the feast?"

Anne didn't answer. She was looking at the activities going on in the Nun camp. Yes, it did seem the Nun were preparing to go home. But what was with all the toymaker shells?

At first, Anne thought the Nun were honoring the creatures that had been killed fleeing the forest. But there were far too many empty shells. None seemed to be damaged. In fact, each shell was handled very carefully, with reverence and sorrow.

Anne shrugged off Daisuke's arms and kicked across the snow toward Misha. "What the hell is going on?"

Misha looked up sulkily from his stove. "Don't freak out now. I've had a hard week."

"*You've* had a hard week? What are you doing to the toymakers?"

But Anne could see what the Nun were doing, couldn't she? They were popping open the toymakers and decanting their innards like chunks of salmon from a tin.

The Nun had a whole assembly line going. One man tended a small clutch of land-galleys, to which he murmured and clicked like they were nervous hens. Another would pick up a toymaker in wood-and-plastic gauntlets and pry off its forward window. A third reached into the shell with a scoop and – *schlup!*

Anne's hands came up to her mouth. "You're killing them."

Daisuke's head jerked around. "Killing? What?"

"They're already dead, Anne," Misha said. "Take a smell."

Anne sniffed. Even in the cold, the stench of toymaker biochemistry should have made the edge of the Dorado forest smell like a snowy sewer. But all she got now was a faint whiff of something deep and rich. Loamy.

Anne let Misha reassure Daisuke that nobody was in danger. No, the destruction was already done, wasn't it? It was just even deeper than she had known.

Anne looked more closely at the stuff being prepared by the nearest Nun butcher.

The butcher removed and discarded a few calamari rings – naked toymaker worms, ringed with eyes and teeth. Black, stinking internal fluid was also quickly mopped away, leaving a brown mass as deeply convoluted as a little brain. The butcher carefully rinsed this wrinkled mass before dropping it into a cook pot. Anne sniffed again.

"Mushroom soup." She turned back to Misha. "Mushroom fucking *soup*?"

"It's a fungus," said Misha. "From the Earth biome. It makes toymakers edible. It must have evolved—"

"I know how it must have evolved!" Anne snapped. There was a toymaker biome capping the mountains on the eastern border of the Earth biome. Nature abhorring vacuums as it did, it was only a matter of time before something from Earth figured out how to digest toymaker tissues.

"And I know we're nowhere near the Earth biome now," she continued. "The Nun brought these magic mushroom spores with them, didn't they?" She even knew when the spores must have been planted. "The go-home dust!"

"What happened?" asked Daisuke.

Anne felt like spitting. "Even back before Farhad brought the forest down, the Nun were killing the toymakers."

Misha held up his hands with an air of weary indifference. "This was all decided before we even crossed into the Dorado biome. We took a stand, with you, against Farhad." His palms turned up. "Win or lose, we knew he would stop giving us supplies."

"He never said that," Daisuke said, taking Farhad's side again.

"Of course he'll starve them out," Anne told him. And to Misha she said, "Of course you'll starve. What'll you do when your mushrooms run out?"

The lines in Misha's face grew deeper and darker. "Our mushrooms should last us long enough to make it back to the Sweet Blood biome, even if you and Daisuke come with us."

Anne took a step back. She'd been about to go with these people. If she had come out here an hour later, would she have even known what they'd done to the toymakers? Or would Anne have just eaten the mushrooms they offered, and wondered where all the toymakers had gone?

"No," she whispered. And louder. "No, Misha! The toymakers trusted the Nun. *I* trusted *you*."

Misha rolled his eyes. "Don't be dramatic. This is something the Nun do on every long voyage they make. The toymakers keep letting them do this, so either they don't mind being eaten or they aren't smart enough to prevent it."

Anne understood all about not being smart enough to prevent disaster. Allowing herself to be led like a lamb to the slaughter. A toymaker choking on spores.

Misha's head twitched to the side and he lowered his voice. "And stop looking so horrified. People are talking about you."

"Ha!" said Anne. "Since when do I care what people say about me? That's always been the trouble with me, hasn't it?" If Anne were a better manipulator, would she have been able to stop these disasters? Or would she have happily joined in the causing of them?

"Well, you're still welcome to tag along. Although before you do,

I suggest trying the soup." Misha smiled grimly and gestured at the cook pot. "The taste takes some getting used to."

★ ★ ★

"I take it you don't plan to return to Imsame with the Nun? A good idea, since we'll arrive back at Imsame before they do," Farhad said. "You're welcome to come up the mountain with us, Anne, Daisuke. In fact, I hope you do." The tycoon leaned back in his chair, fingers steepled. "It would be a shame to let those space suits go to waste."

Farhad shouldn't have been able to corner Anne like this. She wasn't even *in* a corner, just in the middle of the caravan. Farhad looked like he'd simply chanced to be drinking his tea in the breakfast nook by the door, but must have been lying in wait.

"Stop," said Anne. "Just stop."

Farhad raised his eyebrows. "Of course you have my profound gratitude for all the help you've given this expedition. If you want to give up now, I understand, although I am disappointed."

Daisuke frowned. "I don't like what you're doing."

What *was* he doing? Anne felt her own face twisting as she figured it out. "You're trying to fucking *shame* me. No! What did I do wrong? Nothing! Ethically, morally…" she waved her hands, "…speculative-biologically! I figured out this entire eco-economy on my own in two days and you spied on me and used what I learned to destroy this place."

"A high price to pay, but—"

"But fucking what?" Anne welcomed the anger. It was like a bridge over this yawning chasm of terror and despair. And here she was, having walked out to the middle of it with a blindfold on! "What could possibly justify everything you've done?"

Farhad put down his teacup so he could shrug more elaborately. "I would love to tell you, Anne. I would love to *show* you what wonders I believe lie beyond the Howling Mountain wormhole." He picked the teacup back up. "But you've declared very explicitly that you stand against me. How can I reveal my goals to you?"

"In other words your goals are fucking *evil* and you fucking know it! Look behind us, Farhad. What I allowed you to do in the Dorado biome – that's what's shameful, all right?"

Farhad's cheeks darkened and his lips drew back from his teeth. He looked like Anne felt.

Something almost happened. Anne could almost see the spark in the air between them, like the spot of light at the focal point of a magnifying glass.

But his hand came up. Farhad smoothed down his beard, and the mask was back on. The tycoon closed his eyes and exhaled.

"When I was a boy I smuggled myself out of Iran in the back of a pickup truck." He held up a hand to stop Anne from saying, 'So bloody what?'

"I mention that, not because it was very hard and frightening and painful, but because it came between experiences that were…" another deep breath, "…worse. And ever since then, I've done my utmost to make sure that nobody I love ever finds themselves in a similar position ever again." He watched his reflection in the window, superimposed over the ruins and the Nun. "And then, I turn on the news."

"Um," Anne said. She felt like she'd run into a wall that had turned out to be a painted curtain.

Daisuke was caught less flat-footed. "You told us before about your plans to move people to Junction."

"Right." Anne shook herself. "Your grandkids don't need a second Earth, Farhad. They need to fix the one they have."

Farhad looked back at her. "When the *Titanic* was sinking, is that what the people on the lifeboats told the people drowning in the Atlantic Ocean? 'You need to fix the boat you have'?"

Anne floundered, and this time Daisuke was no help. What if he agreed with Farhad? What was the counterargument here?

Farhad didn't give her the time to find it. "I empathize with you," he said. "Both of you. You must be angry and hurt and frustrated that you can't make me care about what you obviously care about so deeply." He held his hands out to her. "But Anne, that's why I hired you. Your passion."

Despite herself, Anne felt moved. But she looked at Daisuke's blank face and understood the trap. What was Farhad trying to distract her from? "What is it exactly that you expect to find on the other side of the Howling Mountain wormhole? What is it you think will save mankind or whatever your crazy plan is?"

He sipped his tea. "I have several contradictory expectations. That's why it's an experiment."

Anne crossed her arms. "That's pretty bloody glib, isn't it?"

The fake half smile slid away, but Farhad didn't look angry. For a moment, he looked away, as if shy or unsure of himself.

"Understanding is like light," he said, apropos of nothing that Anne could see. "Insight. Judgment, however, is like lightning. Do you see? One of them illuminates and nourishes, the other terrifies and destroys."

Anne shook herself. She had to remember what this old villain's game was. "You think I'm being too judgmental? Of who? You? Should I just roll over and let you do what you want?"

He chuckled, any vulnerability gone. "Ah, there's that passion again. I should have predicted it would conflict with mine, and done more, earlier, to align our interests. I apologize deeply for not doing so, and I promise you that I will take actions now to redress my wrongs and make sure I never repeat them."

He stood, and Anne nearly said, 'Okay, bye,' before she realized he was trying to dismiss her.

She stomped a foot. "I cannot *believe* this! I've saved people's lives. I shouldn't feel like this. I shouldn't have this happen to me."

"I feel like that too, sometimes," said Farhad. "Like I want to shake my fist at the sky and curse the God that gave me this life. But God is merciful, Anne. God is compassionate. He gives us the tools we need, if we're just brave enough to take them."

Anne couldn't help but snort. "Unbelievable. You mean God sent you to me?"

Farhad laughed too. "Quite the opposite, Anne. Quite the opposite." He bowed his head slightly. "Thank you, both of you, for all you've done for me so far."

Daisuke's expression was deeply suspicious. "What do you plan to do?"

"Climb the mountain. With you, if you'll accompany us."

"Can you not?" Anne pleaded. One more time, she had to try. "Sometimes you just have to leave things be."

"I'm afraid I can't do that, Anne. When you stop changing the world, you die. If you'll excuse me."

Farhad bowed slightly and walked toward the bridge. Only once he was out of sight did Anne understand that he had gotten the last word. Another win for Farhad.

★ ★ ★

"He knew."

Anne looked around her lab, seeing nothing.

"Farhad knew I'd refuse to work with him, and he knew about this cruelty to toymakers thing the Nun are into. We can't hike back to Imsame on our own, so we have no choice but to just sit here and wait until they get back."

The others were preparing for a hike up to the wormhole at the peak of the mountain. They expected to spend no more than a day on the trip, but they weren't traveling light. The ATV was loaded with, not food, but equipment, including what looked like a winch.

"*Kaeru ka naa.*" Daisuke was standing in the corridor outside the lab, face swinging between Anne and the others like the snout of a nervous golden retriever. "I'm worried that they won't come back."

"You mean they might all get eaten by monsters?" said Anne. "We should be so lucky! Maybe that's what this expedition's been missing. Culling."

Daisuke paced back into the lab. "That isn't funny. What if someone really dies?"

Anne considered the fact that, as bad as she felt, nobody had died on this expedition. The last time she'd been on Junction, there'd been a murder about every two days. Maybe that danger had focused her attention on what mattered. Now, with the immediate stakes so low and the distant-future stakes so high, she felt like she was being ripped apart.

"Well, what are we supposed to do?" she said. "Ask them nicely not to hike up the mountain? They're not going to listen to us. Moon wants wormholes. Farhad wants a new world for his grandchildren to colonize. Boss Rudi wants a dowry for his daughter. Talking to Aimi or Turtle would tip Farhad off. Even Misha doesn't give a damn about

Junction except as a place for his wife's tribe to live."

Daisuke stared at her blankly.

Anne ground her teeth. "What? You think this is *my* fault? You think I've unmasked myself in front of my enemies and alienated my allies. Ha! 'Alienated'. 'Cause you are what you eat, right?"

Daisuke took a breath. "No. I think we should go with Farhad and the others. I think we should protect them."

"Oh no! We are not going with them." Anne crossed her arms. "*I* am not going with them. I will not be a party to whatever Moon is going to do."

"We can stop him."

How many times had Anne heard that one? "How?" she said. "Slimy manipulation? Mouth false promises at him? Tell him what he wants to hear? 'It'll be okay'? 'We'll be fine'? Whatever you're planning to say to me, I don't want to hear it."

Daisuke tried to make Anne look him in the eyes, but she wouldn't. Anne felt cored. Scooped out.

"This was supposed to be a vacation," she said. "This trip has been shitty, Daisuke. Really shitty. We've done more damage to Junction than anything ever. And everyone thinks I'm some sort of harridan for pointing it out, but in five hundred years, do you think people are going to say, 'Boy, it sure is great the first explorers of Junction trashed the place'? No. They're going to say, 'Another world ruined. What a fucking tragedy.'"

Daisuke wasn't listening. He was looking away down the caravan, massaging his sternum, expression pained. "I understand you," he said. "But I also understand Farhad and Moon. If what we discover here can help people, don't we have to discover it?"

"Oh, the 'people' thing," said Anne. "The only difference between people and nature is that people ought to know better. When nature destroys itself, it's just something that nature does sometimes. When people destroy nature, it's evil." Anne wished she'd told Misha all this.

Credit to Daisuke, he looked like he was thinking about what Anne said. Although, he was an actor. It might be that he just *looked* like he was thinking.

"I don't agree," he said. "I think there's no difference between people and nature. I think 'people' is just something that nature does sometimes." His eyebrows came together and he held his palm in front of his face. "It looks into a mirror."

"Very poetic," Anne said. "I'm sure your next TV series will be a big fucking hit."

And you can make it without me. The sentence formed itself in her brain. Right there. *You can make it without me because I am sick of this 'humans are more important than every other species put together' bullshit.* It was true. It was right. It would hurt Daisuke so much to hear it.

Didn't that mean that Daisuke was more important than every other species? Anne shook her head.

Now he was looking at her and Anne knew that it wasn't even enough to *not* say what she was thinking. He was so empathetic he *knew* what she wasn't saying. Silence wouldn't be enough. Anne would have to say something. And not just anything. She'd have to reach into his head and say the thing he wanted her to say, with no clues from him. Because if Daisuke gave her any clues, he wouldn't trust her to be telling the truth.

This was it. This was why Anne hated people. This was why she would spend the rest of her life in the wilderness, if only people didn't drag her back into their stupid bullshit made-up world.

The mind. What a joke that was. *I know what you know about what I know about what you know* and on and on the recursive curse of intelligence. If people were the universe holding up a mirror to itself, that mirror contained nothing but an endless corridor of reflections.

"All this trip we've been debating about how we'd recognize sapient life if we found it." Anne spoke softly, unable to meet Daisuke's eyes. "And I've been saying it's just automatic processes that give the toymakers and cavaliers and coatls the illusion of intelligence. You lot never realized that the same thing is true of us humans. Intelligence is just nature fooling itself."

Daisuke just looked at her.

"Stop it!" The words felt like something snapping off in Anne's throat. "Stop showing me that mask face. You're not fooling anyone. I know you're miserable, Daisuke. Just fucking admit it!"

A muscle jumped on Daisuke's cheek and Anne flinched.

"Goddamn it!" she said. "Don't do this to me. Don't make me figure out what's going on in your head. Just tell me what's wrong."

"You already know." The words were mild enough, but they strained like a dam about to burst.

"You want me to guess? All right, here's a hypothesis for you, Dice." She jabbed her finger at him. "You don't care about Junction. You just want to rescue me from monsters and be the big man. You want to be brave, but you'd stand by and watch this whole place fall apart as long as I'm safe—"

Daisuke slapped a hand to either side of the doorframe. The whites around his eyes showed. The hands he held out to her trembled. He opened his mouth. Closed it, jaw muscles standing out. He shook his head.

He was terrified. The insight clutched Anne's brain with icy fingers. She was scaring her fiancé.

Anne turned away. She could not bear to look at him. She could not bear to be here. She had to get out of the caravan. Run away or make him run away. *Close your eyes. Don't let yourself see.*

"You want me to choose between you and Junction," she said.

It wasn't like a scientific discovery. There was no thrill as the puzzle pieces connected. No wonder at the beauty of the picture they revealed.

Maybe because it wasn't true?

But Anne was too tired to look under yet another rock. To find out more ways she'd been wrong. She was sick of exploration and she just wanted to stop.

Daisuke finally asked, "Anne, are you happy with me?"

Anne let out a laugh. *Speaking of fooling ourselves.* Again, the words were there in her brain. But what *should* she tell him? How *did* Anne feel? She looked inside herself, and it was just a huge mess.

Daisuke shouldn't have to deal with her bullshit. What had he said about telling people what they want to hear? "It's okay, Dice," she said, and smiled. It was like pushing modeling clay around. Just shapes. "I'm happy with you."

"You're lying." Daisuke put his hand over hers. "I love you," he said. "I'm sorry I brought you here."

Anne looked into his eyes and knew he was telling the truth. And what good did that knowledge do? Why ever develop people skills at all, if all you learned with them were things you didn't want to know?

Anne's nose was suddenly full of snot. "Oh shit," she sniffed. Stupid animal body. Press the right button and it starts crying.

"I love you, but you're wrong." Daisuke still hadn't taken his hand away. It was warm and heavy. "Just because people are part of nature, that doesn't mean we don't...there isn't...." His eyes narrowed. "*Sekinin ya gimu to iu imi nai tte itteiru wake ja nainda.* We still have responsibilities and duties."

"Duties like trying to make me happy? It's so exhausting, Daisuke." Crap. She shouldn't have said that. But Anne felt like she would explode if she kept all this inside her.

Or maybe implode. Daisuke's expression was like a collapsing star in her gut.

"I'm sorry. It was a mistake to bring you here." He stood, removing his hand from hers. "But I am here. I have responsibilities and duties. If I ignore them, I am like a clever animal. I will be evil, just like you said."

He turned then, and walked away to join the expedition up the mountain.

Alone, Anne could finally cry. Once she was done, she understood that she couldn't go home, but she couldn't stay here. The only choice left was to stop Farhad by any means necessary.

She still had such a long way to go, but now at least now it was forward. Up that mountain.

When Anne left the caravan, she dutifully locked its doors behind her.

CHAPTER SEVENTEEN
The Lightning and the Tree

Anne stood alone at the base of the Howling Mountain, looking up.

From a distance, it had looked like a cone or pyramid. Closer up, its surface had appeared quilted. Now, it was clear that the quilting wasn't a surface feature. The 'pyramid' was actually composed of giant, blobby lumps, like a pile of melting ice-cream scoops.

It was clearly, unmistakably biological, but no elephant, whale, or redwood tree could contain a tenth of the mass Anne was seeing. The Howling Mountain might outweigh even Pando the aspen grove, Earth's heaviest single organism. But then the mountain was also too small. Australia's Uluru would dwarf this uncomfortable, in-between thing.

Farhad and the others had a head start in the ATV, although now that she looked more closely at the terrain, the vehicle might actually slow them down. Anne had a chance of beating them to the wormhole and…she'd figure that out later. Now, she walked around the perimeter so the party of climbers wouldn't see her coming. So she wouldn't see them. Daisuke was with them, protecting those—

She closed her eyes. No. If Anne wanted to be angry at people, she could have stayed on Earth. Now it was just time to look at the mountain.

Look. It's the mountain.

From this close, its taper looked more like a trick of perspective than its true shape. As if Anne were looking at a rectangle, an obelisk, a road leading to the stars.

The peak was shrouded in mist, but its lower slopes were covered in soil and plant life of various types. Orange wedges of sierpinski-grass, dark green spirals, frost-colored domes, indigo fans like giant bracken fungi, floppy strips like giant dark ribbons, and the brown fur-like plants of the Toymaker biome.

Oh, the toymakers. Anne's breath hitched. She sobbed, vision blurring. Well, why not cry here? There was nobody left around her to care. The mountain didn't. It just waited beyond the veil of tears.

Anne blinked. Squinted. Wiped the tears away and then realized that their blur had revealed the pattern. She unfocused her eyes, the way she had in the Dorado forest, letting the alien plants on the mountainside turn into abstract blotches of color.

And the colors made a pattern.

Anne remembered the mountains around Imsame, as the valley had once been. Warring biomes carved out territories for themselves, claiming gullies and crags as they poisoned the ground for the life of other planets. There were territories like that here too, except they were tiny. Narrow. And the stripes of color didn't follow the shape of the ground under them.

Toymaker plants liked high elevations, and should have formed a cap on the pyramid. Instead, the brown hair-grass trees snaked up the slope in a pair of irregular lines, paralleling a row of those dark ribbons. To the left of that, a broad wedge of sierpinski-grass narrowed to a meter-wide band of coiling orange bramble. It looked like the path a river made to the sea, widening into a delta. Was Anne looking at a pattern of seed dispersal? But what would be spitting out Dorado-biome seeds from the peak? The wormhole? Except the wormhole was supposed to lead to space.

The skin on Anne's arms prickled under her parka. Coatls actively engineered the shapes of their plant life. Cavaliers did, too, and yes, there was the dark green of their ammonite-grass. Anne backed away, trying to get a better angle...yes. When looked at from the side, it was easy to see how those dark green places had been terraced.

The cavaliers had built stairs onto the Howling Mountain. The coatls had clipped together a viny ladder that they could climb. The toymakers had their paths, too, but how could the little wheeled creatures climb them? If Anne could figure that out, she might be able to beat Farhad's party to the peak.

Except now that she traced them with her eyes, none of the paths actually seemed to lead there.

Anne turned and ran, kicking through snow and sierpinski, gaining perspective. When she judged she had enough, she turned and looked again at the mountain. Yes, those stripes of vegetation thinned as they climbed. They converged faster than the shape of the mountain required, so that they would meet at a point about halfway up, just below the bottom of the mist layer. Was that a hint of something in there? Something darker and more complicated than the surface of the mountain?

Who cared about beating Farhad to the top? She could beat him to what was actually important.

Anne clenched her hands in their gloves. This was what she needed. No distractions. No *people*. Just organisms going about their business and Anne watching over them, trying to figure out what was going on.

Because there *was* something going on. Those paths of vegetation looked wrong, groomed, artificial, pasted on top of something else.

Something else, which had something to do with those dark ribbons. They were everywhere on the mountain, underlying the sierpinski and nautilus-grasses, snaking like water around the white domes, bracketed by toymaker plants like the water in an irrigation channel. At the base of the mountain, ribbons draped like the fringe on a homespun skirt.

Anne headed toward the tip of a ribbon. It was the leaden color of the sky before a bad storm, about the width of her body and the thickness of her little finger, bifurcated at the end like the tongue of a snake.

Anne didn't touch it. Instead she found a patch of rock upslope and jumped onto it. Rock crunched under her boots as she followed the ribbon up the slope. As Anne climbed, she saw knobs of harder material growing on its surface, the color and texture of foamed cement. The color and texture of the rock of the mountain, in fact. *Hmm.*

The knobs on the ribbon grew larger and more numerous as Anne walked uphill, until they fused together into a stiff, round sleeve. The sleeve didn't grow upward like a tree would have, but stuck straight out from the mountain, a squished tube more than a meter across. The ribbon ran into this sleeve, or rather, it flopped limply out of it, the rubbery extension of some larger organism growing underground. And there was another sleeve, angling out of the mountainside to form a Y shape with the first. Anne thought of the end of the ribbon, with its similar bifurcation.

Anne imagined this ribbon contracting, thickening, developing a rocky coat, its forked tip growing into new ribbons as it fused with the mountain's skin.

She squinted up the slope, superimposing the gullies and crags she saw with the ice-cream-pile shape of the mountain in general. Yes. The two sleeves Anne had found were at the tip of a mound of outthrust rock. Farther uphill, there was another mound, with its own pair of sleeves. She looked sideways, along the slope. It was hard to see because of the plants in the way, but it looked like the ground dipped, then bulged out again. Another pair of mounds, each tipped with a pair of sleeves of its own.

The ice-cream scoops were branches. Limbs. Trunks joining to form mightier trunks, growing out from the heart of the organism they called the Howling Mountain.

"Ha." The word puffed into fog. Anne was standing on a giant plant, its leaves draping down over petrified bark and the forests of epiphytes that clung to it. A tree shaped like a pile of ice-cream.

Did this hypothesis cast any light on those other plants? Anne looked down the slope and up, following the multicolored trails of the different biomes. They still looked artificial, shooting straight up to a horizontal cleft in the rock right at the edge of the mist.

Except that wasn't exactly rock, was it? The cleft was a larger version of the little gully across the slope from the neighboring branch-mounds. It must be where two huge branches came together, a tree crotch the size of a subway station. And there was definitely something large growing up there.

Why would plants from all these biomes be growing here? Because the coatls and toymakers and cavaliers had brought them. And why would they do that? Why did the toymakers make these periodic migrations to the Howling Mountain? And follow paths up to that point where two big branch-lumps came together?

"There's something up there that they want," Anne said, and shivered. It wasn't just the cold, it was the way her words dissolved uselessly in the air, with nobody to hear them.

Was it dangerous, whatever was up there? Would Daisuke be all right when he reached it?

The thought brought a painful jolt with it. Would the *mountain* be all right? No, it wouldn't be, and between this unique, ancient organism and one particular Japanese man, it was obvious which she had to choose.

It had to be obvious. Why wasn't it *obvious*?

Anne's breath ghosted through her teeth. "So what the hell am I supposed to do?" she asked the flank of the mountain. The only answer it made was to crunch beneath Anne's boots as she climbed.

It was the act of long habit to check the ground before she sat. You never knew what snakes or spiders might be waiting there to inject your ankles with venom. So Anne swung her leg out in an arc and scraped her sturdy boot across the mountainside.

Rock crumbled like old concrete, linguipods leaped from toymaker grass like striped, overly-active snails. The dull gray surface of the ribbon twitched.

Understanding came like a bolt of lightning. Like lightning, a dozen little questing branches of inquiry had been spreading from Anne's brain into the mountain. She'd barely been aware of them, those questions, connections, hypotheses comparing one imaginary world to another, questing for that first brush against the real world. Then, with the brush of a boot against a plant, a path to understanding opened and fire flooded through.

The rock. The ribbon. The cave in the mist. Farhad and Daisuke climbing the other face of the mountain. The point of it all! Toymakers. Their plants growing right here. Their little wheels, which could not possibly roll them up a slope like this. The ribbons could move!

Anne pounced on the ribbon and grasped its edge with both hands.

It felt like grabbing hold of the conveyor belt at an airport baggage carousel. Rubbery tissue jerked in her grip. The smooth surface crinkled like a skeptic's forehead. Rocks and grass hissed, and the entire dark length of the thing slurped up the mountain, dragging Anne with it.

★ ★ ★

"Hey, Daisuke. Come over to my side of the mountain."

Daisuke stared down at his walkie-talkie, then back at the line of people straggling up the mountain behind him.

The slope was gentle, and in places seemed almost to have been carved into stairs. Daisuke didn't have to worry about someone having heart palpitations or falling into a crevasse, so he was able to focus on the next step. The dark green swirls growing over ground like old coral. The crunch under his boots and the breathing of his companions. The labor of his lungs and the burning of his calf muscles. He'd tried not to think about how he'd betrayed Anne, and whatever he was going to do next.

"Anne," he whispered into the microphone, "I'm sorry."

"Yeah, me too. I was a jerk because I didn't know what was going to happen, or more precisely because I knew something bad was going to happen, but now...."

It was good to hear her babble again. Daisuke waited for her to pause for breath. "What happened? Are you all right?"

"Yes. I came to a realization. Come to my side of the mountain and you'll see why."

"Where? What side?"

"Remember when we thought the mountain was a pyramid? It still is, just it's a pyramid made of ice-cream scoops."

Daisuke had very little idea what she was talking about. That was usually a good sign. "You mean the mountain has four sides?"

"Yes, but each face is made of the ossified skin of twigs that branch off one of four big limbs. I'm at the...what do you call it...the apical meristem of the right-hand branch of the south-west limb. What about you?"

Daisuke shook his head. Apical what? What about branches? "I'm halfway up, I think. I'm just below the clouds. There is a..." – what was 'seam' in English? "There is a line around the middle of the mountain, like a belt."

"The seam where the four equatorial trunks meet the apical trunk, yes. Hm."

"Yes?"

"There ought to be a trunk at the foot of the mountain as well. Squashed down small where we can't see it?" A pause. Daisuke could almost hear her mental gears shift. "Anyway. You must be as high as me, then. Good hiking, Dice. If you walked, then you probably used the crevices between mounds. Going up the cavaliers' stairs, right? You must be in the crotch between the two main branches of the north-east limb right now."

Daisuke looked left and right. "There are big mounds on either side of me. Is that right?"

"Exactly right," she crowed. "Climb up the one on your left. I'll tell you how."

That would be much harder than Daisuke's climb so far. He didn't hesitate.

His jump didn't take him as far as it would have in normal gravity, but Daisuke spread his arms and legs and clung like a spider climbing an egg. His walkie-talkie squawked, but he didn't pause. He would explain to Farhad and the others when he reached the top.

He saw Anne's boots first. Anne was standing on top of the mound, in front of a pair of the limp, lead-colored ribbon-plants that seemed to characterize this mountain.

"You had to just fling yourself up here, didn't you?" she said. "You couldn't wait for me to tell you how to ride the ribbon-trees."

"What?" panted Daisuke. "I'm sorry."

"You should be. This is exactly what − no. Later. I'm sorry too, Dice." She knelt, holding a hand out for him to grab. "First, let me show you what I was wrong about. It's big."

★ ★ ★

Anne stood on the mountain with Daisuke and showed him the lands they had passed through. The Toymaker Mountains, blue in the distance. The iridescent shimmer of the glasslands. The rolling, forest-green hills of the Cavalier biome. And last, closest, the Dorado biome. It was orange again.

"Look!" she said. "Don't you see what it *means*? Use your binoculars, Dice. Look at the Dorado trees!"

Because there the trees were. Canopies of living money, rebuilt − they must have been! − by the creatures that valued them.

Daisuke's brows lowered over the eyepieces. "They are shorter and closer to each other than before. They look more like cones. Pine tree shape?"

"Good eye! I'm thinking it's a better shape for snowfall. Maybe the Dorado Planet has seasons." Her words came faster. "The closest thing I can think of on Earth is the blooms you get after rain in the desert or the regrowth after a periodic forest fire. Eucalyptus trees produce fruits that *have* to burn in order to release their seeds. Of course, you also have deciduous trees that lose all their leaves once a year, and or in the case of bamboos, just set seed and die all at once."

Living things died, and suffered, and raged against fate, but the wheel spun on.

God, I've been stupid. No. That wasn't quite it. More fundamentally, Anne had been arrogant. She'd thought she'd understood this wild and complex system of a forest. She'd reduced the Dorado biome to fit into her head, then wept when it got so small. She'd been wrong, and that should be glorious.

She remembered herself, standing in the forest right before it fell apart. She remembered her rage, her hopeless, all-directions war. *That poor woman*, she thought. *She ripped herself apart.* Anne had wasted so much time on anger. No point in being angry about *that* though. "I'm willing to bet this reassembly is something the forest just *does* occasionally. Maybe this is how the trees shuffle genetic material around. And it's not close to being done. Look at all the blue you can see. Construction activity!"

"Do you think the wormhole is still missing? Has it reappeared?"

"I couldn't tell. We'll need to go down there and check after, uh." Anne coughed. "We stop Farhad and Moon."

Daisuke lowered the binoculars and looked at her.

Anne's first impulse was to say, "Of *course* I'm still going after Farhad. What he's doing is evil!" But when she looked back at him and tried to deduce what he wanted, it became clear that Daisuke wanted something else from her. He couldn't tell her what it was, because if he did, it would be meaningless.

If only she had any idea what it was Daisuke wanted.

Anne knew she was over-thinking this, but she didn't have much practice at under-thinking, did she?

"Look, Dice. My theory about myself is that I lost the ability to imagine good things happening." She sliced a hand toward the Dorado forest. "It was so easy to look at a tree and see how it might be cut down, I couldn't see how it might grow again. You know?"

"I know." Daisuke lowered his eyes. "I saw you were angry."

"I couldn't stop it. Just saying 'I don't want to be angry' didn't work. I needed a reason – I'm a scientist, I need reasons – but I couldn't find any. The more I looked, the more problems I saw, the more reasons to lose hope. Finally there was nothing left to examine except...." She hugged herself. "Except for the rocks I couldn't look under. I was afraid of what I might find there."

Daisuke's eyes crinkled up with his smile. "Professor Houlihan," he said in his low, slow TV voice, "will you tell me what you found under those rocks?"

That shocked a laugh from her. "Ha! Right! What I found was our last trip to Junction, you jerk. Remember? I was having this grand old time while you were going insane trying to protect me from a murderer. I didn't even believe there *was* a murderer!"

Daisuke rubbed his chest where a toymaker had shot him. "But you caught her."

"Right. I told myself I was smarter this time. I thought I knew about the danger. I made it my mission to protect Junction, but that conflicted with *your* mission to protect *me*."

Daisuke's eyes were sad now, but he nodded. "You understood that just now?"

"No, I actually figured that out back in the Dorado forest." Anne resisted the urge to look away from him. "I was so angry at you. You'd put me above the future of an entire planet! And you knew that I was angry at you, but I didn't know that *you* knew...." She held her hands up to her head. "I couldn't stand thinking like that, so I didn't try. I didn't figure it out until just now that...," she slowed down listening to herself, "you don't think you're good enough for me."

Daisuke stiffened, blinked and looked away. Shock? Sudden tears? Did that support or disprove her hypothesis?

"You don't think you're smart enough or enough of a conservationist, or good enough for anything but protecting me from alien monsters," Anne probed. "Uh, right?"

"I also thought I was good for listening to your theories," he said, and smiled, although his breath caught.

Ha! Support! This was like figuring out the mountain's biology. The same pieces were there, but now they connected up. All the little bits fit together because that was how they grew.

"Right. I kept seeing you with Farhad and Aimi and thinking,

'They're all manipulators.' I didn't see the difference: you really care about the well-being of the people you're dealing with. You aren't willing to sacrifice people in some grand scheme, like Farhad." She spread her arms. "That's how I want to be too."

"But I want to be like you. I want to not care what they think about me."

"Wait a sec, all those times you told me 'fuck 'em, don't listen to the trolls on the internet,' you were giving advice to *yourself*?"

He shrugged. "I want to be strong like you."

"Strong like a bull in a china shop, maybe. Even when I knew you wanted me on your side, I didn't do anything with the knowledge. That wasn't blissful ignorance, that was willful ignorance. Armor. And if you need to be more like me, I need to be more like you, or else I'll turn out like Moon."

"Probably there is something in between," Daisuke said.

Anne pinched the diamond on her left ring finger. "Let's find that equilibrium."

He looked back at her. He was smiling again, as brilliantly as he ever did on camera. "Let's find it."

He put his arms around her, and Anne returned the embrace. Life could be destroyed in an instant, but in every instant it lived, it grew.

She looked up into Daisuke's eyes. He frowned.

"How can we stop Moon and Farhad from stealing the mountain's wormhole?"

"Or blowing it up?" Anne held him tighter. "I don't know, yet, but I think we can do it. This feels like a good first step, though. Trusting each other?"

As if waltzing, Daisuke turned them around so he could look up at the mountain. Mist swirled just a few meters over them. "If you know a faster way to climb, we can beat them to the peak."

"Assuming that's where the wormhole is. And I'm wondering... hm."

Anne released her fiancé and looked, not up the slope, but horizontally across it. She examined the seam where the apical and equatorial canopies met. She pictured a cube with a melted, petrified tree growing out of each face. What sort of environment would produce a shape like that? What would be going on in the center, where the trunks met?

"Anne?"

"Let's do some exploring. Reconnoiter. Figure out what it is that we're trying to protect."

She pulled Daisuke across the upper slope of the mound. He was holding on tight to her hand, unwilling to let go.

"You missed me," she hypothesized.

"Of course! I was worried! I thought something horrible happened to you."

Anne could sympathize. "I thought about horrible things too. You open a window to the world, and these thoughts swarm in. What if everything I love dies?" She cast about for another ribbon-tree, but couldn't see one.

The fog was all around them now, but Anne could still see the mountain in her head. The equatorial trunk branched and branched again, each bifurcation ninety degrees offset from the one before. There should therefore be another mound above them and a little to the south. If it was tipped with ribbon-trees, those would be dangling....

"That way," she said.

"Yes," said Daisuke. "I'm sorry, Anne. I can't stop worrying about you. I don't want to stop."

"Well, I don't want to stop worrying about Junction, either. What's love if you're not scared of losing it? What's the point? But then, look at this mountain!"

"I can't see it."

"You know what I mean. Visualize it." She led them onward, pulling Daisuke through what felt like very fine spiderwebs. Lead-colored shapes gleamed ahead. Not ribbon-trees, but some huge, round object, an egg as big as a boulder, connected to the ground with a fat stalk. A fruit? A bud? A giant eye on a stalk?

"What's the point of a mountain?" Anne said. "Nothing! Unless somebody looks at it. That's the point of mountains. That's life. That's love! You find something beautiful, you turn to someone, and you say, 'look at that view!'"

Daisuke smiled, but said, "I still don't see anything. Just darkness and mist."

"Hm." Anne pinched the diamond on her ring, thinking. "The mist." She'd been trying to focus through it. Now that she stopped and considered the air in front of her nose....

The stuff retreated when she drew in breath, then advanced again when she exhaled. It trailed cobwebby fingers across her hands, tasting her skin, twisting together into tiny vortices that carried away her sweat and sloughed skin cells. Larger whorls turned more slowly, gathering and distributing resources, forming tunnels to communicate with their neighbors, linking themselves like a ball-and-stick model of tremendous molecules just on the edge of visibility.

"The mist is alive," she said. "And why shouldn't it be?"

"What do you mean?" What did that waver in Daisuke's voice signify? Anne arrived at a hypothesis.

"Don't be scared?"

His hand flexed around hers. "Okay."

"Anyway, perhaps this is some kind of froth of tiny bubbles? Air, lipid membrane, cytoplasm, membrane, more air. But strung together with what?"

From ahead, their came a clunking, as of wooden clocks.

Daisuke held her back. "Wait."

"Don't leap into danger."

He looked around at her. "Okay. Let's stay together."

"And maybe look first?" Anne brought up her binoculars and focused on the vague shapes in the mist. More lead-colored buds, they looked like, even bigger than the one she'd seen before. The largest, a burr-like hairy thing, could have easily fit four people inside it. It sagged sideways on its stalk, fuzzy apex open, revealing a glowing interior. Something moved around it, tocking.

"Toymakers," Anne said. "Either the Nun didn't eat all of theirs after all, or these are wild."

"What are they doing?" asked Daisuke.

"I don't know." There were other shapes moving around the bud, as well. "Okay. Ten steps forward. Ready?"

They stayed quiet and low, which seemed to work. At least, Anne and Daisuke were completely ignored by the aliens.

"Not just toymakers," whispered Anne. "Those are possum-type coatls."

"Any cavaliers?"

"Not that I can see." Or smell? Anne breathed in through her nose, and was rewarded with the sewage-stink of toymakers, as well as a sharp, vinegar-and-cat-piss smell she'd never before had the misfortune to experience.

"A signal for pollinators?" she wondered.

"What?" Daisuke asked.

"I'm guessing that shiny thing over there is the mountain's flower. Like the ribbons are its leaves. So the toymakers and coatls are like bees? Let me watch."

What were the aliens doing? A pollinator would visit a flower, get its equivalents of pollen and nectar, then buzz off. That wasn't what the toymakers and coatls were doing.

The toymakers filed between the fuzzy-bud and one of their mobile fortresses. The coatls were less well-organized. They seemed to be paying each other to dart into the bud, and out again. In both cases, though, the aliens carried things in that didn't come back out.

"They're storing stuff in it," said Anne. "Or maybe feeding it? How does that make sense?"

She looked up the mountain and something clicked. "Oh. Maybe. Come on, Dice, let's go see the cave."

"Yes? What cave?"

They didn't have to walk far before the ground started sloping out from under them. Rock curved as if pulled inward, puckering into a cavern, funnel, an orifice.

"Right," said Anne.

"How did you know there was a cave here?" Daisuke looked around at the deserted mountainside and laughed. "Tell me, Anne. I want you to explain to me."

Anne's first thought was that he was making fun of her. But he wasn't. She could tell from his face. The way he looked at her, cheeks flushed, lips parted. He smiled in a way that made this entire trip worth the cost.

"The toymakers and coatls back there are loading a fuzzy-bud, right? Not feeding it, but caching supplies. Supplies for a trip! A trip to where? A trip to space. And how do you get there?" She stretched her arms toward the cave. "Ta-dah! Through a wormhole."

Daisuke furrowed his brow. "The cave is connected to the peak of the mountain?"

"No! No, the wormhole was never in the peak. It's in the center! Where all the trunks come together."

Now he was smiling again, enjoying playing Watson to her Holmes. "Trunks?"

Anne made the peace sign with one hand, then the other, one coming off the other. "One trunk splits in two branches, which splits in two again, and so on. That cave ahead of us must be the crotch where two big branches come together into a trunk."

Daisuke snickered.

"What?"

"I'm thinking about Misha. He would say, 'This doesn't look like a crotch. It looks like breasts.'"

Anne looked down the slope of their mound, and up the next one. The cave they were headed for in between. "Christ, Daisuke, you must be horny as hell."

He smiled at her. He smiled *hard*. Anne found herself blushing.

"I'm very happy we're together," Daisuke declared. "I'm happy that you're happy. And we're alone together." He grabbed her around the hips.

Oh! Anne considered it. She considered Daisuke. Or perhaps 'relished' was the more accurate word.

Daisuke's hands moved up and down her back. "*Jikan nai*," he growled. "We don't have time."

"You know, I think we might have time. If I'm right about the structure of this organism, Farhad etc. are hiking to the wrong place entirely." Her heart pounded. "And there aren't any aliens hanging around here. We really could.... Oh! Hey!"

That was all the encouragement Daisuke needed. Anne extracted herself, tugging up her suddenly unbuckled trousers.

"Let's, uh, find some soft moss or something first? Then just make sure there's nothing in that cave that's going to eat us."

"Maybe I'll eat you," said Daisuke, but he turned and skipped down the slope into the cave.

The cave was right where Anne had expected it, but it was inexplicably deep. It wasn't just the volume squeezed between the four mounds around it. She had to think of a different word than *mound*. Lobes? Crowns. The branches had *crowns*. And four of them pressed together should leave a gap at the center, tapering to a point.

Except this cave kept going. It was a tunnel, its walls smooth, with gentle lateral ridges. No claw marks, thankfully, nothing that would suggest burrowing. The smooth surface ended abruptly at the lip of the tunnel, where the crunchy, friable rock resumed. The giant buds had sprouted there. Lead-colored ribbons spread from the bases of the buds, lolling down over the multicolored paths that the animals of various biomes had carved into the mountain. Paths that all led here.

Some sort of mutualism? The mountain drags animals up to its equator, where they pollinate the flowers and...?

Anne's foot hit something on the ground. The object rolled like a stone lemon, dragging a skein of shimmery fabric. A vacuum-spinner. A treasure from space.

"Hey, Daisuke," she said, turning. "Come look at this—"

Daisuke's arms came around her. His mouth covered hers.

★ ★ ★

Daisuke fell on Anne like he was drowning and she was a life raft. Her back hit the wall of the cave. The smooth, hard surface pressed into her spine, but Daisuke was unzipping her jacket with a determination she found very flattering. She ran her hands over his shoulders as he bent to nuzzle her breasts.

Pros and cons: Farhad was headed for the peak of the mountain, where he would find nothing. This tunnel was dry and unoccupied. Anne really loved Daisuke, and they had sex only once on this whole trip.

He kept bending. A sharp downward tug on her belt and cold air hit Anne's legs. She broke out in goose bumps, helped not at all by his face, which was pressed between her legs. Daisuke attacked her underpants.

Anne's heart pounded. Heat diffused up her belly and chest like a shot of hard liquor going the opposite direction. Her legs twitched shut around Daisuke's head. His fingers kneaded her thighs.

The wall still pressed into her back. Beyond the overhang, creatures darted through the living mist. Shadows flickered and colors bloomed. The phrase *eating me out* flashed through Anne's mind.

Sensation gathered inside her, collapsing like a star. The two of them slid down the wall as Anne's knees gave out. He was kneeling in front of her now and a live wire ran up from his mouth to the base of her skull. Another. Her legs squeezed together.

"Fuck, I'm going to suffocate you," she said. Then, just, "Fuck!"

She repeated that a couple of times, probably. Mostly, she was just aware of red-and-black darkness, shot with lightning.

Eventually she released him. The heels of her boots sank back to the ground.

Daisuke stood over her, looking very satisfied with himself.

Anne's was satisfied with him too. She reached down to her ankles, where several layers of clothing had collapsed around her boots.

"God, Daisuke," she gasped. "Goddamn. You didn't have to do that. Our jackets are thick enough we could just— Ow!"

Daisuke had somehow gone from flat on his back to on top of her. His arms were around her again and *whoop*.

Anne dug her shoulders into the floor of the cave while Daisuke wrestled with his pants. His expression before had been joyful, but now it was focused. A cat would look that way before it pounced.

This time the operative phrase was *falling upon me*. Anne had the feeling that if a hideous alien beast had materialized out of the mist between herself and her man, he would have torn it apart with his teeth.

There wasn't anything *too* lumpy under her back. Like the wall, the rock was smooth, with gentle lateral ripples as if eroded by millennia of outgushing water. Her bottom was cold, but Daisuke's heat more than made up for it. Anne's skin was so sensitized it felt like she could feel every one of his leg hairs. His weight on hers increased. Perfectly, they slid together.

More sparks. More bolts of lightning. The walls of the cave vibrated like an earthquake. Anne buried her teeth in his shoulder.

The mountain howled.

CHAPTER EIGHTEEN
Climb

And kept howling.

The noise expanded from whistle to siren to freight train to typhoon. Soon it wasn't a sound at all, but a force that fluttered the diaphragm and pulled inexorably down the tunnel.

Anne's ears popped, and the cave was suddenly full of living mist.

It streamed past her, thick with cobweb organisms. Something the size of a hummingbird tumbled past, triangular wings swiveling. A flash of light, a pop like a gun going off, and the animal shot back out of the mouth of the cave.

"A rocket-propelled animal?" Anne could feel her lips and mouth form the words, but could hear nothing over the howl.

A hand grasped hers, let go, got a firmer grip on her wrist. Daisuke tugged, and Anne pushed herself after him. In this case, the heavy gravity helped them, keeping their hands and knees anchored against the smooth floor. The wind, the suction, was still rising though.

The fog was shot through now with whirling whips of dirt. Bits of variously colored vegetation spattered against Anne's face. Blood pounded in her ears.

But she crawled forward. Hand, knee, hand, knee, she and Daisuke pulled each other out.

The intensity of the wind dropped once they left the cave mouth, but very slowly. The funnel-shaped depression in the mountain had no edges, no convenient corners or outcroppings to hide behind. Anne suspected that that was the whole idea.

"Behind the buds!" she yelled over the noise. "Downhill!"

The buds closest to the cave were bent double by the wind, their fuzzy silver heads beating against the ground like wrecking balls. Debris flew up from the ground uphill of them and swirled into the howling maw. The buds themselves, however, stayed anchored to the mountain.

Of course they would, thought Anne. *None of them are ripe yet.*

The wind was dying down. The howling had dropped back to audible levels and the fog seemed to be fighting back. Gossamer cages spun themselves across the cave mouth, fragile as frost crystals, white with frost and trapped debris.

Anne chuckled. "Catching some food of your own, are you? Cheeky little bastards."

"What?" Daisuke shouted at her. "Are you all right?"

"Fine!" It was true. Anne was fine. She hadn't been eaten by the...the.... "Hole-worm!"

Daisuke turned, face white and contorted. "*What?*"

Anne grinned at him.

"What?" he demanded. "Are you all right? What happened?"

"*Somebody* set off the wormhole!"

He glanced back at the cave mouth. "That was the wormhole?" Then back at her. Color was coming back into his face. "Who set off the wormhole?"

Anne rolled her eyes. "It was Moon and Farhad, obviously."

The wind narrowed to a whistle and vanished. The delicate cobwebs of mist melted under the attention of buzzing scavengers. Something popped and darted: another rocket-animal.

Daisuke shook his head groggily. "What did Moon and Farhad do? You told me the mountain is alive?"

"Yeah, but then you distracted me." Anne sniffed. More cat piss and vinegar. Bleh. "I didn't have time to put together the walls of this cave that have been bored into the mountain. And the buds, Daisuke! The fuzzy-buds!"

He turned around and hugged her. She kept talking.

"Why does the Howling Mountain howl? We knew that the sound was probably caused by air rushing through a wormhole into space, but what opens the wormhole? Why does the mountain only howl sometimes? Why did it howl just now?"

He breathed out into her neck. "Are we safe?"

"Yes," Anne said. "Mm. Probably."

"Anne!"

"Unless Farhad and Moon trigger it again." Anne frowned. "We should call them to make sure they're okay. And find out what they did."

Daisuke let go of her and patted his trousers and belt. They were unfastened, but still present. "You don't sound angry at them."

Ridiculously, Anne looked down at herself, as if she could see into her chest and check her heart for malfunctions. "I guess I'm not." That was a stranger revelation than everything she'd just figured out about the Howling Mountain. "I'm actually grateful for them. They set off the wormhole and told me how this mountain works."

Daisuke pressed the squawk button and got a squawk back. If it was possible for a walkie-talkie to sound panicky, this one did.

Farhad's voice came through, thin and shaky. "It seems that nobody in the expedition has been eaten." He explained that his team had cut through one of the 'big round trees' growing under a cave. This had turned out to be a very bad idea. "Anne, I apologize for my act of destruction in the Dorado biome. In the future, I promise you I'll ask for your opinion before I engage in any environmental intervention."

Anne's first thought was, *Yeah, right.* Her second thought, though, was, *You're scared.* Then another thought: *Did he say 'eaten'?*

"There's something big in the mountain, Anne. Stay with Daisuke."

Daisuke's arms tightened around her.

Anne's first thought was, *You're manipulating Daisuke.* The anger came next, pulled behind the first like the next carriage in a train. But there were more thoughts, weren't there, behind this one? Anne followed the train of deduction as if she was figuring out an alien biome's food-web. Right. So, Farhad was trying to trigger Daisuke's overdeveloped protective instincts. But why would he do that? See the previous hypothesis, re: Farhad was terrified. He was grasping at every lever of control, trying to stay on top of the situation when really, what he *should* get was....

"*You* need help from *us*," Anne declared. "You need explanations."

She looked up at the smooth walls of the cave, out at the hard, round, Velcro-covered shells of the buds that only seemed to bloom on one place on the mountain.

"You saw the hole-worm, didn't you?" she said. "It ate the fuzzy-bud when you cut its stem."

"Um. What? I don't quite follow your terminology."

Anne rolled her eyes. "Come to us. We're halfway up the mountain just like you, on the south-eastern face." Anne thought of what Farhad would want to hear. "You're safe. Um. I know how to get us into space."

"What?" said Daisuke at the same time Farhad asked, "How?"

Anne imagined the mountain's interior. Tiny, stone-skinned twigs came together into large branches, which converged with each other until they formed four mighty trunks. No, six, including the top and bottom faces. Here at the surface, the twigs were so small and numerous they were basically a solid mass, although one with lots of tiny air pockets. In the center, though, there would be enormous empty volumes. And nature abhorred a vacuum.

Daisuke stood and zipped up his trousers.

What if a wormhole leading to orbit sat here for a hundred million years? Surely something would evolve that exploited it. Anne imagined a worm boring into the mountain, eating through rock with the aid of, perhaps, an acid that smelled like cat piss and vinegar? The worm would thread itself through and between those internal trunks, its mouth opening outward into the nutritious air, while its anus found the mountain's heart.

You could grow or shrink a wormhole. You could switch it on and off. The worms in the mountain could use this mind-bending rip in space-time to suck food into their mouths. The mountain, in turn, could grow a seed with a fuzzy exterior. That fuzz captures food for the worm. The interior stays safe as it's passed into space, where it can germinate.

A slow, wicked smile spread over Anne's face. She had a hypothesis to test.

★ ★ ★

"Not only wormholes," Daisuke. "But also...hole...worms?"

They had spent about an hour making their way around the waist of the mountain. Now, from the way the ground was sloping, Anne could tell they were getting close to Farhad's camp.

"It makes sense," said Anne. "An entire ecosystem, this entire mountain, has grown up around the suction provided by the wormhole pulling air into orbit."

"So then what happened to Farhad?"

Anne scraped her boots over the mountain's petrified skin. "He cut down a fuzzy-bud to see what would happen, and what happened was a great stonking worm came out of the cave and swallowed it."

"That's what should happen, right?"

"Right. Some kind of mutualism. I'm thinking the stuff stuck to the outside of the capsule is a treat for the worm. An incentive. The stuff inside the capsule is for a seed." Although now that Anne voiced the assumption, it didn't ring true. "Or not. Not sure about that yet."

There had to be a way for things to come down from space as well as go up to it. The vacuum-spinners proved that. What tests could Anne do?

They rounded a pair of ribbon-leaves and came out onto a slope above another cave. Anne could see the ATV and the tent that Farhad's group had pitched among the fuzzy-buds.

"I think we'll need to camp out here for a few days," she said. "See whether the bud stays in space or comes back, and in what condition." Maybe they'd get the chance to have sex again.

"We can do it this time," Anne said, mostly to herself. "We'll keep him from doing anything stupid." She glanced up at Daisuke. "Um. Maybe you'll tell me how I should play this?"

"You should impress them," he told her. "Tell them what you believe is happening and why. Understanding will give them a feeling of control."

"Right."

Anne reviewed her options, straightened her clothes, and descended to meet the others.

It chose that moment to vomit.

There was no noise this time, not so much as a rumble. The cave on this face of the mountain simply welled with clear, foul-smelling jelly.

From their vantage point, Anne and Daisuke watched Farhad and the others flee their tent and scatter from the path of the slow, gloopy avalanche.

"Should we help?" Daisuke asked.

"Naw. It doesn't look like anyone is dumb enough to touch the stuff, and it isn't exactly racing after them."

The vinegar stench grew stronger, but Anne didn't see anything smoking. The jelly just rolled harmlessly around the tent and unripe buds. It stopped. Quivered. Quivered again.

"Oh, I see," said Anne. "There it is."

A fuzzy-bud the size of a compact car appeared in the cave mouth, covered in jelly. It rolled over the lip of the cave, then slid down the rest of the greasy way. Once the bud was back where it had started, the jelly withdrew, sucked back into the cave like a noodle into a pair of lips. Once it was in the open air again, the aperture at the end sagged open. A coatl wriggled out.

"Ha!" Anne shouted, and everyone looked up at her.

★ ★ ★

"You predicted all of that?" asked Farhad, a few minutes later.

He had led the way to meet Anne and Daisuke at the cave. Moon swayed and stumbled behind him, clutching a long plastic tube like a discount wizard's staff. Then came Boss Rudi, with Turtle and Aimi bringing up the rear. Were they holding hands? When had that happened?

Anne felt as if she'd been asleep for the past week, or wearing blinders. Her hand slipped back and reached for Daisuke, who grabbed it.

"Well, no," she admitted. "I didn't think the worm would spit the fuzzy-bud back up so soon. Maybe because it wasn't fully loaded?"

"'Fuzzy-bud'?" said Farhad. "Are we entirely sure about that name?"

"Never mind about the names." Moon came to a stop. The butt of his plastic staff came down as if he wanted to lean on it, but the physicist jerked it back up at the last moment and tucked it under his arm. "She's expecting me to get into one of those things and ride it through the portal."

"Congratulations on experimental support for you hypothesis," Anne said. "How else do you think you're going to get into space?"

Moon looked at her as if she'd thrown a brick of gold at him. On guard, but hoping for more.

"You're excited," Farhad said after a pause. "I'm very glad to see it, but I'd appreciate a slower and more coherent explanation. With an emphasis on safety. How do we get into space now?"

"Okay." Anne pretended she was sitting on a funding committee. "My guess is that there's some kind of cycle. We see this Velcro stuff all over the buds? This fuzz?" She walked toward the buds, realized Farhad and Moon weren't following, and turned around, gesturing. "Well, come on! Do you want me to explain it or not?"

They followed, and Anne lectured. "You already know the mountain is alive. It attracts animals to bring resources to it, which it stores in fuzzy-buds like the one you cut down. That action triggered the hole-worm that lives in the cave to come out and swallow the bud. Although I guess 'bud' isn't the right word for it. I was thinking flowers and fruits at first, but that's not what's going on here. These things aren't seeds, they're more like cargo containers. Space capsules. Is there a bio-word for that? Receptacles? Macro-vesicles?"

Moon groaned and fell into a sitting position. Farhad cleared his throat.

"Let's call it a *capsule-pod*. When it dropped off its stalk, the worm came out and ate it, using the vacuum of space to pull the capsule through its digestive system."

"That doesn't sound safe," said Farhad.

"But we just saw the pod return, right?" Anne gestured at the spent, sagging structure. "The same one you saw depart just a few hours ago."

"We could probably use it for another tent," Daisuke said.

Anne found the next largest pod, still attached to the round and covered with hair. Closer up, she could see that its outer covering was stuffed with detritus, and crawling with small animals. "You see this stuff? None of it left on the pod that came back, is there? The worm slurped it in, scraped it off, and spat the pod back out. The interior was fine. That coatl lived through the experience, anyway."

"What coatl?" Farhad asked.

"I saw it too," said Aimi, cutting short another long explanation that Anne didn't want to sit through. She was fizzing with energy, bouncing on her feet. Where did the logical thread lead?

Farhad bobbed his head, thinking. "If I understand you right, you're saying this mountain is a biological spaceport."

"What this mountain is," Anne said, "is an entire ecosystem evolved to act as an airlock around the wormhole at the center. Ribbon-leaves drag stuff up here from the ground, store it in and on these capsule-pods. Once the pods are full, they close and break off from their stems, which is a signal for the hole-worm to eat them. At some point the toymakers and the cavaliers and coatls and whatever else got into the act too. They bring cargo from all over and deliver it into space."

"Why would the toymakers want to go into space?" asked Farhad. "What do they get out of the deal?"

"That's actually a really good question. I suppose to get resources?" Although now that Anne thought of it, what resources were there in space? "Maybe they have uses for organisms that don't live on the surface of the planet? I'd like to find out."

Farhad nodded as if he got it. "So this is it. This is why Junction's creators built this place."

"Natural selection would do just fine. You have a wormhole to orbit, and something evolves to plug it. This place is no different from a mangrove forest, where selective forces over millions of years reward co-operation."

"Millions of years," Farhad repeated. "If we leave it alone, we won't need to add any other investments. We can just squat on it and charge our fees to passengers."

Anne's skin crawled, but she pasted on a smile.

If Farhad noticed the pro-social fakery, he pretended it was real. Fakery of his own? "But," he said, "that's a lot of assumptions. What if you're wrong and this seed comes apart and gets digested in the worm, along with anyone who's inside?"

"What if coatls can survive things that humans can't?" asked Moon.

"*Now* you're worried about the danger?" Anne asked. "What about all the other stuff you blew the hell up just to see what would happen?"

Daisuke cleared his throat.

"Um," Anne said, "I mean I have an answer to your question—"

But Moon had turned to Farhad. "It'd be safer if we just broke into the wormhole at the center of the mountain and used our own tether and winch."

"No?" said Anne.

"How difficult will it be to cut into the mountain?" Farhad asked Moon, who shrugged.

"You're not cutting into the—" Anne took a deep breath. Trust. Trust! Farhad was thinking about human safety. He would be a fool not to. Anne imagined worst-case scenarios. "Right. Let's say the worm crunches down on us like we're a gobstopper. Or it traps us for a month while its digestive system works. Or its internal processes produce some kind of horrible poison that somehow gets through our space suits...."

The men looked ill.

"That's *still* a safer bet than fucking *walking* down the worm's gullet and taking a chainsaw to its internal organs. How the hell do you think it would react to that?"

Moon stared at her. "I imagine it would die."

"And then what? Do you have equipment to haul its carcass out of the mountain? No." Anne focused on Farhad. "All my plan needs are natural processes that have worked for tens of millions of years, three space suits, and that tether and winch. We bolt the tether to the inside of the capsule-pod and trail it out the door behind us. You haul us in after we're done."

Farhad met her eyes. What was the expression on his face? Pride that Anne was learning to bargain? Shrewd consideration that she might conveniently get herself killed and spare him a lot of explaining later? Satisfaction that his expert had given him an action plan? Just a polite mask while Farhad hummed to himself and imagined his future grandchildren? What did he want? What was he plotting? Did she know that he knew that she...?

Daisuke squeezed her hand. Anne thought of spending the rest of her life with him, and the answer appeared. "Will we have radios?" he asked.

"Yes," said Farhad. "This is more complicated than I expected. I think we should test it first."

"No," Moon looked down. Nodded to himself. "No, I like Anne's plan. It's the fastest way."

"If the pod closes around us, how will we leave it to launch the satellite?" Daisuke asked.

"Who cares?" Moon said.

"You don't care about the satellite?" Daisuke asked.

Farhad put out his hands to silence them. "I'll talk to Turtle and Boss Rudi about that. And maybe some more clothes for you, Anne? You must be cold."

She had to admit that she was.

Farhad bowed. "Then it's a good thing I had your space suits carried all this way up the mountain."

★ ★ ★

Farhad gave the tether a tug. It seemed quite firmly fixed to the inside of the capsule-pod. Some things he was not willing to leave up to the grace of the hole-worm.

"Why do you want me to do this?"

He turned at Anne's voice, but it hadn't come from behind him. Of course, Anne was already inside the capsule-pod. The aperture at the top had sealed shut around the spare tire they had used as a porthole. Farhad was hearing her voice in his headset. *You foolish old man.*

"Are you asking me to abort?" he said. "If you don't want to go—"

"No, I do, but why do you?" He couldn't see her expression, but the voice got softer. "Why do you trust me?" Now that was a defter question than Farhad would have expected from the socially maladroit biologist. Something had happened to her on her climb up the mountain. Anne had made her transformation.

Farhad didn't expect she would thank him, but he still felt pride anyway. It wasn't the first time he'd saved an employee's marriage.

But there was still her question to answer. Farhad checked to make sure they weren't talking over the global channel and said, "I have several reasons to trust you, Anne." He heard her snort and skipped them. "But it's more to the point that I trust Professor Moon rather less."

"Why? Isn't he doing exactly what you want?"

"No, he's doing exactly what *he* wants," Farhad said. "I'm enabling that because it fits within my greater goals. But now that we've come to a potential divergence, I need to be absolutely certain that my experiments get carried out, not just his, and that I am told their results accurately."

Silence over the radio. The aperture was closed now, tight around the spare tire porthole. The edges of the aperture had sawed through the rubber of the tire, but the metal hub and the tether threaded through it seemed fine.

The skin of this capsule-pod would make Farhad a lot of money. It weighed almost nothing – the pods could be sucked into the worm's mouth with the force of air pressure alone, after all – but it had been very difficult to drill into.

Anne had speculated wildly about the material's composition and Farhad had smiled and nodded. What a relief it was to not have to push and pull the biologist everywhere. Instead, he could do what he had always wanted: let Anne ramble, take notes, and make a fortune off her little parenthetical asides. A material as hard as rock and light as air. Soap-bubble semiconductors. Rocket-animals. A biological spaceport. And that was just what she'd discovered on the climb up the mountain. If all it took to get her co-operation was a concession that risked her life? Well, she'd signed the forms.

"Ready," came Moon's voice over the radio, followed by Daisuke's and Anne's. Farhad waved to Turtle, who started up the chainsaw and pressed it to the stalk of the capsule-seed.

It was very much as before. The outer layer of the trunk wasn't fibrous like wood. It was tough like leather, hard like concrete, and soft like wet clay in concentric layers. Turtle said that the first time he'd done this, the hard parts had retracted. A response to damage?

The capsule shuddered and tipped onto its side. It stuck there, hooks digging into the ground.

And the worm arrived.

It flowed like water from the mouth of its cave. Transparent, stinking, salted with multicolored organs and threaded with white vessels that might have been for blood, the amorphous blob spilled down the hillside and washed over the capsule. Gobbets of transparent flesh splashed up with the force of the impact, but they did not fall.

The transition was as fast as blinking. One moment, the hole-worm was a wave of liquid protoplasm cresting over the capsule. The next, it was a solid, glassy tube. The transparent substance of its body had snapped into shape, every chunk sucked back into its smooth walls.

The worm rested. Waves of iridescence washed up and down its length, highlighting diamond facets. A fitful shudder as the organism seated the capsule more securely within itself. Its front end had become a smooth cap, slightly puckered around the place where the tether protruded.

Farhad's ear hairs tickled, and he became aware of a high, teakettle whistle.

"Back!" he shouted to Aimi and Turtle.

The rock around the mouth of the cave was covered in white, serpentine organs. Tentacles? Tree roots? Anchors? What sort of magic phase-changing stuff was this worm made of? Another potential fortune there.

But he was running. He had to run down into the remaining buds, because the whistle had become a roar. A howl. The air ran with living mist.

His ears popped. The mountain hopped under him, as if he stood on the chest of a giant who'd just sneezed. There was a horrible sound. And the hole-worm and capsule were gone.

Farhad swallowed and watched the tether hiss away down into the mountain.

★ ★ ★

The capsule went dark and a sudden noise and acceleration shoved Anne against the inner wall.

"Not anything near what we need," Moon muttered.

"Anne, what's happening?" asked Daisuke.

"Don't worry," she said. "We've just been swallowed."

One nice thing about the space suits was their radios. The roar of the vacuum at the center of the mountain should have been deafening, but all Anne got from it were the rumbles transmitted through her suit pressing against the skin of the capsule.

Something brushed past the wall. Another something. Anne imagined combs, baleen, and the scrubbing cylinders of an automatic car wash. The hole-worm, sucking the nutrition off their capsule's skin? Or maybe there was something more subtle going on here? Kinetosynthesis powered by their movement over biological switches? Magnetosynthesis? In any case, the worm was taking its payment for the journey.

Daisuke switched his helmet light on. It didn't illuminate much except their three huddled bodies and the dirty inner surface of the capsule-seed.

He swallowed a sudden bubble of nausea and said, "Anne, how is our rope?"

She turned to look at it and got a glimpse of the vibrating nylon cord, a *great* deal of transparent mucus, and a flash of light from outside the capsule.

The vibration of their passage rose to a peak and vanished.

"Oh," Moon said. "Hold—"

The capsule-seed filled with wind and light.

CHAPTER NINETEEN

Space Monsters

Anne felt the blast in her whole body. Especially in her waist, where the savage tug on her carabiner tried to rip the belt off her space suit. The air in front of her was white with swirling fog and her back hit something that spun up and away forever.

She blinked up through the top of her helmet. Their impromptu plug was gone. Wisps of fog tore away from the spare tire, flipping end over end like a dropped coin.

And beyond it, the spinning stars.

Her suit radio crackled with Daisuke's voice. "Anne! Anne, are you all right?"

"I'm in space," she whispered. Then, "Uh. I think so." Anne wiggled her arms and legs, and nothing hurt. It was just that she couldn't move. "What happened?" She looked down. "Oh."

Moon said something with lots of *sh* and *kh* sounds in it. Most likely profane. "The capsule-pod exploded!"

"Yeah," Anne agreed, patting the skin of what had once been a spherical pod.

That skin came up to her waist, hugged her legs, and bulged back outward again. The pod looked like a pear, now, the aperture fractured around four fault lines and pursed out into a long bottleneck, which Anne currently plugged.

She was stuck halfway out of the pod like a reversed Winnie the Pooh. No damage to her suit as far as she could tell.

"Yeah, that actually makes a lot of sense. Normally the air and water would diffuse out of the aperture of the pod and into the body of the worm, where I guess it would release them slowly. But the hubcap airlock we rigged screwed up the system. Good thing we have our own tether and space suits, otherwise we'd be floating in, uh, space." And dead.

Anne closed her eyes and told her heart to slow down. Too late for second-guessing now.

She should have told that to Moon. "Why didn't you predict this?" he demanded.

Anne wiggled irritably and the pod's skin flexed around her. "I'm not actually omniscient. You're the one who kept rushing the preparations." And at Daisuke's noises. "No, I'm sure my suit's still good. I'm just stuck."

"Farhad to Moon," came another voice. "Come in, Moon. Come in, Anne. Daisuke? Are you there?"

At least the relays in the tether were undamaged. "We're here," Anne answered. "We're through." She kept her eyes closed. The spinning was making her dizzy, and she had this pervasive sense of falling.

"How's the tether on your side?"

A pause, then Daisuke answered, "I think it is still firmly attached to the inside of the pod. Moon, help me pull Anne back inside."

"Uh, tether looks good." At least, they didn't seem to be drifting anywhere. They just stopped twisting one way and began untwisting in the other. That meant the tether had to be under tension, which meant it was still anchored to a mountain on the surface of Junction.

How did that work? They went right through one end of the worm and out the other, with the worm itself threaded through the wormhole, straddling both sides of the...surface? Meniscus? Event horizon? The boundary must extend all the way through the worm's cross section. Otherwise it wouldn't be able to pass things into orbit. Or circulate blood to its nether regions. Every second it sat there, however much mass of blood and air and everything else had to be magicked into and out of Junction's gravity well.

Where did the energy come from to do that? And what if you had two worms, one above the other, each threaded through different ends of the same wormhole? Something could drop from the mouth of the top worm into the mouth of the bottom one, get teleported back to the top one, and fall again, forever. Anne began to understand why wormholes upset Moon so much.

"Excellent!" Farhad said. "Scientists, you may begin your science!"

"Can we bring Anne back inside?" asked Daisuke.

"Pushing her out would be easier," Moon said.

"Here, let me see if I can pull myself out." Anne placed her hands on the lips of the aperture. The edges resisted like cold caramel, cracking off and bending. "Give my feet a push, would you?"

"Yes, Anne. Moon, help me."

"No. I'm busy."

"Busy doing what?" Anne asked. "What could you possibly be busy with inside a three-meter-across pod floating in space?"

"He's trying to open the plastic tube. What is that, Professor? Is it important?"

Silence from Moon, a sigh from Daisuke, and ineffectual shoves and nudges while he figured out leverage in free fall. Anne felt pressure on the soles of her feet, and rocky skin crumbled around her waist. Her arms windmilled as she found herself sliding out of the neck of the bottle.

There was a moment of intense nausea. Without gravity, Anne's brain couldn't decide whether she was rising up the tether, or sliding down headfirst.

She closed her eyes and swallowed, willing her inner ears to accept the first interpretation. There were stars out there, weren't there? Stars were in the sky.

Except now the stars were all around her. And, as the capsule, tether, and Anne spun, more celestial objects joined in the carousel. A yellow sun and blue planet passed back and forth across Anne's view, as if the universe had decided that she belonged at its center.

"Okay," she said. "There's a planet out here."

"Is it Junction?" asked Moon urgently. "No. No, it can't be Junction."

"Isn't that the whole point of this operation? Figuring that out?" Another pause as the tether reached the end of its spin in one direction and started in on the other. Anne closed her eyes and focused on not throwing up.

"Exactly. It is time to launch the nanosat," Farhad said over the radio. "Then we'll see if I can pick up its signal."

"What about the spin?" asked Daisuke.

"None of that matters," Moon growled. He grunted as if pushing on something. "The only thing that's important is...*oof!* This...."

The intersuit radios worked great. Anne heard Farhad's sigh as if he was breathing in her ear. "Daisuke, would you see if you can poke your head out the hole, then? Just shove the nanosat out."

"This is such a bullshit operation," Anne muttered, looking down.

Daisuke looked back up at her, his body angled somewhere between the horizontal and vertical. In one hand he held the tether, cradling the toaster-sized nanosat in his other arm.

It was only because she happened to be looking in that direction that Anne saw the flock of animals. They were the size and shape of muffins, but moving faster than thrown javelins. They hit the capsule muffin-top-first, stuck for a second, then bounced off at an angle. The capsule's spin slowed.

"What happened?" Daisuke demanded.

"Ha," Anne said. "Momentum parasites."

"There are living things out there?" He shook his head in the helmet. "Of course, that's why we came here. Anne, I'm going to give you the nanosat. Will you grab it?"

Anne reached down to grab the little machine. She'd had dogs that wouldn't fit in a box this big. "I just throw it somewhere?"

"There's no need to throw anything," said Moon. "If we're orbiting the planet, you can just hold it out and let it go. Now, Daisuke, will you please come help me?"

Were they orbiting the planet? Anne watched the blue-and-white disk slide past, as big as half the sky. They were spinning slowly enough now that she could make out the shapes of clouds and continents, but she couldn't tell if they were sinking toward it or rising away.

Anne held the nanosat out and let go of it. The cube neither fell nor rose nor went anywhere at all. It just sat there in the space where she'd placed it, with just a bit of wobble. Anne thought about that.

Nanosat and Anne faced each other. Anne faced the blue planet, at the moment at least, with the sun at her back. At her feet was the capsule-pod. Above her head....

Anne grabbed the tether and leaned back, looking down...up... *along* the twisted nylon to the wormhole.

At least that's what Anne assumed was up there. All she could see right now was a giant pearly mushroom. At first, Anne thought that was the cloud of air blown out of the capsule-pod. Except there seemed to be an awful lot of it. Air hemorrhaging out of Junction's atmosphere? But that should look like a jet, shouldn't it? This cloud spread very slowly, gaining bulges and wrinkles, shot through with tiny, darting shapes. It was hard to judge how large those shapes were, but they swarmed, swung, and blasted about on puffs of exhaust. Laser light flickered.

A spring-shaped animal twisted out of the cloud, compressed flat, and sprang off. It left a crater behind.

"Not a cloud, then, but some kind of gel? An excellent way of conserving resources, make sure that the air and water don't get away," Anne said. "Maybe the worm is related to the living mist. Or uses living mist as a symbiote? Or is the mist even alive in its own right? Maybe it's just an excretion." That would make sense, given the speed they were going and the number of spines on the capsule-pod. "Without an awful lot of lubrication, we would have torn this worm a new one."

"Ugh," said Moon and Daisuke.

"Anne, is the nanosat broadcasting?" Farhad asked.

Anne checked. "The little green light is on."

"I'm not getting anything yet," Farhad said.

"Good. Finally something makes sense." Another grunt. "Daisuke, help me open this."

Anne turned her attention back to the gel cloud. Small objects pelted it like hailstones. More momentum parasites? Some managed to chip a few pieces off it. That gel must be hardening quickly.

And beyond it....

At first she thought they were unusually bright, unusually colored stars. Then she saw one with a cage around it. Others were covered in foam or shimmering bubbles or bloomed with the mucus-clouds of other hole-worms. Others shone unprotected, transmitting light from some distant part of space.

"It's the Nightbow," Anne said.

"The what?"

"The ring of wormholes around Junction. You saw it on our first night here. There."

She twisted her head around. The wormholes seemed to form a ceiling above her head. "We must be to the right or left of it. Sticking out sideways, and spinning."

Moon managed to disagree with her while saying she was right. "You mean we're above or below the plane of an equatorial portal ring. That's the best configuration for placing things in orbit. Above some *other* planet." Moon was still trying to open his tube.

"Everything all right up there?" asked Farhad.

"Moon's frustrated," Daisuke said. "He can't open his pipe. Is there a machine inside?"

Anne decided not to get involved. Better to take in the scenery while she was in a position to enjoy it.

"We can bring you back and try again," Farhad offered.

"No! No time. No second chances." Moon's voice descended into a growl.

The spinning wasn't so bad now. If Anne circled the tether with her arms and jumped off the capsule at just the right angle....

"Oh! The wall moved," Daisuke said.

Moon said, "Anne, what are you doing?"

She was spinning, was what she was doing. Contrary to the spin of the capsule. That meant that relative to Junction, Anne was more or less stationary.

And she could finally look at it.

The planet shone blue below her. Swirled with clouds, ringed by wormholes and life. Objects down there in the atmosphere, like black arrowheads, their noses shining, silhouetted themselves against the colors of their planet.

Sunlight refracted off air that pooled like tears over the lens of an eye. Algae-colored oceans exhaled clouds. And past fractal coastlines, over land wrinkled and upthrust by opposed tectonic forces, a boiling chaos of colors – green, red, brown, yellow – as different kinds of life battled each other. The planet was a patchwork, at once seething with competition and timeless in stability. A battlefield and a mosaic as lovely as a butterfly's wing.

"Look," she whispered to herself. "Look at this view."

"Oh," Farhad said in her suit radio. "Wait! I'm getting something! Yes. Yes! We're receiving a signal from the nanosat. You're in orbit!

You're above me. You're orbiting Junction!"

Anne smiled behind her visor. "I know."

★ ★ ★

Moon's hands twitched and he lost his grip on the tube. Again!

He was going to die. Here or down on some planet, it didn't matter. His brain would scramble itself and he'd never know why – *why!* – one face of the portal had brought him into the same light cone as the other.

"Moon? What's wrong? Are you all right?"

It was Daisuke again with his stupid questions. Moon put his hands up to his faceplate, trying to hide his tears.

"Moon, come in. Come in, son!" That was Farhad, the cruel old manipulator.

"I'm...." But he couldn't say 'fine'. Some things were just impossible. "I'm done. I give up. I can't understand these things."

"The wormholes?"

Moon twitched again. His heart sped up, flushing warm blood through his extremities. What a ridiculous sack of meat the human body was. "You're still calling them wormholes. They can't be wormholes. They're something else. Something with its own internal energy source. Something that protects the people traveling through it. A user interface."

"So, son," said Farhad. "Use it."

"Use it." Moon blinked and droplets floated away from his eyes. "Yes." A strange laxness had come into his limbs. A kind of peace. He would never know how the portals worked. He could only mash his pitiful paws against them and see what happened. Was that enough? Maybe when the monkey beeped the car's horn enough, he might attract the owner's attention. Maybe the owner would give the monkey what it needed.

The plastic pipe floated between Moon and Daisuke, spinning like a baton. Moon reached for it.

"All right," he said. "Daisuke. Help me with this."

★ ★ ★

Anne breathed a sigh of relief. She had no idea what Moon was going on about, but Daisuke and Farhad would know. Trust. She would trust them to work their people-magic on Moon while she got down to the business of understanding this orbital ecosystem.

She was reminded of blue-water diving. Out in the ocean, you found yourself floating in a medium that seemed to extend to infinity in every direction. Here, there weren't even bubbles to follow to the surface. Only stars.

And some things that weren't stars.

The easiest to spot were the disks. They were right in front of her, if very far away. Perfect circles, at least as far as Anne could tell, which ranged in shade from 'dirty snow' to 'coal', these latter only visible when they passed in front of something else. Most of the circles, though, were somewhere in between, a color Anne decided to call 'pigeon's tummy'.

The disks looked rather like a bloom of moon-jellies seen from above. Except these creatures didn't seem to be moving – no, that sort of thinking didn't work up here. Of course, the disks had to be whizzing about the planet just as fast as Anne was. Say instead that they weren't visibly changing position relative to Anne or each other, although Anne did have the impression that the largest ones were spinning.

Spinning. Anne's fingers clenched in her gloves, as if to clutch around that little black velvet box. The gift from the Nun, the bait on Farhad's hook. Anne was looking at vacuum-spinners.

Unfurled, the skirts of the spinners were each many kilometers across. The organisms had angled themselves – yes! – to catch the sun, presenting their biggest profile to Anne. They would also have to be spinning against Junction's magnetic field. The only place they could spin and face the sun, then, would be if they were hovering above Junction's day–night terminator.

No, of course, not *hovering*; the spinners were orbiting as well. They would be in a ring, but tilted perpendicular to the equator-girdling Nightbow. The ring of spinners would pass over the poles instead. That would explain what Anne was seeing now, which was a wall of variously shaded disks, stretching above and below, curving to outline Junction's horizon.

Anne imagined those organisms spinning, orbiting, pushed away from the sun by the pressure of light and toward the equator by the charged particles they captured. How did they stay on the right path? Minute adjustments of the shade and shape of their skirts? Her eyes crossed. When she focused again, the arcing curtain of spinners had changed. The ones farthest away, at the ends of the arc, were farther apart, and the ones more directly in front of her were larger. *Aha.* They hadn't moved; Anne had. Her part of the Nightbow was carrying her toward the ring of spinners.

What happened in the places where the two rings met? That should be interesting.

Moon groaned over the radio.

"Is everything all right?" Farhad asked.

"This pipe is very hard to open with space suit gloves," said Daisuke, his voice earnest.

"Sorry," Farhad said. "I didn't think of that. Should I reel you in and try—"

"No!" Moon started shouting before Farhad could finish. "I can open it. I'm so close!"

"Close to what?" Daisuke asked.

Anne wanted to tell him to just take the damn pipe away from Moon. They could figure out what was in it when they got back to Junction.

But Daisuke's plan was more subtle. "I think that you're obsessed with wormholes, Professor Moon."

"Portals!"

"Okay, okay. Try it this way. Hold it."

The capsule twisted under Anne, rotating around the tether.

"Whoa," said Anne. "How's it going down there?"

"Moon's feet are on the wall and he is twisting us around," Daisuke answered. "He's using himself and the whole capsule and tether and worm as a giant wrench." Moon grunted, and Daisuke said, "It's very frustrating, isn't it? The portals don't make sense to you. Even after you destroyed one and passed through another. The third one you stole, didn't you?"

"No," Moon said, utterly unconvincingly. "Like this. Give it back. Now hold it orthogonally. No, not that orthogonal. Like you're lifting weights. Yes."

"Don't be ridiculous, Daisuke," said Farhad. "How would one move a wormhole?"

The capsule twisted north-to-south, pressing the tether against the side of the hole.

"Christ," Anne said. "Hey, boys! Stop...well actually keep on it. I can see something under the capsule. I mean, uh, below the plane of the Nightbow."

There were things down there. Or possibly up. *Pole-ward*, Anne decided to call that direction. Out of the plane of the Nightbow, past her feet and the capsule-pod, objects moved. Organisms. Wrinkled and silver-gray objects like regularized meteors. The closest was rising sedately, rimmed with the light of Junction's sun.

"I don't know how you did it," said Daisuke. "I was distracted at the time. But if you could move a wormhole, that would be a very important discovery. If you could move a wormhole *through* another wormhole, that would be much more. If that was possible, you could move wormholes from Junction to Earth. You could sell them and make a fortune. Right, Farhad?"

Moon giggled. It was the sort of noise someone made when he could no longer control himself. "Who cares about the Earth? It's as much a distraction as Junction. Pretty animals and lights."

"Now, Daisuke, it is absolutely *not* my intent to sell wormholes to anyone who asks for one."

Anne knew the feeling in her chest, as if someone was draining the air in her lungs out the bottom. Farhad was about to say something political.

"Junction is a bottleneck, don't you see? If the entire effort has to go through the highlands of New Guinea, we won't be able to get nearly enough people off the Earth in time. But if Canada has one wormhole, for example, and Sweden has another."

"If people know that wormholes can be moved, anything can happen," Daisuke said. "Bombs. Wars! The powerful countries will collect all the wormholes they can find on Junction and hide them."

"Assuming someone doesn't try to send an aircraft carrier through a wormhole and cause it to evaporate and lose it forever." Anne couldn't sit down in free fall, but she dangled against the tether. "Shit," she said.

"World War Three," said Daisuke.

"The destruction of Junction!" Anne said. Blood hammered in her temples. "This is it. This is what this whole mission was really about. You came here to *mine* Junction of its wormholes."

"Who cares?" Moon said. "Aside from you? You just want to preserve Junction as a playground for yourself. So what if there's an ecological disaster, so what if there's a war? I've cracked the universe open and seen what's inside."

Anne saw the opening. Daisuke must have too. "So," he said, "what *do* you see, Professor Moon?"

"I've discovered *nothing*," Moon said. "After *everything* I've done. All the hope and fear in your eyes when you look at me. 'Moon, don't kill the pretty animals. Don't destroy the geopolitical order.' I have the power to grant or deny you whatever I want, and I still don't know *how*!"

Silence, then, Farhad said over the radio, "All right, I'm hauling you back. Forget the pipe, Moon. We can try to pass it through the wormhole you found in the Cavalier biome. Or somewhere else. Daisuke? Don't interfere. Come in, Daisuke! Come in!"

Something flashed on the surface of the meteor. Again. And a third time. Anne's eyes, attracted by the light, caught on familiar shapes. Mounds. Crowns of prickly growth, fuzzed with leaves like giant lead-colored ribbons. A shape like six clumps of broccoli stuck trunk-to-trunk and smooshed into a pyramid. The asteroid looked, in other words, like the Howling Mountain. Although much smaller....

Anne squinted.

Now the orbiting, living mountain looked bigger. And bigger still. It was moving much faster than Anne had realized. It was just that so much of that movement was *right toward* them.

"Guys?" she said. "I think we're going to need to abandon ship."

Of course the guys both said, "What?"

"Come in," said Farhad, which was harder to explain.

The space broccoli now filled the entire lower half of Anne's world.

"No!" Moon said. "It has to be now, there's no time!"

"You're panicking, Moon. There is still time. When America invades and collects all the portals, they'll put them in a research facility. You can head that facility, son."

The tether jerked. A vibration ran down it. Farhad was reeling them in. A second ago, Anne would have thought that was a bad thing. Now....

"Come on, son," said Farhad. "We've talked about this. My plan is the only way for you to make your discoveries while your brain still works."

A gleam against the blackness of space. Three shadows against the blue of Junction. Anne blinked and they were gone, but she had an impression of something long and thin, with a glow at its tail.

"Come on, son," Farhad repeated. "Moon. Come in!"

"Missiles," Anne said. "But I think they missed." Even Anne's tiny glimpse could only have come as the missiles passed her.

She turned, looking away from the mountain-ship, to see four bright sparks. Rocket engines? But why would the mountain fire missiles *past* the capsule? Was there something else waiting in space?

One of the missiles flipped.

It was as fast as flicking a light switch. A puff of white vapor and the drive flare flattened and vanished behind a dark, irregular oval. The nose of the missile was hard to see against the backdrop of space, but it seemed to be growing larger. Closer.

"Moon, come in!" Farhad's voice was strangely calm.

Of course! The mountain-ship was much too bulky to swoop around swallowing things in orbit. It would have trained rocket-animals. Mutualists like hunting falcons would snatch its prey for it.

"Moon, come in. Anne, come in. Daisuke, come in."

"Farhad, would you shut up!" Anne snarled. "Daisuke and Moon, get out of the pod right the fuck now!"

"Anne, I haven't said anything!" Now Farhad sounded as panicked as he should. "You're panicking. Come in." And calm again.

"Moon. Come. In."

The hair's bristled on Anne's neck. She gripped the tether tighter and bared her teeth at the mountain. The ship. A monkey might snarl like that at a zoologist with a net.

Exhaust sputtered around the outline of the mountain, aligning the clyclopean mouth that opened at its peak. "Come! In! Anne! Moon! Daisuke! Get out of the pod right the fuck now! Come! In!"

"Yes," said Moon. "*Yes.*"

Anne's stomach lurched. Or, rather, it settled. The sensation was pleasant after the floating feeling of free-fall, as if she were....

Was she accelerating? She looked around, but the missiles were still incoming, three of them on course to push three astronauts into that mouth. But the acceleration from the missiles would push her forward. This acceleration was pushing her up. Or pulling her down.

Dust settled around Anne's feet, onto the surface of the pod.

"Oh. Gravity," Anne said, and the pod blew out from under her.

CHAPTER TWENTY

The Purpose of Junction

It was as if Moon had uncorked a hurricane.

The cap of the pipe flew out of Moon's gloved fingers with the force of a gunshot. He could feel the concussion through his suit. He could *hear* it. *Bang.*

His eyes snapped closed, leaving afterimages burned onto his retinas: Daisuke's snarling face, his hands on Moon's wrists, Moon's own hands on the pipe, and the brilliant, orange-and-blue sphere of the wormhole.

Moon had known this was going to happen. Of course, what else could happen? If portals existed, and you could change their size, change their position, put one in a bottle, and pass it through another wormhole, what else *could* happen but violence and madness?

Now, though, there was nothing but howling wind, white with ice crystals. Segmented sticks smashed against squirming animals. A creature like a fish made of coiled ribbon bucked and belched as pressure differential unspooled its body. An entire world's atmosphere vomiting from the hole that Moon had made.

Detritus rattled and squelched against Moon. Something tugged on his wrists and waist. Something pressed against his belly. Those would be Daisuke's grip, the carabiner attached to the tether, and the butt end of the pipe. Yes, those vectors all lined up with Moon's predictions.

Except where was the impact on his back? Moon had expected to be thrown into the wall of the capsule. He'd also expected more spin than this. Moon had tried to align the pipe with his center of gravity, but Daisuke had been trying to wrestle the pipe out of his grip at the time. Moon was sure he hadn't achieved a ninety-degree angle with his belly. And where was the wall of the capsule?

The wind cleared, the pressure eased. The wormhole at the end of his pipe had vanished, and Moon could see the wall of the capsule now, flipping away into space behind Daisuke's shoulder, already thirty meters away or more.

Moon and Daisuke, clinging to each other, now spun in empty space.

Moon could explain that. The force of air outgassing from the portal had blown the capsule-pod. And most likely torn the pod inside-out.

Moon was in space, and Daisuke was with him. The carabiners that clipped them to the tether were designed to give way before the fabric of their suits, and so they had. All very sensible, post facto. But he hadn't predicted this. He hadn't predicted *this*!

Moon laughed. He was tethered to Daisuke, but not to any other reference point. The two of them were floating free in space! He laughed so hard he choked. He wept and gasped in his helmet. Moon had achieved the impossible. He had moved a portal through a portal. Everything would change now! Everything would be destroyed and remade! It was glorious.

New vectors of movement. Not around, as one would expect from the dynamics of gas escaping a roughly spherical volume, but back and forth. Ah, of course, that was oscillation caused by the observer being shaken. Another fascinating result of his experiment. The opening of a portal between vacuum and a planetary atmosphere causes a destructive outgassing, the death of the experimenter in space, and the violent anger of his companions. Moon should have predicted that too.

★ ★ ★

Daisuke grabbed the pipe and the wormhole vanished.

It was as if he'd flicked a switch. Daisuke's glove closed around the white PVC plastic and the misty, orange-blue heart of the hurricane blinked out. The tension in his stomach slacked. Gravity no longer pulled him toward the end of the pipe. The storm continued, but with each moment it was weaker.

The pipe was empty. No, it had some dirt inside, drifting up and out. Little sparkling specks. Daisuke put his thumb over the hole, plugging it, controlling what he could.

Ice, doubloons, and dead animals flew out into space. So did Daisuke and Moon.

The physicist's eyes were open now, but he didn't seem to see Daisuke. Moon howled, his face compressed around the hole of his mouth. He might have been screaming in despair, but the sound coming through the suit radio was laughter.

Daisuke shook him. Although with nothing to brace himself against, the motion was more like doing one-handed pushups. "Moon! Professor Moon! Dohyun!"

"Daisuke! Where are you? Shit!" That was Anne. Daisuke couldn't see her.

"Anne. I'm all right." Junction and its sun swung crazily around them as he and Moon tumbled. "My suit is not broken. Moon, is your suit broken? Anne, are you all right? We are..." he tried to control his breathing, "...falling."

Anne cursed again. "I can see that. Okay. What do I do? How do I solve this?"

"Anne?" Farhad said over the radio. "What's going on? What happened? Did Moon open the pipe?"

And then, in an entirely different tone, Farhad's voice said, "Come in. Come in, Moon. Come in, Daisuke."

★ ★ ★

"Oh right," said Anne. "You."

She was maybe a quarter of the way up the tether, all four limbs wrapped around it as it pulled her toward the wormhole like a huge, contracting rubber band. That would be great if her fiancé wasn't spinning off into space, an increasingly ridiculous distance away, the target of a flying, talking, hungry mountain.

Anne fought panic. She had to think. Observe. If she turned her head, she could see the sparks of the two missiles on their way to intercept Daisuke and Moon. Anne had several theories as to why, but maybe this time she had an easy way to test them.

"Hey," she said. "Hey you. Mountain-ship. Why did you fire missiles at us? *Are* you the Mountain-ship? Or the Zookeepers? One of those rocket-animals? Are you some other animal? Some kind of sit-and-wait ambush thing, with a radio lure, evolved to eat explorers? Or are you actually Farhad and I'm just going mad up here?" She was babbling.

The response wasn't much better. "You? The Zookeepers?" It switched to Farhad's voice. "Come in! To." And back to hers. "The mountain-ship? One of-anima-other animal d-wait a radio-l? Are you-ing mad up here?" And Daisuke: "I'm all right."

Moon made a disgusted noise. "This is ridiculous," he said. "*I* don't have any idea what you're talking about, and I'm a human who speaks English."

Anne stared at the gray pyramid rising between her and Junction. Was there even a message behind that gibberish? A mind? Would it be worth her time to imagine that she was talking to someone? Here she was again, in that corridor of mirrors. How could one intelligence ever know for certain it wasn't just talking to itself?

"Oh shit," she said. "This is the purpose of Junction."

"Anne?" It was Farhad. "What do you see? Is there some solution?"

Anne waved a hand at the blue planet hanging in front of her. "This planet isn't someone's ruined zoo. We're not the conquerors here, or even the looters. We're the *specimens!*"

Someone was trying to talk over her, but Anne didn't let them. Or it, as the case might be.

"Remember the toymakers and the cavaliers and the coatls? *Almost* intelligence. *Not quite* something you could talk to. And their concentration increased as we got closer to the mountain. They were pulled there. *We* were pulled here!"

"You think we were destined to come here?" Moon asked. For once, his voice contained no hint of sarcasm.

"Are insects destined to fall into a drop trap? No. You bury a little plastic cup with a sieve on the top, and bugs of the right size fall into it. We went up the Howling Mountain, got in the capsule, rode it through the hole-worm and the wormhole." She watched the ship grind out another revolution. "And now here comes someone to collect us."

Her own voice answered her. "The mountain-ship? Of the Nightbow in the capsule, the hole-worm and the wormhole." The mountain's voice switched to Moon's: "Portals!" and back to hers:

"The Howling Mountain. There's a planet out here. Of Junction."

"I think it agrees with me," said Anne.

"What are you suggesting, Anne?" Farhad asked. "Do you think this…this mountain-ship will collect you and put you safely back on Junction?"

"Well, biologists do sometimes put the animals they trap back where they found them," Anne said, "if they don't take them to the lab."

"Or kill them and dissect them on the spot! No. No, do not allow the mountain-ship to collect you," Farhad said, as if he had any say in the matter.

"Okay," said Anne. "Okay. Let me think. There would surely be easier ways to kill us, if that was the purpose of the mountain-ship. It makes much more sense if those rockets really are meant to push us gently into—"

"Its mouth?" Moon said.

"Come in! Come. Its mouth."

"You're not helping," Anne told the ship.

"Anne, it's all right."

"Mountain-ship, would you shut up?"

"Anne, I said that," said Daisuke. "It is all right. Moon and I will test your hypothesis for you. The rockets will pick us up. And you can climb back to Junction. You can get help for us. Right?"

Anne looked up the tether. She might be able to climb this rope, find some way past the foam cloud, and climb up the hole-worm's digestive tract to make it back to the surface of Junction.

"Wait just a minute, what sort of help can I get?" she said.

"Anne, I think he's right," that was Farhad. "You have my word—"

"Shut up, both of you! You're trying to manipulate me into leaving you, Dice, and I won't do it." Her hands shook as she fumbled around her waist, searching for the carabiner that attached her to the tether.

"It's better for two people to die than three, right?" said Daisuke.

A shudder climbed Anne's body. She'd been trying not to think about death. Could she get herself captured by the mountain as well? Or, if she was wrong, get blown up by its missiles, or just fall forever through space.

"You have my word. Push us, mountain-ship! Your hypothesis for you. The rockets will pick us up." The mountain-ship played back one of Anne's sobs too.

Anne took her hands away from her belt and put them back around the tether.

"Don't give up," said Daisuke, but his voice was hollow. Was that the sound of someone losing hope? Anne tried to hold on to her own. She pulled the tether through her hands, sliding herself 'up' toward the wormhole and its bolus of frozen mucus.

"There's got to be something," she said. "Daisuke, Moon. Do you two have any way to come back to me?"

"I don't know. I don't think so."

A cough. "Reaction mass," Moon said. "A whole planet's atmosphere worth of gas."

"Are you all right, Moon?" asked Daisuke, or possibly it was the mountain-ship.

"Shut up. Take your thumb off the end of my pipe...no, wait!"

"Wait!" echoed the mountain-ship. Then, eerily, "No."

Anne stiffened, but nothing happened. As far as she could tell, the two men were still spinning away below her.

"What happened?" she asked.

Moon swore under his breath. "What should have happened was the pipe should have rocketed away from Daisuke's hand as soon as he unstoppered my pipe. Instead, the portal must have shut down."

"Why did it shut down?" Daisuke's voice trembled.

"There's no air around us, obviously," said Moon. "The portals don't work unless there's breathable air on both faces."

Anne breathed a sigh of relief.

"All right," Farhad said. "Let's not do anything before we've all agreed on it, right?"

"And while we're waiting, the missiles will hit us," Moon said.

Anne looked and found them. "They've flipped over again," she said. "They're burning away from you."

"Yes, I can see the plumes," said Moon.

Anne raised her eyes and saw what he meant. The plume of her own missile was like a little sun, growing quickly.

"Slowing down to match velocities with us? Maybe they do intend to pick us up gently. Maybe they do intend to pick us up gently."

Was that Moon repeating himself, or the mountain-ship agreeing with him?

"Three missiles," said Anne. "Three passengers in the capsule. How did it know?"

"Wait," Daisuke said. "I'm thinking about air."

"Good for you," said Moon.

"Inside the capsule-pod, why did the pórtal open? There was no air inside the pod when you opened it."

"What are you talking about? I..." Moon's breathing came faster. "I don't know. I didn't even think of that. There was no air in the pod. Of course. How did I make that hurricane? Why did the portal open? It shouldn't have opened. But I knew it would. And just now...why?"

"Professor Moon, how can we use the portal?" Daisuke asked.

"We can't." Moon's voice was as hard and heavy as the mountain bearing down on them. "You're right. It shouldn't have worked at all. The experiment should have been an utter waste. I came up here for nothing!"

"Are you all right? Don't give up."

That was Daisuke's voice again in her ears, but somehow, Anne didn't think that it was Daisuke speaking them.

"Are you all right?" Now it was Anne's voice. "Come back to me?" Daisuke's again. "Breathe. Stay calm. Come back to me. Come in. Air. Air. Air. Air. Air."

Anne watched the mountain spin. "What are you telling us?"

It answered in Daisuke's voice: "The portal. The portal open. Open."

The missile streaked under her. Anne got a glimpse of a tangled mat of metal-colored tendrils, a puff of mist, a long silver-gray trunk, and a skirt of fire. Then it was past, receding toward the open peak of the mountain-ship. The rocket-animal − rocket-tree? − had missed her.

"It's better for two people to die than three, right?" came Daisuke's voice.

★ ★ ★

Daisuke cursed, but the ship didn't repeat him.

"Dice, that was the ship talking, wasn't it?" Anne said over the radio.

"Yes," he said. "But I still agree with it." What else could he do? If he could reach out and shove Anne back through the wormhole, he would.

"I don't think it understands what it's saying," Anne said. "Maybe it doesn't know what *die* means." But she was grasping at straws.

"Anne, I think it's time for you to find a way home." That was Farhad. His voice was heavy. "You'll get more than your research station. You'll get everything it is in my power to give. Daisuke, she will be the empress of Junction. Moon, every child will learn your name in school."

Daisuke knew he had no reason to believe this old villain, but he took comfort where he could get it. "Thank you," he said.

He expected Anne to rage against Farhad for trying to manipulate her. Instead, she said, "Wait a sec. That isn't Moon's tropism."

"What?" said Daisuke.

But Anne was still talking as she climbed, her voice that soft, musing murmur it got when most of her brain was involved in speculative science. "He doesn't even want to be the next Einstein. Not really. Not anymore. If he did, he'd give a damn about his reputation. He wouldn't keep Farhad's secrets for him, and Farhad would know that. Oh! That's why Farhad keeps calling Moon 'son'. He knows that Moon doesn't want science anymore."

"No!" Moon said. "I do! That's why I'm so angry that—"

"Moon wants a miracle. He wants to bring his father back."

Radio silence. Daisuke stared through his visor and Moon's into the man's eyes. Stars, planet, and orbital biome turned around them.

The physicist should have sneered. He should have waved a dismissive hand and said, 'Don't be stupid. That would be impossible.' Instead, he whispered, "How did you know?"

"I observed you," Anne said. "I know what kind of animal you are, Moon. You thought you were using wormholes to discover the new physics. But even if you were rushing to make your mark before the Alzheimer's gets you, that wouldn't explain how fast you're going. The corners you cut. You're frantic. In that way, you are like Farhad. You're not frightened for just yourself. You think you can save your father."

"Air," said the mountain-ship.

"I thought your father was dead," said Daisuke.

"As if that matters!" Moon snorted. "How can you still not see! We've *been* through the portals! You know they violate causality!"

"You mean," Daisuke suggested, "that they send us to places beyond our light cone?"

"You're just parroting words you don't understand! I might as well talk to the mountain."

"Moon, don't be a dipshit."

"Sorry," Moon said, and Anne wondered whether she could have saved everyone a lot of trouble if she'd had this exchange with him at the start of the expedition.

"Open," said the mountain. "Open. Come in."

Moon met Daisuke's eyes through their visors. "You idiots! You're so blinded by faster than light travel you can't see the applications: perpetual motion! Time travel!"

"I think I get the first one," Anne said. "You put one wormhole on top of the other and you'll fall through them forever."

"Baby stuff! Look!" Moon thrashed as if trying to escape his suit and explode. "You time-dilate Portal A. Accelerate it. Portal B continues to age normally, but Portal A stays young. For you and Portal B, a day or a year have passed, but for Portal A, it's still yesterday, it's still last year. Now if you go *through* Portal B, you have traveled into the past."

"Okay?" said Anne.

"What 'okay'? Don't you see what that means? You care about the environment so much. What if we could go back in time and make sure the environment is never damaged? We could un-do anything!"

"Well, if we had a handy pair of wormholes," Anne said. "One of which had already been conveniently accelerated by someone. Who? Friendly god-aliens who knew what we needed before we did?"

A light was growing on Daisuke's side.

"Yes," Moon said. He let go of the pipe that contained his stolen wormhole.

"Come in —ack to me," said the mountain-ship. "Two passengers."

"No," Moon said. "One passenger."

"One passenger," echoed the mountain-ship.

"Wait, what are you— Oof!"

Daisuke was still several logical steps behind the conversation, trying to figure out how time travel worked. Moon's shove took him entirely by surprise.

The force moved down Daisuke's arms and shoulders, rocking him backward. Moon drifted in the opposite direction, torso rotating away as his legs pointed toward Daisuke's chest. Moon's knees bent.

"Wait!" This time, Daisuke could see exactly what Moon was trying to do. But how could Daisuke stop him? Grab the man's ankles and throw off his launch? Doom both of them rather than save both? What was it Farhad had said about win-win scenarios?

Daisuke kept his arms spread, but he said, "Moon. Are you certain you want to do this?"

The physicist didn't answer with words. No doubt he thought that speaking would be a waste of time.

Moon just kicked Daisuke hard in the chest, and sent himself flying into space.

He spun as he flew, like an arrow aimed at the mountain-ship. Silent, except for the breathing on the suit radio. Daisuke tried to find the right words to tell him.

"It's all right, Moon," he said. "You're on the right course now."

"And brace for impact," came Anne's voice.

Moon's body, tiny now with distance, curled into a ball.

Then a flash. Fire. A long, smooth body. Tangled, dully gleaming branches like a huge bush made of lead. Moon vanished into that tangle and was gone. The bright spot of the missile's exhaust receded.

"It got me," Moon panted. "It got me!"

Daisuke turned his head in his helmet, following the rocket-tree as it streaked toward its home mountain. The mountain was close now, and the rocket soon had to flip and fire in the opposite direction, slowing itself as it made ready to dock and deliver its cargo.

"Come in," said the voice on their radio. "Come in."

"Thank you," Moon said. "I—"

Daisuke lost whatever the physicist had to say in the roar of interference as the last rocket-tree blasted past.

A near miss. Moon's kick had sent Daisuke flying, and he wasn't even singed by the exhaust. The missile-shaped organism flew straight past him, returning home with its siblings.

"You were right? All those crazy guesses and speculations and you managed to get it right?" Moon sounded angry now. "How can you *do* that?"

Anne wasn't listening.

★ ★ ★

Daisuke wasn't going to make it. Anne could see it. Moon's kick had been almost perfect, but Daisuke would miss the tether.

Anne unclipped her carabiner, braced her feet against the cloud of solidified snot the hole-worm had made, and jumped.

"Stop! What's going on?" Farhad cried.

"Anne. No." Daisuke didn't scream the words. His voice just broke under their weight.

"Not now," she said. "I have an idea. Is your thumb still on the top of that tube?"

"Anne? Anne?" That was either Moon or the mountain-ship.

"Anne, you idiot!" No, *that* was Moon. She could hear his teeth gnashing from here. "The tube won't work. The wormholes only open if there's breathable...oh! Wait. Oh. Sorry I called you an idiot."

"It's okay."

"Moon, Houlihan! Make sense!" Farhad ordered.

A sigh from the physicist. "Why do portals work that way? Why didn't the portal work that way in the capsule-pod? Because we're not dealing with physical laws. These are safety features, created by somebody. There seem to be overrides."

Anne watched Daisuke swell in her visor. She was close enough now to see the tears in his eyes.

Farhad's voice wavered. "Anne, are you certain about this?"

"Oh, do you want certainty?" she asked. "What kind of scientist do you think I am?"

She hit Daisuke. He caught her.

They spun round and round, over and over, and in another direction that Anne thought might be called 'yaw'. Her stomach heaved, but she focused on the pressure against her left glove and right wrist. Daisuke's fingers. She looked through the top of her helmet at Daisuke's face.

Pulling him closer actually sped up one of the round-and-round spins, but Anne didn't care. The movement brought Daisuke's face closer. He was spinning the same way she was, which meant that, from her perspective, Daisuke was the only thing standing still.

Him and that bottled wormhole.

Anne looked down at the pipe in his right hand. Frost sparkled around the rim where his thumb stoppered it.

The wormhole wasn't an astronomical phenomenon. It was a tool. A device made by people. Beings with a conscience, perhaps? Mercy and compassion?

"I'll hug you," she said. "You put the pipe between us."

Daisuke got it. He held the pipe, one hand around it, the other under its base. She checked that they were aimed correctly.

Anne pulled him closer and the universe wheeled.

"Okay, Dice. Take your thumb off the end. And please," she prayed, "take us home."

Like a spring bubbling up in the desert, light shone from the pipe. Gravity bloomed between them.

CHAPTER TWENTY-ONE

Wonder and Wormholes

The universe turned upside down. Then in a circle, and back the other way. Junction and its sun danced merrily around the maypole of Anne and Daisuke's long axis.

Anne couldn't do much but hold on. Daisuke didn't look like he was doing the steering either. Sweat ran up, down, and across his face as he fought to keep his grip on the pipe. The bottled wormhole sputtered and sparked, twitching like a snake as it twisted them around itself. The jet of air it blasted into space was the very least of the magic it was working.

Junction wobbled to a stop before Anne. It hung there blue and white, girdled by life and wormholes. A swarm of black specks swirled briefly across the planet's shining face. Tiny organisms a meter away, or were they farther and larger? Anne couldn't say.

Static burst in her ears, resolving into the question, "All right?"

The light from the pipe blinked out. Something bopped Anne on the top of her helmet.

"Oh!" said Daisuke and let go of the pipe. His hands scrabbled above them.

Anne looked up to see the lumpy, yogurt-colored surface of the hole-worm's ball of mucus. It seemed like so long since she'd stood on that thing.

She resisted the urge to push off of Daisuke. The action might very well fling him back into the void. Instead, she reached up and grasped at the hardened mucus. The tips of her gloves found a crest, the edge of a crater where some orbiting creature had smacked into the bolus. She pinched the crater wall, pulled on it, and – thank Newton! – found herself moving in the direction she wanted to go.

Anne hung there for a moment, breathing. Blue and gold light slid along the pipe as it spun under her feet, apparently exhausted. Anne grabbed it, and slipped it through her belt.

"Did you make it? Are you safe?"

"Is that you, Farhad?" Anne asked. "Or should I say thank you to the mountain-ship?"

"Thank you!" said Daisuke.

"Thank you!" his voice echoed back, then switched to Anne's: "Mountain-ship?"

Anne turned her head and found the mountain-ship. It had risen farther, so it was partly occluded by the tiny horizon/roof of the mucus ball to which Anne clung. "Thank you," she said again.

"Yes. And you have my thanks too, whatever you are," Farhad said. "Anne and Daisuke, you should be able to find the tether now and crawl up it. Tell me when to activate the winch on our side. And...." His voice lost its air of command. "Moon? Are you there, son?"

"I'm here." And an echo. "I'm here."

The mountain-ship seemed to be spinning up. Long, dull-shining leaves spread out from it like the ribbons in the hair of a dancing girl.

"The rocket delivered me," Moon said. "It threw me into some sort of internal chamber where I was caught by several layers of appendages. I am now suspended in some sort of gel. I am falling very slowly through it. I believe that this is an airlock."

How could they hear him? Was the mountain relaying his signals? Nice of it, if so.

"That's fine, Moon. That's fine. Uh, Anne, what's next for him?"

Anne's first impulse was to tell the truth, which was that she had no idea. But on the assumption that Moon wanted reassurance, and Farhad absolution, she said, "Well, he might be safe. An airlock means air, right?"

"Safe," the mountain-ship repeated in her voice. Anne hoped it understood English better now. She hoped Moon would be all right.

Anne pulled herself 'upward' until she was clinging like a spider to the surface of the mucus ball.

"Hey," she said. "Moon. Thank you for saving Daisuke."

"Thank yourself. You're the one who manipulated me into kicking off him."

"Jesus Christ, you're an asshole. All I did was tell you the truth."

"Yes. Me too." Moon's voice was sad. "I'm sorry I didn't tell you the truth earlier. I'm sorry we could never talk to each other."

The mountain-ship was almost out of sight now, its wide base only just peeking out from behind the curve of Anne's ball. The long white plume of its rocket stretched across half the sky.

"Me too," Anne said. "Say hi to the alien overlords for me?"

"I found the tether," said Daisuke. "Anne, come to me. Then I think if we crawl to the opposite side of this ball, we will find the wormhole."

They found more than just one. As they crawled around the curve of the mucus ball, the whole Nightbow came into view. Ranks of wormholes curved off into the distance on all sides, and drifted slowly in layers over their heads. The mountain-ship was making for one of these.

"Moon," Anne said. "You're in the interchange. I think you're about to pass through a wormhole."

A heavy sigh from him. "Would you stop calling them wormholes, Anne?"

"You still want to have this argument with me?" Anne tried to imagine what must be going through his head. "Fine. We'll call them whatever you want. We'll call them *Moons*, if that will make you happy."

"That will be very confusing," said Daisuke.

Moon's chuckle was nearly drowned by the static. "Do you know what my name means? *Moon* means *gateway*, as in the Namdaemun."

Anne watched the narrow peak of the mountain-ship angle toward a particular green-white bubble.

"Just call them *portals*," Moon said. "Call them privileged perspectives in space-time. Or, hm. Just one perspective. Yes, that might work. One portal with ten thousand faces, and we are the bugs that crawl across them."

The peak of the mountain-ship kissed the portal.

"Um," Anne said, "you can go ahead and ask the Zookeepers whether you're right?"

He laughed. "No, you're still thinking the portals are artifacts, but they're not. There is only one portal, and it is the creator!"

Farhad said, "Godspeed, son."

The portal expanded and the mountain-ship seemed to twist. The stars of Junction vanished, replaced by other lights. Moving lights.

On the other side of the portal, sparks drifted and darted like insects, parting to reveal, not a planet but a glittering tangle of branches. A forest canopy the size of a continent.

The fish-eye lens of the portal bent those branches into the fingers of cupped palms. They seemed to hold their distant sun. Anne thought of trees, stabilizing soil, fixing carbon, channeling great gobs of water from the ground into the air, which they also made. That was the ultimate free lunch: from valueless regolith, atmosphere, and stellar radiation, life built itself.

The view continued to expand with the mountain-ship. Now Anne could see other mountain-ships drifting over the lead-colored canopy like bees hovering over the crown of an oak. That structure must be the size of the moon at least. And beyond it rose the rim of a planet.

White and green clouds swirled over blue-black depths. Streams of gas and life swirled in immortal hurricanes. The shadows of other moons tracked across the titanic face of a living gas giant.

"What is that?" Daisuke asked.

"The Terminus." That was Anne's voice, but she hadn't opened her mouth.

"Godspeed," said the mountain-ship, and the portal collapsed behind it. The jet of gas from its rocket dissipated, leaving behind the ranks of orbiting portals. The Nightbow wound on, as stable as ever.

★ ★ ★

The trip back to Junction was very interesting.

The hole-worm cascaded over them, and did not digest their space suits. All it did was swallow them.

Weight returned with gentle pressure, as if they were riding a train. Where did this energy come from? Where did their orbital velocity go? Anne had the impression of vast, secret spaces. An entire alien landscape seen through a pinhole. Moon thought the portals were all one big thing. Anne thought they contained even greater multitudes.

For a while, she just held on to the tether, relishing the feeling of weight. Her boots on the ground.

Daisuke turned on his torch, illuminating a long, upward-sloping tunnel. Wetness glistened on smooth ribbed walls. The tether went right through the middle. "All right," he said, "let's climb."

The climb was much less interesting. After the first ten minutes of slowly pulling themselves through pulsing darkness, Anne wanted to talk.

"Daisuke," she said, "are you familiar with the phrase 'manna from heaven'?"

"Something about magic?"

"No, that's *mana* with one N. From video games. *Manna* with two *N*s is from the Bible. When the Jews escaped Egypt and they were wandering in the desert, God dropped food on them, like fish in an aquarium."

Farhad groaned over the radio, but Daisuke said, "All right?"

Anne watched the worm's gut pulse on the walls. "Well, I was thinking about this system that shuttles materials back and forth between Junction's orbit and its surface. Food from heaven on earth, food from earth in heaven. Except it isn't a one-time thing. It doesn't just drop onto your head miraculously one day, it happens every day. For a hundred million years."

"I don't understand."

"The people who built this place – the Zookeepers, or Moon's portal-god – knew all about sustainability," Anne said. "They had at least a hundred *million* years of foresight. They didn't just build machines that built machines, they set up the system that caused the machines to evolve! With nothing but dust and starlight and one second after another, they made all of this. Everything we've seen." Anne pulled herself up another step. "I think that's the only way you can really make anything."

Silence on the radio, except for the ragged breathing from her and Daisuke and Farhad. The bodies of three people, surviving from second to second.

Finally, they stood in the tunnel mouth. Anne looked out over

272 • DANIEL M. BENSEN

the dark and hazy Toymaker Mountains, the rolling Cavalier biome and the orange tangle of the Dorado forest, thicker now. Living mist rose in the last gusts from the exhausted hole-worm – curtains layered with subtle shapes. High clouds floated above, dotted with kelp-tree balloons. And below down the slope, there were human faces.

Farhad and Aimi. Turtle and Boss Rudi. Misha was gone, but Anne would find him again. The humans' mouths opened and closed. Turtle waved his hands in joy. Farhad wiped away tears.

Anne waved back. She could finally unclasp her helmet and breathe some fresh air. The air smelled of rock, strange soil, and the cat piss of whatever enzyme the hole-worm used to break down its dried mucus.

And everyone was shouting.

Farhad put his arms around Anne. She couldn't feel him squeezing through her suit, but he sure did rock her back and forth.

The others took their turns. Turtle, Aimi, even Boss Rudi. They'd been worried about her, Anne realized. They really cared about her.

They cared so much that it took almost half an hour before Farhad said, "We need to talk about what we're going to tell people when we get back."

Anne turned to him. "All right. Say your piece."

Farhad hung his head, leaning toward her. "Anne, I want to thank you."

"Uh, yeah?"

"You made me realize something. Something that's been driving me for a long time."

"Yeah, no problem," said Anne. She was still uncomfortable around Farhad and didn't really want to talk to him. That made her think. Maybe there was something under that discomfort for her to discover. "Uh, I mean, yeah? What did you realize?"

Farhad's eyes crinkled as if he'd read her thoughts. But then he looked away, expression uncertain. "When I was a teenager, I was smuggled into Turkey in the back of a pickup truck."

Yeah, I know, you told me, Anne didn't say. She waited.

"I remember hiding under a tarp, behind a crate of some foul chemical or other, thinking, *If I can just make it across the border.*" Farhad shook himself. "But of course, once I made it to Turkey, my troubles weren't over. Nor when I reached England, nor America. When I came to Junction and the Howling Mountain, I thought that we would find something here that would repay my sacrifices. Instead, you found another mountain. A mountain in space."

Farhad's voice didn't falter, but his shoulders jerked. His hands flew to his face, where they hid his eyes as his shoulders jerked again.

Anne had zero idea of what to do. Was Farhad crying? Should she...run away? Pretend nothing was happening? Comfort him? How? She looked around at Daisuke for help, but then she didn't need it. She remembered the living mist, and how they'd reached through it for each other.

"You're crying," Anne said. "You must be sad because...because there's always another mountain."

Farhad jerked again and said, "Ha!", which was ambiguous as hell. Should she laugh with him? Give him a hug? Anne couldn't bring herself to do that. But she could stand here and make sure this old man knew he wasn't alone.

"You can never really arrive anywhere, can you?" Anne groped for understanding. "You can never say, all right, I got to the finish line. I'm done. You just have to keep climbing and climbing forever. What with Junction and the Howling Mountain, and the Interchange and the Terminus beyond *that*...."

Anne wasn't looking at Farhad anymore, but over his head. Her voice had gotten faster and louder. She bounced on her toes.

"Ha!" said Farhad again, and sniffed. "Professor Houlihan, you're excited."

"Damn right I'm excited. There's so much to learn!"

"There is, indeed. The amount of things we have to learn never ends." Farhad straightened. "And that's a good thing. Thank you for reminding me of that."

Anne felt the urge to end the conversation there. But that was an urge that Farhad was projecting, wasn't it? She resisted. And made a mental note to learn that trick herself.

"That's all well and good," she said. "Deep psychological insights and all. Good on you. But now what? We go back to civilization and tell them we've discovered the Zookeepers? Oh, and by the way, we can move around and destroy wormholes."

"Maybe because people know about the Zookeepers, they will be afraid to interfere with the wormholes," said Daisuke.

Anne and Farhad both snorted.

"Come on, Dice," she said. "The looming threat of alien retribution will make people want to steal and destroy wormholes *faster*."

Farhad's eyes flicked up to the sky. "If it isn't already too late."

"So, we keep everything a secret," Daisuke said, but Farhad was already shaking his head.

"No. We'll tell the world what it needs to know. Portals are tools, and their makers are still here, actively using them. Our next play in this game should be to—" he glanced at Anne and caught himself, "— but I won't tell you how to spin the news. In fact, what you said just now, both of you, that conversation, was perfect. Just repeat that."

He smiled, which made Anne even more suspicious. "Wait a moment. Is *that* why you brought me here? I'm the one who sent the news about the wormhole to the whole world. Daisuke's the face of happy shiny international co-operation on Junction. And you want us to break your story."

Farhad shrugged. "It's your story too, isn't it?"

Daisuke chuckled as if at a clever chess move, but Anne just shook off the appeal to her ego. Farhad ought to know by now that that wouldn't work.

"No," she said, and pointed at the ground. "It's Junction's story."

Daisuke and Farhad both nodded, but she could tell that Farhad was faking it. He still had no idea what she was talking about.

She decided to try to make him understand one more time. "Junction has a lot more value than as a site to extract resources from. When you mine the mountain, the stuff you mined out of it is gone. But when you learn something new, you get something for nothing."

Ignorance turned into knowledge, ugliness into beauty, meaningless *stuff* became part of a plant or an animal.

"Yes, yes, but what if the world needs those portals?" Farhad glanced up at the sky again, and the alien armadas it might contain. "At a time like this, can you really sit on top of this treasure trove and refuse to let others make use of it?"

No, *this* was the way to get to him. Anne could almost see it. "What do you want to do with Junction? Keep your grandkids safe, right?"

He blinked at her. Caught his breath. "Yes," he said.

"Thinking about the next generation is like thinking about the next, what, fifty, one hundred years? The Zookeepers think in terms of *millions* of years," she said. "If you can do that, if you extend your plans out to infinity, then your own goals will demand that you treat yourself – and other people, and *everything* – sustainably."

"That assumes I think Earth has another million years," Farhad said. "Or even fifty."

Anne understood his problem. For all Farhad's talk of faith, he didn't really have any. He couldn't imagine the Earth surviving the century. He didn't think he had time, so he grabbed what he could and didn't care what he destroyed in the process.

"Nothing we learn can fix Earth unless we believe the Earth *can* be fixed," said Anne. "Junction can give us new biochemistry, all right, and even new physics, but that's not as important as inspiration."

She flung up her arms. "I mean, look at it! This planet is a machine designed a hundred million years ago, and it *still works*! That's sustainability you can sink your teeth into! You can walk through it. You can climb up it and into *space*, Farhad! Junction is a beacon. It's a promise. We can learn how to do this!"

Farhad took a step back from her, eyes round. Suddenly he looked much younger. "Wow. Say *that* to the journalists. Please!"

"I think she means," Daisuke said, "that in the long run, wonder will be a more profitable export than wormholes."

"Yes, Daisuke. Yes, I see that." Farhad put his hand up to his mouth and stroked his goatee. He looked almost normal again, but he couldn't fool Anne. Under his hand, Farhad was grinning like a little boy. "I agree."

★ ★ ★

"How much of that was the truth?"

"All of it."

Anne and Daisuke lay on their bed, letting the caravan carry them toward home. It was time to return the Dorado portal to its forest, see whether the portal in the Kenzan Crater had reappeared, and tell Earth their shattering news.

"Except I noticed you used words like *beacon* and *promise*. In space, you called Junction a trap."

"Well, I was trying to get Moon to leave." Anne snuggled up under Daisuke's arm.

Muscles slid across his chest as he gestured. "But what if it's true? What if he goes to meet the Zookeepers? What if he comes back next year and he's the Emperor of the Milky Way?"

"Biologists don't usually elect their lab animals to high positions of power, Daisuke."

"Biologists might become excited when they see a new species, and go look for more."

Anne nodded, pulling her knees up so his body could warm them. "I've been thinking about that. The mountain-ship was testing us, but what exactly was it measuring?"

"Intelligence, you said."

"Yeah, but what is intelligence? I think the ship gave us a choice: stay or go somewhere else. At first, I thought that that was because we'd passed some threshold of personhood and suddenly our consent mattered. As if the Zookeepers were bound by human moral philosophy. But I wonder." She rolled onto her back, looking at the ceiling. "I wonder if it wasn't the beginning of a new test. Something more subtle than cracking our language."

Daisuke rolled onto his side and put his arm across her. "What sort of test?"

"Think about it this way: Junction is a hundred million years old. We tore through it in less than a week. If it were that fragile, we could never have found Junction the way it is. I think something special has happened to us. I think the portals were watching us and listening. I think they were trying to teach us something: 'Welcome. Enjoy our hospitality. Help yourselves while we decide what sort of animal you are.'"

"What do you think they have discovered about us?"

"Well, we certainly led them a merry chase, didn't we? What would you do if one of your lab rats figured out how to get out of its cage and open the door and take a taxi away from your lab?"

"I think if I had a lab rat that did that," Daisuke said, "I'd follow it."

The Nightbow spun above them, filled with mountains.

ACKNOWLEGMENTS

If writing *Junction* was like pulling a monster from the depths, *Interchange* was like strapping on a scuba tank and going hunting. I made it back intact thanks to the following people.

Turns out wormholes as I described them in *Junction* don't make sense! Thanks to Michael Tabachnik for some real wormhole physics and Robert Dawson for nixing a couple of bad wormhole ideas and helping me understand why they were bad. David DeGraff read through the whole damn manuscript, propping up Moon's explanations where he could, unraveling character motivations, and generally raising the level of conversation.

On the squishier side, Alessandro Allievi gave me some non-standard biochemistry, Vladimir Nikolov helped with the lifecycle of mountain-ships and Anne and Daisuke's relationship, and Anatoly Belikovski provided the hole-worm's vacuum-curing Kevlar mucus. Oscar Lozada and Alexander Brown didn't buy the evolutionary biology of the Dorado biome and made suggestions for how to render it more plausible. Thomas Duffy did a great deal of depth-adding and sanity-checking in the Dorado biome as well the orbital biome. You know when ideas are bouncing between people and the ideas just get bigger and better? It's a treasure.

And then there are those even squishier humans! Franz Anthony painted an excellent shmoo picture, very graciously talked with me about names and backstories for the Indonesian characters, and gave me the Indonesian text. Emil Minchev helped me with narrative flow, Timothy Morris corrected Australian cultural references, and Mami Kojima corrected my Japanese. T.J. Berg told me what kind of grant proposal Anne must have written before *Junction*, the sort of operation she'd want to put together in *Interchange*, and generally blessed me with a ton of science advice and suggested reading. I got to...some of it. Eeson Rajendra loved the sights and sounds of *Junction* and told me so, a welcome ego-boost. Copy editor

Imogen Howson not only picked her way across my shattered quotation marks and elipses, but compiled a glossary of all the made-up words in *Junction* so she could make sure they matched the made-up words in *Interchange*. Katheryn Anderson told me why Anne should say no to eccentric millionaires. And of course Pavlina read a much earlier draft than everyone else and told me all the places where I was wrong.

Now for the research. For physics, I used *Spooky Action at a Distance* by George Musser, *The Mathematical Universe* by Max Tegmark, *The Ascent of Gravity* by Marcus Chown, *A Briefer History of Time* by Stephen Hawking, and *Extreme Medicine* by Kevin Fong. The paper Moon read about the hollow earth was 'A Geocosmos: Mapping Outer Space Into a Hollow Earth' by Mostafa Abdelkader.

For biology, its evolution, and its exploration I had *I Contain Multitudes* by Ed Yong, *The Wood for the Trees* by Richard Fortey, *Plant Science: An Introduction to Botany* by Catherine Kerr, *The Making of the Fittest* by Sean B. Carroll, and three papers in early ecology: 'The Lake as Microcosm' by Stephen A. Forbes, 'The Ecological Relations of the Vegetation on the Sand Dunes of Lake Michigan' by Henry Chandler Coles, and 'Nature and the Structure of Climax' by Frederic E. Clements.

Humans, those trickiest of animals, were somewhat more fully illuminated by Ray Dalio's *Principles*, Ashlee Vance's Elon Musk biography, Brené Brown's *Daring Greatly*, and most of all *Never Split the Difference* by Christopher Voss.

My heroes Terry Pratchett, Lois McMaster Bujold, and Greg Egan helped me find a way to live and write. The atmosphere, themes, and ideas of *Interchange* were inspired and informed by the work of Alastair Reynolds, Sue Burke, Der-Shing Helmer, and the music of Against the Current, Goosehouse, and John Murphy's 'Adagio in D Minor'.

Finally, thanks to my agent Jennie Goloboy, and my editor, Don D'Auria, who got this project off the ground in the first place. Hacking away at a story day after day, it's easy to forget that somebody might actually read it at some point. Thanks for being those readers. Thanks for helping me reach more.

FLAME TREE PRESS
FICTION WITHOUT FRONTIERS
Award-Winning Authors & Original Voices

Flame Tree Press is the trade fiction imprint of Flame Tree Publishing, focusing on excellent writing in horror and the supernatural, crime and mystery, science fiction and fantasy. Our aim is to explore beyond the boundaries of the everyday, with tales from both award-winning authors and original voices.

•

Other titles available by Daniel M. Bensen:
Junction

You may also enjoy:
The Sentient by Nadia Afifi
American Dreams by Kenneth Bromberg
Second Lives by P.D. Cacek
The City Among the Stars by Francis Carsac
Vulcan's Forge by Robert Mitchell Evans
The Widening Gyre by Michael R. Johnston
The Blood-Dimmed Tide by Michael R. Johnston
The Sky Woman by J.D. Moyer
The Guardian by J.D. Moyer
The Goblets Immortal by Beth Overmyer
The Apocalypse Strain by Jason Parent
The Gemini Experiment by Brian Pinkerton
The Nirvana Effect by Brian Pinkerton
A Killing Fire by Faye Snowden
Fearless by Allen Stroud
The Bad Neighbor by David Tallerman
A Savage Generation by David Tallerman
Screams from the Void by Anne Tibbets
Ten Thousand Thunders by Brian Trent
Two Lives: Tales of Life, Love & Crime by A Yi

Horror titles available include:
The Haunting of Henderson Close by Catherine Cavendish
The Garden of Bewitchment by Catherine Cavendish
Black Wings by Megan Hart
Those Who Came Before by J.H. Moncrieff

•

Join our mailing list for free short stories, new release details, news about our authors and special promotions:

flametreepress.com